THE
DAUGHTERS
OF
GENTLEMEN

A FRANCES DOUGHTY MYSTERY

THE
DAUGHTERS
OF
GENTLEMEN

LINDA STRATMANN

The
Mystery
Press

To
Nige, Sabine, Karen and Simon
Because four Furlongs always go the extra half mile

First published 2012

The Mystery Press, an imprint of The History Press
The Mill, Brimscombe Port
Stroud, Gloucestershire, GL5 2QG
www.thehistorypress.co.uk

British Library Cataloguing in Publication Data.
A catalogue record for this book is available from the British Library.

ISBN 978 0 7524 6475 6

Typesetting and origination by The History Press
Manufacturing managed by Jellyfish Print Solutions Ltd
Printed in India

CHAPTER ONE

Algernon Fiske was a very worried man. For some years he had been accustomed to living in the state of pleasurable equilibrium to which he felt he should be entitled, but suddenly all had been thrown into anxiety and confusion.

His late father had been a successful grocer, and while Mr Fiske would have been the first to state that grocers were splendid fellows he had declined to become one himself. The rent of several shops had enabled him to subsist on his true passion, English literature, and he enjoyed a modest celebrity as an author, lecturer and reviewer of books. His interests were especially directed towards the education of the impressionable young, and since he was the father of two girls he was particularly concerned with the prudent development of the female brain. His wife Edith was the daughter of a clergyman, whom he had selected not for love or beauty or fortune but for her good temper and the excellence of her mind.

A woman's intellect was, he believed, too often neglected. Was it not the duty of womankind to conduct the management of the home, that haven of comfort so essential to the successful man? And while a nursemaid was more than adequate to tend to the bodily comforts of the very young, it was to their mother that they should turn for stimulation of the mind during their tenderest years. As he watched his infant daughters, Charlotte and Sophia, grow into sturdy and serious little girls, he began to wonder what school might be best for their development into the young women he hoped they would become, and lighted upon a small but promising establishment whose proprietors, Professor Edward Venn and his wife Honoria, appeared to be suitable in almost every way. The only small drawback was the Professor's delicate state of health, which ill-equipped him for the burden of administration.

Thus it was that Algernon Fiske MA became patron and governor of the Bayswater Academy for the Education of Young Ladies. He was soon joined by two other gentlemen with similar concerns, landowner Roderick Matthews, whose market gardens supplied the denizens of Bayswater with fruit, vegetables and fresh flowers, and Bartholomew Paskall, property agent. Under their guidance the little school moved to a larger establishment in respectable but not showy Chepstow Place and opened its doors to more pupils, the carefully brought up daughters of Bayswater gentlemen of substance. The unfortunate early death of Professor Venn, whose long hours of toil on a great work of history was both a fine example to society and his downfall, might have threatened the future of the school, but Mrs Venn had bravely stepped into his place. In all its years of existence there had been no suggestion that the school was anything other than the most perfect of its kind. This was the situation until the afternoon of Wednesday, 3rd March 1880, when fourteen-year-old Charlotte Fiske was unexpectedly escorted home by one of her teachers in a state of great distress.

Miss Bell (grammar, spelling and elocution) was quick to reassure the Fiskes that their daughter had done nothing wrong. That morning, Charlotte had discovered an item of printed matter in her desk that appeared to have been placed there by a prankster, but, being a sensitive girl, she had been upset by the incident and the school had thought it advisable that she return home for the afternoon to be comforted by her family. Edith Fiske was a shrewd woman who felt sure that Miss Bell, who loved the English language so much that she normally put it to constant use, was keeping something back. She ordered her cook to prepare a glass of warm milk, and as Charlotte sipped the soothing liquid, she carefully questioned her daughter.

'Well, my dear?' asked Algernon, a few minutes later, peering over his spectacles as his wife entered his study. There was a book of poetry on the desk before him. He had been struggling to compose a review and was trying to determine whether it was a greater kindness to the author to say only what good there was in his work, or tell him the truth and risk hurting his feelings.

'It is both better and worse than I had feared,' said Edith. 'Charlotte assures me that she read very little of the offending item, but it was enough to learn that it was a treatise attempting to persuade young girls that they ought not to marry.'

'Ought not to marry!' exclaimed Algernon, astounded. 'On what grounds?'

'Thankfully,' said Edith, dryly, 'Charlotte did not read sufficient to discover that.'

Fiske threw aside his pen. 'But why would anyone send our daughter such a thing? I hope she has taken no notice of what it says.'

'She will not,' said Edith. 'You may leave that to me. But you, Algy dear, must go to the school at once and speak to Mrs Venn. The person who did this must be found and stopped. Who knows what wickedness they may commit in future?'

Algernon sighed and looked down at his barely commenced review of the works of aspiring poet Augustus Mellifloe, a task that had suddenly acquired more relish, especially in view of the keen wind making hollow mocking sounds down the chimney.

'Don't worry, my dear,' said Edith, briskly. 'I will deal with Mr Mellifloe. And remember to wear your muffler.' Resignedly, Fiske rose from his desk. Edith took his place, selected a pen, tested the sharpness of its nib, and set to work.

Fiske returned home an hour later, his face grey with misery, and sank into an armchair. 'The whole school has been under the most hideous attack!' he exclaimed. Edith had, in his absence, completed the review to her satisfaction, although not, in all probability, to the satisfaction of Mr Mellifloe, and was stitching a lace edging to a new cap while simultaneously reading a book on English history, achieving this feat with a device of her own invention which held the pages of the volume open as she worked. She now abandoned both activities to give her unhappy husband her full attention and pour him a warming glass of sherry.

Fiske had learned that the morning class, which consisted of twelve girls, had assembled in the schoolroom to do an hour of quiet study on whatever subjects had been individually assigned. When Charlotte Fiske opened her arithmetic book a piece of folded paper had fluttered out. She had begun to read it when Miss Baverstock (music, deportment and dancing) who had been supervising the class, noticed the paper and investigated. Miss Baverstock decided to take Charlotte and the paper to see Mrs Venn (headmistress, history and geography) when a horrid thought struck her. She quickly ordered all the other girls to go up to the common room, and arranged for Mlle Girard (French, and plain and fancy needlework) to supervise them.

Mrs Venn, having perused the paper with understandable distaste, and establishing that Charlotte had no knowledge of how it had arrived in her desk, at once comprehended Miss Baverstock's way of thinking and both women went down to the empty schoolroom, leaving Charlotte to be comforted by Miss Bell. Every desk was opened and thoroughly searched, and in every one there was an identical paper, each one neatly tucked into the pages of a book. Mrs Venn then set about interviewing all the girls individually, but none of them had as yet discovered the pamphlets placed in their desks or had any idea how they might have come to be there. Mrs Venn concluded that it was merely chance that it had been Charlotte Fiske who had been the first to find hers.

'And what was your opinion of the item in question?' asked Edith.

'I did not see it myself,' confessed her husband, 'but I am told that it has been most carefully removed from innocent eyes. One hopes that it will never be seen again.'

Edith frowned and returned to her sewing. 'What does Mrs Venn propose to do?' she asked.

Fiske hesitated. Everything had been so very clear when he had spoken to the headmistress, but now, having to explain the position to his wife, he found it less easy to justify. 'It is my understanding that she considers no further action to be necessary.'

Edith raised an eyebrow. 'That is very surprising,' she said.

'She believes that the whole incident may have been no more than a childish mischief, the culprit being one of the girls who would not have understood the meaning of the publication,' said Fiske. 'Having spoken most firmly to all the pupils, she is convinced that the girl, whoever she may be, is now so thoroughly frightened by what she has done that she regrets her transgression and it will not recur.'

'And do you share this view?' asked Edith. There was something subtle in her tone that her husband could not help but find alarming.

'I would like to,' he said, hopefully.

Edith stopped sewing and looked at him with a direct stare that was all too familiar. 'But you are understandably afraid that she may be mistaken.'

He sighed. 'Supposing it is no thoughtless prank, but a plot by strident mannish women to affect the minds of our girls?'

'Then,' she informed him, 'you must be concerned that such a thing may happen again.'

'I am,' he said unhappily.

'And who knows what indecent material they may select for their next attempt?'

Fiske shuddered. 'I wish I knew what to do.'

'Mr Paskall and Mr Matthews both have daughters at the school,' Edith observed. 'It would seem appropriate to advise them of the situation.'

'Yes! Yes of course!' Fiske rose from his chair. 'I will go and see them at once. In fact, I will call a meeting – an extraordinary meeting of the governors. This thing must be stopped. Our girls must be protected at all costs!' He was visibly trembling as he left the room. Edith nodded approval, took up her scissors and cut a thread.

Later that evening Mr Fiske sat dejectedly in Bartholomew Paskall's study in company with Mr Paskall and Roderick Matthews. The three men, although all in their late forties and joined in a common purpose, were remarkably unalike: Mr Fiske, short, slightly portly, with greying side whiskers and a thinning pate; Matthews, tall with a broad forehead, glossy dark hair and trim beard, drawing languidly on a cigar, Paskall, thin and intense with a nose like an eagle's beak. While Fiske's study was warmly lined with the leather backs of lovingly bound volumes, and Matthews' spoke more of leisure than work, Paskall's was an extension of his business, the shelves stuffed with cracked ledgers and bundles of papers tied with string. The desk was piled high with newspapers and political pamphlets, since Paskall, to his considerable pride, had recently been selected as one of the two Conservative candidates for Marylebone in the forthcoming General Election. Those with their fingers on the parliamentary pulse confidently predicted that this would take place in the autumn.

'Of course you were right to alert us, Fiske,' said Matthews, whose two youngest daughters Amelia and Dorothea and a ward, Wilhelmina, were all pupils of the school, 'and right too to get the whole story from Mrs Venn. But the question is, what's to be done?'

'I don't think this is a childish prank,' said Paskall, frowning. 'And neither do I think it is some confederation of women who may be easily dismissed as misguided. It is more serious than that. It is a personal attack on *me*. I have political enemies, and the success of the Conservatives in the recent by-elections makes my victory in the autumn almost certain. Someone seeks to destroy me by creating a scandal in the school. Of course I am concerned for my daughters, but Beatrice and Leticia are sensible girls and they will listen to me.'

'Oh, I don't smell politics in this,' said Matthews, nonchalantly. 'It could be some rival school about to open its doors and hoping to gain pupils by discrediting us.'

'One thing we dare not do is make a public statement,' said Fiske. 'To deny wrongdoing would simply arouse suspicion where there was none before. Neither should we have anything to do with the police.'

'I doubt they'd be interested, Fiske,' said Matthews dismissively. 'From what you say it isn't even a crime.'

'Can you imagine if anyone were to see policemen going into the school?' said Paskall, his voice faint with horror. 'And as for detectives—'

'I would never condone persons of that sort speaking to our girls,' said Fiske. 'These men are in daily contact with the lowest type of criminals, and some of them are little better than criminals themselves. Many have actually been dismissed from the police force, for what reasons I dread to imagine.'

For a moment or two the only sound in the room was that of Matthews sucking at his cigar and a squally wind rattling the window and driving raindrops against the pane like pebbles.

'Why not ask Mrs Venn to make enquiries?' suggested Fiske. 'She is a sensible woman.'

'From what you have told us, Mrs Venn prefers that no enquiries should be made,' said Paskall. 'I agree that we should appoint someone, but it should be an individual with no involvement in the work of the school.'

'What about a female detective?' said Matthews with a laugh, which quickly evaporated when he realised that his two associates had taken his joke seriously.

'Is such a person entirely respectable?' asked Fiske. 'It seems a very strange sort of proceeding for a woman.'

Paskall suddenly pulled a recent copy of the *Bayswater Chronicle* from the pile of newspapers on his desk. 'Did you hear about Miss Doughty, the chemist's daughter?' he asked, and turned to the inner page of local news. 'Reading between the lines she danced rings round the police and it is she we must thank for solving the murder of Mr Garton.' He proffered the paper to the others and they examined a column headed 'My Remarkable Career by a Lady Detective.'

'What do you suggest?' asked Fiske when he had read the item.

'It can do no harm to engage her to look into the matter,' said Paskall. 'If the young lady can unmask murderers then I think she will be equal to this. The family is respectable, and I understand that her reputation is beyond reproach.'

Matthews put down his cigar and looked around for the brandy. 'Agreed,' he said, and somehow – and Mr Fiske never learned how – it was all settled in a moment that he should go to the chemist shop in Westbourne Grove and engage Frances Doughty as a detective.

The next morning Mr Fiske was unsurprised to discover that after the recent tragedies and charges of murder which had centred around Doughty's chemist shop, the business was under new management. The shop was bustling with ladies, all casting simpering looks at the new young pharmacist Mr Jacobs, from whom he learned that Miss Doughty had not yet vacated the apartments next door. There, he presented his card to the maid-servant, a burly young woman with a face like a disgruntled bulldog, and was shown upstairs to a parlour, almost bereft of comforts, a large box suggesting that arrangements were being made to move to new accommodation.

Miss Doughty was very young, scarcely old enough to have left school herself, but that, to Mr Fiske's mind, was to her advantage, as she might thereby gain the confidence of the girls. He was impressed by her calmness and composure, and as she listened to him, saw that she was already considering the difficulty and how she might resolve it. There was no hint of frivolity about Miss Doughty, no trace of unwarranted orna-ment or vanity, or a mind distracted by thoughts of romance. Miss Doughty would never have put a flower in her bonnet and made eyes at Mr Jacobs. Fiske departed, feeling a new con-fidence.

Frances was left alone for a while, and despite her cool exte-rior, her heart was thudding with excitement. Only an hour before she had been facing the dull but not unpleasant pros-pect of becoming a dependent of her Uncle Cornelius, a kindly man who she knew would attend to her comfort and happiness. Her main regret had been that Cornelius had no place for her maid, Sarah, who had been a quietly loyal and steadfast pres-ence in her life for the last ten years. Sarah had first come to the Doughtys as a squat fifteen year old with an expression of deep gloom and the capacity for ungrudging hard work, and had become someone in whom Frances placed a confidence and trust that she would have shared only with a mother or sister. Cornelius had recommended Sarah to a family in Maida Vale, something Frances was still gathering the courage to mention, as she suspected that Sarah's feelings on the subject were even stronger than her own.

Mr Fiske's request had startled her, but it had opened a window that afforded her a view of a quite different future, and she had been bold enough to accept. Now that she had done so, doubts came crowding in and she took a clean scrap of paper and began to calculate how they might live. She had a little money left after paying her father's debts, and Mr Fiske had been kind enough to advance her some funds for expenses. Against that she had to set the cost of lodgings and other necessaries. Her conclusion was that she had a month to achieve success. Even if this engagement proved to be her only one, it would be an adventure, and she reassured herself that at the end of a month she would be very little poorer than at present.

She was so engrossed in her task that she did not see Sarah approach until a substantial shadow fell upon the paper.

'You won't send me away, will you?' said Sarah. 'I'll work for nothing. I'll do extra washing and cleaning, it won't be any trouble.'

Frances smiled reassurance. 'I hope it will never come to that,' she said. 'No, it seems that I must hang out my shingle as a private detective.'

'Oh!' exclaimed Sarah, relieved. 'Only I thought the gentleman might have come about —,' she rubbed her broad red hands on her apron. 'Because I wouldn't have gone away and left you and there's no one could have made me, so there!' She pondered this new development and a smile spread across her face. 'A detective!' she said. 'And you'll be the best one in London – or in the world – which is about the same thing, really.'

'But the best news is, I am being well paid for the work, and will be able to rent accommodation once we leave here. I must write to my uncle at once and advise him that I will not after all be taking advantage of his kindness.' Frances had already decided to inform Cornelius that she was about to be employed by a girls' school, which was very nearly the truth. Not long ago she would have hesitated about telling even a small untruth, but that time was past. She was becoming more practised at gentle deceit, something she felt sure would be a useful skill in her new calling.

'There are lots of very respectable apartments to let hereabouts,' said Sarah. 'Only —,' a new concern clouded her features, 'they mostly have a housekeeper, and a washerwoman that calls, and I don't suppose you'll need a maid of all work.'

'That is true,' said Frances, 'but what I will need is a lady companion on whom I know I can rely. Perhaps you might apply for the position?'

'I'd like nothing better!' was the eager response.

'Then that is settled, and without the need for an advertisement.'

After fortifying themselves with tea and bread and butter, the two women set about their errands, Sarah to view apartments and Frances to undertake her first visit to the Bayswater Academy for the Education of Young Ladies, where Mr Fiske had preceded her to make an appointment.

The school occupied a single-fronted premises, with a ground floor, commodious basement and two upper storeys. Neatly kept, it nestled amongst the homes of professional gentlemen and elderly persons of the middle classes who enjoyed comfortable annuities. As Frances rang the bell, she wondered briefly if she was equal to her appointed task, but she pushed the thought aside, and determined that necessity would lend her whatever resources of skill and character she needed. After all, she thought reassuringly, with this inquiry she would not be required to solve a murder.

CHAPTER TWO

The door was opened by a diminutive maidservant with a pointed chin, sharp nose, sparkling eyes and more bounce in her manner than Frances would have thought appropriate.

'Miss Doughty to see Mrs Venn,' said Frances.

'You're expected,' said the maid tartly. 'Follow me.'

Frances, realising that her position in the house ranked just a fraction above tradesperson, entered a narrow high-ceilinged hallway, the walls adorned with botanical prints and pastel-shaded maps, and followed the maid up a flight of stairs to a heavy polished door, the brass plate announcing 'Mrs H. Venn, Headmistress'.

As Frances was ushered into the study, the headmistress rose to meet her with a coolness of manner which was more than mere formality. Frances recognised at once to her considerable dismay that she was not wanted there, and the tight-lipped politeness of Mrs Venn's greeting only confirmed that impression. She realised with some concern that when Mr Fiske had engaged her he had almost certainly done so without previously consulting Mrs Venn, something the lady could only have seen as a personal affront.

Mrs Venn was a lady of more than middle height and aged about forty-five. Her carriage was dignified without being unnaturally rigid, her air that of confidence in her own domain. She wore a plain costume of stout dark cloth with a bunch of keys at her waist, a fob watch on a chain about her neck, and a discreet mourning brooch at her throat. Her hair, once pale brown, now streaked with grey, was swept into a high knot. She had never been beautiful, but the approach of the middle time of life had lent her a poise that was not unflattering.

The study was small and well lined with books and ledgers, the desk neither too cluttered, which would have indicated a disordered mind, nor too bare, which would have suggested idleness. Everything was tidily arranged, and Frances felt sure that Mrs Venn would be able to lay her hand on any document required at a moment's notice. There was a small, framed portrait on the wall, a painting in oils of a gentleman with bushy brows and a wide mouth with a pendulous lower lip that gave him a mournful if eccentrically intelligent look. Frances suspected that this was the late Professor Venn. There was also, very prominently displayed, a photograph of the front of the school building, with a group of three gentlemen – one of whom Frances recognised as Mr Fiske – standing on the steps handing a key to the Professor, with Mrs Venn a decorous shadow at his side. Of the other two gentlemen, whom Frances assumed were Fiske's fellow governors, one was tall with a proud handsome face, while the other had a less flattering profile. Behind them was a small group of demure and identically dressed schoolgirls.

'I must apologise for this intrusion,' Frances began, in what she hoped was a suitably mollifying tone. 'It is my intention to carry out what I have been asked to do with the least possible disruption to the work of the school.'

If there was a softening of Mrs Venn's expression, the device that could have measured it had not yet been constructed. 'Since the governors have appointed you to make enquiries, I will of course extend my full co-operation to enable you to complete them speedily,' said the headmistress, in a voice that could have attracted frost. 'My own opinion is that the whole matter is a trivial, childish piece of mischief, best forgotten.'

'That is my thought exactly,' said Frances, deeming it best to start by agreeing as far as possible with whatever the headmistress might say. Mrs Venn waved her to a seat and Frances took out her notebook and pencil, while Mrs Venn resumed her place behind the desk and sat in almost regal pose, her hands clasped comfortably before her. 'I would like to begin by seeing a copy of the pamphlet.'

'I am afraid that is not possible,' said Mrs Venn.

Frances smiled. 'I know that I am very young, but I will do my best not to be shocked by its contents.'

'I meant,' said Mrs Venn, 'that they have been destroyed. On finding them my one thought was to protect my girls. Had I known that the governors would appoint someone to look into the matter I would of course have retained one for you to see.'

'Well, that is a setback,' Frances admitted, 'but I am sure I will find a copy elsewhere. In the meantime could you tell me as much as you can remember about it – the title and the author – the publisher?'

'I did not make a note of the publisher,' said Mrs Venn. 'I doubt if a respectable establishment was employed. It was an unpleasant, cheap thing, little more than a page folded in two and the interior printed. The title was something like "Why Marry?", or some such nonsense. The author did not have the courage to provide a name.'

'And the object of the pamphlet was to persuade girls not to marry?'

'It appeared so. The entire tenor was most objectionable.'

Frances made a note in her book. 'Can you recall any of its content?'

'Miss Doughty, I have better employment for my mind than memorising material fit only for the fireplace.' Mrs Venn gave a tilt of the chin that told Frances that she had now said all she would say on that subject.

A chart on the wall was a boldly lettered timetable of lessons, and Frances rose and studied it carefully. 'I understand that Charlotte Fiske discovered the pamphlet in her arithmetic book at approximately nine o'clock yesterday morning. According to this timetable, the last time she would without doubt have opened that book was in a lesson which was held the previous morning between eleven and twelve o'clock. If the pamphlet had been there then, she would have seen it, so it must have been placed there between those times. I will need to interview Charlotte, of course, but I will also require a list of all persons who were in the school between those hours, and a copy of this timetable. I will also need to see the schoolroom.'

Mrs Venn's expression did not change, but the fingers of one hand tapped on the back of the other in a small gesture of annoyance. 'Very well,' she said at last, taking a copy of the timetable from her desk drawer and handing it to Frances. 'I will compose a list for you of all pupils, teaching staff and servants. I do not, of course, know what callers there were at the servants' entrance, you must speak to the housemaid Matilda about that. I received three visitors on the afternoon of March 2nd. Mr Julius Sandcourt, the husband of a former pupil, came at two o'clock to discuss his desire to invest in the future of the school. He was here for about half an hour. Mrs Sandcourt is the eldest daughter of Mr Roderick Matthews, one of the governors. I then received a visit from Mr Fiske, with whom you are already acquainted, and he brought with him a Mr Miggs, who is establishing a new business publishing educational books. They wish me to write a book about the instruction of girls. They were here between four and five o'clock and took tea. I think we may assume that none of these visitors wish any harm either to the school or its pupils.'

'I agree,' said Frances, although she added all those names together with that of the third governor, Mr Paskall, to the list of people to whom she might speak. Even if someone was not a suspect, she thought their knowledge of the school might provide an insight which would lead to the culprit. 'How long have the servants been with the school?'

'I have no reason to suspect their involvement, if that is what you mean,' said Mrs Venn. 'The housemaid, Matilda, has been with us since the school opened, some ten years ago. She is due to be married very soon, and has every expectation of happiness. Mrs Robson, the cook, has been with us for seven years. Her husband, of whom I understand she has no complaint, is a coachman and they reside in Porchester Mews. Mrs Thorn, a widow, comes in to help with the cleaning twice a week, on Mondays and Fridays, as she has done for a similar length of time.'

Frances wrote this down. 'And now I would like to speak to Charlotte and see the schoolroom.'

Mrs Venn consulted her watch. 'There is a lesson about to conclude in a few minutes. Let us go down.'

Frances learned that there were two schoolrooms, both on the ground floor. They did not connect and each had a separate entrance from the hallway. At the far end of the house another door gave access to stairs, which led to the basement kitchen and a room where meals were taken.

Mrs Venn first showed Frances the front room, which was currently unoccupied. Because of its size and the generous natural light, it was used for music, dance, deportment and art. There was a small pianoforte in one corner and a cupboard for paints and brushes. The walls were tastefully decorated with examples of the girls' work, which showed that the most recent subject studied was a vase of flowers, and there was also a pretty display of painted fans and posies of dried flowers embellished with ribbon. Frances inspected the room and made polite compliments, until the movement of feet next door told her that the French lesson with Mlle Girard had ended. They passed into the hallway, where the teacher, a dainty little woman of about twenty-five, was ushering the girls from the room. The pupils, who appeared to range in age from twelve to seventeen, were clad in plain grey dresses and spotless white pinafores, each girl's hair shining as if brushed only moments ago, and tied with a grey bow. Mrs Venn spoke briefly to Mlle Girard, who cast her dark eyes and an arched eyebrow at Frances. She then spoke to one of the girls before departing with her youthful train following, leaving Charlotte Fiske, who was already starting to look afraid, in the custody of Mrs Venn.

'Come with me, Charlotte,' said Mrs Venn, in a far kinder tone than she had reserved for Frances. 'This is Miss Doughty, who would like to ask you some questions.'

Charlotte was fourteen but looked younger. She re-entered the schoolroom timidly, and Frances realised that with her awkward height, she must tower over the girl. She wondered what Charlotte was most afraid of – being blamed herself, or causing another's disgrace.

The schoolroom was comfortably large enough for a class of twelve. There were individual wooden desks with lids, arranged in three rows of four, a higher desk and chair for the teacher, and a large cupboard for stationery. A blackboard rested on an easel and had already been thoroughly scoured. A chart on the wall listed which girls were responsible for such tasks as cleaning the board after each lesson, the supply of ink, and ensuring that the room was tidy before being vacated. There were maps on display, some framed embroidery samplers, and a portrait of the Queen. Frances would have preferred to speak to Charlotte alone, but Mrs Venn at once went to the instructor's chair, sat down, took up a pen and looked immovable.

'Charlotte,' said Frances gently, 'Your father has asked me to find out who put the pamphlets in the desks. I know it was very upsetting for everyone, so when I know who that person is I would like to speak to them and ask them not to do it again.'

Charlotte's lower lip trembled. 'I don't know who did it – really I don't!'

'And I believe you,' Frances reassured her. 'But I am hoping you may be able to help me. I know that you are a clever girl and your Papa and Mama are very proud of you.' Charlotte looked less afraid and managed a little smile. 'So – would you like to show me where you found the pamphlet?'

Charlotte went to a desk on the far side of the room and opened the lid. Inside Frances saw a pencil case and a pile of exercise books with covers of different colours denoting the subject within – green for botany, blue for French, pink for arithmetic and so on. Charlotte's name, written with a studied effort at neatness, was on every book. The French book was on top of the pile and Frances picked it up, to see immediately underneath it a primer of French phrases and a book of nouns and verbs. 'So when you have just completed a lesson, the books for that lesson are generally to be found on top,' said Frances. 'Can you show me which book the pamphlet was in?'

Charlotte quickly rifled through the desk and found her arithmetic primer, a volume of about a hundred pages and some smaller booklets of about eight pages each, which were sets of exercises. 'It was in here,' said Charlotte, holding out a booklet devoted to the subject of long division.

Frances took the booklet. 'Whereabouts in your desk was this yesterday morning?' she asked.

'It was inside my arithmetic book. That was underneath most of the others.'

'And when did you last look at these exercises?'

'At the lesson the day before.'

'You are sure that the pamphlet was not there then?'

'Oh yes, quite sure,' said Charlotte. At that moment the door-bell sounded.

Frances turned to the headmistress. 'Mrs Venn, I believe you conducted the search of the other desks?'

'Together with Miss Baverstock, yes,' said Mrs Venn, somewhat taken aback to be made the object of questioning in front of one of her pupils.

'I suppose that no note was made of exactly where each pamphlet was found?'

The headmistress set her mouth in a firm line of displeasure.

'I am sure that at the time no such need was anticipated,' said Frances.

'You are correct. All I can tell you is that they were in locations similar to that Charlotte has described.'

'Tucked well away so that someone making a routine inspection of the desks would not have seen them,' said Frances.

'Exactly so.'

There was a knock on the door and the maidservant entered.

'Yes Matilda, what is it?' asked Mrs Venn.

'It's Mr Rawsthorne to see you Ma'am.'

Frances wondered why the prominent Bayswater solicitor had come calling. He was also her own family's solicitor and a friend to her father, who had given them much sympathetic assistance during the recent distressing time. She knew that he had two young daughters and thought it possible that they were pupils at the school.

'He says it's very important,' added Matilda.

From her expression, the headmistress was clearly unhappy about leaving the room. She glanced at her watch and sighed. 'Very well, show him up to my study.' She rose and handed Frances a sheet of paper, on which she had been writing during the interview the list Frances had required of staff, pupils and servants. 'Charlotte – the next lesson is deportment and will take place in *one minute*. Do not be late!'

As soon as Mrs Venn had departed, Frances managed to fold her tall frame into one of the girls' chairs, so that she was more on a level with Charlotte.' Just one or two more questions,' she said. 'When you found the pamphlet, you began to read it, didn't you, because of course you were curious to know what it was.'

Charlotte began to look afraid again. 'Yes, but – I don't remember anything!'

'I am sure,' said Frances, soothingly, 'that your Papa and Mama are *very* pleased to know that you recall nothing of what was in the pamphlet, and Mrs Venn shares that view. I, on the other hand, am very sorry to hear it, as it would help me a great deal.'

Charlotte frowned and contemplated her feet.

'Perhaps if you could try to remember just a little. I am told that the title was "Why Marry?" Is that correct?'

'Yes, I think so,' said Charlotte grudgingly. 'I didn't really understand what it meant.'

'And had the author been courageous enough to put his or her name to it?'

'No. There was no name, only – A Friend to Women.'

'I see,' said Frances, smiling encouragement, 'how very interesting! I wonder what that charitable person had to say? I would be *most* entertained to find out!'

The girl's lips moved but no sound emerged.

Frances leaned forward and spoke in a confidential tone. 'You have my promise that I will say nothing of what you tell me.'

Charlotte glanced quickly over her shoulder at the door, then took a deep breath. 'It said – that before a woman marries she should discover all of the man's character – but that many women, on finding it out, would choose not to marry at all. But I don't know what that means and I didn't read any more!'

Frances felt quite sure that Charlotte had read more, but was also certain that this was all she would tell.

When Charlotte had scurried away to her lesson, Frances made some notes and considered what she had learned. For a person to enter the schoolroom and distribute the pamphlets by simply placing one in each desk was a task that could be accomplished in less than a minute. To extract a booklet, put the pamphlet inside and then conceal it between the pages of a book and then tuck it securely away, and do this twelve times, was altogether a lengthier operation. The culprit must have had the leisure to do it, with reason to feel confident that he or she would not be interrupted, and might also have been someone who would have been able to explain away their presence should another person unexpectedly appear. Frances looked at the timetable. After the Tuesday arithmetic lesson ended at twelve the class had been split into two, the older girls remaining in the schoolroom for history with Mrs Venn and the younger transferring to the front room for music with Miss Baverstock. Following this there was an hour when the girls and staff all took luncheon together. In the afternoon there had been four lessons, but at no time had the schoolroom been unused. Lessons ended at five o'clock, when the pupils who did not board had been collected and those who did had afternoon prayers then made their ablutions, had supper, and went to bed. The obvious time to put the pamphlets in the desks was between five, when classes ended for the day, and nine the following morning.

The list provided by Mrs Venn showed that only three pupils boarded, the daughters – aged twelve, thirteen and fifteen – of a gentleman called Younge. The only servant who boarded was the housemaid, Matilda, and of the teaching staff, only Mrs Venn, Miss Baverstock and Miss Bell. Mlle Girard and Mr Copley (botany, painting and drawing) resided elsewhere.

She was deep in thought when Mrs Venn returned. 'I would like to view the rest of the premises and see where those who reside here are accommodated,' said Frances.

'Of course,' said Mrs Venn with glacial politeness.

Mrs Venn, Frances found, slept in a small but comfortably appointed room that adjoined her study, which also served as a washroom and dressing room. On the same floor was a bedroom for the accommodation of Miss Baverstock and Miss Bell, a water closet, a wash room, and a common room where the girls did needlework and informal study and had tea. On the second floor was a girls' dormitory, a storeroom, and a small room for Matilda. The basement was divided into two, a kitchen and a room where meals were taken. There were twelve places set at a long table for the pupils and a smaller table for the teaching staff. The servants, after bringing in the meals, ate in the kitchen. Frances thought it very possible that one of them might have been able to slip away to the schoolroom for a few minutes without arousing suspicion.

Matilda and Mrs Robson were working in the kitchen, the former stirring a pot of soup and the latter, with heavily floured arms, putting the finishing touches to a large, thick-crusted pie of savoury aspect. Mrs Robson stopped what she was doing as the headmistress and Frances entered, and stood respectfully by the table, but Matilda simply looked around briefly and went on stirring.

'I trust that that is all you need to see?' enquired Mrs Venn.

'It is,' said Frances, sitting down. 'And after such hard work I would welcome a cup of tea.'

Mrs Venn paused a little longer than was necessary. 'Matilda,' she said at last, 'please provide Miss Doughty with a cup of tea before she departs.' Without a word, Matilda put her spoon down and went to fetch the teapot.

Frances glanced at the timetable. 'I will return after two o'clock to speak to Mr Copley, Mlle Girard, Miss Baverstock and Miss Bell. I would be grateful if a private room could be provided. At five I would like to see the three girls who board here.'

'Of course,' said Mrs Venn, with an effort at being accommodating, 'I will make the arrangements.'

'This is all about those silly papers in the girls' desks, isn't it?' said Mrs Robson, when Mrs Venn had left. 'I hope you don't think *we* had anything to do with it?'

'Not at all,' said Frances. 'But you may be able to help me by letting me know what visitors came to the house between twelve on Tuesday and nine the next morning?'

'Mr Sandcourt came on the Tuesday,' said Matilda, bustling with the teapot, which Frances saw was being filled for more than one, 'and then Mr Fiske with Mr Miggs.'

'And they all had appointments?'

'They did, and I took them straight up to see Mrs Venn, and showed them out when they went.'

'No one else was here? No one who might have waited in the hallway?'

Matilda shook her head. Mrs Robson put the pie in the oven and opened a box of currant biscuits and they all sat down to tea.

'Were there any visitors on the Wednesday morning?' asked Frances.

'Not at the front door, no,' said Matilda.

'There were the usual delivery men at the kitchen door, and Mrs Armstrong, who collects the linens to go to the washhouse,' said Mrs Robson, 'but none of them even came inside let alone went upstairs.'

'And Davey came to see me,' said Matilda with a superior smile. 'My intended. I gave him a cup of tea.'

'Mrs Venn has no objection to your young man calling here?' asked Frances with some surprise.

'None at all,' said Matilda, firmly.

'Can you think of anyone who might have had the opportunity to put something in the girls' desks – or who might have wanted to do such a thing?'

Both the servants shook their heads. 'I can't see what all the fuss is about,' said Mrs Robson.

'What was in the papers?' asked Matilda, with a sly little laugh and a mischievous twinkle in her eyes. 'It wasn't one of those romance stories with pirates and brigands? Can I see one?'

'They were not stories at all, so I understand,' said Frances, 'but they have been burnt so I have not been able to examine one.' Matilda looked disappointed.

'Well,' said Mrs Robson, 'If Mrs Venn has burnt them then it must be for the best.' She gave a firm nod, gulped the rest of her tea and went back to work.

There was no more to be discovered so Frances finished her tea and departed. Thus far, she reflected as she walked home, her enquiries had resulted in the conclusion that those people who had the opportunity to put the pamphlets in the desks were the very ones who had no motive to do so. She was left with two very important questions. At some point in the future she would firstly have to ask Mrs Venn for the real reason she had destroyed the pamphlets, and, secondly, what it was that she was afraid of, but that time had not yet come.

CHAPTER THREE

Frances returned to her almost desolate rooms in Westbourne Grove and ate a simple dish of boiled eggs, then Sarah conjured a wonderful pudding from old bread, apples and sugar. She had not yet succeeded in finding a suitable apartment, and Frances gathered from Sarah that the cost of respectable lodgings for two was greater than she had supposed and more than Frances could reasonably spare from her carefully hoarded resources. Nevertheless, when the meal was done, Sarah voyaged forth again with a tangible air of optimism, leaving Frances to study the notes of her interviews. Alone, with her few possessions packed in boxes around her, Frances contemplated her future, and hoped that she had not given Sarah false hopes of success. One commission was all very well, but she had not given any thought as to how she was to find another. She wondered about the cost of putting an advertisement in the *Bayswater Chronicle*. 'Lady detective. Discretion assured.' If nothing else that would attract the ladies in Bayswater who had bad husbands, and Frances felt confident that there would be many of those.

For the present her thoughts revolved around the possible motives for the placement of the pamphlets in the school. Mr Fiske had already told her of Mrs Venn's impeccable history, but she wondered if there was something to be learned from the circumstances of the three governors – not what they proudly showed to the world, but those matters on which they preferred to remain silent.

When Sarah returned she brought with her two unexpected visitors. Charles Knight and Sebastian Taylor. 'Chas' and 'Barstie', as they were familiarly known, were two businessmen, as inseparable as brothers, who had befriended Frances very recently. She had wisely decided quite early in the acquaintance not to ask them the nature of their business. While their fortunes ebbed and flowed, sometimes with startling suddenness, the one thing that remained constant was their abject fear of an individual who they knew only as 'The Filleter'. Frances had only encountered him once, a black-clad, repellently odorous and greasy young man with a thin sharp knife at his hip. The mere mention of his name was enough to put them to flight.

When Frances had last seen them, they were smartly dressed, but leaving Bayswater as fast as their legs could carry them. Today, while glad of their company, she was sorry to see that they were clad in garments which, while once worn proudly by gentlemen of fashion, would nowadays be rejected by all but the most desperate pawnbroker.

Frances greeted them warmly, and, noticing a jaded look which they were polite enough to try and conceal, sent Sarah to bring them tea, bread and potted meat, which they consumed with considerable relish.

'I will be taking new apartments soon,' declared Frances. 'When I am settled, I would be very pleased for you to call. I hope that you intend to remain in Bayswater?'

'We are even now in search of suitable accommodation in this immediate area,' replied Barstie, waving a languid hand as if all the amenities of the district were laid out for his choosing. 'Bayswater is quite the pinnacle of gentility for those of us who prefer to live useful lives.'

'We have the strongest possible reasons to be drawn to its opportunities, its multitudes and its delights,' said Chas. The tea and food had restored his strength and his rounded face glowed pink with energy. 'My friend has an ardent romantic nature and wishes to lay his heart at the feet of a young lady with considerable financial expectations. The young lady, sadly, is immune to his protestations — in short, she will not have him. But he will not abandon his quest.'

'Now don't pretend that *your* heart is unengaged,' said Barstie. 'Bayswater also holds the key to your happiness.'

'Happiness is a full purse, and something in the bank,' said Chas. 'All my business is here, and no man, not even a *certain person* whose name I will not mention for fear of soiling my lips, will keep me from it. I mean to make my fortune, Miss Doughty, and then I hope to be worthy of a young lady of exceptional qualities. A young lady who knows the value of things – who I can entrust with my heart, my life, even my books of account.'

'She must be very remarkable,' said Frances, who had once received an unsubtle hint that the business acumen she had gained during the years working in her father's shop had stirred Mr Knight's tender interest.

'Oh, she is, she is. But I have not spoken one word of devotion – nor will I until my fortune is secure!' He nodded very significantly.

'Well, gentlemen, if you have not yet found suitable accommodation – I hesitate to mention it as it is hardly more than bare rooms —,' she saw their faces brighten and pressed on. 'Although I am leaving very soon, I do have the use of this property for two or three more days before Mr Jacobs brings his effects. You are very welcome to stay until then. There are two quite unoccupied rooms above.'

'That is very kind of you,' said Barstie, casually. 'I think, Chas, we may consider availing ourselves of the offer.'

Chas frowned. 'Er – as to the question of rent —'

'Oh please don't think of it,' said Frances. She pretended not to notice their palpable relief.

'Such generosity!' said Chas, beaming. 'We accept at once!'

Frances decided not to raise the question of their luggage, which might cause them embarrassment as she was fairly certain there was none. 'There is, however, one little service you might perform for me,' she went on. 'I need information about three gentlemen who reside in Bayswater. Their business and family circumstances.'

Chas and Barstie exchanged worried glances. 'This is not another case of murder, Miss Doughty?' asked Barstie anxiously.

'Oh, no,' she reassured him, 'nothing so terrible as that. I would like to know if these gentlemen might have rivals – or enemies, even. Whether justified or not. Even the most respectable of men may make enemies who envy them their success.'

Chas and Barstie both nodded sagely as if they had whole armies of envious rivals. 'Let us know their names and we will find out everything we can,' said Chas.

'They are Mr Algernon Fiske, who is an author I believe, Mr Roderick Matthews, a market gardener, and Mr Bartholomew Paskall, property agent.'

'They are known to us by repute only, though not personally,' said Chas.

'I would also like to know something of the circumstances of Mr Julius Sandcourt, who is married to Mr Matthews' eldest daughter, and an associate of Mr Fiske's called Miggs,' Frances added. 'I will meet any expenses of your enquiries of course.' She paused. 'In advance – why not?' She found a few shillings in her purse and handed them over. 'Now, gentlemen, I have an appointment very shortly, but if you were to join me for supper at seven, I would be delighted.'

The arrangements completed, Frances returned to Chepstow Place, where Matilda admitted her to the school and asked with a smirk if she had solved the puzzle yet.

'Not yet,' said Frances, 'unless there is something *you* can tell me.'

'Oh I've said all I know, which isn't anything,' said Matilda. 'Mr Copley's waiting for you. Now I'd be very surprised if *he* didn't know something.'

Frances was ushered into the art room, where she found Mr Copley carefully arranging chairs in the largest circle the room would permit. In the centre of the circle was a small table on which sat a cut-glass vase, which held a fresh posy of spring flowers. Copley, a small sprucely dressed man of about thirty with a prematurely receding hairline, looked up with a smile as Frances entered the room.

'Ah, Miss Doughty, how may I assist you?' he enquired brightly, flapping his hand at Matilda by way of dismissal. She turned and flounced back to the kitchen.

'I was hoping you would be so good as to answer some questions,' said Frances.

'Of course! Of course! And you may assist *me*, Miss Doughty,' he said, placing a chair beside the little table, 'by seating yourself here.'

Frances sat and took out her notebook while Mr Copley bustled about, checking the view of the table from each of the seats in the circle. 'I understand that you do not lodge in the school,' Frances asked.

'Oh dear me, no, that would be quite improper. I have my own rooms in the Grove. Some might call my humble abode an attic, but to me, Miss Doughty, it is a place near to heaven. There I have a little studio where the light illuminates my work and I may grow my garden of precious flowers near the window. If I might impose on you, Miss Doughty, could you lean a little more to the left? Just so!'

Frances, trying to accommodate him while also writing in her notebook, said, 'And what classes do you teach here?'

'Botany twice a week, drawing twice and painting twice. All at 3 p.m. There is a school in Kensington where I have classes every morning. I also have other employment illustrating books, and in my leisure moments I am inspired by my own notions of Art. Perhaps if you might place your left hand on the table?' He rotated the vase about an inch, stepped back to gaze at it, and sighed. 'The most beautiful thing in the world to me is the flower. The delicate fragile petals, as they just begin to open, the hint of dewy moisture within. So innocent! So pure! How it lifts my spirits to see it.'

Frances took a moment from her new occupation as artist's model to make a note. 'Please could you tell me exactly where you were between midday on Tuesday the second of March and nine the following morning?'

He gazed at her. 'You are very young, Miss Doughty.'

'I am nineteen,' she said. 'And I would be obliged if you would answer my question.'

He licked his lips. 'Barely more than a schoolgirl yourself.' He sat down. 'Let me see. On Tuesday I was as usual at the school for boys in Kensington, where I taught two classes in botany and draughtsmanship, the first at nine o'clock and the second at eleven o'clock. The hour between classes I spent in the staffroom looking at the pupils' work. I was then permitted to take a light luncheon with the pupils and staff. I was here from two o'clock, preparing the room for my class. I took class between three and four and then I returned home, where I remained until the next morning. On the Wednesday morning I was again in Kensington.'

'When you were here on Tuesday, did you have any occasion to enter the schoolroom?' asked Frances.

'None at all.'

'And did you see anyone enter or leave, or was there perhaps some person standing in the hallway?'

He pondered this. 'If I had seen one of the staff or pupils or servants enter or leave it would not be so unusual that I would remember it particularly. I have no recollection of seeing any visitors that day.'

Frances paused, for she was about to pose a question which she would never formerly have considered asking a single man. 'If you would forgive me for asking a question which may seem impertinent – what is your opinion of marriage?'

Mr Copley's eyes opened wide and there was a flush of colour in his cheeks, then he straightened a little in his chair. 'I – I believe marriage to be the highest and most holy of aspirations,' he said at last. 'I hope to be married myself one day.'

'You did not see any of the pamphlets that were placed in the girls' desks?'

'No, I did not.'

'Can you suggest why someone might want to place them there?'

He made an expressive gesture of helplessness. 'I cannot possibly imagine.'

'I am asking everyone the same question.' Frances waited for a reply.

Mr Copley thought for a while and then uttered a sorrowful sigh. 'There are individuals in this world who, sadly, cannot see a thing of purity and perfection without wanting to besmirch it. I both despise and pity such persons.'

'Can you name a suspect?' asked Frances hopefully.

'I spoke in the abstract, of course. I have no acquaintanceships in such circles. I expect, however, that they would already be known to the police.'

Frances thought of Matilda's hint about Mr Copley. Did the girl really know something or was she simply amusing herself with groundless insinuations? 'As an artist,' she said, 'you are more skilled than most in observation. Is there no one here whose behaviour or expression has seemed different lately?'

He shook his head. 'I am sorry, Miss Doughty, it is as much a mystery to me as it is to us all.'

Frances thanked him, and though he had not been able to help, one comment had led to a thought. While the placing of the pamphlets was not in itself a crime, perhaps the culprit had committed other acts which were of a criminal nature. She determined to pay a visit to Paddington Green police station in the near future. Even if she learned nothing there, it would be an opportunity for some agreeable conversation with Constable Brown.

Frances rang for Matilda, who did not trouble herself to attend promptly but arrived in her own time, and advised her that Mrs Venn had set aside the common room for the remaining interviews. Matilda then left Frances to make her own way upstairs.

Mlle Girard was seated comfortably before a good fire warming her toes, which were encased in embroidered slippers. Some papers lay piled on a table nearby, which Frances could see were exercises in translation, and her needlework box was open at her feet. She was engaged in crochet work, which, from her expression of contentment, was a far more pleasurable activity than correcting the clumsy French of girls for whom the language held no charm. Mlle Girard interested Frances because she had not, as far as she could recall, ever met a French person and was curious as to what a French lady's manners might be. Her father had never spoken a great deal about the French, largely because if the subject ever arose in the newspapers he dismissed it as beneath his contempt.

Mlle Girard arose and greeted Frances most politely, although Frances thought that the teacher regarded her as not quite an equal. She was a trim young woman with eyes that always seemed to be asking a question.

'Thank you for agreeing to speak to me,' said Frances.

'Oh but I am delighted to do anything that might help,' said the teacher in a softly pretty accent, settling herself again. Her fingers, slim as spider's legs, moved nimbly as she worked a delicate blue and white scalloped edging around a dainty handkerchief.

Frances was not an admirer of ornament for its own sake, but knew that there were many who were; ladies who used it to draw attention to their beauty and men who decorated their wives to demonstrate their own prosperity. She sat down, placed her hands on her lap and laced her long fingers. For the briefest of moments Frances wondered if, had she not been fated to grow tall enough to look men in the eye, her life now would be different from the way it was, and if that would be a good thing or bad? She had never longed for beauty, but thought how useful it would be as an enchantment to persuade people to tell her the truth.

'I see you are admiring my craftwork,' said Mlle Girard with a sweet smile. 'It is very elegant, is it not? A pattern given to me by my grandmother.'

'How long have you been teaching here?' asked Frances.

'Two years.'

'And do you have any thoughts as to why someone might have wanted to play this curious trick on the school?'

The teacher gave a slight shrug. 'No, it has never crossed my mind. It was upsetting for the girls and of course Mrs Venn, but I imagine it was what you call a practical joke, something from the English sense of humour. I have noticed, especially amongst young men, but sometimes girls as well, a fondness for jokes which can be cruel and cause much unhappiness, and for no other reason than pleasure in the joke itself. I find it very strange, but that is the way.'

'Between midday on Tuesday and nine on Wednesday morning, did you see anything that you thought was unusual – someone in the school who is not normally here – or someone you expected to be here but was not behaving in their usual manner?'

'No, nothing of that kind at all.'

'On the Wednesday morning, when the pamphlets were found, what were you doing?'

'I do not lodge here, you understand, I have my own apartments where I also on occasion take private pupils for lessons in the French language. I came here at nine, and was arranging some displays of the girls' needlework in the art and music room. I knew nothing of the affair until Miss Baverstock asked me to take charge of the girls in the common room while she spoke to Mrs Venn on an urgent matter. Of course I complied.'

'And how did the girls behave?'

'They seemed very – unsettled. I saw that Charlotte had gone with Miss Baverstock, and I asked them what had occurred. They said that Charlotte had found something in her desk and was being questioned about it. I asked if they knew what this thing was and they said it was a paper, but they had not seen what kind. I think, although they are girls and have as much mischief in them as any young lady, they were concerned about Charlotte and were wondering if she might be punished.'

'I doubt that one of the girls was responsible,' said Frances. 'It is hard to see how a pupil might have come by twelve copies of such a pamphlet.'

'That is what I think,' said Mlle Girard. 'It is someone who does not usually come here – you need to look outside the school and not inside.' Frances suspected that she was right.

'I hope you will not think me impudent, but I would like to ask your opinion of marriage,' said Frances.

Mlle Girard smiled. 'It is not something that may be enjoyed in comfort and happiness without money. A sensible person will take care not to marry before he or she is provided for. There is a gentleman in Switzerland – we hope, in a year from now, to be united.'

The interview completed, Mlle Girard put away her crochet, took up her papers and departed, to be replaced by Miss Baverstock, a tall lady of about fifty with a severe expression and, as suited a teacher of deportment, a back as straight as a ruler. Her hair, the colour of wet clay, was braided and wrapped about her head in long coils. Frances decided not to ask her about marriage.

'I believe that you have taught at the school since it began,' said Frances.

'I have. Prior to the opening of the school I took private lessons, here in Bayswater.' Miss Baverstock studied Frances disapprovingly, and shook her head. 'May I say, Miss Doughty, that your carriage leaves something to be desired? Do you do a great deal of reading? There is nothing wrong in that, of course, if the material is suitable, but I find that girls who read often have slumped shoulders, and there is almost nothing as bad in a young lady as slumped shoulders.'

'Oh,' said Frances, immediately adjusting her posture.

'That is better,' said Miss Baverstock with a nod. 'Let us proceed.'

'Can you tell me in your own words about how you discovered the pamphlet in Charlotte's desk? I would like you to start your account from when the class began.'

Miss Baverstock briefly pursed her lips. 'You have a tidy mind, Miss Doughty. I admire that. Very well, I will do as you request. The girls were in their places just before nine, and once I had checked and corrected their postures they began their work. I was engaged in some correspondence. Then one of the girls – Helena Younge – came to ask me about the method of making a decorated garland. We spoke for a minute or two then, as she returned to her place, she must have brushed against the booklet in Charlotte's hand, and it fell. As it did so, I heard Charlotte give a little gasp and I saw the paper fall to the floor. It looked unfamiliar and I went to look at it. I think you can imagine my feelings on seeing its true nature.'

'What happened then?' asked Frances.

'I naturally asked Charlotte what this meant and she said she had discovered the paper in her arithmetic book but was at a loss to know how it had come to be there. I decided to take her to see Mrs Venn, and then – and how glad I am that I did – I wondered if the other girls had received similar missives. I asked them if they had and they assured me that they had not, but it then occurred to me that they might not yet have discovered anything, so I asked them all to go up to the common room.'

'Where they were supervised by Mlle Girard?'

'Exactly. I then took Charlotte to see Mrs Venn and afterwards Mrs Venn and I looked in all the desks, where we were horrified to find an identical pamphlet in every one.'

'Do you recall which books they were hidden in?' asked Frances, without much hope that she would.

'I am afraid not. Is that important?'

'I don't know. Perhaps not. But all the papers were very well hidden?'

'Oh yes. It is quite possible that some of the girls might not have found theirs until the next day.'

'Did you at any time from about twelve the previous day to the time the pamphlet was found see anyone in the school who ought not to have been there? Or someone in or near the schoolroom who did not usually go to that part of the house?'

'No one at all.'

'You have not observed anyone behaving in an unaccustomed manner?'

'I have not.'

'You lodge here, I believe?'

'Yes, I share a room with Miss Bell. I slept soundly that night as I usually do and noticed nothing unusual or out of place.'

Frances looked at her notes again, Miss Baverstock observing her calmly. The teacher made no comment on Frances' youthfulness and lack of experience of the world but she did not need to speak to do so.

'Have you any thoughts you might share with me as to who might have done this – or why?' asked Frances.

Miss Baverstock made a sour grimace. 'I will not name any names, Miss Doughty, but I will say this – there are persons in this world who, unhappily, take a malicious delight in causing upset to other people. They do it for pleasure, Miss Doughty, and it is disgraceful! I will say no more.'

When Miss Baverstock had departed Frances sat silently for a time wondering if there was anything of importance she had missed, any question she had omitted to ask which might have provided greater enlightenment. It was one thing to ask and learn nothing because there was nothing to learn, quite another to feel, as she did, that she had failed to learn something because she had not explored sufficiently.

Miss Bell arrived, a lady in her early thirties, who, from her appearance, was still living in hope that she would not always be in the single state. There was too much lace on her bosom, one too many frills on her cap, and a faded flower pinned above her heart. She dabbed at her eyes with a colourfully embellished handkerchief. 'The poor, poor girls!' she exclaimed. 'What a dreadful thing to happen. I see them all as if they were my very own, you know. Not,' she gave a little laugh, 'that I am old enough to have such large daughters, but I feel for them as if they were my family.'

'Charlotte must have been very distressed,' said Frances.

'Oh she was! I have never seen a girl cry so. She thought she would be blamed for it all, you see, though why she might think so I really can't say. The other girls found her distress very alarming.'

Miss Bell, like Miss Baverstock, had seen nothing at all suspicious during the time when the pamphlets must have been put in the girls' desks. 'As to who might have done this thing – I really can't imagine! Why warn the girls against the married state when it is the pinnacle of a woman's happiness! I wonder if some lady who hoped to marry but could not find a husband wished to deter her rivals so that she might have a better chance. I can think of no other reason.'

Frances' interview with the three Younge sisters was similarly unhelpful. They stood quietly in a row like a set of china dolls, regarding her with large, brown, reproachful eyes, as if her questions were an affront to their merit. None of them had seen or heard anything of note and Helena, while agreeing that her apron might have brushed by Charlotte as she returned to her desk, seemed astonished that anyone should invest this incident with any significance.

Before she left, Frances spoke briefly to Mrs Venn to advise her that she had completed her enquiries for that day, and would be reporting her conclusions in due course. In fact Frances had no conclusions, nor, on the basis of what she had learned, did she think was she likely to have any, but she was not about to admit it. Mrs Venn showed no interest in the results of Frances' endeavours, but expressed a hope that her work would be over very soon, and rang for Matilda. The housemaid was looking even more pleased with herself than usual. There was the edge of a paper protruding from her apron pocket which, Frances thought, had not been there before. When the maid saw that Frances had noticed it, she pushed it deep into her pocket, out of sight.

CHAPTER FOUR

On her way home Frances called to see Mr Fiske. On being told by the servant that he was in conference with a gentleman, Frances extracted the information that the gentleman concerned was the aspiring publisher, Mr Miggs, and said that this was very convenient as she wished to see them both. After exercising some firmness, she was admitted to their presence. Mr Miggs, she found, was a man of about twenty-five, impeccably dressed but with the most unattractive set of Dundreary whiskers she had ever seen and an intensely serious expression, as if he hoped that by denying his youthfulness he might thereby command greater respect. He professed himself charmed to be introduced to Frances, about whom he had read in the newspapers, and presented her with a crisp little business card which he extracted from a silver case. Mr Fiske, on seeing Frances, was at first hopeful that she had come to say she had resolved the problem of the pamphlets, then disappointed to find that she had not, then astonished that she wanted to question him, puzzled that she wanted to question Mr Miggs too, and finally alarmed that she also wished to speak to Mr Sandcourt. Frances, who had for many years been used to dealing with the petulant and unpredictable mood changes of her father, had no difficulty at all in managing Mr Fiske. She quickly confirmed that neither he nor Mr Miggs had entered the schoolroom on their visit to the Academy, and secured a letter of introduction to Mr Sandcourt.

Julius Sandcourt was what was popularly called a self-made man, though whether he had constructed himself on humble foundations or from the broken remains of other men, Frances did not know. There had been a pretty society wedding a year before, when Selina Matthews, then just twenty-two, had married Mr Sandcourt, whose wealth and age were said to be greater even than those of her father. The Sandcourts lived in one of the superior premises on Inverness Terrace, and kept six servants and two carriages. Frances had intended to present a note asking for an appointment but Mr Fiske's letter was sufficient to admit her to the drawing room where Mr Sandcourt, his wife and another young lady were engaged in conversation. Frances might once have been impressed by the evidence she saw about her of wealth; the fine furniture, rich upholstery, paintings and porcelain heavy with the dull gleam of gilding, with which the room was almost oppressively filled, but she had learned that money alone did not make for happiness, and resolved to judge only on what she found.

Her first impression of Mr Sandcourt was that he was not, despite his name, an Englishman. The cast of his features; the mouth, nose, cheekbones and brows too large for an already broad face; the wiry grey hair and tint of his skin denoted a more exotic origin. As he rose to greet her she saw that he was several inches shorter than she, and rather stout, nevertheless he had a charming smile. Selina's face – as white and beautiful as a marble statue – was surmounted by a mass of shining, almost black, hair, elegantly arranged, her features and colouring sufficiently like that of one of the school governors in Mrs Venn's photograph to proclaim her as his daughter. Her gown was of the latest French fashion, something Frances had only ever seen in shop windows, the elaborate trimmings designed more to display wealth than to please the eye. She would, on her husband's arm, have appeared as a rich jewel pinned to his sleeve. Selina, when she glanced at her husband, which she did infrequently, did so with a well-practised expression of warm regard.

Their companion was Lydia Matthews, who was aged about twenty and, despite every artifice, could not boast even one tenth of her sister's beauty. Her parchment paleness gave her a sickly look, and this was not enhanced by hair of an indeterminate shade between light brown and faded red, swept back from sharply pinched features. While Mr Sandcourt was courteous and friendly towards Frances, and Selina gazed on her with curiosity, Lydia regarded the visitor as if she had been a scullery maid, who had ventured where she had no permission to be.

'Thank you for agreeing to see me,' said Frances.

'But I am very pleased to see *you*, Miss Doughty,' said Sandcourt, with an accent less of Eastern Europe than East London. 'I read about you in the newspapers, and a very exciting read it was too.' He signalled to the maid to bring some refreshment. 'If I ever need the services of a detective, I shall think of you first!'

Out of the corner of her eye Frances saw Lydia's mouth twitch.

'I have come on behalf of Mr Fiske,' Frances began, not sure how to introduce the subject.

'Oh, it must be about those stupid papers at the school,' said Lydia loudly. 'I'm sure I don't know why he troubles himself!'

Frances realised that Lydia must have heard about the incident from her younger sisters, and thought that Mr Fiske's hope that the affair might be kept secret was an ambition that had collapsed long ago. It was probably the subject of animated gossip at every tea table in Bayswater.

'Mr Fiske has supported the school for many years,' said Selina, her voice altogether more soothing than her sister's. 'I expect you know, Miss Doughty, that Lydia and I were both pupils there. It is a fine school.'

'Oh, it is good enough, I suppose,' said Lydia, carelessly, 'but why should we think of it now?'

Selina made a slight gesture, the fingertips of one hand curving in lightly to touch her abdomen. 'Julius intends to become a patron,' she said. The maid brought a tray with sherry and sweet biscuits. Selina waved it aside, but Lydia nibbled a biscuit and Frances accepted one, while Sandcourt poured himself a large sherry and took a handful of biscuits without troubling himself about a plate.

'I have visited the school and met Mrs Venn,' said Sandcourt. 'She seems like a good sort of woman.'

'You were there on Tuesday, I believe?' asked Frances.

'I was.'

'It is believed that the pamphlets were placed in the girls' desks either on the Tuesday or the Wednesday,' said Frances.

'I hope you don't suspect Mr Sandcourt!' exclaimed Lydia. 'That would be the stupidest thing I ever heard!'

'Not at all,' said Frances hastily, 'I only meant —'

'I know what you meant,' said Sandcourt, cheerily, 'and I can tell you I saw no one about when I called apart from the maid and Mrs Venn. But it's not a serious matter, is it? Perhaps it was meant to be an advertisement. There's any number of little printing works after contracts to produce posters and pamphlets and looking for cheap ways to advertise.'

'But the nature of the material . . .' queried Frances, 'and the location . . . ?'

'It has us all talking, though, and trying to find out who did it!' he said with a chuckle. 'It'll be some young business type who'll come up with a smile and then try to make his name out of it. I should like to meet *him*.'

Lydia laughed. 'I think Miss Doughty put them there on purpose to make a name for herself!' she said. 'Then she will blame it on some servant and be in all the newspapers again.'

Selina allowed a slight frown to ripple across her flawless forehead. 'Are you feeling well, my dear?' asked Sandcourt.

'If I may, I would like to rest now,' she said softly.

'But it's almost dinner time! You must eat, you know.'

She nodded. 'I know. Have a little light supper sent up in about an hour and I will see what I can manage.'

Sandcourt eased himself out of his chair and escorted his wife to the drawing room door. Frances took the cue to depart. 'If you don't mind my mentioning it,' she said to Selina, 'I understand that sipping a little aerated water may help the – er – discomfort.' Selina gave a faint smile.

That evening, Chas and Barstie returned, freshly suited and booted and almost rosy cheeked with confidence. They had been hard at work on Frances' commission and were bursting with information, which they imparted over a simple supper of soup, bread, cheese, pickles and cold meat. 'Mr Fiske professes to be an author, which is a highly unprofitable occupation except for those rare few who catch the public fancy such as Mr Dickens,' said Chas. 'His main assets are a string of grocery shops and a clever wife. He also had the great good fortune never to have invested in the Bayswater Bank.'

Frances, whose recent success in exposing the activities of a scoundrel had precipitated the sudden and disastrous failure of the Bayswater Bank, felt a momentary twinge of guilt, but she quickly reminded herself that had she not revealed the crimes when she did the crash would still have come but much later, and would therefore have been far worse.

'His associate Mr Arthur Miggs is employed by the Grant Publishing Company of Farringdon, but plans to start his own business. He is energetic, ambitious, and, by all accounts, honest to a fault.'

'I became acquainted with Mr Sandcourt today,' Frances observed. 'He struck me as very pleasant.'

'Or Sandrovitch, as he was once known,' said Barstie. 'He made his fortune in the fur trade. It is said he has warehouses and workshops all over London.'

'I also met Mrs Sandcourt and her younger sister, Lydia,' Frances added, 'and I was struck by how unalike they are, both in appearance and character. I can guess that Mrs Sandcourt most closely resembles her father, but I have never seen Mrs Matthews. Is she alive?'

'She is not,' said Barstie. 'I believe she was an invalid for some years and was taken to Italy in the hope that she would improve. She regained her strength and even became a mother again, but it was too much for her and she died soon afterwards.'

'Does Miss Lydia have a sweetheart?' asked Frances, thinking it very unlikely.

'No, but she has set her cap at so many it is all but worn out,' said Chas. 'She is like a pickled lime – sharp, and not to everyone's taste.'

'Surely her father's wealth will attract a suitor?' said Frances.

'Ah, well, as to wealth . . .' Chas shook his head. 'There are many kinds of wealth. There is property you may safely dispose of and property which you would rather not. Then there is wealth as land and what lies on it, and wealth you may put in your pocket. There is money you may enjoy freely and money which is already spoken for before you get it.'

'And Mr Matthews' wealth?'

'He has land and buildings on a nice little estate at Havenhill, not far from Uxbridge, which he uses to produce his income, but he has suffered lately as so many have with the downturn in trade, and he also made large losses when the bank crashed. He is not ruined, and neither is he poor, but he has a large family. One son has gone abroad to make his own way in business and one daughter is married, but there are three boys at school, three girls unmarried and a ward. How is all that to be paid for?'

'One or two wards?' asked Barstie, thoughtfully.

'That hardly matters,' replied Chas. 'Any number of wards are cheaper than one daughter. Grateful for whatever they are allowed. Related through some cousin or other of his late wife.'

'But there is a rumour —,' said Barstie with a smile.

'Not just a rumour but a very popular belief —,' said Chas significantly.

'Practically a certainty —,' added Barstie.

'That Mr Matthews hopes to mend his fortunes by marriage.'

Money and marriage, thought Frances. How closely they were related. Even though the law now permitted married women to keep what they earned or inherited after they were wed, it was still believed to be in their own interests that such property as they possessed on marriage should pass to their husbands.

'When is the wedding to be?' asked Frances.

'Oh, never, if I hear it right,' said Chas. 'The lady in question is none other than Mr Paskall's sister, a duchess no less, and a widow, who has a fortune and a most determined mind of her own.'

'And intends to hold on to them both,' said Barstie.

'Mr Paskall has alluded in the newspapers to his noble connection,' said Frances, 'chiefly when he discusses the coming election, but I had not realised it was so close as a sister. How did that come about?'

'It is a pretty tale,' said Chas. 'The lady is Margaret, Duchess of Kenworth, and all by the strangest chance.' Having ensured the attention of his audience, Chas helped himself to more cold meat and refreshed his teacup before proceeding.

'The first Duke had three sons and she married the youngest one. But it was not a prudent marriage for it was all for love and nothing else. And no sooner were they wed than she found that her husband was addicted to the bottle and had squandered what little fortune he had. Luckily for the lady the two older brothers were sympathetic to her position, but then it suited them to be. To avoid scandal and trouble to themselves they agreed to pay their unfortunate brother an allowance, but only so long as he never touched a penny of it and his wife consented to look after him. Peace of mind and respectability, and all to be had on the cheap, or so they thought, because no one would have given twopence for their brother's chances of living another six months. But the lady still loved him and devoted herself to him, and under her care he was very much improved, and I am told that when he was sober he was a good husband. They had a daughter, who is said to be very beautiful and delicately brought up. But here is where the hand of fate can be seen. The eldest brother, who was by then the second Duke, married a lady who, while excellent in almost every way, was unable to supply him with an heir. He urged his brother – the second son – to marry, and the poor fellow was on his way to pay court to the lady of his choice when he suffered an unfortunate accident and died. Ten or so years later, the Duke himself passed on, and the youngest brother – on the longest possible odds – found himself the third Duke, with land and money and plate and paintings, not that he was able to enjoy them for long.'

'And these will all belong to the Duchess's husband if she marries again?' asked Frances.

'The landed estate, by settlement, will come to the daughter when she is 21 – she is now 14 – but the rest, and one may only guess the value, is rich pickings for ardent gentlemen. There were suitors paying their addresses even before she was in semi–mourning. Several tried to persuade her that she was not able to manage her fortune, which would be better placed in their hands, but she would not listen.'

'And,' said Barstie, 'she has proved herself to be an excellent manager, with clever investments and careful living. Her only ambition now is to give her daughter every refinement and see her married well.'

'So Mr Matthews is a fortune hunter,' said Frances, 'and cares nothing for the lady.'

'I think he is,' said Chas, airily, 'as are all men in one way or another. If the daughter was 21 I hardly think he would have troubled himself about the mother.'

'What does Mr Paskall think of Mr Matthews paying court to his sister?' asked Frances.

'Ah, what did I tell you, Barstie?' said Chas with a smile of triumph. 'Miss Doughty sees all that there is to see!'

'Oh, I wish that was true,' sighed Frances.

'Mr Paskall and Mr Matthews are, like Barstie and me, old friends, who first became acquainted at school. And a wonderful pair of *harum scarum* rascals they were in their youth, always up to pranks, though they wouldn't want to be reminded of that *now*.

'Mr Paskall, who, as I am sure you know, hopes to be voted in for the Conservatives at the next election, was one of the many who made losses when the Bayswater Bank collapsed, though he has kept very quiet about it and would deny it to your face if asked. He would dearly love to lay his hands on his sister's fortune, but she will let him have none of it, even as a loan. She is afraid that he will lose it, as he lost the rest. Not one penny will she let him have, for she knows that once she has weakened and allowed him some then he will be constantly returning to her for more. *But* supposing she was to marry Mr Matthews, her fortune would then become his and *he* would be very amenable to lending Mr Paskall the funds he requires.'

'And what of the daughter?' exclaimed Frances. 'His own niece? Would he leave her poor?'

'She will have enough to meet Mr Paskall's ambitions,' said Barstie. 'He would rather she marry a tradesman with money than a title with none.'

'But I expect her mother wants her fortune to attract a husband in the high life,' said Frances. 'How has the daughter been educated?'

'By private tutor, in keeping with her mother's desires.'

'Oh, and one more thing,' said Chas. 'Matthews, Paskall and Fiske are the governors of the Bayswater Academy for the Education of Young Ladies, where those scurrilous pamphlets were left the other day. But I expect you already know that.' He winked at Frances.

CHAPTER FIVE

At eight the following morning Frances returned to Chepstow Place, painfully aware that, as yet, she had no suspects, very little idea of what the pamphlets had contained, and no clues at all as to why inappropriate reading matter had been put in the girls' desks. She had no grand plan in mind but there were pupils to whom she had not yet spoken and she supposed that she should interview everyone, including Mr Fiske's fellow governors, before she admitted defeat.

She was met at the door not by the housemaid, but by Miss Bell, who was clutching a handkerchief and looked flustered. 'Miss Doughty,' she said, 'I am so sorry, we are all at sixes and sevens today. Please come in, Mrs Venn would like to see you at once. She has something very particular to impart.'

Miss Bell was unusually silent on the reason for her agitation, which suggested to Frances that the headmistress had reserved for herself the pleasure of revealing the information. After showing Frances up to the study, Miss Bell hovered for a moment on the landing as if unsure which way to turn, then, with a sudden little lurch of decision, hurried downstairs.

As Mrs Venn greeted her visitor there was a smile playing around her lips, but it was not the kind of smile Frances cared to see. Dignity was obviously required and she braced herself.

'Good morning Miss Doughty,' said Mrs Venn genially. 'You will be pleased to know, as I am, that your work here is complete. We have discovered the culprit. It was the housemaid, Matilda Springett.'

'Oh,' said Frances, 'has she confessed?'

Mrs Venn looked less happy for a moment, then she recovered her air of superiority. 'As good as. She has run away. Her bed was not slept in last night and she has not appeared for duty this morning. Clearly the result of a guilty conscience.'

'Only yesterday,' Frances reminded her, 'you told me that Matilda has been employed by you since the school opened. If you had any reason to complain of her you did not mention it to me. You obviously regarded her as trustworthy.'

Mrs Venn did not like to be reminded of her earlier statement. 'I did, until now,' she said firmly.

The two women looked at each other for a few moments. 'I expect you have many other duties, as do I,' said Mrs Venn, rising as if to conduct Frances from the room.

Frances smiled, because while Mrs Venn had assumed that her investigation was ended, she felt suddenly sure that it had only just begun. To Mr Venn's astonishment, therefore, Frances did not follow her to the door, but remained where she was. The headmistress was understandably unused to her direct orders being resisted, and Frances was in the mood to challenge her.

'I *do* have one pressing duty,' said Frances, 'and that is to complete my investigations to my own satisfaction. And now I would like to see Matilda's room. If she has run away she may be in some trouble and there could be some indication there as to where she is.'

Mrs Venn paused, and appeared to be struggling with the good sense of this suggestion. 'Very well,' she said at last. 'Follow me.'

Matilda's room was on the second storey, small and plainly furnished with a bedstead and washstand and a wooden clothes chest. A small box was underneath the bed. The ashes in the tiny fireplace were as cold as the room. Mrs Venn stood by the doorway, her expression stern and watchful as Frances examined the contents of the chest. She found a plain gown suitable for Sunday best, shoes, a shawl and underlinen, but no coat or bonnet, which suggested that Matilda had gone out wearing her servants' gown, coat and boots. The apron was folded on the bed and Frances searched the pockets but found nothing. The note she had seen earlier, whatever it was, had gone. She lifted the small box onto the bed and sat beside it. It was unlocked, and, throwing the lid back, Frances found inside a small purse which contained a few copper coins, a nosegay of dried flowers, a letter from Davey assuring Matilda that she would always be his Valentine, and a cheap brooch. Frances felt uncomfortable about rummaging through another person's possessions but knew that there were times, as in a court of law, when delicacy would not assist justice. In the bottom of the box was a pair of old leather slippers, the soles worn into holes. Frances was wondering if these were a keepsake, as they seemed to have no other use, when she noticed something stuffed into the toe of one slipper – a handkerchief. She pulled it out and, as it opened, a cascade of coins fell out onto the bed. They were gold sovereigns. She looked up at Mrs Venn, who was as astonished as she.

'And what are Matilda's wages?' asked Frances. She picked up the coins and counted them, then piled them neatly on the lid of the box.

Mrs Venn stared at the unexpected hoard. '£20 a year, due quarterly. But the money is not paid at that time. Neither servants nor staff are permitted to keep anything of value in their rooms. Wages are placed to the individual's account in my strongbox and small amounts handed out weekly.'

'There is £20 here. Do you know where Matilda might have obtained such a sum?'

Mrs Venn sat down on the bed, her face creased with thought. 'She may have saved it over a number of years, I suppose, but why keep it in her room – why not with me, where it would be safer?'

Frances examined the coins and shook her head. 'These are recently minted. They were not saved over a long period of time.'

'Perhaps she saved the money in a smaller denomination and then changed it?' Mrs Venn suggested.

'But again, why hide the savings in her room?' asked Frances. 'There was no reason to keep it from you. Or was there?'

Consternation and even a little fear was in the headmistress's expression as she shook her head. 'No, none at all.'

'So this cannot have been come by honestly. Indeed, it may have been payment for putting the pamphlets in the desks, although it does seem excessive for such a trivial commission. Which suggests that either the matter is not trivial or there have been others. What do you have to say to that?'

'I am sorry but I really don't know what to say,' said Mrs Venn unhappily.

'So we have two difficulties now,' declared Frances, 'and the conundrum is far from solved. If Matilda has indeed run away, why would she leave so large a sum of money behind? And if, as we now suspect, it was she who placed the pamphlets in the desks, it was not for any reason of her own but for payment, and so the real culprit is as mysterious as before.'

Frances had pressed her advantage and now had some leisure to feel sympathy for the headmistress, who had clearly received a shock. 'Mrs Venn, I wish you to be perfectly frank with me. Nothing must be hidden. Matilda may be in danger and I can see that you are concerned for her welfare. Tell me first of all – does she have family or friends who might have seen her?'

Mrs Venn looked relieved. 'You are not going to inform the police?'

'I will speak to her family first. There may be some simple explanation. If not, then the police must be told.'

'She may have gone to her mother,' suggested Mrs Venn.

'That is my hope.' She turned to look closely at Frances and for the first time her expression suggested a measure of confidence. 'I would go there myself, but —,' she paused and looked uncomfortable. 'There is something you should know. May I be assured of your complete discretion?'

'Of course.'

'Matilda's family live in Salem Gardens, near Moscow Road. Her mother is a widow and supports herself by taking in lodgers, which is why Matilda has a room here. She has a brother, I believe, and there is a young man, a friend of his called Davey who wishes to marry her. Also —,' there was the faintest flush of embarrassment on her cheeks, 'There is a child living with them.'

'A child?' said Frances.

Mrs Venn nodded. 'There is no easy way to say this. Matilda has a child. A little girl about seven years of age. Her mother cares for her.'

'And – forgive me if this is an indelicate question, but I need to know all the truth – is her sweetheart the child's father?'

'No, she has only known him a year or two. It is the old story, I am afraid. Matilda was very young and trusting, and a man who lodged at her mother's house promised her marriage. When he realised her unhappy position he abandoned her. The world, Miss Doughty,' said the headmistress with a sigh, 'is full of such scoundrels, as it is of innocent girls who suffer the blame while the men go free to ruin others.'

'If Matilda has a child and a sweetheart and £20 in gold,' said Frances, 'it is very hard to understand why she should run away.' She rose. 'I will go and speak to her mother. Could you supply me with a letter on the school's notepaper so that I may introduce myself?'

'I will do that at once,' said Mrs Venn. She took charge of the sovereigns and they returned to her study, where she locked the coins in her strongbox and penned the required letter. 'Miss Doughty,' she said, 'I would be very obliged to you if you were to remember at all times the importance of the school's reputation. We rely absolutely on the confidence and trust which our patrons place in us. They send us their best of treasures – their beloved daughters – and they must know that I will care for the girls as if they were my very own. One tiny suggestion of the smallest stain upon the school's record would be a disaster of the greatest magnitude. I have already told you more than most people know.'

The unanswered questions trembled upon Frances' lips, but she did not ask them. If she had simply scored a victory over the headmistress, that would have left them still at defiance, but she now had the opportunity to earn the lady's trust and respect, and with that would come the confidences she needed.

Salem Gardens was a narrow street of small terraced houses. The 'gardens' in question were not apparent to the passer-by, and were presumably at the back of each premises, although Frances doubted that a great deal of gardening as she understood it was being carried out. The sounds of hammering nails, sawing wood, and beating of metal, as well as a strong whiff of laundry soap and borax showed that the enterprising denizens had used the space to establish their own businesses. As she sought out the house of Matilda's mother she passed a chimneysweep carrying his brushes and poles and wearing the grime of his employment like a black greatcoat, a carpenter striding to work with a canvas bag of tools slung across his shoulder, a carrier with parcels on a handcart, and boys taking barrows of vegetables from door to door. Children too young to be in the parochial school were clustered in doorways, but they were decently dressed, and as clean as could well be expected.

Frances knocked at the door of a tidily kept house and it was opened by a woman of about fifty whose compact figure, dark enquiring eyes and the sharp tilt of her nose at once identified her as Matilda's mother.

'Mrs Springett – my name is Frances Doughty and I have come from the Bayswater Academy,' began Frances. She offered the letter of introduction, and Mrs Springett looked at it with a frown. 'May I come in?'

Mrs Springett spent a great deal of time reading the letter then bit her lip and looked sorrowful, as if the visit was both unwelcome but expected. At last, she nodded and stood aside. 'Is it about Tilda?' she said, resignedly.

'Yes,' said Frances, 'is she here? May I speak with her?'

She entered a small narrow hallway with stairs directly ahead leading to the upper floor. The front room, judging from its lace-curtained exterior, was a small parlour kept for Sunday best and special occasions, and Mrs Springett led Frances to the back room, where there was a fire roaring in the grate, a scrubbed wooden table, plain chairs and a simple dresser with pans, kettles, teapots, crockery and flat irons. An armchair stood by the fire, and there was a workbox and a pile of garments to be mended, all of it male working clothes. A door at the rear led to a small scullery, from which Frances assumed the garden space and outhouse could be reached.

'She's not here,' said Mrs Springett, in answer to Frances' question. 'She lodges at the school, but you'll know that if you've come from there. She should be there now.' She stared at Frances with some anxiety and seemed about to ask a question, then changed her mind. 'I was about to make a cup of tea. Please, sit down.'

Frances sat while Mrs Springett made tea. It was obvious that the lady was not simply flustered but actually alarmed by the visit. It would have been natural for her to ask what Frances wanted with Matilda, but it was fear, not courtesy that prevented her from enquiring.

'She's a good girl,' declared Mrs Springett, bringing the tea things to the table on a tray. 'She never gave me any trouble. And if there's things she has done in the past which she regrets, well, we all make mistakes when we are young, and she never meant to hurt anyone.'

'When did you last see Matilda?' asked Frances.

'On Sunday, at church. She comes here every Sunday and then afterwards she walks out a while with Davey — he's her intended. He lodges here.' Mrs Springett poured the tea and then sat down, her eyes full of questions.

'That was five days ago,' said Frances. 'Have you heard from her since then — received a note from her, or sent her one?'

'No.' There was a sharp, nervous gasp. 'Miss Doughty — what has happened? What has she done?'

'I'm not sure,' said Frances. 'It may be nothing. She was at the school yesterday as usual during the day, but it seems that she went out at night and has not yet returned. I saw her with a note and wondered if she had an appointment.'

Mrs Springett lowered her cup, the tea untasted. Her hands began to shake. 'I don't know. She didn't come here.'

'Can you think of somewhere she might have gone? She has a brother who lives here, doesn't she? Perhaps he knows where she is.'

'Yes — Jem. But he's said nothing to me about Tilda, and nor has Davey.'

'Is there family elsewhere that she might have gone to visit?'

Mrs Springett shook her head. 'None hereabouts.'

'I understand she has a child,' said Frances gently.

Mrs Springett took some time to stare at the table and rubbed her hand over its surface back and forth as if trying to smooth out the grain of the wood. 'That is true,' she said at last. 'A little girl.'

'Is she here?' asked Frances, but she could see no signs of a child in the house, and wondered if the girl had been one of the little group playing outside, although none had looked the right age.

Mrs Springett shook her head. 'At school,' she said at last.

'Is she a boarder or a day scholar? Might Matilda have gone to see her?'

'She won't have gone there,' said Mrs Springett, quickly.

'Can you be sure of that?'

She nodded. 'Yes. Very sure.'

Frances hesitated and chose her words carefully. 'Mrs Springett, we had a curious incident at the school recently. Quite harmless – someone playing a prank – some pamphlets were put in the girls' desks. I was asked to find out who did it, and several people have said that it might have been Matilda. If she thought that we suspected her she might have been afraid and run away to hide. I would like to find Matilda; not to blame her or cause her any disquiet, but because Mrs Venn has a high regard for her and is concerned for her safety. If you should happen to hear from your daughter, please could you ask her to write to Mrs Venn and reassure her that she is safe? I am sure that if she was to return the matter could be resolved quite easily.'

A great many contrasting emotions were passing across Mrs Springett's face, but Frances' comments appeared to have calmed her initial anxiety. 'Yes – I will. Pamphlets, you say? What kind of pamphlets are they?'

'I have not seen them but I have been told they were a discourse addressed to young women on the subject of marriage,' said Frances, deliberately avoiding further description so as to judge Mrs Springett's response. 'Have you seen any such pamphlets in Matilda's possession? Has she ever mentioned them to you?'

Mrs Springett shook her head. 'I suppose someone might have given her something on the subject as she is due to be married soon, but I have not seen one.'

'I expect Matilda is looking forward to the wedding,' said Frances, now confident that Mrs Springett had not seen any pamphlets. 'When is that to be?'

'In April. There'll be lodgings coming free in Moscow Road, and they'll live there. Davey's a good young man; he's a carpenter and has worked up quite a nice little business in the area.'

'I think I ought to speak to your son and also to Davey. They may have heard from Matilda since last night. And if you could let me know the name and address of the school your grand-daughter attends —'

'No. I've said. Tilda won't have gone there.'

'How old is the little girl?'

'She's —,' Mrs Springett appeared to be struggling to remember. 'Seven – yes, seven.'

'And her name?'

'Edie.' She suddenly leaned forward. 'Miss Doughty – we never mention the child in front of Davey. It upsets him.'

Frances, knowing that Davey was not the child's father, suspected that he had not even been told of Edie's existence, and guessed that Mrs Springett was understandably concerned that should he learn of it, a cloud might be cast over the forthcoming wedding. She wondered what was being hidden and if it had any connection with Matilda's disappearance. There were, she knew, places which did not deserve the name of schools where unwanted children could be minded for a fee. Had the child been sent to such a place and was Mrs Springett ashamed to admit it? Perhaps the little girl was one of those sad mites born with some disease or deform-ity yet which nature had somehow kept alive, and was being kept from the eyes of the world? She knew that it would be hopeless to press Mrs Springett further at this juncture but thought it possible that she might have to do so in future. She would very much have liked to search the house and garden, to see if there were any signs that Matilda had been there recently, but did not feel that this was something she was in a position to insist upon.

'I will abide by your request, of course,' said Frances, finishing her tea. She wrote her address on the letter of introduction. 'If you should hear anything at all, or if you should discover one of the pamphlets in the house, please send me a note. I will return this evening to speak to your son and to Davey.'

Mrs Springett nodded dolefully.

Frances wondered if she might ask Chas and Barstie to keep a lookout for Matilda, but it seemed improbable that they would recognise her, as their substantial memories only extended to persons with rather more capital than £20.

'I don't suppose,' Frances asked Mrs Springett, 'that you have a portrait of Matilda?'

'No,' said Mrs Springett, 'we're going to have one done special, for the wedding.'

That was a disappointment, but Frances suddenly thought where she might obtain an image to assist in the search.

She returned to Westbourne Grove via the imposing terraces of Kensington Gardens Square, and sat and looked at her notebook again. Not only was there still a long list of people to whom she had not yet spoken, but the pamphlet itself was eluding her, forever out of her grasp, like something that had existed only in storybooks. What, she wondered, if the copies Mrs Venn had burnt were the only ones ever to be printed, and the answers to all her questions lay in ashes?

CHAPTER SIX

Sarah, who had been hunting for apartments with all the determination of a sportsman out for a good kill, returned in a state of some satisfaction as she had found one that she felt sure would suit in Westbourne Park Road. She described its merits and extracted a promise from Frances that they would go together and see it without any delay, but recognised with some concern that Frances' introspective mood was not a happy one. A hard stare was all that was required to induce Frances to reveal what she would have told no other person, that she was far from confident that she would be able to succeed in solving what had seemed at first to be such a simple problem, and was afraid that their entire future would depend on her ability to do so.

Sarah's first instinct was to deal with difficulties by the liberal application of food, especially as she knew that Frances could sometimes be too preoccupied to eat, even when hungry. She ensured that Frances sat at the parlour table and prepared fried eggs and ham, with relish and buttered toast for them both, then sat down to eat, with the unspoken expectation that Frances do the same.

Frances obediently picked up her knife and fork, and as they ate, told Sarah the full story of what she had found so far, which she realised could be described in *précis* as: the pamphlet was missing, Matilda was missing, and everyone she spoke to was either hiding secrets or telling lies.

'The thing is,' said Sarah, thoughtfully, 'you've asked me to be a lady's companion, and I would like that more than anything, but I'm not really sure what it means. It has to at least mean helping you, doesn't it?'

'We will make of it what seems best to us,' said Frances with a smile.

'Well, as it looks like in the new place I won't have half the work I did before, then I wondered if I could be a sort of detective apprentice. And I could go out and about and do the things you might be too busy for. And if you directed me, then I'd know what questions to ask.'

Frances felt some of the weight of duty lifted from her shoulders, although none of the anxiety. 'I can think of nothing I would like better,' she said. 'Consider yourself my trusted assistant in all things!'

'Well, first off,' said Sarah, 'why not get Tom to look for that maid what's run off, because if he can't find her no one can!'

Tom Smith was a relative of Sarah's who had been the errand boy at the chemist shop when it was owned by the Doughtys and now worked for Mr Jacobs. With quick feet, sharp eyes, natural cunning and a keen sense of opportunity, he was, at the age of about ten, clearly a lad who would go far in the world. No one better than he knew all the by-ways and alleyways of Bayswater, and he could worm his way into the hearts and confidence of servant girls with an innocent look and a boundless appetite for pastry.

'That's an excellent idea,' said Frances. 'He will be paid for his work, of course.'

'Jam tart and sixpence,' said Sarah, who knew Tom's price. 'And the next thing – only – I expect you've already thought of this, but —'

'Yes?' asked Frances eagerly.

'Well, this pamphlet – do you know if it was done special to be put in the school or is it just one you can go into a bookshop and get?'

Frances stared at Sarah. 'Do you know, I had been thinking it must have been printed specially, but you're right, it might be one that anyone could buy if they knew where to get it.'

'Well then,' said Sarah, 'why don't I go to all the newsagents and booksellers hereabouts and ask if they know about it. I might even find one.'

'That will be your first commission as my assistant,' said Frances. 'And see if you or Tom can discover anything more about Matilda Springett than we already know that might help us find her. If I can find Matilda and the pamphlet, then I think I have the answers to everything.'

The meal done, Sarah and Frances took the short walk to Westbourne Park Road, where Frances was introduced to Mrs Embleton. Mrs Embleton was a breed of person with whom Frances had never previously been closely acquainted – a lodging-house keeper, and it was her character as much as the rooms which interested Frances. Mrs Embleton, who was a widow of about forty-five, was friendly and obliging without being intrusive, and respectable without any false pretentions to being genteel. She made it clear in the nicest possible way that the apartments were let only to single ladies of good reputation. Gentlemen callers were permitted 'within reason'. She did not explain what this meant and Frances guessed that if one had to enquire then it would be a sign that the enquirer was not the kind of person Mrs Embleton wished to have in her apartments.

The house was the property of a gentleman who had worked in the City, and had prospered so well that he had retired to live in the country. It was beautifully appointed both inside and out. When her employer had lived there, Mrs Embleton had been the housekeeper, and he had since engaged her to let the accommodation, collect the rents and generally provide simple services to the ladies who took the apartments, of which there were three.

The ground floor had already been let to two elderly ladies who were sisters, and their maid, who, said Mrs Embleton, lived very quietly, and almost never went out except to church. The second floor, which consisted of only two rooms, was occupied by a spinster, who spent her days engaged in works of a charitable nature. Frances quailed in the face of such uncompromising virtue and wondered what Mrs Embleton would say if she realised that her prospective tenant was a private detective.

The rooms to let were on the first floor and consisted of a cosy parlour, a bedroom and another room which might usefully be a second bedroom, dressing room or study. There was even a bathroom and a quite separate water closet on the landing. Mrs Embleton lived in comfortable rooms in the basement, where there was also a large kitchen. She was willing to provide breakfast and plain dinners, although she was not averse to her 'ladies' or their servants using the cooking facilities if they so wished, as long as all was kept spotless and tidy. A washerwoman called once a week to deal with the linens for an extra charge, and a woman was engaged to clean the shared portions of the house and would be willing to clean the apartments by separate arrangement.

Compared with the frugally kept rooms beside the shop in Westbourne Grove – which was the only home Frances had ever known and where she had worked behind the counter and in the stockroom from early to late, cared for her dying brother and ailing father and shared the work of the house with Sarah – this snug apartment with its comfortable furnishings and modern fittings made Frances feel that she had never been intended by providence to live in this way. Mrs Embleton mentioned a price which Frances knew was more than she could reasonably afford. It was almost as if in a dream that she agreed, in a voice that sounded like quite another person's, to move in on the following day.

Sarah went to arrange a carrier and also to visit newsagents and booksellers, while Frances returned to the disheartening reality of her fruitless enquiries at the school, arriving shortly before Mr Copley was about to take his next lesson. He had prepared an arrangement of fans and was carefully draping them in the folds of a silk handkerchief. 'Miss Doughty, may I assist you?' he asked.

'You may,' she said. 'I see that your artistic tastes are for drawings of objects rather than persons, but I had wondered if you were also able to do portraiture. I need something very particular.'

He gave an arch little smile. 'Why, Miss Doughty, whatever *can* you mean?'

'I would like you to draw a portrait of Matilda Springett,' she said. 'You will be aware of course that she is missing. I would like a picture to assist those looking for her.'

The smile vanished. 'Well, I should be able to undertake that,' he said, but without any great enthusiasm. 'I have to say her sudden departure is not entirely unexpected. I always thought there was something dishonest about the girl. I had it in mind to tell Mrs Venn of my suspicions, although I had no proof, it was all in her manner, which ranged from the negligent to the downright insolent. Why Mrs Venn tolerated her nonsense I cannot say. Are there valuables missing?'

'Not as far as I am aware,' said Frances. 'Why did you say nothing of this before? Did you not think she might have been the person who put the pamphlets in the girls' desks?'

'Not unless there was money in it, which I doubt,' he said. 'The girl thought of little else. I have heard her boasting of how much she had put by and how she would not be a servant for much longer, but have servants of her own.'

'To whom did she make this boast?' asked Frances. 'Was it to you?'

'Of course not – I would hardly engage in conversation with such a person as that!'

'Then who?'

He looked away, awkwardly. 'I really can't recall now.'

'You must try to remember, it could be of some importance.'

He made no reply, but took up a sheet of drawing paper and began to sketch. Frances watched as the strokes of his pencil produced an excellent likeness of Matilda, her face tilted up with a knowing, almost challenging expression.

'There,' he said, handing the paper to Frances. 'I am sure the minx will be found, most probably in police custody, or a — a place I decline to mention.'

Frances took her departure and hurried to the chemist shop, where she was fortunate to encounter Tom as he was leaving with a knapsack full of deliveries. 'Good afternoon, Tom,' she said. 'My word, you are looking very smart today!' It had always been something of an effort for Sarah to keep Tom clean and tidy, something Mr Jacobs appeared to have achieved almost in an instant.

Tom grinned and puffed out his chest. 'Afternoon, Miss,' he said, with a salute. 'Togged out to the nines, ain't I? A real tip-topper!' He was wearing a suit of dark blue cloth, with a neat jacket edged in braid and the words 'Cyril Jacobs, chemist, Westbourne

Grove' embroidered on the collar, and the same legend around the band of his peaked cap, which made him, thought Frances, into a kind of perambulating advertisement. The jacket sported shiny gilt buttons of which he was obviously very proud, as he inspected them and rubbed them with a sleeve as if they were in danger of losing their brightness if not given special attention. Her father, she thought, would never have thought of such a thing, or countenanced the expense if he had.

'I have a commission for you,' said Frances, 'if you are able to take it. I can pay you sixpence, and Sarah will make a jam tart.'

'Mmmm!' he said, licking his lips as if already tasting the treat. Frances showed him the portrait. 'This is Matilda Springett, who is the maid at the Bayswater Academy for the Education of Young Ladies on Chepstow Road and has not been seen since eight o'clock last night,' she said. 'If you should see her, don't speak to her or you may frighten her away, but come to me at once and tell me where she is. Her mother lives in Salem Gardens, so if she goes there let me know. In any case, once your work is done for the day, come and tell me anything you have learned about her.'

'I will,' he said, ''n tell Sarah to make it raspberry jam, 'cos that's the best!'

Frances next determined to interview Mr Paskall, whose office was on Westbourne Grove, not far from Mr Whiteley's row of fashionable shops. There was a brass plate at the door, a little scratched by insistent shoulders, but buffed to a presentable shine and engraved with the words 'Bartholomew Paskall & Son, Property Agents, Management and Insurance.' She ascended a steep narrow stair to the upper floor, where a trim young clerk sat in the outer office trying to look important. Above his desk, and the most impressive thing that anyone would see on entering the room, was a large framed portrait of Bartholomew Paskall, striking a pose that would not have looked inappropriate on a Roman emperor, with bright blue eyes staring down imperiously from under bushy brows, his nose a disagreeably large hook. It was hard to imagine him as Chas and Barstie had described him in his youth, an inky-fingered schoolboy cheeking his masters and cutting class.

'My name is Frances Doughty,' she told the clerk. 'I would like to see Mr Paskall.'

'Mr Paskall senior is not in the office at present,' said the clerk. 'I am not expecting to see him today. Have you come about a property? I could see if Mr Paskall junior is available.'

Frances was giving some thought to this, as she was unsure if Paskall junior would be able to help, when the door to the inner office opened and a young man emerged, a similar yet rather less forbidding version of his father. 'Bennett,' he said, handing a large bundle of correspondence to the clerk, 'could you see these letters are put in the post immediately – they must be delivered today.'

'Yes, Mr Paskall,' said the clerk, 'and there is a Miss Doughty here —'

Young Paskall's eyes opened wide. 'Not the famous Miss Frances Doughty!' he exclaimed.

'Well, I'm not so sure about being famous . . .' said Frances awkwardly.

'Oh, but I beg to differ! This is quite an honour. I expect it's my father you want to see, but come into the office and I'll see if I can be of any help. Bennett – please note that in future this lady is *always* to be admitted.'

Frances was ushered into a room that succeeded in being both large and cluttered, as if twenty different tasks were all being carried out at once and jostling each other for precedence. 'Do take a seat,' said her host eagerly. 'May I offer you any refreshment?'

'Thank you, no,' said Frances, sitting in a creakily overstuffed leather chair, while young Paskall, pushing a wing of long hair from his forehead, took a seat behind the desk, which was covered in folders stuffed with papers, some of them open, their contents cascading out in such disarray that there was the danger of an unintentional exchange of material. On either side of the room were long tables stacked high with similarly overfull folders, tied up with string. The walls were lined with shelves of law books, some of them of such antiquity that they were thick with dust. Pens, pencils, loose papers that seemed to belong to nothing at all, and bottles of ink were abundant, and there was a litter of printed advertising notices. Frances picked one up. It was describing a property to let and was the product of a local printer. Although it was not a quality item, the paper and print were good enough. Mrs Venn had suggested that the mysterious pamphlet had been a cheap production. Had she merely been expressing an opinion based on its disreputable contents or had this been an accurate description of the work of a less competent printer?

'I read about your exploits in the *Bayswater Chronicle*,' said Paskall, with an admiring look.

'It was very much exaggerated,' said Frances, modestly.

'Sensational if only half of it was true, and now I understand that father has engaged you in some detective work regarding that strange matter at the school.'

'Yes, I was hoping to ask him if he might have visited the school on either Tuesday or Wednesday, when we think the pamphlets were put there, and if so, whether he saw anything that could be important.'

'Hmm – let me see if I can help you.' Paskall picked up a large leather-bound book, which Frances assumed was an appointment diary, and studied it. 'Ah yes, Tuesday – he met with clients in the morning and was here in the afternoon, then he was at the Conservative club in the evening. On Wednesday he was in the office all day. So – nothing at the school by prior arrangement. In any case, I believe Mr Fiske is the man who deals with all matters relating to the school. Father is rarely there.'

'Have you ever been there?'

'No, I have no involvement with the school at all. Father might bring me in as a governor if his parliamentary duties become too arduous – you know, don't you, that he is a prospective Conservative candidate for Marylebone?'

'So I understand.'

'In fact, it is father's belief that this whole pamphlet business is a plot by his political enemies.'

'Really?' said Frances. 'But the pamphlets were found two days ago. These enemies have been very quiet since. In fact they have failed to make any capital out of it.'

Paskall was silent for a moment then nodded. 'An excellent observation.'

'Do you have an opinion as to the culprit?'

'I'm afraid not. But if, as you believe, there is no political motive, it must surely be a quite trivial affair.'

Frances decided to say nothing about the twenty sovereigns which suggested otherwise. 'That may be the case, but since I began my enquiries the maidservant at the school has run away. Either she was responsible or she is afraid that she will be blamed, but there must naturally be concerns about her safety.'

'Of course,' he said, solemnly. 'Is she a young person?'

'She is.'

'Then we must hope that nothing scandalous is involved. Have you been engaged to find her?'

'Not explicitly, but I hope that if I do she will admit that she was the agent of the person who wished the pamphlets to be put in the school, and give me a name. I am sure that with kind questioning she will tell me the truth.' Frances was not in fact confident of this, but thought that a combination of gentle persuasion with Sarah's strong and inflexible presence behind her might be just what was needed.

'Another triumph for Miss Doughty!' exclaimed young Paskall. 'Please do not hesitate to apply to me for any help you may require. After all, father has a lot to occupy him at present, and if I could relieve just one of his concerns it would make his life less exhausting. When I next see him I will be sure to ask about his last visits to the school and if he saw anything of importance there.'

'Thank you,' said Frances. She rose. 'I will take up no more of your time for today.'

'Please do return if you have any more questions,' he said courteously 'After all,' he added with a smile that held no detectable hint of satire, 'it is not often we entertain a Bayswater celebrity in our offices.'

Frances returned to the school in the hope that Matilda might have reappeared, but no one had heard anything from her. She then went back to her apartments in case there was a message but there was none. Wearily she made some tea, and found that Sarah had provided a fruitcake, a slice of which was very welcome. Sarah came back in time to share the tea and cake, and reported that none of the local newsagents had heard of a pamphlet called 'Why Marry?' 'One did say that it was the sort of thing what would have been written by what he called "bluestocking ladies", whatever they may be. I don't think he approved of them very much.'

'Men do not care for females with minds of their own,' said Frances. 'But we do have minds and can think and reason and learn if we are allowed to. We have different ways, that is all, different spheres of thought. Who is to say which is preferable? Both are of advantage to society.'

'He did give me this,' said Sarah, handing Frances a small printed sheet. 'He said it might help me find the sort of lady I was looking for, only I'm not sure I liked the way he said it.'

The paper was headed 'Bayswater Women's Suffrage Society', and read:

> Join us, sisters, to agitate for the granting of female suffrage and an end to the gross injustice under which your countrywomen have long suffered. Give women the vote, that a valuable host may be added to the electoral body, so the country may be wisely, economically, and mercifully governed. Let the distaff become a sceptre!

The paper was attributed to a Miss E. Gilbert and gave an address in Chilworth Street, which was not far distant and which Frances knew to be a terrace of handsome and lofty buildings, many of which were highly respectable lodging houses. Such a lady, thought Frances, might well be opposed to the idea of marriage, or at the very least believe that it was not the only role in life a woman might seek. 'Did you learn anything about Matilda?' she asked.

'Only that she has a sweetheart who is kind and hardworking and amenable to being under her thumb. She is a small person but I was told she has a very large thumb.'

'Perhaps they have gone away together and married in secret,' said Frances hopefully. 'If she felt in any danger she might think it would give her some measure of protection.'

🌸

Later that day, Tom came to report on what he had found. He had not seen Matilda and neither had she returned home. Her mother, brother and Davey had all been out looking for her.

'That is all very well, but have they told the police?' asked Frances.

'There's no coppers been to the 'ouse,' said Tom. 'Not today and not before.'

Frances shook her head. 'If they don't tell the police soon, then I will,' she said.

Tom sat down to a large jam tart and a mug of cocoa, while Sarah stood staring in wonder at his new uniform and scrubbed face.

Frances, meanwhile, had a letter to write. It was addressed to Miss E. Gilbert of the Bayswater Women's Suffrage Society, and requested the pleasure of an interview.

CHAPTER SEVEN

The carrier came early next morning when the Grove was coming to life. Delivery carts rumbled along the roadway, and the carriages of early customers were already prowling. Shutters went up with a rattle and a bang, and shop assistants in neat uniforms scurried to take their places. The sweepers were already out and the swish of their busy brushes and the footsteps of passers-by were like the background refrain of an orchestra, to which the clank of harness, the snorting of horses in the cold air, and the shouts of drivers added a contrasting measure. Frances, who had grown up with this morning chorus, had no idea of how she might feel to leave it. To the rooms of her old home, now bare, she had already said her farewells, and concluded that while she ought perhaps to have shed some tears, that she had rarely been happy there. The recent discovery that her father had lied to her, as indeed had her Uncle Cornelius, about the loss of her mother, although both with her interests at heart, had meant she was leaving her past behind with even less regret than she might have done.

Sarah looked at her with a worried expression but Frances smiled reassuringly and said only that they had better get the boxes. Between the carrier and the two women, assisted by Chas and Barstie, they soon loaded the cart and it was a matter of minutes to reach their new home.

Leaving Sarah to unpack their possessions, Frances hurried to Salem Gardens, where she found a neglected pot of broth cooling beside the fire and Mrs Springett sitting at the table with two young men, all deep in conference. The dark haired muscular man with intense brooding eyes was similar enough to his mother to be identified as Jem Springett, while the other, taller and more slightly built with yellow hair who sat anxiously twisting and untwisting his fingers, was undoubtedly the sweetheart, Davey.

'Miss Doughty – do you have any news of Matilda?' asked Mrs Springett jumping up, her face bright with anticipation.

'I am sorry, I have learned nothing,' Frances admitted. 'I was hoping when I came here that she might have returned.'

The unhappy mother wrung her hands in distraction and paced back and forth. 'Davey and Jem have been out and about day and night looking everywhere they can think of, and I have asked all the neighbours if they have seen her, but no one knows where she can have gone.' Jem got up to comfort her with a rough but affectionate hug, but tears started in her eyes and she had neither the energy nor the will to mop them away.

Frances sat at the table and faced Davey. 'I am looking into the matter of some pamphlets that were distributed at the school,' she said. 'Do you know if Matilda had anything to do with that?'

Davey looked mystified. 'I don't know anything about any pamphlets,' he said.

'What are you saying?' exclaimed Jem. 'That she did something wrong?'

'No, not at all, but it did cause some – consternation.'

'And why do they send you here, asking us questions?' Jem demanded. 'Mother was very upset after you called before, and we don't want you coming back!'

'I have been engaged to make enquiries by the school governors,' Frances explained.

'I told you so!' declared Davey. 'This is the detective lady who was in all the papers! If she is clever enough to find out murderers she'll soon have Tilly safe home!' The innocent hope in his voice both touched Frances' heart and made her afraid. How she wished that she had a world of experience that could have prepared her for this, and a whole army of assistant detectives.

'When did you last see Matilda?' she asked Davey.

'It was on Tuesday,' he replied readily. 'I know I'm not supposed to, but she said it would be allright, so I went to the back door and she gave me a cup of tea. I was only there a few minutes. There was no harm in it.'

'And how did she seem to you? Was she happy, or perhaps worried about something?'

'Oh no, she was very happy. We talked about —,' he blushed a little, 'about how it wasn't long before we were wed.'

'It's a costly business, starting a new home,' said Frances. 'Was Matilda concerned about the expense?'

'No; well I have my work and I'm going to start up my own carpentry shop, and Tilly has something put by . . .' His voice trailed to silence and he looked down. Frances could see that he was holding something back, though whether it had anything to do with Matilda's disappearance or the pamphlets it was impossible to say. He gulped suddenly. 'Oh I do hope she is safe! I know she is a good and faithful girl and would never run off with another man!'

'Have you sent her a note in the last few days or has she sent you one?'

Davey shook his head. Frances thought that questions regarding the twenty sovereigns might be better left for another time, when Matilda's mother and brother were not there. She turned to Jem, who regarded her with a surly look, his dark eyes fierce under heavy brows. 'I am sure that if you had seen her or could offer any clue as to where she is, you would tell me,' she said.

'I would,' he said firmly.

'Have the police been told she is missing?'

Mrs Springett and Jem exchanged worried glances. 'No,' whispered the mother. 'It would be best not — how would they know where to look? We will find her.'

'I think,' said Frances, rising to her feet, 'that if Matilda is not heard from today, you should go to the police.'

Mrs Springett seemed to shrink inwards, as if her body had been eaten away from within by anxiety, but Davey looked up and nodded. 'I'll go,' he said. 'Even if she is in some sort of trouble, she's still my girl and I'll stand by her.'

'We might have to at that,' said Jem, gruffly.

'I hope it won't come to that,' said Mrs Springett, laying her hand on her son's arm and pressing it for comfort. 'Besides, what can the police do, who don't know her? It's best for her family to look out for her.' She took a deep breath, pulled her shoulders back, and made herself once more the Springett matriarch. 'Now then, Jem, Davey, you'd better both get something to eat to keep your strength up, and then you can go out looking again.'

Frances prepared to leave, wishing she had the authority not only to search the house but take each member of the family individually and shake them hard to dislodge their secrets. As she went to the door there was a tapping of the knocker and Mrs Springett, her son and Davey all leaped in sudden excitement. 'Oh, please let it be her!' gasped Mrs Springett, making a dash for the door to wrench it open. Frances saw Davey's face brighten with hope and Jem's angry scowl suddenly smoothed.

There was disappointment outside, however. A woman clad in a plain stuff dress with her sleeves rolled to her elbows, her arms reddened from hot water, stood at the door.

'Oh, it's you, Eliza,' said Mrs Springett, forgetting manners in her emotion and turning her back to hide her face.

'Has anything been heard?' asked Davey.

Eliza came in, wiping her hands on her apron. 'It's only —,' she said, and stopped.

Mrs Springett whirled to confront her neighbour. 'Have you seen her?'

'No, no I've not and I don't want to come here worrying you about nothing, but you'll hear about it soon enough from someone else, and I thought —,' she passed a thick forearm across her forehead. 'There's a woman's body been found. In the Serpentine.'

Mrs Springett gave a little scream and Davey exclaimed, 'Oh don't say that!'

Jem put his arm about his mother. 'Come on, then, Mrs Brooks, best give it all,' he said.

Eliza seemed to be regretting her intrusion. 'It's some poor creature who's drowned herself and they don't know who she is. I mean, there's all sorts of women throw themselves into the Serpentine, but I know Tilda and she never had any reason to do anything like that so I'm sure it can't be her.'

Davey shook his head. 'No, it won't be my Tilly. She'd never do anything like that.'

'Right – well, I'd best go then,' said Mrs Brooks with some embarrassment, and backed away.

Mrs Springett began to cry and Jem hugged her tightly. 'Now then, Mother, no need for that. I'll go straight there and have a look just so we know for sure it's not our Tilda. I'll find a carrier's cart to take me and I'll be there and back in no time. Davey, you can go out looking for her, and Mother you wait in, in case she comes back. Mrs Brooks!' he called after the retreating figure of the neighbour, who stopped reluctantly. 'Come on in and sit with Mother while we go out. Do I go to the Receiving House? Is that where they have the body?'

The neighbour nodded and crept back indoors, while Jem hurried out followed by Davey. 'Well,' said Mrs Brooks after a pause, 'I'd better make some tea.' Mrs Springett sank into a chair, her hands clasped over her mouth.

Frances helped Mrs Brooks with the tea and took the opportunity to question her. 'When was the body found?' she asked softly. She hoped her question would not disturb Mrs Springett, but a glance told her that that lady was locked deep in her own nightmare.

Mrs Brooks was so flustered that she didn't think to ask who the stranger was. 'Nigh on an hour ago, and if it hadn't been found then it would have lain in the dark till morning. It was under one of the arches of the bridge. One of the boatmen pulled it out, and took it up to the Receiving House, but there was nothing they could do.' She leaned closer. 'I know that it was a woman,' she whispered, 'a young woman. Perhaps she was up on the bridge and threw herself over into the water.'

They drank tea in a silence that was broken only by Mrs Springett's whimpers. Deaths in the Serpentine, Frances knew, were not uncommon, though more usually in the warmer months when the waters were in regular use by bathers and boats and there were accidents. Sometimes it was no accident, but a deliberate act of terrible desperation. Mrs Brooks tried to coax Mrs Springett into taking some tea, and Frances took advantage of the distraction to slip upstairs and look about, but saw no sign that Matilda had been there recently. She returned to the parlour after a quick glance into the front room, which was, as she had surmised, for Sunday and holiday best, and explained her absence by admitting with some embarrassment that she had been looking for the WC. 'It's out back,' said Mrs Brooks, as if it could scarcely be anywhere else, and Frances went through the scullery to the garden, where there was a small outhouse and a shed with a washing boiler. She pried for as long as she could without it exciting comment, but everything was as it should be.

An hour passed before Jem returned. When he flung the door open and Frances saw the shocked and stricken expression on his face, she left the house at once.

As Frances hurried down Salem Gardens with the anguished cries of Mrs Springett echoing down the street, she could not help but think that she might bear some responsibility for the tragedy. Had it not been her rigorously pursued enquiries, her determination to find out the truth that had impelled Matilda to run away? She imagined the girl afraid, not knowing where to turn for help, lost in the dark, and stumbling to her doom. Or was there a still greater horror awaiting the bereaved family? Could guilt and despair have led the housemaid to take her own life? From the little she had seen of Matilda, Frances had to agree with Davey; such an action was not in the girl's character. It was not as if Matilda, soon to be a bride, had to worry about losing her place. Davey seemed like a good man, and Mrs Springett a caring mother. Frances was suddenly accosted with an unpleasant and unworthy wave of self-pity. Her own mother, as she had only recently discovered in a revelation that had changed all she had ever believed about that parent, had cared nothing for her.

Frances stopped walking for a moment and had a firm word with herself. She had done without a mother's care since she was three years old and nothing she had learned could undo that or make her any less the person she was now. Skirting around the stables of Queen's Mews she was soon in Chepstow Place, where she rang the bell at the school door. Two or three minutes passed and she was about to ring again when the door was opened by a flustered looking maid of about sixteen. Frances had no difficulty in gaining admission and impressing upon the girl the urgency of her need to see Mrs Venn at once.

The expression on Mrs Venn's face as she was conducted into the study suggested uncomfortably to Frances that she was looking neither calm nor controlled. 'I apologise for this intrusion, but I am the bearer of bad news,' she began.

Mrs Venn waved Frances to a seat, poured water into a glass from a carafe and handed it to her. Frances sank gratefully into the chair clutching the glass, and took several sips. 'I have just come from seeing Mrs Springett and while I was there she was informed that Matilda is dead. The poor girl was found in the Serpentine. Her brother has identified the body.'

Mrs Venn was shocked, rather than grieved. 'That is very terrible news,' she said. 'I assume – I hope – that it was an accident.'

'That remains to be seen,' said Frances. 'I expect there will be an inquest. But questions will undoubtedly be asked.' She felt steadier, and put the glass down. 'Thus far, I have been required to keep confidential the incidents that have taken place in the school, and since it seems that no actual crime has been committed, merely an indiscretion, I was agreeable to that, but now that a death has occurred, and the death of someone who was suspected of being the culprit, it will be necessary to reveal the truth.'

Mrs Venn shook her head. 'I cannot agree to that,' she said. 'Exposing the school to gossip and scandal will not bring the poor girl back to life, and our suspicions will only fuel rumours that she took a desperate course of action. Are her family not in pain enough that they must suffer this additional distress?'

Frances sensed that the plight of Matilda's family was not of great moment to Mrs Venn, who had mentioned them only to strengthen her argument. 'Nevertheless, the truth may come out whether you wish it to or not,' she said. 'I have already found in my enquiries that the rumour has spread well beyond these walls.' There was no mistaking the expression of keen suffering that passed briefly across the headmistress's features before she was able to compose herself. 'I will need to arrange a meeting with the governors to find if they wish me to continue my enquiries,' added Frances, 'but I will advise them that I should do so, since it is my belief that Matilda was only the agent of another. Her death may not put an end to incidents of this nature.' She took a deep breath and squared her shoulders. 'And now, Mrs Venn, before I proceed any further, I would like you to tell me the *real* reason you destroyed the pamphlets.'

The headmistress's expression suggested astonishment that such a question could even be asked. 'Pardon me,' she said with great dignity, 'but I believe I told you so at our very first meeting.'

Frances paused, looking for the right words with which to indicate that she thought that Mrs Venn had been telling untruths. It was only an impression, and she had neither proof nor power to force an admission. At that moment there was a ring at the doorbell, followed almost immediately by a loud, insistent knocking.

'Whoever can that be?' said Mrs Venn, rising quickly from her chair. Soon afterwards heavy footsteps were heard almost running up the stairs and the door of the study burst open to admit a figure all too familiar to Frances. The new housemaid hovered behind him, her hands waving like the flippers of a performing seal, stammering, 'Mrs Venn – I'm sorry – but it's the police!'

'That will do, Hannah, please leave us,' said Mrs Venn curtly. Hannah, who was obviously finding her new position a source of anxiety, disappeared with a little squeal of fright.

'Inspector Sharrock, Paddington police,' said the new arrival, taking a large handkerchief from his pocket, applying it to his nose, which looked even coarser and redder than Frances remembered it, and making a noise like several trombones. He stopped in mid blast when he saw Frances and gazed at her suspiciously. 'Miss Doughty,' he said, between sniffling nose-wipes, 'I hardly expected to see *you* here.'

'Miss Doughty is employed by the school,' said Mrs Venn, hastily.

'Ah,' said the Inspector with a nod of understanding, and Frances saw that the headmistress's clever comment had suggested to him that she was there in a teaching capacity. She decided not to enlighten him.

'Inspector, I assume that you are here about my housemaid, Matilda Springett. We have only this very moment received the sad news,' said Mrs Venn. Given the suddenness and nature of the intrusion she had offered him neither a seat nor refreshment, but he seemed not to expect them.

Sharrock narrowed his eyes and looked at Frances. 'I see – well I have a few questions to ask and then I'll be on my way.'

He took a notebook and pencil from his pocket. 'Can you tell me when you last saw Miss Springett?'

There was a sudden cry from far below, piercing enough to travel up the stairs and through the closed door of the study. 'That would be my constable giving the news to the cook,' said Sharrock. Frances wondered if the constable in question was Wilfred Brown, whose company she found far more pleasant than that of the Inspector. Constable Brown was a good-natured young man who had shown her great kindness during the tribulations of the last few weeks, and she wished, not for the first time, that she had met him a few years ago, when he was single.

'I last saw her on Thursday,' said Mrs Venn.

'Two days ago,' said Sharrock. 'And you, Miss Doughty?'

Frances pushed away the foolish daydream. 'The same.'

He peered at them both over his notebook. 'When on Thursday?'

'In the evening,' said Mrs Venn. 'It was about eight o'clock. She was not required later on, and I assumed that she had completed her duties and gone to bed. On Friday morning I realised that she was not on the premises and saw that her bed had not been slept in.'

The pencil scratched busily. 'And how long has Miss Springett been employed here?'

'A little over ten years. From the opening of the school.'

He nodded thoughtfully. 'Then you must have found her reliable and a good worker to have employed her for so long.'

'Indeed.'

'So much so, that when she went missing overnight for no good reason, you took action at once, and engaged a new maid to take her place,' said Sharrock.

'I —,' Mrs Venn remained calm but a slight flush appeared on either cheek. 'I had no reason to believe that anything amiss had occurred.'

'Why? Had she disappeared before?' Sharrock demanded. 'But no, she can't have done, can she, because you have just told me she was reliable. Maidservants who go off on their own without so much as a by your leave will soon find themselves without employment, so I understand.'

'Matilda has a sweetheart – they are due to be married soon
—,' Mrs Venn sighed, '*were* due, I should say. I thought that the
excitement had turned her head and she was with him.'

'And this sweetheart would be —?'

'Davey Harris. He lodges with Matilda's mother in Salem
Gardens.'

'Inspector,' said Frances. 'It is not true to suggest that Mrs
Venn took no action to find Matilda. She sent me to Salem
Gardens to see if she was there.'

'Ah, doing a little light detective work were we Miss Doughty?'
asked Sharrock with more than a touch of mockery. 'How very
unlike you. And what did you find when you went there?'

'I spoke to Mrs Springett, who informed me that she and
her son had not seen Matilda since church on Sunday and Mr
Harris not since Tuesday. They had all assumed that she was
here. I returned there today to see if there was any news and
found that Mr Harris and Matilda's family had been out making
enquiries and looking for her.'

'Really? You must all have been very concerned for her safety,'
said Sharrock. Frances saw the trap and refused to be drawn.

'I do not believe that anything could have been achieved by
informing you when she had only been gone for a day,' said Mrs
Venn defensively.

Sharrock strode rapidly to the desk and faced the headmistress. 'We might not have started our own enquiries at that stage,
but I could have given her description to my constables and
asked them to keep their eyes open. As it was, neither you nor
her family reported her absence to the police. I can't help wondering if she ran off because she was in some sort of trouble
– trouble that both you and the Springetts would rather we
didn't know about. Trouble that might have led to her death.'

'How did she die?' asked Frances, trying to avoid an awkward
silence.

'That will be for the inquest to decide,' said Sharrock. 'There's
to be a post-mortem examination.'

'But it *was* an accident?' said Mrs Venn. 'I was told she had
been found in the Serpentine, so I presume she fell in and was
drowned.'

Sharrock looked as if he was about to sneeze, and blew his nose again with even greater force than before. 'I expect that would suit you very well, if you don't mind my saying so. Keep it all quiet, no publicity, no gossip, never mind about the girl.'

Mrs Venn gasped at being spoken to in this way. Frances felt a moment of envy for the Inspector, able to speak his mind as he wished and not worry about causing offence. 'I am sure you must have you own opinion,' she said.

'I do,' he said, 'which I am not inclined to share.'

'Inspector,' said Frances softly, 'I can assure you that Matilda was very content in her place here, and there can be no suggestion that this unfortunate occurrence is connected in any way with the school. You will appreciate that the daughters of some of the leading citizens of Bayswater, including Mr Paskall, a future member of parliament so I understand, are educated here. For the reassurance of anxious parents, it would be advisable if the cause of Matilda's unhappy death could be established as soon as possible. We can only hope that it was simply an accident – a stumble in the dark that could have happened to anyone.' She waited, hoping for some confidence, but Sharrock simply pursed his lips and wrote in his notebook again.

'Oh pray heaven the poor girl did not do anything desperate!' said Mrs Venn.

'Oh? Was she the type to do that?' asked the Inspector.

'Not in the slightest! And even if she had some secret sorrow, she knew she could have come to me and I would have listened to her sympathetically. And her mother is a kindly woman who would have helped her in any difficulty.'

'Is there anything else you would like to tell me, Mrs Venn?' asked Sharrock.

Frances gave the headmistress a very pointed look which that lady found it impossible to ignore. She gave a groan of resignation.

'Matilda,' she began. The Inspector raised a shaggy eyebrow. 'We suspected that she might have . . .' She looked pained and Frances took pity on her.

'It is thought that she might have committed a small indiscretion,' she said. 'Nothing of a criminal nature – the possession of cheap literature.'

'Oh, I *see*,' said Sharrock with a knowing smile, and Frances saw that it was unnecessary for her to elaborate.

'You understand that as a school it is essential to be beyond the smallest reproach,' she went on. 'I was intending to ask her about it when she ran away. I thought – we thought —'

He nodded sagely. '*You* thought that the maid was so frightened of your reputation as the terror of malefactors that she had gone away to hide rather that have you question her?'

'I'm not sure I would express it quite in that way,' said Frances. 'There is another matter you should know. On Thursday afternoon I saw Matilda with a note. It may have had nothing to do with what has happened, but it is possible that it was to make an appointment for a meeting later that day.'

'We didn't find a note on the body,' said Sharrock. 'Perhaps it will still be in her room.' He looked at Frances suspiciously. 'You don't know where this note is?'

'I do not,' said Frances.

'I did ask Mrs Robson if Matilda had received any visitors or messages,' said Mrs Venn, 'and she told me that someone had delivered a note at the kitchen door that morning. Whoever it was did not come in, and she did not see the person.' Sharrock wrote laboriously in his book.

The study door opened and a young constable who Frances did not recognise peered in. 'Nothing, Sir,' he said, and Frances realised that Matilda's room had been searched. She glanced at Mrs Venn, who remained stonily determined not to mention that Matilda's twenty sovereigns were in her strongbox.

'Very well,' said Sharrock, 'but I can tell you now, both of you, that I am not entirely satisfied with your co-operation and you may be sure that I will return as soon as the inquest has delivered its verdict. Good-day.'

The Inspector pulled out his handkerchief, applied it to his nose, and departed. From down the hallway came the melancholy sound of the brass instrument section of a small orchestra.

Frances turned to Mrs Venn, whose face had lost all hint of colour. 'If the police are concerned that Matilda's death was more than an accident, we can no longer withhold from them the precise reasons why I am here,' she said. 'We may both already have committed a crime! My duty to the law must outweigh any promises of confidentiality I have made. We may assume that nothing will now be decided until next week, but it is my intention to go to the police and tell them everything I know that may have a bearing on the matter. And since it is the school governors who employ me, and not you, I will be obliged to inform them that my enquiries are being impeded by the fact that you are keeping information from me.'

'Miss Doughty,' exclaimed the headmistress in desperation, 'you must believe me – I do not know who wrote the pamphlets or why, neither do I know who put them in the girls' desks or what possible motive they can have had for doing so.'

'Then why did you destroy them?' asked Frances bluntly.

'I have already told you – it was not material I wished anyone here to see. Please – I must ask you expressly not to reveal anything that might do damage to the school. What if you were to say something and then it later appeared that it was unnecessary for you to do so?'

'Well,' said Frances, after some thought, 'I will say nothing for now, but I cannot promise that this will always be the case. I agree that it is unpleasant to think of such material being placed before innocent young girls. Whoever did so is prepared to stoop very low indeed, and may do so again.'

'If their only wish is to destroy everything I have worked for, they may already have succeeded,' said Mrs Venn unhappily.

Frances remained certain that Mrs Venn had not told her the truth. She knew that she could use the authority of the governors to try and force the information from her, but to do so would make an enemy of the lady, and she felt that she needed her as an ally.

Later that day Tom brought two notes for Frances that had been delivered to her previous address. Her recent messages had resulted in an invitation to take afternoon tea with Miss Gilbert on Monday, and an appointment later that same evening to call at Mr Paskall's residence to discuss the investigation with the three governors. It was more than ever essential that she locate a copy of the pamphlet and see it for herself.

CHAPTER EIGHT

After church on Sunday morning Frances suggested to Sarah that they take a walk in Hyde Park. It was a natural spot for refreshment and entertainment for people of all classes. On Sundays between the hours of twelve, when congregations emerged from morning service, and two, when they returned home for dinner, the park played host to a great variety of visitors, some of them ostentatiously holding Bibles and hymn books to demonstrate their piety, whether they had actually been to church or not. In winter when the Serpentine was frozen, gentlemen and not a few ladies donned their skates and displayed their athleticism on the ice, while the women and children who stood watching, muffled in scarves and shawls, munched on hot chestnuts fresh from the vendor's brazier. In the summer there were concerts and teas, and the Serpentine was crowded with swimmers and boats. March was only a promise of summer, but the air was invigorating, the freshness of new greenery made dull days brighter and visitors could almost feel as if they were enjoying the countryside without going to all the trouble of leaving town. It was an excursion which Frances had seldom been permitted in the past, since her father had deplored anything smacking of entertainment on a Sunday afternoon, and would, she was sure, have had her working in the chemist shop's stockroom making up mixtures and lotions if he could have squared this activity with his principles. She recalled only a few brief happy afternoons when the sun had shone and she had walked in the park with her brother, and listened to the speakers who in recent years had had the freedom to stand on a box and talk about any subject that moved them. It was an extraordinary thing to do and she had secretly wondered what that must be like.

Frances and Sarah walked down the long curving drive that divided Hyde Park from Kensington Gardens. The grasslands of the park were emerging from their faded winter gloom and here and there a few scattered clumps of flowers had prodded their way through the turf to enliven the scene. As they approached the Serpentine they could see through the heavy clustering bushes and bare black branches of trees, the still grey water mirroring the clouds that hung thickly above. There were a few spots of rain, but the breeze of the last few days had stilled and the cool air had lost its sting.

As they neared the bridge they passed the Magazine, the old munitions store, which in recent years had also served as the Park's police station. Hyde Park, so her uncle had told her, had once been a most lawless place, with thieves and footpads roaming the darkness, but nowadays it was patrolled by police both by day and night, and no one in distress need ever be far from help.

'What I don't understand,' said Sarah, echoing Frances' thoughts on the subject, 'is how Matilda came to fall in without anyone noticing? I'm sure if *I* was to fall in, I would make a great noise about it and then all the police and boatmen would come and pull me out.'

'It is not well lit at night, I understand,' said Frances, grappling with the image of perspiring attendants hauling Sarah's water-soaked bulk from the Serpentine, 'but I agree, the police and boatmen are very diligent, and one is always reading in the newspapers about them rescuing bathers in distress.'

'And then there are the poor souls who come here to put an end to themselves,' said Sarah with a shake of her head, 'but from what I've heard of Matilda Springett she wasn't the sort to do that. Too much salt and pepper about that girl. I could see her stepping into danger, careless-like, but not taking her own life deliberate.'

'Perhaps she was playing a silly game as people do, and fell from the bridge and struck her head,' said Frances, but she hardly believed that herself. Matilda had impressed her as a girl with more than a hint of daring, but not that kind of foolhardiness which would have led her to risk her life for a senseless game.

The road curved into the approach for the bridge, and Frances, examining the width and height of the stone parapet and comparing it with her memory of Matilda's small stature, found it hard to imagine how anyone so diminutive could topple from the bridge by accident. Up ahead, Frances saw two figures, a man in the Sunday best suit of an artisan and a woman in black with a heavy veil, being supported by him. Both were standing by the parapet staring disconsolately into the water below. To her discomfiture she recognised Jem Springett, and felt sure that the lady with him was his mother. Both had a mournful restless air, as if they were hoping that peering into the still cold water where Matilda had died might bring them enlightenment.

Frances was unsure if she should approach them and as she paused, her mind was made up for her as Jem saw her and walked his mother over to greet her. 'Miss Doughty,' he said, with less hostility than he had shown her before.

Frances greeted them and introduced Sarah as her companion, Miss Smith.

'Mother wanted to come here, to try and see – try and understand – but it's very hard. We don't even know why Tilda came here.'

'It was the very last place my girl was alive,' whispered his mother.

'Perhaps she came here to meet someone,' Frances suggested.

'I can't imagine who that might be,' said Jem. 'She said nothing to us.' He hesitated. 'It's been said, Miss Doughty, that you are a detective.'

'I am,' said Frances.

'I don't really know what it is detectives do, unless it's to go about and ask a lot of questions that sometimes the police don't think to ask,' he said. 'Would you help us? We want to find out what happened to Tilda.'

'It's a little early to think of that,' said Frances. 'Let us wait until after the inquest has brought in its verdict. Things may be much clearer then.'

'You didn't see her poor body,' said Jem, and his mother gave a small wail of distress. 'It was clear enough to me. Great dark bruises on her neck. Someone, Miss Doughty,' his lips trembled with grief and anger, 'someone took my little sister by the throat and choked the life out of her, and then they threw her in the water, hoping she would be found a suicide. But there was no water coming out of her – she was put in already dead.'

'Oh!' exclaimed Frances, appalled at this revelation. 'I am most distressed to hear it – what a terrible thing for all of you. Mr Harris must be desolate with grief.' She glanced quickly about, but Davey was not within sight.

'That's another thing,' said Jem, grimly. 'Davey is a good, steady man, a quiet temperate soul, and he thought the world of our Tilda and was working all hours to make a home for them when they were wed. And now the police are asking him questions about where he was when it happened.'

'Davey,' said Mrs Springett, her voice little more than a croak, 'who wouldn't hurt the smallest creature, not a mouse, not a fly! Why would they think he could do such a thing?'

'It is the first thing they think of,' said Frances, 'a sweethearts' quarrel, jealousy – it does happen very often, but I am sure they will soon realise their mistake.'

'Only they think they have their man,' said Jem. 'Davey was out that night – he went to see his sister who lives out Marylebone way – they think he could have met up with Tilda here on his way home.'

'But there are many hundreds of people who could have been here that evening!' said Frances.

'What they're saying is, she wouldn't have trusted a stranger to get so close. And Davey has some scratches on his arms, like a woman's nails.'

'I see. How does he explain those?'

Jem sighed. 'His sister sometimes takes too much to drink, if you understand me, and then she hardly knows where she is or what she's doing. She sees things that she thinks are attacking her and then she needs to be pacified. Davey said she did scratch him that night. But of course she'll have no memory of it.'

Frances reassured him that she would do whatever she could. She learned that the inquest would open the following morning at Mount Street Infirmary, a place she had often read about, where coroner's juries met to contemplate the sodden corpses of the unhappy or the unlucky, taken from the Serpentine. Frances promised to attend, and she and Sarah took their leave of the grieving pair and left them still staring into the water, like mystics searching for a truth that would not appear.

Frances and Sarah walked back along the bridge with Frances deep in thought. At last she said, 'If what Jem Springett said is true, then it was undoubtedly murder, but it seems like a curious place to carry it out, within such a very short distance of a police station.'

'If she was throttled, very quick, then she wouldn't have had a chance to call out,' said Sarah.

'True, which means that the murderer was standing very close to her and took her by surprise. The police are right – it was someone she knew and trusted.'

'Her sweetheart,' growled Sarah.

'Or perhaps a woman, who she felt posed no threat. I do think it unlikely that this was a woman's crime, but Matilda was small and slight enough to be killed in that way by a stronger female.'

Frances stopped suddenly. 'And there is another thing,' she said. 'Jem thought that Matilda was strangled on the bridge just above the place where her body was found, and then thrown over the parapet into the water. Did no one hear a splash? Such a sound would carry a long way at night and the police must surely be alert for noises of that very nature.'

They were walking beside a mass of large bushes and trees, some of them heavy with pale blossoms, and the space opened to reveal a small narrow path sloping down to the bank of the Serpentine. 'I wonder . . . ,' murmured Frances, and turned to follow the path. At the water's edge she found a wooden boathouse with a gabled roof, and a row of ten narrow rowing boats drawn up beside it, all furnished with oars and boathooks. Set slightly behind the boathouse was a building surrounded by railings, its imposing entrance flanked by noble columns. Above the doorway was inscribed 'Receiving House. Royal Humane Society.'

'Oh, this is where they take the poor souls they pull out of the water,' declared Sarah. 'There's many a creature doesn't know which way to turn, what with drink and debt, and throws themselves in. Or the young men who go swimming to impress the ladies and then faint. I've heard they've got all sorts in there – doctors, nurses, medicines, hot blankets, warm baths. And they do things to try and squeeze the water out.' She clenched her hands as if wringing out a sponge, then shook her head. 'Never does any good.'

Frances followed the path that skirted the Serpentine in the direction of the bridge. She could now see that in addition to the five arches spanning the water, there was also a deep arch at either end of the bridge forming a tunnel over the lakeside pathway. Frances stepped into the damp hollow darkness of the tunnel and stared up at the stonework above. 'I wonder,' she said, and turned to Sarah. 'What do you think? Would this be a good place for a secret meeting?'

'Good place to get murdered,' said Sarah.

'My thought exactly,' said Frances. 'But Matilda would never have come to such a spot to meet someone she felt she could not trust. Someone must have gained her confidence and then betrayed her. And once the poor girl was dead, she could easily be carried to the water's edge and put in without making a noise. I wonder how the body came to be lodged under the arch of the bridge – there is no current to carry it there.'

Sarah glanced back at the row of boats. 'Perhaps he used one of the boathooks to push her further out so it would look as if she had jumped off the bridge. But he wasn't very clever – he didn't think about the marks on her throat showing up.'

Frances recalled something she had read in a medical book. 'There was not enough light to really see any marks at the time,' she said, 'and bruises can look much darker two days after death.'

As they walked back to the gate Frances realised that Sarah was unusually quiet, a worried expression furrowing her broad features. Frances stopped suddenly and turned to face her companion. 'Sarah, I can see that something is troubling you,' she said.

Sarah looked awkward for a moment. 'If you don't mind, I'd like to say what I think plainly and straight out.'

'I would welcome it if you were always to do so,' said Frances. 'You know me better than anyone alive and I value your opinion on everything.'

Sarah looked encouraged by the thought, but was still uneasy about what she was about to say. 'The thing is – what happened to Matilda – well, the person what killed her might have done it so she wouldn't speak out against him and let on that it was him who told her to put the pamphlets in the school. And if that person was to find out that *you* are asking questions, then he might come after you as well. So what I was going to say was that I don't want you going out meeting people on your own at night in dark places. So if you got a note that said you had to go somewhere then I want to go along with you and keep you safe.'

Frances, who knew from personal observation that Sarah's powerful fists could fell a man with a single blow, smiled and nodded. 'That is very good advice,' she said, 'and I will make sure to have you as my personal guard.' Sarah looked relieved. The two women linked arms and walked on together like two companionable yet very unalike sisters.

At nine o'clock on Monday the inquest on Matilda opened in the boardroom of the infirmary near Grosvenor Square. The infirmary was part of the parish workhouse, a large, plain build-ing of some antiquity, which had suffered over the years from a number of reconstructions forced upon it by rising demands for accommodation, and the understandable feeling of the guard-ians that it was undesirable for paupers to be sleeping four to a bed.

As anticipated, the hearing was brief and poorly attended. Mrs Springett was a silent, veiled figure supported by her son. Davey, who was presumably still under suspicion, was not present. There was one newspaperman, who did nothing but draw caricatures in his notepad and was obviously waiting for something more interesting. The court took evidence of identi-fication from Jem, after which the proceedings were adjourned for a week. Frances next called at Paddington Green police station but Inspector Sharrock was out with his constable. She learned only that Davey Harris was still being questioned by the police, but had not yet been charged with any offence, and left a message saying that she would return. Back at the apart-ment, she and Sarah ate a small and gloomy luncheon of a chop with potatoes, with Frances too preoccupied to even consider pudding.

That afternoon, with Sarah scouring ladies' reading rooms for the elusive pamphlet, Frances, promising faithfully to be home before dark, called at Chilworth Street to meet the ladies of the Bayswater Women's Suffrage Society. She was met at the door by a respectable looking maid who conducted her to a first-floor apartment.

'Miss Doughty!' exclaimed a lady of buxom figure and a girlish deportment quite out of keeping with her age, which was about forty. 'You cannot imagine my *delight* when I received your letter! I am Esme Gilbert and this is my dearest and most trusted friend and companion, Marianne John.' A tiny and very slender lady with frizzy, slightly greying hair and timid eyes sat in an armchair by the fire, embroidering what appeared to be a banner large enough to span a church hall. She looked up and gave a shy but friendly smile.

The room was furnished with the intention of being very warm and comfortable. There were no hard chairs with stiff wooden backs which might oblige the occupant to sit with painful but polite rigidity, but all was softness, and cushions, and doilies. The door was heavily draped in a burgundy coloured damask curtain, a small round table was covered in overlapping lace cloths, and a padded couch dripped silken shawls, its arms cradled in embroideries. Frances had never seen so many fringes and tassels in one room. A side table with a pretty cutwork cloth was piled neatly with books and pamphlets, and a bentwood coat stand held not coats but about twenty purple sashes.

'Miss Doughty, it is quite impossible for me to adequately express how much the ladies of Bayswater hold you in admiration,' enthused Miss Gilbert. 'You are a bright and shining example of the woman not only of today but the future. Please take a seat – here, by me —,' she plumped onto the couch and patted the place beside her. 'There will be tea and scones very shortly. Have you ever considered joining our campaign? I have a great deal of literature for you to read which I know you will find of the utmost interest. And we have a meeting planned on Wednesday evening – you *must* come. We are in Westbourne Hall on the Grove, a most suitable place, which I believe can hold up to one thousand persons, and I have every confidence that all the places will be taken, and more demanded. It is a sad state of affairs that there is no larger meeting hall in Bayswater and I have written to the newspapers several times on that very subject.'

'I wish you every success,' said Frances politely and sat down, while Miss John quietly stitched away. The maidservant brought in a well-laden tray, which she placed on a folding table in front of the couch, and Miss Gilbert busied herself pouring tea.

'Would you perhaps consider making a short speech to the throng? We are expecting many persons of influence in Bayswater, including several gentlemen, to whom we must perforce at the present time look for our demands to be met. Once we have more women in positions of authority it is on our sisters in the struggle that we may then depend to carry the banner forward. You see, Miss Doughty, and I do hope it will not be long before we can address each other on more familiar terms, you have shown to the *world* what it is that a woman can do, that a woman's intelligence is the equal, or even the better of any man. If anyone says to me that a woman's mind is not as good as a man's, that she can deal only with the frivolous or gentler considerations, I say to them at once "What about Miss Doughty – *she* will prove you wrong!" Scone and butter?'

'Thank you,' said Frances, accepting tea and a scone. 'You have given me a great deal to consider. I will certainly come to your meeting, but as I have never before made a public speech I think that on this occasion I will watch others and learn how it is done.'

'But you will at the very least honour us by taking a seat on the platform?' urged Miss Gilbert. 'My dear Marianne says, and I agree with her, that your patronage of our great cause will add greatly to our powers of persuasion.'

'I am very flattered,' said Frances, 'and I will sit on the platform and will, I am sure, feel very insignificant in the company of so many prestigious persons. I hope, however, that you may be able to do me some small service.'

'Whatever is in my power!' Miss Gilbert gave a little gasp of anticipation. 'Are you tracking down another murderer? How *very* exciting!'

'Oh, nothing as remarkable as that,' said Frances, which was not, she told herself, a lie as she was still officially only engaged to find the person behind the pamphlets. 'I am interested in an item of literature and it was suggested to me that you would know where I might find it. None of the newsagents or bookshops in Bayswater seem to have heard of it.'

'Well, now, let me show you some of our publications,' said Miss Gilbert, bouncing out of her seat and going to the side table. 'What was the title?'

'It was called "Why Marry?" and the author was called "A friend to women". The tenor of the pamphlet was, I understand, to persuade young women not to enter the married state.'

Miss Gilbert returned to her seat clutching a bundle of pamphlets. 'That sounds most interesting, but I cannot say I have ever seen or heard of it. Marianne is a great reader and would, I feel certain, have mentioned such a thing to me. I assume, Miss Doughty, as you find this subject so interesting, that *you* have no plans to marry?'

'No, there is no gentlemen to whom I wish to attach myself.' Frances was suddenly assailed by visions of a certain young constable's nut-brown moustache but thrust the inappropriate thought aside.

'I hope you do not live alone?' said Miss Gilbert, anxiously. 'You are – and my comment is offered only in the spirit of friendship and sisterhood – very young to be alone in the world.'

'Indeed, no,' Frances reassured her, 'I have a loyal friend and companion, a lady in whom I place the utmost trust.'

Miss Gilbert smiled and nodded with approval. 'I see that we understand each other perfectly. Dear Marianne is more to me than just a friend. She is my rock, my anchor, my bright beacon! How fortunate you are!'

Miss John laid her sewing aside for a moment and took tea in dainty sips, then carefully cut a quarter of a scone and laid it delicately on her plate. 'I have heard,' she whispered, 'that pamphlets of a *most advanced nature* have recently been placed in a girls' school.'

Miss Gilbert, about to take a large bite of a scone, stopped and stared at Frances. 'Is *that* your interest? Oh do tell!'

'I would take it as a very great favour if you were to treat my enquiries with confidence,' said Frances, in a conspiratorial tone, and the ladies, with the thrilling sense that they were now a part of a secret mission, quickly agreed.

With Miss Gilbert temporarily incapacitated from speaking by a superfluity of jam, Frances took the opportunity to glance through the Society's pamphlets, which were mainly concerned with the campaign to extend the suffrage to women, but also urging for a change in the laws governing the property of women to permit them to retain ownership after marriage. All the pamphlets were printed on good quality paper, and all bore the name of the author.

Frances, who had neither property nor any prospect of marriage, had never given a great deal of thought to the question of women's property rights, but now she considered it, thought it very insulting to assume that a woman might not do with her own property as she pleased, and must by law hand it over to her husband on marriage, a man who might prove to be a scoundrel or a fool. She wondered what 'A friend to women' might have to say on the subject.

Since Westbourne Hall lay at a point half way between Frances' apartments and Chilworth Street, it was agreed that she and Sarah would meet Miss Gilbert and Miss John outside the hall at a quarter to seven on Wednesday evening. Tickets, Miss Gilbert assured Frances with a twinkling eye, would not be a difficulty. Frances, clutching a sheaf of literature, succeeded in extricating herself from the warmth of the lady's regard and returned home.

Later that evening, Frances and Sarah were seated in Mr Paskall's study facing that gentleman and the other two governors. It had taken a certain amount of obstinate persistence on Frances' part to ensure that Sarah should also be in attendance. On their arrival it had been assumed without question that Sarah was a maidservant who was best accommodated in the basement kitchen, but on it being revealed that Frances regarded her as a trusted assistant whose presence was essential to the proceedings, some alarm ensued. Eventually, it was agreed that Sarah should be admitted to the meeting, and so she sat arms folded, with an expression of intense concentration while the men, when they dared to look at her, which was not often, regarded her as they might have done had Frances instead arrived with a trained wild beast which she had assured them was under her complete control, but which they feared might turn savage and bite them at any moment. In this they were probably nearer the truth than they imagined.

Frances looked at the three governors, two of whom she had not previously met – Paskall his bright blue eyes keen as a hawk, his thin frame hunched and alive with nervous energy, Matthews laconic and relaxed, but, thought Frances, with a certain calculating intelligence in his dark eyes. She felt no liking for either of them, but had some sympathy with Mr Fiske who, it seemed, did all the actual work of the board, while the other two always appeared to have things to do of too great importance to be able to spare any time to assist him.

'I am most intrigued,' said Matthews, fiddling in a leisurely way with his cigar holder, 'as to the reason we are here. As I understand it, the whole matter has been settled. If this is simply about recompense then I am agreeable to anything you gentlemen may consider reasonable. Fiske, can you see it it?' He took out a cigar and began to roll it gently between his fingers. Frances felt sure he would not light it while she was there, and this was his way of suggesting that the interview, having not even properly started, was about to conclude.

'Yes, yes,' said Paskall impatiently, 'I concur. I am a very busy man, Miss Doughty, and can waste no more time on this.'

'I am not here about finances,' said Frances firmly, 'and neither is it my belief that the enquiry is at an end.'

'Oh?' said Paskall, 'but I thought that wretched girl who drowned herself is the culprit!'

'That is my suspicion,' said Frances, 'but until we have the verdict of the inquest, we do not know the manner of her death and I would not attempt to pre-judge the matter. There is also the question of her motive.'

'A silly prank, surely,' said Matthews with a dismissive wave of his hand. 'She was probably weak-minded, and jumped into the Serpentine because she was afraid of losing her place.'

'She was neither,' said Frances. 'I believe that she was a moderately clever and artful girl who somehow became involved in something more dangerous than she thought. And she had everything to live for, and no fear of losing her place, as she was soon to be married. Matilda may have distributed those pamphlets but I think she was being directed to do it by someone else.'

'And who might that be?' asked Matthews.

'That I do not yet know,' Frances admitted.

Paskall suddenly leaned forward and thumped on his desk. 'You see! I was right!' he exclaimed. 'Miss Doughty has hit upon it! This is a plot by my political enemies! The maid was just a tool, probably bribed, and then —,' he suddenly paled, gulped with fright and pressed his knuckles to his mouth.

'What is it now, Paskall?' asked Matthews, wearily.

'But don't you see?' said Paskall, gesturing with trembling hands. 'There are powerful men involved, men who will stop at nothing! Perhaps the girl was killed to ensure her silence!'

'Don't be ridiculous,' said Matthews, but it was muttered under his breath and Paskall probably didn't hear.

'What do you think, Miss Doughty?' asked Paskall nervously.

'As I have said, we will not know the truth until we hear the verdict of the inquest, but,' she paused and proceeded cautiously, 'having said that, I do have confidential information which suggests that murder is not an impossibility.'

Matthews said nothing, but opened his eyes wide and quite forgot about his cigar.

'What do you propose?' asked Fiske in alarm.

'If Matilda did meet her death by violent means that is a matter for the police. They have already made a visit to the school and interviewed Mrs Venn and myself.' Paskall groaned and Fiske shook his head in despair. 'They are currently interviewing Matilda's sweetheart, Davey Harris, but there is no real evidence to suggest he is the culprit. Your concern, I know, is to resolve the question of the pamphlets, which may or may not be connected with Matilda's death, and it is that which I wish to continue investigating.'

'Do the police know about them?' asked Paskall.

'They have been told that Matilda was suspected of being in possession of unsuitable literature,' said Frances. 'You appreciate that I have been placed in a very difficult position as I believe that neither you nor Mrs Venn wish the police to be told the whole truth of the matter. Should it become clear to me that the information is material I will have no alternative but to tell them everything.'

'Well, we must hope it will not come to that,' said Fiske. 'Perhaps the young man will confess.'

'But he may be innocent,' said Frances. 'In fact, I think he is. And neither he nor Matilda's family know anything about the pamphlets. Do you agree that I should continue my investigation?'

All three men nodded.

'That is good, because I need to ask all of you some questions.'

Matthews, who now seemed to regard the meeting as affording him far more entertainment that he had anticipated, happily put his cigar case back in his pocket. 'Question away, Miss Doughty.'

'My enquiries have shown that the pamphlets must have been placed in the desks at some time between twelve on Tuesday 2 March, when Charlotte last used her arithmetic book, and nine the next morning when the discovery was made. I know that Mr Fiske and Mr Miggs paid a visit to the school during that time, but I would like to ask you, Mr Matthews and Mr Paskall, if you visited the school between those hours and if so, did you see anything of note? Was there any person there you might not have expected to see, or was there anything in Matilda's manner that was unusual?'

'Oh, I have not been there for many months,' said Paskall, 'and neither has Mrs Paskall.'

Matthews shook his head. 'Can't recall the last time I stepped through the door,' he said.

Paskall and Matthews both looked at Mr Fiske.

'I can assure you that both I and Mr Miggs were shown straight to Mrs Venn's study and then departed after the meeting,' said Fiske. 'I saw no one else. Now you mention it, I did think that the maidservant was not so respectful as she might have been.'

'I assume that none of you gentlemen have seen the pamphlets in question?'

They shook their heads. 'My difficulty is that Mrs Venn, not realising that someone would be appointed to investigate, destroyed them before I arrived. She said that they were unsuitable for young minds.'

There was a knock on the door and Paskall's housemaid entered with a telegram on a small tray. 'Urgent for you, Sir,' she said.

Paskall leaped from his chair as if fired from a catapult, tore open the message and, having read it, almost collapsed back again. 'Gentlemen!' he exclaimed breathlessly, waving the paper aloft, 'the hour is at hand!'

'Whatever do you mean?' said Matthews.

'There was an announcement made in the House tonight! Quite unexpected! Lord Beaconsfield is dissolving parliament early.'

'Then there is to be an election soon?' asked Fiske.

'Yes – very soon – oh my word – *this month*!' Paskall was half excited and half alarmed. 'But there is so much to do, so much to be settled that I thought I had months to achieve!' He turned to Frances. 'This business at the school must be solved without delay, and with no breath of scandal! I must go to the Conservative club at once – there are meetings to be arranged – Matthews – we have a great deal to discuss!' Paskall ran to the study door and wrenched it open. 'Theodore! Come here – I need you urgently!'

The tousled head of Paskall junior soon appeared at the door 'Now then father, where's the fire?'

'Oh it's good news! The best! But we need to make haste! I'm to be in parliament before the month is out!' He thrust the paper at his son, who read it with some pleasure, then, looking up, saw Frances.

⟩

'Well, bless me if isn't the lady detective! Have you come to take us all prisoner?'

'I am merely reporting on my progress in the matter of the pamphlets,' said Frances, 'and now I believe the meeting has concluded.'

'I think,' said Fiske, 'it is safe for you to assume that your services continue to be required, and that all necessary expenses will be met. But there was one thing I was about to say. I called upon Mrs Venn on the afternoon that Charlotte was sent home, and asked to see the pamphlets, but she told me that they were locked in her strongbox and the key had been mislaid. It seemed so unlike her, but she was obviously distressed by the incident and not her usual self and so I let it pass. I assumed that by the time you had gone there she would have found the key. Now you tell me they have been destroyed. Some servant's mistake, I suppose, but very unfortunate.'

Frances stared at him. 'Mr Fiske, when you engaged me in this matter you told me that you had been unable to view the pamphlets yourself, and when I spoke to Mrs Venn she said that they had been destroyed. I assumed therefore that you had not seen them for that reason. Are you now telling me that she destroyed them *after* your visit to her and not before?'

'Well – I —,' he looked dismayed. 'That does seem to be the case.'

Frances was suddenly angry, both with Mrs Venn and with herself. Now she was sure that the headmistress had lied to her. What if the pamphlets had been in the strongbox all along? What if they were there still? She must demand to examine the contents at the first opportunity.

As Frances hurried along the street, she was seething with annoyance. 'We are going to the school,' she told Sarah. 'I need to speak to Mrs Venn and it will not wait!'

CHAPTER NINE

By the time Frances reached the school and had waited impatiently outside for her ringing to be acknowledged, she was sufficiently incensed to push her way past the unfortunate Hannah and head for the stairs. The maid squeaked and backed against the wall as Sarah, unstoppable as a road-steamer and almost as wide, followed on. Without pausing to knock, Frances flung open the door of the headmistress's study, and was pleased to find that lady at her desk.

'What is the meaning of this?' demanded Mrs Venn. 'This is most unseemly and unworthy behaviour!'

Frances strode into the room. 'There will be no more seemliness until I have answers,' she said.

'And who is this – person?' said Mrs Venn, with a gesture of distaste.

'Miss Smith is my trusted assistant,' said Frances, advancing as far as the desk and leaning on it almost as Inspector Sharrock might have done, while Sarah folded her arms and stood at the door. 'I have been lied to, Mrs Venn, and I will be lied to no longer. I have just spoken to Mr Fiske, who has told me that on his first visit to you after Charlotte was sent home you told him that the pamphlets were in your strongbox. Yet the very next day when I came here, I found you had destroyed them. Or have you? Are they still there? I demand to see the contents of the box this very moment.'

Mrs Venn gaped in astonishment, but there was no mistaking the alarm in her eyes however much she might try to brazen out the situation. 'Mr Fiske may have been mistaken – confused . . .' she began.

'I think not,' said Frances. 'I think you are lying to me still.'

'This is an insult!' exclaimed Mrs Venn.

'It is one you have brought on yourself. The box. *Now.*'

There was a pause, then at last Mrs Venn rose and unlocked the iron-bound box that stood on a side table, and threw back the lid. 'There,' she said, turning and walking back to the desk. 'See for yourself.'

Frances peered into the box, but to her disappointment saw no papers, only neatly arranged and labelled pouches of money, and a few trinkets. One of the pouches, she knew, held the money found in Matilda's slipper and Frances was about to suggest it be sent to the girl's family, but decided that its presence there was evidence and it should be left as it was.

'I trust that is what you came to see,' said the headmistress, with a small smile of triumph.

Frances stood and thought for a moment, then she sat down. 'Assuming — and this in my opinion is a very large assumption — that you were telling Mr Fiske the truth when you told him you had locked the pamphlets away, I suggest to you that the key was not mislaid at all, and you were lying so as to avoid showing them to him.'

Mrs Venn bristled at the accusation but said nothing.

Frances, feeling surer of her ground, continued. 'Then he went away, but you must have been afraid that he would not let the matter drop. So who was it you feared? Not Mr Fiske — I doubt that anyone fears Mr Fiske — not the other governors, who never seem to come here. Not the police or detectives who you knew would *never* have been brought here. Who then?'

Mrs Venn moved back to her seat. 'I see,' she said, 'that you are a young lady who will not be deflected from her purpose. Mrs Fiske is of a very similar disposition. You should make the lady's acquaintance. You will have a great deal in common.'

Frances nodded. 'And you knew that Mrs Fiske, mindful of the welfare of her daughters, would come here and demand to see what her husband had failed to see, and would not rest until she had done so.'

'Yes.'

'And that was when you destroyed them?'

'It was.'

'No doubt you told her it was done to protect the girls, just as you told me, but that was not the real reason, was it?'

The headmistress was silent.

'Mrs Venn,' said Frances urgently, 'I have spoken to Jem Springett who saw Matilda's body. He believes that she may have been murdered. Whether it pleases you or not we may soon find the school alive with uniformed policemen. And then I *know* that Inspector Sharrock will drag the truth out of you and he will not be as gentle as I am.'

Mrs Venn suddenly started to tremble in dismay and tears spilled from her eyes and rolled down her face. Frances allowed her a few moments to compose herself and dry her eyes. It was Frances' turn to give the other woman a drink of water. 'The pamphlet contained a libel against the school,' said the headmistress at last. 'An allegation as untrue as it was disgusting.'

'Was anyone named?' asked Frances.

'No. And I will say no more since I do not wish to be guilty of spreading this unpleasantness myself. Miss Doughty, you can see how dangerous this is for the school. Do not force me to reveal this lie to others who may be foolish enough to believe it!'

'Very well,' said Frances, evenly, 'but I still need to know more. A libel you say, therefore something that you know is untrue, but presumably it is impossible for you to prove it is untrue, or you would not have felt unable to deal with it. I understand the nature of cruel rumour – my own father was a victim of it and it almost destroyed us. I will not ask you to repeat the accusation, but tell me this – was there anything in the pamphlet – and I am assuming now that you read it in its entirety – which suggested to you that it was written by a teacher or former teacher, or perhaps a former pupil? Is that where I should be looking for the culprit? Is there amongst those persons anyone who would have borne some ill-will towards the school or even yourself? Was a teacher dismissed, a pupil expelled?'

Mrs Venn thought deeply and despondently, then shook her head. 'I have never had occasion to dismiss either a servant or a member of the teaching staff. Those who have left have either ceased to work due to age, or have departed in order to marry, or have found a situation that suited them better. All have expressed how fond they were of the school. The current staff – and I would stake my life on it – are beyond reproach and most loyal. Neither have I ever sent a pupil away. Many of the girls have made excellent marriages. I have regular letters from several of them, and they visit me and say how happy they were here.'

'But did the author demonstrate some personal knowledge of the school?'

'I think,' said Mrs Venn unwillingly, 'that the author had some knowledge.'

'Very well,' said Frances, 'in that case I would like you to supply me with a list of all the staff who have ever taught here and also all the pupils. Then we will go through the list and you will tell me of anyone who you know to be deceased or residing abroad.'

'It is growing late,' said Mrs Venn, wearily.

'The sooner we make a start the sooner we will be done,' said Frances.

Fortunately for Frances' enquiries, the school had during much of its existence been even smaller than at present. Initially, all of the teaching had been the responsibility of Mrs Venn and Miss Baverstock. Another lady had joined them later, but she had died several years ago. Professor Venn had been the figurehead of the school but had not actually taught, his days being devoted to his great work of history which would, due to his early death, never be published. He had suffered from breathlessness and pains in the chest, and his doctor had diagnosed degeneration of the heart. Mrs Venn, feeling it was inappropriate to have an invalid on the premises, had placed him in a sanatorium, where, as she had personally assured herself, he had received the best possible care until his final fatal collapse some weeks later. The only member of staff who had left recently was a teacher of arithmetic and science, who last January had, at the age of forty-four, been unexpectedly swept off her feet at an anatomy lecture, had married on St Valentine's Day, and was currently enjoying wedded bliss in the south of France. There had been some difficulty in replacing her and her classes had had to be shared between Mrs Venn and Miss Baverstock, who had been finding the extra call upon their time extremely arduous. Mrs Venn uttered a sigh, then on a sudden thought gave

Frances a speculative look and with a few swift questions established that she had useful experience in both disciplines. Before Frances knew it, she had been engaged for chemistry and arithmetic lessons once a week each, as a temporary measure only.

Frances examined a list of sixteen girls, all of whom were former pupils. Two, Selina Matthews and her sister Lydia, she had already met. Mrs Venn gave her to understand that neither of these could be the author of the pamphlet unless their grammar had undergone a very marked improvement since they left the school. Girls tended to join when aged between ten and thirteen and stay until they were eighteen. Two girls were an exception, Selina Matthews (later Mrs Sandcourt), and Caroline Clare, who had become pupils at the school on the same day at the age of fifteen. Mrs Venn explained that Caroline was a distant cousin of Roderick Matthews' late wife, and the date that she and Selina entered the school coincided with his first becoming a governor. Selina had left a year later to go to finishing school, it being felt that her personal attractions were more likely to secure her a good marriage than any intellectual capability. Since her marriage she had, however, become a devoted patroness of the school, donating and awarding prizes, and even taking a table selling lace and embroideries at the Christmas bazaar.

Three of the sixteen girls had married wealthy merchants and now lived abroad, while five had married in London and still wrote to and visited Mrs Venn and said how much they would like to send their daughters to the school, and recommended it to their friends. Four of the unmarried girls were betrothed, and two hinted that happiness would soon be theirs, which left Lydia Matthews, who lived in constant hope of matrimony, and Caroline Clare, who had gone abroad several years ago, her situation unknown. All her girls, said Mrs Venn, were ornaments of the community, and she could not imagine a reason why any of them would want to harm the reputation of the school.

When they were done Frances rose to leave, and the two women faced each other. 'Mrs Venn,' said Frances, 'I apologise for the rudeness with which I entered your study, and any impolite words I may have uttered. I believe we both appreciate that we can only resolve this matter by working together.'

Mrs Venn nodded. 'I agree,' she said, 'and I too must apologise for being less than open.'

Awkwardly they shook hands, like the two parties to a quarrel who had determined to make things up.

On the following morning Frances made her way to Salem Gardens to see if the Springetts had any further news, but she knocked on the front door in vain. She was just turning away when the door of the next house opened and the neighbour, Mrs Brooks, looked out.

'Oh, it's you,' she said, wiping hot suds from reddened forearms, 'They're not at home. They're out arranging the funeral.'

'Do you know if Mr Harris has come back?' asked Frances.

'No, the police have still got him, more to their shame,' said Mrs Brooks indignantly.

'I am sorry to hear that; I hope they may soon learn their mistake.' Frances was about to return home when, on a thought, she said, 'I suppose you have known the family for some years?'

'Oh, yes, ten twelve year I've lived here, longer than anyone on the street.'

'I only met Matilda two or three times but I thought she was a clever and sensible girl,' said Frances, who knew that her only means of making progress was to pay compliments to the dead maid.

'She was always a good girl to her mother,' declared Mrs Brooks, 'came to see her every Sunday, and saved out of her earnings and gave her something to help her out, five shillings a week, regular as anything.'

'A good girl indeed,' agreed Frances. 'Five shillings. That would have been most of her wages. I suppose you must remember when Edie was born?'

'Hmm, yes,' said the neighbour unwillingly, 'but they don't like to talk about that, so I don't know how you heard of it.'

'Mrs Venn mentioned her to me,' said Frances. 'She is a kind and generous lady and was happy to allow Matilda to return to her duties after the child was born. There are many employers who would not have permitted it.'

'That's true enough,' said Mrs Brooks. 'Well, this isn't getting the washing done.' She turned to go back in.

'I had expected to find the child living with Mrs Springett,' persisted Frances, 'but she is not. Is she at school?'

'I don't know what you mean,' said Mrs Brooks, stopping and staring back at Frances with a puzzled look. 'The child died in less than a year. The doctor said her little insides were all twisted and the food wouldn't go down proper.'

'Oh,' said Frances, confused, 'but Mrs Springett said —,' she paused. 'I must have made a mistake. Is there another child, perhaps? One aged about seven, who is at school?'

'No, there was just the one. Matilda was young and she was led on – it's happened to many a girl, believing a man's lies. After that she kept herself respectable and was happy to wait till a good man made her an honest offer.'

'And Edie would be seven if she had lived?'

'Yes, I think so. Only don't you go talking about her in front of Davey, they won't be holding with that.'

'I understand,' said Frances.

As she walked away she tried to remember the first conversation she had had with Mrs Springett. There was no doubt in her mind that Matilda's mother had told her that the child, Edie, was aged seven and at school, and Mrs Venn seemed honestly to believe this. Indeed, Frances felt sure that had Mrs Venn known that there was no child living at the Springetts, she would never have mentioned her existence. It was only Frances' intended visit to Salem Gardens that had prompted the grudgingly given confidence. There was no reason why Mrs Venn should necessarily have known that the child had died, although now Frances thought about it, Matilda must surely have been absent from her work for the funeral. Had the maid not attended the funeral of her own child, or had she given a false reason when asking permission to be absent from her duties? But why had she concealed the death from Mrs Venn? Had she concealed it from others, too? What had she been hiding? Frances suspected that any friends or neighbours of the Springetts who had not known them before the child's death would not have been told of it.

It was at least clear to Frances why Mrs Springett had lied; it was because she had come to the house saying she was from the school, something Matilda's mother had found very disturbing even before she learned that her daughter was missing. Mrs Springett must have thought that Frances had come to ask about the child, and had been very anxious that Mrs Venn should not know the truth. What else had Matilda done that her mother did not want revealed? And did any of this have anything to do with Matilda's death? Frances had to remind herself that she was not investigating a murder, only the distribution of pamphlets, yet she could not help feeling that the two were connected.

The streets of Bayswater were even busier than usual, and there was a rumbling of pre-election excitement in the atmosphere. Messengers scurried back and forth, groups of men stood talking animatedly on street corners, and someone had called an impromptu meeting where a crowd had collected to hear a debate on whether Lord Beaconsfield or Mr Gladstone was the better man, and what was to be done about Ireland. The air was chill and some enterprising individual was making a quick profit on the sale of hot meat pies.

Frances returned to the school to take the first of the arithmetic lessons to which she had impulsively agreed. Mrs Venn introduced her to the girls and then sat quietly at the back of the schoolroom to observe the new teacher. Frances did not find the headmistress's presence intrusive, rather it was comforting as she felt it gave her more authority. For the first time, Frances faced the entire class of twelve pupils. Apart from the three doll-eyed Younge girls and Charlotte Fiske, she had not had the opportunity of meeting them before. Sophia Fiske she identified at once as a slightly younger version of Charlotte, although she had a confident, intelligent look that her elder sister lacked. Mr

Rawsthorne's daughters were small round girls, only a year apart in age, who glanced at each other often as if sharing some private amusement. The younger of Mr Paskall's two daughters had been fortunate enough to inherit her features from her mother, but the eldest had her father's hawk-like profile and an insolent superior stare, as if challenging observers to notice and comment upon her unusual looks. The two Matthews girls, smaller versions of Selina, gazed at Frances suspiciously, as if she was an exhibit in a display of fairground curiosities. A thin and palely freckled girl with sand coloured hair and eyes of a faded blue was Wilhelmina Danforth, Matthews' seventeen-year-old ward.

None of them, thought Frances, could appreciate how fortunate they were to enjoy a good education in pleasant surroundings, an education, moreover, which would continue until they were young women about to enter society. She herself had been briefly schooled in crowded classes by harassed teachers overwhelmed by numbers, where she had been expected to absorb only the basic skills which her father had deemed would fit her for a life assisting him in a menial capacity. She had loved her brother Frederick, but how she had envied him the schooling her father had felt no qualms about affording him. She had studied her brother's schoolbooks in private, alone, with, she suspected, far more eagerness and relish than he had ever shown, read every book on her father's shelves, and then later prepared herself to take the examinations which would have entered her to study as a pharmacist. That, at least, had met with her father's grudging approval, and, when he could spare the time from training Frederick, he had given her further instruction. And then, in an instant, the life she had planned for herself was gone, her brother's accident and lingering death requiring her to be his constant nurse, as she had later been to her distressed and fading father. Work and self-reliance was to be her life, whereas these girls were destined to be wives and mothers, cosseted and protected by men. She wondered which fate was the better.

Frances appreciated that she had been given a simple class to teach, and did not find the task too arduous. She had been told what the girls were studying and which exercises were appropriate to their ages, and after demonstrating by use of a board and chalk how they were to proceed, assigned them their work. Her time was then occupied in marking completed exercises as they were handed in on slips of paper, and helping any girls who were experiencing difficulties. There was room for her to walk between the desks and so she decided to take a tour of the classroom and observe the girls working, which they did quietly and diligently. After a while Mrs Venn, with a nod and a smile of satisfaction, left the room.

As Frances took her seat again, she saw a hand go up. It was Sophia Fiske. 'Miss Doughty, it's true, isn't it, that you're a detective?'

Frances smiled. 'That is one occupation I have, yes, but at this very moment, I am a teacher.'

The other girls said nothing, but all of them had glanced at Sophia with interest. 'But you are watching us, aren't you?' said Sophia. 'Are we all suspected?'

'I have no suspects at present,' said Frances, 'but if any of you has anything to say to me, I would be pleased to discuss it privately after class.'

The girls, after another glance at Sophia, all bent their heads and returned to their arithmetic. Sophia, after a flicker of the eye towards her sister, did so, too. Frances set them an exercise to do, and when the lesson ended and the class left to go to deportment and dance, she sat alone, examining the papers. None of the girls stayed behind to speak to her and she completed her work uninterrupted.

Mrs Venn came to invite her to take luncheon with the staff, and made some polite compliments about her abilities as a teacher. 'That is kind of you to say so,' said Frances, 'and it is as well that I have some small talent in that direction, since I may seek to make my living in that way, if my investigation is unsuccessful.'

'And no more is known about poor Matilda?'

'The police are questioning her sweetheart, Mr Harris, and I feel strongly that they have made a very great mistake. I think I will go up to the police station this afternoon and see if there is any news.'

'Is it quite proper for you to go to such a place?' asked Mrs Venn, with some dismay.

'Quite possibly not,' said Frances, 'but I have been to far worse in search of the truth. Incidentally, I discovered something this morning which I think you may not know. Were you aware that Matilda's daughter Edie had passed away?'

'No, I was not,' said Mrs Venn. 'I am very sorry to hear it, of course. Matilda said nothing to me about it, and I did not detect anything in her manner to suggest she had suffered such a loss, neither did she request leave to attend the funeral. Was it very recent?'

Frances studied Mrs Venn's expression and felt quite sure that she was being truthful. 'Not at all – the child did not attain her first birthday.'

They were walking down the corridor towards the basement stairs and, as she spoke, Frances saw the headmistress stop suddenly and her body almost swayed against the wall as if she was about to faint, then she quickly put out her hand and recovered herself. If the news of Edie's death had come as a surprise the fact that it had been so long ago was a palpable shock.

'How curious,' said Frances, 'since you knew of the child's existence, that she said nothing.'

Mrs Venn took a small handkerchief from her pocket and pressed it to her face, then she shook her head. After a moment or two she said, 'I do remember, it would have been about that time, I expect, Matilda did ask permission to go home as she said her mother was unwell and required nursing. She was there for about a week.'

'Perhaps,' said Frances, 'she went to help her mother care for Edie until her death. Why do you think she lied to you?'

'I really can't imagine,' said Mrs Venn, 'and of course it is now most unlikely that we will ever know.' She walked firmly on.

Luncheon was soup, bread, cold meat and milk pudding, and while Frances had a good appetite, she saw that Mrs Venn ate little and appeared distracted. Once the meal was over, she prepared to leave and found that the headmistress too had an errand. 'While I believe it is most improper to intrude on a family's recent grief,' she explained, 'I feel it is my duty to pay a call on Mrs Springett and see if there is anything I can do to assist her at this sad time.' As she left, her face set and determined, she did not appear to be carrying with her the packet of money found in Matilda's box, and Frances decided not to prompt her about it.

Frances turned her steps towards Paddington Green police station. She had hoped to see the cheerful face of Constable Brown, but instead found Inspector Sharrock in discussion with the sergeant at the desk. His face had grown redder and his nose was swollen like a giant but unappetizing raspberry, due to what was undoubtedly a heavy cold and catarrh, neither of which was calculated to improve his normally touchy temper.

'Oh no!' he exclaimed as she entered. 'What is it *this* time, Miss Doughty? Treason? Mutiny on the high seas? Better let me know at once so I can go out and arrest the villains. That would save us all a lot of time.'

Frances ignored the jibe. 'I wish to speak to someone in confidence,' she said.

'Well you can't see Constable Brown, if that was what you were hoping. He's been transferred to the Detective Division.'

Frances tried not to let her disappointment show.

'I do have other constables, you know. Some of them are even single.'

The sergeant hid a smile behind his moustache, and Sharrock wiped his nose on a large and unpleasantly soiled handkerchief. 'Come on, then, Miss Doughty,' he said heavily, 'into my office and I can give you a minute or two, but no more.'

'Have you tried Friar's Balsam?' she asked as she followed him into the office, which she was sorry to see was no less chaotic than the last time she had been there.

'I've got better things to do with my time than hang over a basin of hot water,' he said, throwing himself into a chair, which uttered a noisy squeal of protest. 'Now, what is it?'

Frances looked about to see if there was a seat which might be either free of heaps of paper or clean, or preferably both. She remained standing. 'As you may recall, I mentioned that Matilda Springett was thought to have been in possession of unsuitable reading matter.'

'Yes, and it's over half of Paddington that she gave them to the girls to read,' said Sharrock. 'Have you read them?'

'No, I have not.'

'Unwise of the girl, but it's not exactly a police matter. Why should I be interested, unless you have brought samples?'

'It appears that Mrs Venn disposed of the items rather than risk having them fall into innocent hands, but it has since occurred to her that the publisher might have further copies. She is anxious to trace the publisher so that he might agree to withdraw them. I had wondered if the publisher or seller might be already known to you for offences such as publication of criminal literature; maybe libel or slander. If you could advise me of any such, I would be most obliged.'

'Libel and slander?' said Sharrock. 'We don't get a lot of that round here. Stealing, yes, fighting, yes, and doing just about anything while drunk. But I'll keep my eyes open. No doubt with the election on its way we'll have libel and slander thick as snowflakes.' He sneezed noisily and Frances backed away in distaste.

'Jem Springett told me that when he identified the body of his sister he saw bruises on her throat,' she said. 'He was certain that she had been murdered.'

Sharrock grunted. 'Yes, well neither of you is a doctor, and nor am I, so let's leave all that till we get a verdict at the inquest.'

'But you are treating Matilda's death as murder, or you would not still be holding Davey Harris in custody. Do you suspect him?'

'And what is that to you?' Sharrock demanded.

'It is not my personal concern,' said Frances, 'but Mrs Springett and her son and their neighbour Mrs Brooks are unanimous in their belief that Mr Harris would never have harmed Matilda.'

'Well all that is very interesting, but it's not exactly evidence is it?' said Sharrock. 'If I freed every suspect whose friends thought he was an angel we'd be in a right pickle.'

The door opened and the sergeant peered in. 'He's ready to go now, Sir.'

'Oh, that's wonderful!' said Sharrock gloomily. 'All right, I'll have a word.' He heaved himself out of his chair and pointed a warning finger at her. 'And you, Miss Doughty, are not, and I repeat *not*, to go poking your nose where young ladies have no business. You've got yourself quite a reputation, and it isn't a good one. There's people round here are saying you are some sort of a detective. I hope you know better than that.'

He stamped out, closing the door behind him, but Frances quickly pulled it open and saw a constable bringing Davey

Harris from the cells, while the sergeant returned to him such property as had been in his pockets on his arrest.

'Now mind, this doesn't mean we don't have our suspicions!' said Sharrock to Davey, who stood with his head down, blinking despondently. 'I'll be keeping my eye on you, I can promise you that!' Davey hurried away and Sharrock headed back to the office and scowled as he saw Frances in the doorway. 'Now, unless you have a photograph of the murderer caught in the act with his name pinned to his chest, you can go, and I don't expect to see you here again.' He slumped into his chair again and submitted to a fit of coughing and sneezing.

Frances was eager to leave and rushed out after Davey Harris. She knew that Sharrock in his annoyance had made a slip in admitting that as far as the police were concerned Matilda had been murdered. 'Mr Harris!' she exclaimed, and Davey paused and looked around. 'I hope you remember me, I'm Miss Doughty – I called at Mrs Springett's house. I was in the police station just now to ask if there was any news.'

He gazed at her mournfully and shivered. 'No, no news. I'd best get home.' He walked quickly on.

'They'll be pleased to see you,' said Frances, trotting alongside him, gathering her skirts so she could keep pace. 'They never believed that you had done anything wrong, and neither did I.'

'Nor would I. Why would I harm my girl? It was just that I had some scratches on my arm, and – well – it was the way it looked. Lucky for me someone remembered seeing me with them earlier in the day.'

'If you don't mind my asking,' said Frances, 'can you tell me if Matilda ever earned any money apart from her wages from the school? She must have been eager to save up for the wedding, and it may be that she did some extra work. Perhaps someone paid her to distribute pamphlets. Was she ever a member of the Bayswater Women's Suffrage Society?'

He stopped and stared at her. 'Women's suffrage? No, my Tilly never bothered herself about things like that.'

'But she was able to save towards the wedding, and give her mother money every week. Perhaps the Society paid her to hand out pamphlets for them. It's harmless enough, though the school did believe the material to be a little advanced for its pupils.'

'No.' He shook his head. 'She never did anything like that, not as far as I know. She did have some money put by for the wedding, but she didn't say how much.'

'But surely she can't have saved up *and* helped her mother out of her wages from the school.'

He dragged both hands through his hair. 'Why do you want to know all this?' he groaned. 'She was a good girl – the very best, she'd never have done anything wrong.'

'I am sure you are right,' said Frances soothingly, 'and I believe that the school is quite wrong in suspecting that Matilda may have done something – inadvisable. If I could be reassured that any money she came by was from an honest source, then that would remove any stain of suspicion from her memory.'

He chewed his lower lip and thought about this, then walked back and forth a pace or two, shivering. Finally he stood still. 'Well, she told me not to say anything, but —'

Frances waited, expectantly. She had done all the gentle prodding she could, and now allowed the gap of silence to draw him in.

'I suppose it's all one, now,' he said with a sigh. 'She got given money by a charity. Only she wasn't to tell anyone about it as they only had so much to give, and so they picked out deserving cases, special, and helped them.'

'What charity was this?' asked Frances.

'I don't know anything about it, but Tilly said to me that there was a kind lady who gave money to girls who were about to be wed. And she had got some money from her and was keeping it for our wedding.'

'Did she tell you the name of the lady?'

He shook his head. 'No, only that she was a fine lady who liked to do good.'

'Did she see the lady often?'

'I don't believe she saw her more than the once. But she did say that she was hoping to see her again, and that she would have more money from her – quite a lot more – and it would help set me up in business properly, maybe get a little workshop.'

Frances looked into Davey's simple, grief-torn face, and wondered what it was that Matilda had strayed into that had got her killed.

Chapter Ten

estbourne Hall on the Grove was a building with a charmingly ornate four-storey façade, and was much used in Bayswater for concerts and meetings of all kinds. Frances recalled having once been taken there by her uncle for a musical entertainment, but in recent years the demands of first her brother's and then her father's illness had prevented any such amusements. In any case, her father had disapproved of the theatre and regarded attendance at political meetings as pointless for a female.

The carriage hired by Miss Gilbert and Miss John appeared promptly at a quarter to seven. Miss John, with a sweet smile and her eyes sparkling with suppressed excitement, carefully cradled a large parcel which Frances was sure contained her new banner. Miss Gilbert, all noisy enthusiasm with a stream of words bubbling from her lips, was momentarily silenced when introduced to Sarah. After the usual politenesses, she turned her head aside and murmured something that sounded like 'remarkable.'

Frances was interested to see that the people crowding around the Hall and presenting their tickets to the doorkeepers were respectably dressed and well-behaved, and there were a number of men amongst them. She said as much to Miss Gilbert, who smiled in a very satisfied way.

'Many gentlemen are enlightened enough to support our cause,' she said, 'and with the election about to descend upon us this is an important and most opportune time. I have it on very good authority that Mr Grant, one of the Liberal candidates, is a sympathiser, and I will ask him to state it explicitly the very first chance I have. While gentlemen cannot yet look to us for votes they ought not to ignore the influence of ladies upon the outcome of the election. Many men of sense will, I am sure, listen to their wives and sisters when making their decisions. I shall be addressing the meeting on that point and also urging the drawing up of a petition to be presented to the new parliament on the subject both of female suffrage and the property rights of married women. They cannot refuse us! They will not!'

'Oh no,' whispered Miss John, shyly, 'I am sure they will not.'

Frances, looking about her at the assemblage, noted that Sarah was viewing the great throng with less pleasure than she, and realised that there was almost no one present of the artisan class and certainly no servants. There must, she thought, be many who would have liked to be there and would have benefitted greatly from it, but were prevented from doing so by pressing duties, or were forbidden to attend by husbands or employers outraged by the mere idea of women having minds, opinions and possibly even demands. Was the female vote only to be enjoyed by ladies of property and position? It was a more complex matter than she had supposed and one to which she would have to give a great deal of thought.

Miss Gilbert marched proudly into the hall, as if at the head of an army, and led Frances to where a platform had been made ready with tables and chairs. The body of the hall was filled with rows of closely packed seats, and these were quickly being occupied. Frances could not help wondering, and hoped that she would not seem cynical in this, if the attendees were all prompted by an interest in female suffrage, or whether some were simply there as a way of passing the time, there being little in the way of alternative entertainment until the political parties arranged their public meetings. There were a few newspaper men present, who could easily be distinguished by their busy pencils, and she recognised in particular Mr Gillan of the *Bayswater Chronicle*, whose unduly melodramatic style of reporting had, she felt, contributed in no small way to her current notoriety.

Miss Gilbert ascended the platform with great pride and confidence, Miss John pattering behind her, and together they unfurled the banner which pronounced the society's name in large letters, draping it across the table so that no one might have any doubt of the reasons they were there. A few people were looking about restively, as if hoping for free refreshments, of which they were disappointed to see none. There was a table which was unhappily bereft of teacups and plates of bread and butter, but was well stocked with piles of pamphlets for sale. Sarah went to examine them, electing to remain in the body of the hall as an extra pair of eyes.

Frances found that apart from her companions and herself, the platform was occupied by two more ladies and two gentlemen, one of middle age and the other a slender young man with long hair and an expression of devoted earnestness.

Miss Gilbert opened the proceedings by welcoming all-comers to the inaugural meeting of the Bayswater Women's Suffrage Society. She then introduced the individuals on the platform, affording Frances considerable embarrassment as she eulogised on her superior skills as a detective, which, she assured everyone present, were proof, if any were needed, that a woman's intelligence was more than competent to deal with political questions. The other ladies on the platform were Mrs Bartwell, who sat with some distinction (and, thought Frances immovable *avoirdupois*) on a school board, and Mrs Edith Fiske, whose literary accomplishments, said Miss Gilbert, were well known to everyone present. Frances, having had Mrs Fiske recommended to her by Mrs Venn, albeit in a satirical humour, as a lady of superior qualities, could not help but steal a glance at her, and found that Mrs Fiske was regarding her with more than usual interest. She saw a lady of undoubted plainness of face, but with a firmness and resolution in the set of her form which suggested that she was someone who knew how to make her wishes not only known, but come about.

The middle-aged man on the platform was a Mr Hawkins, who had tried but failed to be selected by the Liberals as their parliamentary candidate, and was, suspected Frances, attempting to make a name for himself by supporting the New Thing, on the grounds that if women were to be enfranchised, he would thereby double his support. The youthful looking gentleman was introduced as Jonathan Quayle, a poet who had recently dedicated a small volume to the cause.

Miss Gilbert then made her opening address, starting by assuring her listeners that the new Bayswater Society was officially affiliated to The National Society for Women's Suffrage and enjoyed the full approval of that organisation. Letters of support, she announced, had been received from many notables, including that enlightened and worthy gentleman Mr Jacob Bright MP, as well as Mrs Fawcett, the wife of Mr Fawcett MP, Mrs Garrett Anderson MD, and Miss Isabella Skinner Clarke, of the Pharmaceutical Society. There was polite applause.

Miss Gilbert then talked at some length of the various Bills that had already been before Parliament on the question of women's suffrage, all of which had, to date, been defeated, but which nevertheless gave her great cause for hope, since by the numbers of the votes and intensity of debate it could be shown that support for the measure was increasing, and must increase still further with time until eventually they would win success. She spoke with great energy, punctuating her talk by bouncing on her heels at moments of high emotion, and spreading her arms wide as if about to embrace the audience.

They owed, she said, a great debt of gratitude to the tireless work of the National Society, and she therefore proposed the first motion of the evening, namely the Bayswater Society's approval of and support for the objects of the National Society. This motion being unobjectionable, it was carried unanimously. Her second motion concerned a new petition to be sent to parliament the instant the forthcoming election had been decided. Since Miss Gilbert was content to take upon herself the entire work of framing the petition the meeting was happy to agree with her proposals.

Mr Hawkins rose to speak in support of the notion that all property holders ought to have the vote, regardless of sex. The opponents of previous Bills which had sought to extend the suffrage had said that if women got the vote then the next thing they would ask for would be seats in Parliament, something for which they were unsuited. He personally did not think the House of Commons would be any the worse for women members and in fact a great deal better. There were shouts of 'Hear! Hear!' from the floor, and a number of voices proposed Miss Gilbert for Prime Minister, that lady declining to admit of any unworthiness for the honour.

Mrs Fiske was next to speak and showed great composure and dignity of address. She expounded on the hardships that women suffered, which could only be rectified by their being given proper representation. Every aspect of a woman's life was ruled by the legislature yet they had no say in its selection and could take no part in framing the law. She was convinced that there were as many women as there were men fully equal to the task, and the foundation of women's future was a proper education. It was the duty of every mother of girls to prepare them to take part in government. A few men were opposed to the measure of women's suffrage, but their views could easily be shown to be fallacious, and it was not they who were the enemy. Far more dangerous were those who by their indolence and apathy and want of intelligence failed to see how vital the enfranchisement of women was for the good of society as a whole.

Mr Quayle addressed the meeting with an air of nervous diffidence. He began by reading a little poem of his own authorship, with a modesty about its merits that Frances thought to be entirely justified, nevertheless, its theme, the moral superiority of women, was appropriate and his words were well received. Frances had never had any great pleasure in poetry as she could not see how a sentiment well expressed and truthful could be made any better by trying to fit it into a rhyme. Fortunately Mr Quayle gave the remainder of his address in prose. It was the view of some, said Mr Quayle, that only single women or widows should have the vote, since to give it to married women might threaten domestic harmony. Mr Quayle professed himself to be a great admirer of the female sex and believed that all women of full age whether married or not should be entitled to vote, and who could say that a married woman might not have a better understanding of the issues affecting families, more sense and compassion and a cooler head than the man to whom she was united? There was a murmur of sympathy about the hall. How unfair it was, he went on, that a woman should have her own property taken from her control by the simple fact of being married, and possibly given to someone less able and intelligent than herself? A person of great wit had once said, he added with a smile, that before a woman married she should discover all of the man's character, but many women having done so would choose not to marry at all. There was a small ripple of amusement around the hall, and several people, all female, shouted 'Hear! Hear!' with a feeling that spoke of personal experience.

But Frances heard nothing. If someone had spoken to her directly at that moment she would not have been able to respond. Jonathan Quayle had used almost the very words that Charlotte had remembered from the missing pamphlet. For all Frances knew other words in Quayle's speech had also been derived from it. Was Quayle the author of the pamphlet? Did he know the author? He had most certainly read it, and it was possible that he still had a copy. Frances was determined that nothing must now deflect her from obtaining the pamphlet.

As soon as the meeting was over, Frances, at grave risk of being very impolite to all those around her and exciting prurient gossip, quickly sought out the young poet.

'Mr Quayle,' she began, entirely forgetting in her eagerness the formalities of a preamble, 'it is essential that I enlist your help on a matter of very great importance.'

'Miss Doughty, it would be an honour to assist you,' he said, gallantly.

'For reasons I am not at liberty to divulge, I am trying to find a pamphlet with the title "Why Marry?"' she said, almost breathless in her haste to say the words. 'Tonight I heard you quote from it – are you the author?'

'Oh, I have never written any pamphlet, only my little poems,' he said.

'Then you must have read it,' she urged. 'Perhaps you still have a copy. If so, I would like to purchase it.'

He smiled. 'There should be no difficulty about that. There are so many pamphlets in my house and I often pick them up and read them. My dear wife, Flora, takes a great interest in the Women's Suffrage Society and it is she who distributes its publications.'

'When you say "distributes" – do you mean she gives them out to interested persons?' asked Frances.

'No, all the business is done by post,' said Quayle. 'The pamphlets are sent to us by the printers, and we keep them at the house.

They are advertised in the newspapers, and Flora receives the funds, makes up the packets and sends them out.'

At that moment Sarah, who had been looking at the publications for sale in the hall, came up to the platform and shook her head.

'Is Mrs Quayle here tonight?' Frances asked, 'I would very much like to speak to her.'

'No, my dear Flora is devoted to our home and rarely strays forth,' he said fondly. 'She is a very timid girl. Why don't I speak to her this evening and see if she has any copies left of the pamphlet you are looking for. If you could supply me with your address I will ensure that she sends one to you, and please accept it with our compliments.'

Whether this was an innocent or deliberate deflection Frances could not know. 'That is very kind of you, but I must impose upon you further. I wish to see it tonight.'

For a moment he was taken aback by her boldness, then he recovered. 'I see that Miss Gilbert has not underestimated you, Miss Doughty. Very well, I will secure a cab. I have a little house in Fulham.'

'Thank you. There will be three of us to travel as my companion Miss Smith will accompany us.'

'Oh!' he exclaimed, as Sarah loomed into view, as if daring him to attempt even the smallest incorrectness. 'Of course. That will be —,' he laughed nervously, 'most appropriate.'

The crowds were streaming from the hall, most of the audience in urgent search of refreshment. In the Grove, posters blazoned with the names of the Conservative candidates had, during the course of the meeting, appeared in the windows of nearby taverns and boys with bundles of leaflets were taking the opportunity of the sudden activity to hand out the election addresses of the Conservatives. There were no answering publications for the Liberals, who, it appeared, had been somewhat remiss in their arrangements. Frances quickly thanked the Misses Gilbert and John and assured them of her support for the Society before she and Sarah joined Mr Quayle in the cab.

Flora, said Quayle, who seemed inspired to heights of impassioned lyricism at the mere thought of his wife, was the most beautiful, delicate, shy and sweetly feminine girl in the whole world. They had met because her mother, Mrs Gribling, a good and respectable lady with an interest in literature, occasionally held small gatherings of poets who thereby had the opportunity to read their humble offerings aloud. Many a starving poet, he declared, would have expired for his art had it not been for Mrs Gribling's bread and butter. Flora, who had kept house for her mother, had on those occasions only been seen when tea was to be served. This done she would retire quickly to another room, like a fragile flower afraid of withering in the sun. And yet, he thought, and yet – he uttered a sigh – perhaps there had been something in his poetry which had induced her to creep to the door of the parlour and listen. For his part, he had fallen in love with her on the very instant that he had seen her.

Quayle assured Frances that he believed strongly in the development of women's intellect and would have been more than content if Flora had taken a leading part in the Women's Suffrage Society. Had she desired to take the platform and make a speech, he would have been the first to applaud, but this, she had assured him, was not to her taste. She loved their little home and wanted nothing more than to make it agreeable for him. They had been married for less than a year, and for domestic bliss and comfort he could recommend nothing better. Feeling it necessary to explain that he did not earn a living from his poetry, something that Frances had already guessed, Quayle said that he had been fortunate in receiving a legacy from a generous aunt, this and his daily work as a clerk of accounts was more than enough for their small wants. Frances was largely silent as Quayle enthused about his little house as if it were a palace in miniature and his wife the queen of both his home and heart. Sarah said nothing, her face stonily impassive.

Quayle understood, however, that there were marriages which resulted in great unhappiness for both parties and did not disagree with the writer of the pamphlet that careful thought should be given before entering the married state. Want of money, the dissipation of unsuitable husbands, and contrasts of character were, in his opinion, the chief causes of marital misery.

The Quayles lived in a terraced property not far from the Fulham Road. There was no resident servant, only a woman who came in to do the heavy work, and of course a washer-woman, but everything else Flora liked to do for herself. As Quayle opened the front door, she peered around from the parlour into the hallway, like a bashful child. Her simple dress showed her delicate figure to advantage, and her face was very pale, with good features, and surrounded by a mass of lustrous golden hair. Unlike Selina Sandcourt, who knew she was beautiful, and that her beauty was her fortune, Flora Quayle seemed quite unaware of the advantages that nature had been kind enough to bestow upon her. She was for a moment alarmed at the appearance of two strangers on her doorstep, but her pleasure at seeing her husband was unmistakable.

'Flora, my dear, here are Miss Doughty and Miss Smith who attended the meeting tonight and are most anxious to acquire one of your pamphlets. If you would be so kind as to provide some cocoa I will find what is needed.' He hurried upstairs and Flora conducted Frances and Sarah into a small but well-kept parlour, so tidy and spotless that no army of assiduous maid-servants could have left it better.

'I hope we are not imposing upon you,' said Frances, 'but I was so moved by the speeches tonight that I simply had to know more, and there was something your husband said which was inspired by a pamphlet – I felt I had to obtain a copy without delay.'

'Not at all,' said Flora, 'please be seated and I will bring the cocoa, it is already made, as I knew Jonathan would want a cup.'

They were soon settled, by which time Quayle had returned and Frances had to suppress her excitement as she saw he held a paper. 'Ah, I remember this one, now,' he said, 'and it was a curious thing – it was not sent by the usual printer, and there seem to have been no orders. Perhaps they have failed to advertise it.'

'May I see?' asked Frances. Her cup rattled a little in the saucer as she set it down.

'Oh,' said Flora quietly, lowering her gaze to the tabletop. 'Yes. I thought it strange, too.'

'I have read several of the publications given to me by Miss Gilbert,' said Frances, 'and they were all on good quality paper and printed by Grant and Co. of Farringdon. This one is altogether thinner and by —,' she looked at the back, which read only 'Printed for the author by Soho Printworks Dean Street, W.' 'Not a firm I am acquainted with. Well, this is quite the mystery. And were they delivered here by hand, or did they come in the post?'

'By hand, I believe,' said Flora.

'Is it a recent publication?'

'I think so,' said Quayle. 'We received it in the last month.'

'And what is your current stock?'

'There are three dozen.'

Frances wrote her new address on a slip of paper and handed it to Quayle. 'I would very much like to speak to the author. If you should learn anything, would you write to me?'

They both agreed, and Frances finished her cocoa with as much speed as was commensurate with politeness and not burning her mouth, and after attempting to pay for the pamphlet, an offer they refused to countenance, made her departure.

It was too dark to read in the cab home, but Frances, holding on to her prize, was content to wait. 'I have to teach a chemistry class tomorrow,' she told Sarah, 'but I would like you to go to Dean Street and find out all you can about the person who ordered the copies of this pamphlet.' Flora, she thought, had been very quiet at their meeting, but then that, according to her husband, was the nature of the girl. Even if Flora had not recognised Frances' name from the newspapers – and Frances was unsure if her fame had spread as far as Fulham – she would soon be apprised by her husband of the nature of their visitor's profession and the urgency with which she had demanded the pamphlet. She wondered if Flora had any more information to impart and if she might expect to receive a note requesting a private interview.

It was late when they returned, but not so late that Frances could not light a lamp and sit down to read.

Why Marry?
By
A Friend to Women

Do not think because I am a friend to women that I am thereby an enemy to men. There are many good, kind and worthy men, but there are also those who may appear to possess every manly virtue and yet time and circumstance will reveal them to harbour evil in their nature so terrible that it can hardly be named.

A young girl, still with the pallor of the schoolroom on her cheek, taught sufficient arithmetic only that she might understand a butcher's account, and enough French to recite a little poetry, yet thoroughly educated in the art of decorative fans, and instilled with all the horrors that might befall her if she allows her shoulders to slump, is hardly qualified to judge the character of a suitor by outward appearance and manners. Her papa and mama have, with the best of intentions, selected him as worthy of their daughter's respect and love, but they judge him only by his fortune, and whether he can provide the kind of establishment of which they hope she may be mistress. They, of course, do not have to live subservient to him, tend to his demands, and endure his faults. The disagreement of husband and wife is a great cause of unhappiness, but worse than this is neglect, cruelty and – painful as it is to relate – shameful and corrupt dissipation.

Do not, my young reader, dearer to me than a sister, be eager to rush into matrimony. Your relatives may tell you that it is the summit of every woman's ambition, and it is true that a married woman may be a happy creature who expects all married women to be as happy as she, but if she is miserable then she wishes for nothing better than company in her misery. Before a woman agrees to marry she must first come to know and understand all the character of the man, but I fear that once she knows his character, she may decide not to marry.

You, who know nothing of the world and its wickedness, have been taught that it is the duty of Man to protect Woman, and that he has been placed in ascendancy over her by nature, custom and law, in order to carry out this duty. What woman would complain of this if all men were diligent and kind and selfless, but there are some who inhabit the world like monsters and consume and destroy all that is good and pure for their own pleasure. The authority placed in their undeserving hands will be abused, and lead to the ruin and despair of the innocent. What of the wife, so cruelly betrayed? How will she seem in society, except that she will conceal her suffering from the world and speak only to praise the husband who has broken her heart. His intemperance will be spoken of as an illness bravely borne, his uncontrolled appetites kept hidden behind a locked door suggesting only industry and application of the mind. How much better it would have been for his poor wife if she had never known him, how gladly now she would accept eternal spinsterhood rather than endure the torment of life with such a man as this.

Youth is full of optimism, and age may seem dry and bitter by comparison, but that is the fruit of knowledge. Gather your knowledge, let it ripen, use it well. Do not be led astray by fair words and fair faces until you know enough to judge what may lie beneath.

Frances laid the pamphlet aside, and for a time sat silently in thought. At last she retired to her bed, but sleep did not come to her until well into the night.

CHAPTER ELEVEN

Frances had read the pamphlet several times but the next morning, before she had even had her breakfast, she re-read it. The message was abundantly clear, and she now understood what had so terrified Mrs Venn and why the headmistress had ordered the destruction of every copy rather than risk having any member of the board of governors see it.

Frances was, on reflection, feeling a little embarrassed by the rapidity with which she had left the meeting the previous night and, concerned that she might have appeared impolite, wrote a letter to Miss Gilbert and Miss John, apologising for her sudden departure, which she said had arisen from unforeseen circumstances, thanking them for their kind invitation and asking to be advised of any future gatherings. She added that she was thinking of writing a pamphlet herself on the subject of professions for women, and needed a reliable and economical printer who would be able to make a few dozen copies. She had heard of the Soho Printworks in Dean Street and wondered if they knew of anyone who had used that company and could recommend it.

Frances returned to the school to take her first chemistry lesson, giving herself an hour to make the necessary arrangements. Miss Bell was on hand and advised her that these classes were always held in the schoolroom, and Frances was surprised to learn that her predecessor had not felt it necessary to prepare the room in any way. A careful search of the stationery cupboard and the second floor storeroom revealed nothing that might assist her in imparting any useful information to the girls. She found it hard to understand how she was expected to teach chemistry when there was no laboratory, no equipment and, indeed, no chemicals. 'Oh it is not as if we are expecting the girls to be chemists and handle all those smelly things,' said Miss Bell brightly, when apprised of the problem.

'What did the previous lady teach?' asked Frances.

'I really can't say – does it matter?' Miss Bell gave a girlish trill of laughter and scurried away.

The class, Frances discovered when her pupils had assembled, had been learning about the elements and where they were to be found and their uses to mankind. The information had been illuminated by a collection of grey pebbles in a box. When Frances opened the box to display the pebbles the girls regarded them with expressions of deep gloom. Frances closed the box and set it aside, deciding to draw on her years of work in her father's chemist shop and teach something she knew.

Frances told the girls about simple home remedies for common ailments, and how to make soothing skin lotions and preparations for the hair. To her delight, the subject captured the interest of the class, and the girls had a multitude of questions to ask, especially concerning Frances' professional experiences, and wanted to know how pills and mixtures and ointments were made. Somehow, the lesson developed into a conversation, and the subject turned to poisons. Frances found herself describing the properties of arsenic, strychnine, antimony, chloroform and sugar of lead, and the lethal doses and symptoms of poisoning of those substances. The girls listened eagerly and the sound of their excited chatter and keen questioning must have been clearly audible in the hallway for the door opened and Mrs Venn peered in with a worried expression, but, seeing the girls enthusiastically clamouring for information, she simply smiled, nodded and withdrew. Several of the girls wanted to know if pharmacy was a good thing for women to do and Frances spoke warmly of her idol, Isabella Skinner Clarke, the first woman to be a full member of the Pharmaceutical Society, and how she had pioneered the path that others might follow. There was even, she informed them, a London School of Medicine for Women, where they might learn to be doctors. Before Frances knew it the lesson was over and the class filed out with sighs of regret.

The next lesson was deportment, and the girls marched to the front classroom in straight-backed military fashion, with Miss Baverstock rapping out her denunciation of slumped shoulders.

Frances learned that Mrs Venn was at work in her study, and with some concern at what she was about to do, went upstairs.

Her task was made all the harder because this was the first occasion on which the headmistress had appeared pleased to see her, and she had assumed that the visit was simply to report on the success of the chemistry lesson. 'Mrs Venn,' said Frances, with as little preamble as possible, 'I have found a copy of the pamphlet.'

It was fortunate that Miss Baverstock did not view Mrs Venn's posture at that moment. 'I suppose we must discuss it,' she said.

They faced each other in silence for a while, and there was no mistaking the pain of the headmistress or the regret of the younger woman for being the cause of that pain. Frances placed her copy of the pamphlet on the desk between them. Mrs Venn made no attempt to touch it, indeed she recoiled from its presence as if it carried some vile infection. 'The school described in the pamphlet is this one,' said Frances at last.

'I fear you are correct,' said Mrs Venn.

'The suffering wife is yourself and the erring husband is Professor Venn.'

'Oh but so much of the error was mine,' said Mrs Venn, with great emotion. 'I thought I could influence him for good, but I was mistaken.'

'What was the nature of his intemperance?' asked Frances. 'Wine, perhaps?'

Mrs Venn gave a dry laugh. 'I wish it had been. I would have found it easier to blame him. No, it was morphine. You of course will understand the subtle dangers of that drug. He had been given it with good intentions after an operation, but he could never erase the craving from his body. It sapped the goodness from him — what little there had been. I will be frank with you. I married him for companionship, he married me for money. When he was drugged he was at least manageable, but at other times I am sorry to say he showed me violence. His study, where I let it be known that he was writing a great work of scholarship, was little more than a den of indulgence. There was no great work and there never could be. But he was so often charming, and to the world he seemed to be a fine example of scholarship and exemplary propriety, and thus he earned respect and admiration for the thing he only appeared to be. It amused me a little when Mr Fiske said he felt that the school needed the overall guidance of a man, which in truth was something it had never had.'

'Who knew of the Professor's weakness?' asked Frances.

'Miss Baverstock, of course,' said Mrs Venn. 'There have been many occasions when she was obliged to assist me and she has been an invaluable support in times of trial. Dr Montgomery, our physician. I regret that his advanced age made it easier for my husband to persuade him to supply the drug. He is long deceased. And —,' she paused, 'Matilda also knew. It was never my intention that she should, but she once found him in a desperate state and saw some of his bottles and syringes. It was impossible to conceal it and she did from time to time help me care for him.'

'I had wondered,' said Frances, 'at Matilda being allowed more liberty than I would have expected. Your kindness in not dismissing her when you discovered her condition, her familiar manners and your tolerance of her sweetheart frequenting the premises. I take it that was the price of her silence. Did she demand money too?'

'Sometimes, yes,' the headmistress admitted reluctantly.

'The money found in her room? Was that from you?'

'No,' said Mrs Venn, with an emphatic shake of the head. 'I never at any time paid her such a sum. And if I had, why would she hide it from me?'

'It is easy to see why Matilda concealed from you the fact that her child had died.'

'Yes, sometimes she would tell me the child was ill and I would allow her an afternoon visit, and I admit I sometimes gave her money for medicine. I see now that my kindness was abused. You must think me a foolish, credulous woman.'

'Far from it,' said Frances. 'You have more than the ordinary sympathy for young girls who have been led astray by the selfishness of men.' There followed a long silence, as Mrs Venn fought and defeated the ghosts of past memories. Frances wondered what those memories might be, but let it pass.

'But tell me, what of the girls who were pupils at the school at the time of your husband's illness. Did any of them know about his condition?'

Mrs Venn touched a folded handkerchief to her palms. 'I don't believe so. I did my best to protect them. They were given to understand that his absences were due to his work, and they were carefully supervised at all times.'

'The nurses at the sanatorium would have known.'

'I asked the supervising physician to be discreet for the sake of the school, and I know he was. The nurses worked under his direction. My husband's case was not the first of its kind there.'

Frances understood now. Not the first or indeed the only case. It was for the treatment of such cases as Professor Venn's that the sanatorium existed, and discretion was its most valuable service.

'What prompted you to have your husband removed there?'

Mrs Venn struggled to speak, but eventually, and it was almost a relief, she did so. 'One night,' she said, 'I found him wandering in the house in a state of —' her voice declined almost to a whisper, 'semi-undress.' Her bosom heaved convulsively and for a moment it was an effort to get her breath. 'I was able to take him back to his room, but I knew then that it was not safe for him to remain on the premises. I was only glad that there were no girls boarding at the time.'

Frances fetched the water carafe and served them both. 'Mrs Venn, this is a delicate matter, but the pamphlet made other allegations – it suggested the possibility of another kind of intemperance.'

Mrs Venn closed her eyes and tears escaped from below her lashes and streaked her pale cheeks. She pressed the handkerchief to her face. Frances went to pour more water but Mrs Venn, recovering, shook her head. 'Thankfully there is no proof – no suggestion even – that any of my girls was subjected to an insult, or witnessed anything that might have caused her distress. The writer talks of a locked door, and is therefore giving in to conjecture only. It is very unpleasant to consider the kind of imagination that might conjure up such a thing. But the allegation alone will give great pain to any parent whose girls attended the school during my husband's lifetime, and the mere fact that

I endured his presence here when I knew his faults will call my judgement into question. The scandal could well ruin me.' She dried her eyes. 'Have you shown the pamphlet to the governors?'

'No, I have only just located it, and have not yet told them I have done so,' said Frances. 'It may not be necessary to show it to them. You have said that the matter it contains is libellous, and I appreciate that it would cause unnecessary distress, and arouse suspicions where none is warranted. I have not, after all, been asked to do anything other than discover the person who placed the copies in the school, and their motives for doing so, and reassure the governors that it will not happen again. I may do all of those things without letting them read the item in question.'

'Thank you,' said Mrs Venn gratefully.

'The document itself has provided few clues,' said Frances. 'I have found only that it was printed by a company called the Soho Printworks in Dean Street. Do you know anything of that company?'

Mrs Venn shook her head. 'No, the name is not familiar to me, and I do not know of anyone connected with that part of London.' She paused. 'Unless . . .'

'Yes?' asked Frances.

'No — there may have been something mentioned to me recently concerning Soho, but I can't recall it now. My mind is very confused and preoccupied. It may mean nothing.'

There was a Westminster directory on Mrs Venn's bookshelf, a recent edition, unlike the one in Frances' father's library, which was ten years old. He used to complain bitterly that it listed businesses that no longer existed, but refused to go to the expense of a new one. 'With your permission,' said Frances, reaching for the directory. Mrs Venn nodded. Frances soon found the Soho Printworks on Dean Street, but saw nothing else that caught her eye. She replaced the book. 'You will be sure to let me know if you remember anything?'

'Yes — yes of course.'

With that assurance Frances took her leave, and though she now knew a great deal more, felt that she was still no closer to identifying the author of the pamphlet.

❧

Sarah had not yet returned from her errand, but Frances found four letters awaiting her that had been delivered to the chemist shop and brought to her door by Tom. All were from women requesting her services as a detective, and she wondered if they had been sent in response to her appearance at the Bayswater Women's Suffrage Society meeting. A lady of quality suspected a previously trusted servant of stealing from her and wanted the matter investigated with the utmost secrecy and discretion. Another lady whose husband was a jeweller, asked Frances to look into the affairs of a young man who was courting her daughter, and who, she believed was being less than truthful about his prospects. The wife of a travelling salesman, who was only ever at home on Saturday and Sunday, had found to her great distress that his supposed employers had never heard of him, and wanted to know where he spent his time from Monday to Friday, while the wife of a senior clerk who worked in a tea merchant's office from Monday to Friday, was curious to discover where he spent his weekends.

Frances wrote to all these correspondents making appointments for them to call and reflected on the alarming and unexpected development that she now had not one mystery to investigate but five. She wondered what other detectives did in that situation. There was no one to whom she could go for advice and she was obliged to have recourse to her own common sense. At the very least she would need to purchase a bigger notebook, some new stationery, and folders in which to keep the papers in each case separate. Perhaps she should even get a small strong box and have some business cards printed. And she surely ought to take a regular newspaper. The *Bayswater Chronicle*, of course, *The Times* or the *Morning Post*, and the *Illustrated Police News*. Almost as soon as the plans were made she felt a chill of anxiety. She had spent the last few days, when not concentrating on the task in hand, concerned that her new enterprise would not be a success. That worry had now been replaced by a new one; that she might not be equal to the amount of work that was suddenly being demanded of her. At least, she reassured herself, she now could afford to stay in her new home for a little longer. Application and economy were surely all that was required, and she was no stranger to either.

Sarah returned from Soho, having spoken to a young assistant at the Soho Printworks, who remembered receiving the copy for the pamphlets a month ago. Four dozen had been printed and they were collected in person a week later. The lady who had both brought the copy and paid for and taken away the pamphlets had given her name as Mrs Jones, and he could recall nothing of her appearance except that she was respectably dressed and, he thought, between the ages of forty and fifty. The lady had also been careful to take the original handwritten piece away with her. It followed that three dozen of the pamphlets had been sent to Flora Quayle, and the remaining ones were the dozen distributed at the school.

Frances showed Sarah the four letters she had received, but Sarah seemed unperturbed by the sudden arrival of new work and commented that if *she* was in the house with the thieving servant she would get to the bottom of the mystery in five minutes, that Frances' 'business friends' – Frances assumed Sarah meant Chas and Barstie – would have all the answers about the young suitor, while Tom's sharp eyes and quick feet would soon reveal what the two husbands were up to.

Frances was considerably heartened by this, and the discussion moved to the pamphlet, and Professor Venn's intemperance.

'If I only knew who Matilda was meeting in Hyde Park,' said Frances. She had never believed as Davey so innocently did in the 'fine lady' and her charitable offerings. The idea that a 'fine lady' would agree to meet a maidservant under the arch of the Serpentine Bridge at night was surely ridiculous. Her almanac had confirmed that on the night of Matilda's death the moon had been in its last quarter and waning, giving the murderer even more cover of darkness than usual. The charitable lady was undoubtedly a fiction and Matilda, she felt sure, had been meeting someone of quite another character, for no very respectable purpose, and wished to conceal this fact from Davey, her family and the school.

'Perhaps she was meeting the woman who had the pamphlets printed,' Frances pondered. 'I remember Matilda's expression when she touched the note. She was very pleased about some-thing and I think I can guess what it was. She was expecting either to receive money or a new commission that would bring her money. Did she ask for too much? Did she threaten to reveal a secret? What was so important that she was killed for it? As far as I know the only ladies between the age of forty and fifty who were at the school when the pamphlets were placed there were Mrs Venn, and Miss Baverstock. Both of them knew about Professor Venn's unfortunate habits, but neither have any reason to want to harm the school; very much the opposite, and if Matilda had wanted to speak to either of them in confidence she did not have to go to Hyde Park to do it.'

'She might have told her mother about Professor Venn, and his funny ways,' suggested Sarah.

'So she might,' agreed Frances. 'And Mrs Springett is the right age, but all the same the style of the pamphlet is not some-thing either she or Matilda could have written, and of course, she would not have needed to see her in secret.'

'Perhaps she was meeting a fancy man,' said Sarah.

'Davey, you mean? But why meet him there?'

'No, I meant some other man. It might even have been the one who fathered the child. If she was pretending to Mrs Venn that her little girl was still alive, so as to get money off her, why not pretend the same to the father so as to get money off him, too?'

It was a theory which Frances had to admit entirely suited the character of the girl.

'As far as anyone knows she hasn't seen the child's father in years, although it is possible that she could have met him again by chance, and seen an opportunity,' said Frances. 'The last anyone heard of him he was a lodger at Mrs Springett's house.'

'Suppose he's come on in the world,' suggested Sarah, 'and he's got a good situation, and a wife.'

More than that, thought Frances, supposing he had not only bettered himself but become something of a public figure, per-haps someone with a reputation for moral correctness who would be most anxious to conceal any hint of such an asso-ciation in his past. Could he be the source of Matilda's £20?

And she had told Davey that she was about to get a great deal more. If her demands had increased and it looked as though they might never end, then her blackmail victim had become her killer.

Frances knew this was a police matter, and it was no part of her commission to find out who had killed Matilda. Both of these sensible thoughts were cast aside by her natural curiosity. She persuaded herself that by looking into the question she could dismiss from her mind the idea that Matilda's murder was connected with her distribution of the pamphlets at the school. There was one person who Frances thought might be willing to speak to her on the subject. She returned to Salem Gardens and knocked on the door of the Springetts' neighbour, Mrs Brooks.

CHAPTER TWELVE

It was a few moments before Mrs Brooks came to the door, her face red and glowing, haloed in a cloud of starch-laden vapour. 'Oh,' she said, 'well they're in now, and Davey's back.'

'I hope you don't mind,' said Frances, 'but it's you I wish to speak to.'

She shrugged. 'Well I don't know nothing, but you can come in if you like.'

The back parlour and most of the scullery had been given over to ironing. A long wooden table was covered with a thick cloth, and there were several hot irons, some light with fine points, and some as heavy as doorstops, towering heaps of linen awaiting them, bowls of water to be sprinkled for steam, and piles of neatly folded sheets and pillowcases.

'I just wanted to ask if you could remember who was living at Mrs Springett's when Matilda came home to have her child,' said Frances. 'Of course I can't speak to Mrs Springett about that with Davey there.'

'I don't know why you'd want to know that,' said Mrs Brooks. 'There's tea in the pot if you want a cup.'

'Thank you,' said Frances and helped herself. In the over-heated atmosphere of the house an almost constant supply of a refreshing beverage was essential. 'I will be open with you Mrs Brooks,' she said. 'Although I am teaching at the school, I am also a detective, and I am making some private enquiries on behalf of the governors. I regret that for reasons of great confidentiality I am not at liberty to tell you any more.'

Mrs Brooks looked very surprised, and stared at Frances as if she was some new creature in the zoological gardens which had just arrived from a country she had never heard of and could not imagine.

'As a part of those enquiries I need to speak to the people who were living next door seven or eight years ago. I was hoping you might recall some names.'

Mrs Brooks, while considering the question, took up a flat iron from the hearth, tested its temperature with a licked finger, and, satisfied with the sizzle, began to apply it to linen in a series of brutal thumps. 'Well, there was Jinny, of course, that's Mrs Springett, and Barney, that was her old man, only he wasn't too well – he died not long after, and Jem – no, I tell a lie, he was from home then, on his apprenticeship. And then there was the two lodgers.'

'Two?' asked Frances, surprised.

'Yes, I remember that particular, because when Tilda came home unexpected she had to share a bedroom with Jinny because the lodgers had the other.'

'Do you remember their names?' asked Frances, taking out her notebook.

Mrs Brooks screwed up her face but after some thought shook her head. 'No, I can't after all this time – Watson maybe, or Wilson or Wigson or . . . no, it's gone.'

'Not the same name for both, surely?' said Frances. 'Or were they related?'

'Oh yes, they were sisters.'

'Oh!' said Frances, taken aback. 'And had they been there long? Were there no male lodgers before?'

'No, never any men lodging there before Davey, and Jinny only allowed *him* because he was a friend of Jem and she knew him to be very quiet and respectable.'

'Forgive me,' said Frances, 'but I had been given to understand that the father of Matilda's child was someone who once lodged with her mother.'

'Then you've been told wrong,' said Mrs Brooks. 'It was a messenger boy what came to the school and talked a lot of nothing and turned her head with his ways. I expect you know the type.'

Frances did not know the type and was not sure why Mrs Brooks thought she might.

Matilda, she now realised, had been a young woman who, while her position in society was always destined to be a humble one, was prepared to undertake anything short of substantial wickedness in order to improve her prospects. Her specialty was the blackmail of anyone who had reason to fear information in her possession. The true identity of the father of her child could never be known, and Matilda was probably willing to point the finger at anyone who would pay her money rather than be identified. Was the messenger boy story true? Or had Matilda even persuaded Mrs Venn that the father was her own husband, and extracted money from her in return for her silence? The child had been called Edie, and Professor Venn's Christian name was Edward. Could that be coincidence or a part of Matilda's blackmail plan?

With a wedding due to take place, and hopes of establishing Davey in a comfortable business, Matilda must have started to increase her demands. Frances very much doubted, however, that Mrs Venn, even if physically able to strangle the girl, was prepared to commit such a cold-blooded act. Matilda was a possible source of the insinuations about Professor Venn in the pamphlet. She could not have written it herself, so who might she have told? Would she have told anyone? The girl, Frances reflected, had been a highly successful blackmailer for several years, and must have known that her secrets were only valuable while she alone guarded them.

At teatime Chas and Barstie came to see Frances bearing one of Mr Whiteley's best fruitcakes and a pot of jam, and looking flushed with optimism. Water was soon set to boil and what had been planned as a meal of bread and butter became a feast.

'Bayswater,' said Chas, draining his teacup and setting it down with a satisfied smile, 'is the land of opportunity for those who know how to take advantage of it. Especially,' he added, with a significant wink, 'when election time rolls around! All the to-ings and fro-ings and excitement and plain downright panic, and everything is an emergency and has to be done expressly and on the instant and money no object! Oh yes!' He rubbed his hands together. 'Money – no – object!'

'Bayswater,' said Barstie dreamily, 'is a pond – a smooth still pond with little fish and big fish all swimming about minding their own business, but you only have to stir it and the big fish try to swallow the little ones while all the refuse that has settled in the depths comes up for everyone to see.' He sighed with pleasurable anticipation.

'How very glad I am,' said Chas, 'that I was never a patron of the Bayswater Bank.' Barstie said nothing but glanced at Chas as if to suggest that had he been, the losses he would have sustained in the recent crash would not have been extensive. 'Mr Paskall, on the other hand, is in a most precarious position, and he and his son have been working night and day to avoid the dread hand of the bailiffs. I have even heard it hinted that a *certain person*, who I decline to name, has been involved.' He shuddered. 'Fortunately that unpleasant fellow has not been seen around here lately, which does not mean of course that he is *not* here. Desperate times indeed, and doubly so now. There's to be a big meeting at the offices of the Paddington Conservative Association tomorrow evening and if Paskall can't convince them that he isn't about to go bankrupt, it's the end of him as a candidate.'

'But he hopes he has found a way out of the difficulty,' said Barstie. 'You may expect a very important announcement in the morning newspapers!'

Chas nodded. 'Barstie here has been in and out of Mr Paskall's office almost as much as the man himself, and has been privy to all the arrangements.'

'A marriage is to be announced that will solve everything!' said Barstie. 'If all goes to plan, generous funds will be flowing into the Paskall coffers very soon.'

But is Mr Paskall not already a married man?' said Frances.

'He is,' said Chas, 'but his old friend Mr Matthews is a widower.'

'You don't mean an engagement between Mr Matthews and the Duchess?' asked Frances.

They nodded.

'But you advised me only a few days ago that the lady was immune to persuasion.'

'Matters have changed,' said Chas. 'Mr Paskall is certain to be elected to parliament, and his influence in these parts is such that his recommendation will be enough to secure victory for others whose fortunes have hung in the balance. I have even heard it said —'

'Possibly by Mr Paskall's own agents,' said Barstie.

'I have heard it said,' continued Chas, flicking a pellet of bread at his friend, 'that Paskall is certain to gain a high office sooner rather than later. What sister would deny assistance to a brother destined for ministerial status?'

'But what of her daughter, who she dotes upon?' asked Frances. 'Have there been provisions made for her?'

'All attended to,' said Barstie. 'Mr Rawsthorne has been very ingenious and drawn up a settlement that satisfies the wishes of the mother and secures the girl's fortune, while leaving sufficient to save Mr Paskall from ruin.'

'And,' said Chas, 'my spies tell me that there may be another betrothal in the wind.'

'Paskall and Matthews,' said Barstie. 'The two fathers have been very hugger-mugger with a scheme to unite their families, though whether the young parties involved have been told of it, I can't say.'

Chas grimaced. 'If young Paskall knows of a plan to marry him to Miss Vinegar, and he is *not* on the next steamer to Australia, he is a braver man than I am.'

'I suppose,' said Frances, 'that you are now far too busy with election business to undertake a commission for me.'

Their protests were loud and long, after which Frances told them of the recent correspondence concerning the suspicious suitor, and Chas said that he would be willing to place a substantial wager that the man's name would shortly be appearing on a list of Bayswater bankrupts.

When they had departed, Frances and Sarah spent a quiet and comfortable evening, Sarah occupied with some mending while Frances made a list of every woman she could think of aged between forty and fifty who might have even the remotest connection with the school and who might have been the lady who had taken the pamphlet to be printed in Soho. There were, she realised, when she had completed her list, many more she would not know of, the aunts of past pupils, for example, or relatives of teachers, and as to ladies who had some doubts about the advisability of marriage, well, she had recently shared a hall with several hundred. Only a large force of policemen could hope to interview all of *them*.

She was now in a terrible dilemma. It was her duty to report her recent findings to the governors of the school, and it was possible that one of them might, without realising it, have information that could further her enquiries and even locate the mystery woman, but if she so much as revealed the name of the printer, who might well retain copies of work done, then the governors, or Mrs Fiske, if her husband confided in her, which she felt sure he did, would thereby be enabled to obtain a copy of the pamphlet and see the wicked insinuations it contained. There would follow a scandal from which the school would never recover.

The next morning as anticipated, the society columns of the newspapers carried the announcement of the forthcoming nuptials of the Duchess of Kenworth and Mr Roderick Matthews. Frances had decided to follow the news of the election so that she would be fully informed about politics when she was eventually permitted to vote; an improvement that she was sure could not be far distant. She learned that Mr Gladstone had made a lengthy address denouncing the Conservative government's foreign policy and the Conservative candidates had made an address entirely approving of the government's foreign policy. Mr Grant, a local man who had once been the director of Grant and Co., printers, of Farringdon, and was now one of the Liberal candidates for Marylebone, had made a speech attributing the recent trade depression to the neglect of home affairs for foreign affairs and strongly recommended the repeal of Schedule D of the Income Tax, which seemed very sensible to Frances. Perhaps, she thought, if wives and mothers and educated spinsters were permitted to vote, brave young men would no longer be sent half way across the world to die for some cause they hardly understood – they would be at home with their families leading happy and productive lives. Her brother had read books about the glories of war, of battles and charges and victories won, which he had thought very admirable, but Uncle Cornelius, who was old enough to remember the Crimea, had said sadly that it was not like that at all, and spoke of cold and rain and mud and cholera.

There were two more letters that morning, one from a lady who had met a very pleasant and eligible gentleman in Hyde Park and wished to know something of his antecedents, and one from Mr Arthur Miggs, the young publisher, who asked Frances to discover the identity of *Aquila* who wrote literary reviews in the *Chronicle* and other papers, and had been unkind about a recent volume he had published on behalf of a client.

The client, Frances learned, was also unforthcoming about his name unless he, or possibly even she, had been christened Augustus Mellifloe. Mr Miggs had enclosed a clipping from a weekday newspaper. It read:

> The author of *Mes Petites Chansonettes* has none of the qualities that go to make up the complete poet. He lacks both the power to evoke sympathy in the reader, and the variety of imagination and expression that he requires if he hopes to please; relying too heavily on consistency of metre which quickly becomes monotonous, elaborate rhyming which detracts from what sense there is in his verses, and noble sentiments so trite that only the most depraved individual would disagree with them. The brief introduction to this mercifully slim volume in which he dedicates the poems to his mother is the best of his work.

Frances could easily see that Mr Mellifloe had good reason to be upset at this item, but, not having read the work in question, was unable to judge whether *Aquila* was correct. Fortunately there was amongst her father's small library a handbook of business law, from which she learned that an expression of opinion as opposed to a statement of fact was unlikely to result in a successful prosecution for libel. As to discovering the identity of *Aquila*, Frances could see that if Mr Miggs was to do so, another kind of criminal charge might be the result. She wrote a letter advising him that she was too busy to take the case, and suggesting that he approach *Aquila* through the medium of the newspaper in question, perhaps with a polite suggestion that the review might be published again in modified form.

The morning and afternoon were spent meeting her new clients. The lady with suspicions of her servant arrived by carriage and was more than pleased to accept the services of Sarah as a general house cleaner, which would permit her free access to all parts of the property. She looked with some apprehension at Sarah's large hands, all but obscuring the piece of needlework she was engaged in, and said, though she hardly liked to mention it, that once the culprit was discovered, the matter should be dealt with as peaceably as possible.

Frances next met the lady whose daughter was being pursued by an ardent suitor, a gentleman who had declared his romantic attachment within days of the first meeting and was even now pressing for a wedding date to be set. She extracted sufficient details to supply Chas and Barstie with what they required, and wrote them a letter.

The two ladies whose husbands were mysteriously absent for part of the week were both small and plump and well-dressed and liked the colour mauve. They wore identical lockets, had the same sad expression and provided Frances with portraits of the same man. Frances promised them that the matter would be settled without delay.

She was not expecting another visitor that day so was surprised when Mrs Embleton came up and said that a lady had called and wished to speak to her. The lady's name was Mrs Fiske. Frances asked for her to be shown up immediately and refreshments brought.

'Miss Doughty,' said Mrs Fiske, 'it is to my regret that we have been unable to make each other's acquaintance sooner.'

'I, too, have greatly looked forward to meeting you,' said Frances. 'May I introduce my associate Miss Smith.' She ushered the visitor to a seat. 'How may I assist you?'

'You are perhaps too young to fully appreciate a mother's anxiety for her daughters,' said Mrs Fiske, 'but it is that which brings me here. You have met Charlotte and Sophia, and I think you will have observed that they are quite different in character. Charlotte is a gentle, timid, tractable girl, while Sophia, although two years her junior, has the stronger will and a better mind.'

'Both girls have merit,' said Frances diplomatically.

'They speak very highly of your chemistry lesson. Sophia has said that when she is older she would like to become a chemist or even enter the medical profession. I have not yet broken this news to her father.' She paused, and it was a very particular kind of pause which always preceded a query of some delicacy. 'I have come to ask if you have discovered the origins of the pamphlets that were distributed at the school.'

'I am continuing my enquiries,' said Frances, 'and I have made some progress, but I have not yet identified the person who arranged for them to be placed there or the motive behind the action.'

'May I ask, since you are now teaching at the school, whether you have had cause to observe anything of . . . an unfortunate nature – anything you would consider inappropriate, or that gives you any reason to believe that the girls may be in danger of any kind? I have been to the school and spoken to Mrs Venn and I have not observed anything untoward, but you, an independent person working within its walls – you may have another view.'

'You surprise me by that suggestion,' said Frances. 'In my brief acquaintance with Mrs Venn I have judged her always to have the best interests of the girls at heart. She protects them as she would do if they were her own.'

Mrs Fiske looked somewhat relieved. 'I am glad to hear it. You are aware, of course, that only Charlotte of all the girls actually read the pamphlet, and she claims to recall or at least to understand nothing of what she read, and I hope that may be the case, but I think sometimes she has bad dreams and talks in her sleep. Sophia has heard things she ought not to have heard and has made some remarks to me about the school, which if true . . . ' she shook her head. 'I have tried to question her but she is more difficult to manage than her sister, and now she has become silent on the subject as she knows I mean to pursue it, and she will not be moved. I have spoken to Mrs Venn and Miss Baverstock who tell me that they perused little more than the title, and none of the other teachers saw it at all. If I could only find a copy then I could satisfy myself as to its contents.'

'But how would that assist you?' asked Frances. 'The words of a person who places anonymous and unsuitable literature in the desks of schoolgirls can hardly be trustworthy. They may have been motivated by malice, jealousy, business rivalry or even a disturbance of the mind, and are therefore to be dismissed.'

'I understand that,' said Mrs Fiske, 'but a mother will always worry about her babes. Her mind is full of terrible fears of things that will probably never happen but it is her duty as a mother to anticipate them and take steps to prevent any possibility that they might occur.'

'Can you tell me what it is that Sophia has said?' asked Frances.

'Things that should never pass the lips of any young girl, let alone one of just twelve,' said Mrs Fiske grimly. 'She said that a wicked man lives in the school, behind a locked door, and there he does wicked things. He is a bad husband and makes his wife very unhappy. She asked me the meaning of the word 'dissipation'. I hardly knew what to say.'

Frances thought carefully. Sophia's knowledge was rather more detailed than might have been learned from Charlotte talking in her sleep, but the girls' desks were too far apart in the class for Sophia to have been able to read Charlotte's copy of the pamphlet. She suspected that Sophia, the more intelligent and manipulative of the two, had simply prised the information from her sister. Mrs Fiske probably thought so too, but had preferred to suggest otherwise.

'There is no man living at the school, of that I can assure you,' said Frances. 'There is a single gentleman who teaches art, but he lives elsewhere and has no room of his own on the premises. I believe the only man ever to live in the school was Professor Venn, and he died several years ago. Neither is there any locked door. Please reassure Sophia that she has nothing to be afraid of.'

'Oh, Sophia is not afraid,' said Mrs Fiske, 'but Miss Bell overheard her telling these tales to the younger girls, to put them in their place, and some of them are afraid. I am sorry to have to say it but Sophia will sometimes "Queen" it over the younger girls and even a few of the older ones and they are quite used to doing her bidding. Miss Bell told me that about two weeks ago Sophia played a game with them, marching them round and round and saying she was taking them to see the "Friend to Women" who lives in Soho. I wish I knew what she meant by it.'

'*Two* weeks ago?' said Frances. 'Surely not!'

'Why, what does it matter? It was the same day that the girls performed a dance display – *that* I do remember. About a week before Charlotte found that dreadful pamphlet.'

'Oh,' said Frances, '*now* I understand.'

As she indeed did – she understood that a great deal of her efforts of the last eight days had been wasted, and she needed to re-think the events that had taken place in the school for perhaps as long as the last month.

The next morning Frances returned to the school and this time there were two people she especially wanted to see, Miss Baverstock and Mlle Girard. She now knew exactly what it was that had troubled her when she had spoken to the French mistress, that tiny feeling of almost ticklish discomfort at the back of her mind that somewhere there was a small but possibly crucial gap of time unaccounted for. She had initially received the impression that on the morning that Charlotte had found the pamphlet, all the girls had been under continuous supervision and therefore unable to consult with each other about what story they would tell, a circumstance which had made their agreement convincing. This, she now discovered, had not been the case. Miss Baverstock, pinned down relentlessly and made to recount events in detail as they had happened moment by moment, told Frances that her first reaction on finding the pamphlet had been to take Charlotte to Mrs Venn and she had been making for the door when it had occurred to her that the other girls' desks should be searched. She had told the rest of the class to go up to the common room, where she believed Mlle Girard was marking compositions. She then followed them up the stairs, taking Charlotte to Mrs Venn's study, when she heard a sound behind her, and, believing it was one of the girls lagging behind, turned around and saw Mlle Girard leave the art and music room. She quickly requested Mlle Girard to remain there for a conference, took Charlotte into Mrs Venn's study, and explained what had occurred. She then returned to the hallway, where she discussed the situation with Mlle Girard and asked her to sit with the class in the common room, which she did. The girls had therefore been unsupervised for at least two or three minutes, which was, Frances thought, ample time for a domineering child such as Sophia to tell them all what to do.

Frances next demanded to question Charlotte again. Told by Miss Baverstock that Charlotte was in a reading class she asked for Charlotte to be removed from the class. Told that this was not possible, she replied that it was entirely possible and not only that but she could prove it by going into the classroom and removing Charlotte herself. Miss Baverstock went to fetch Charlotte.

Behind the closed doors of the art room, garlanded by the sickly scent of too many dried flowers, Frances bluntly advised the cowering girl that she knew what had happened. 'I think that while Miss Baverstock was looking at the pamphlet that fell from your desk, Sophia ordered you by some signal to say nothing. Then, when she came home after school, she told you that the girls had agreed that they would all say that they had never seen the pamphlets before. Everyone had to stand by that story, because none of you wanted anyone to know that when the pamphlets were found you had all had them in your possession for at least a week, and you had all read them. Isn't that true?'

Charlotte burst into tears.

'I will take your response to imply the answer "yes",' said Frances. 'And now I must start from the beginning and find out exactly when the pamphlets were put in your desks, so I may learn who put them there. You cannot avoid answering my questions by crying. I will wait all day for you to stop if I have to.'

Charlotte sniffled and gulped and stopped. 'When you first found the pamphlets, were they tucked away securely in a book or was that something you did yourselves to hide them?'

'We hid them later,' Charlotte admitted. 'When we found them they were just thrown on top of the books.'

'So, placing them in the desks was the work of perhaps a minute at most,' Frances surmised. 'And on what day did you first find them?'

'I can't remember,' said Charlotte, looking as if she was about to cry again.

Frances was merciless. 'You can and you will,' she demanded. 'Do you know how much time I have wasted because not one single one of you could tell the truth? You are the daughters of gentlemen, and this is not the kind of behaviour your parents expect of you.'

Charlotte dissolved into fresh sobs and all that Frances could extract from her was that she had found the pamphlet on the morning after the dance display. A consultation with Mrs Venn and Miss Baverstock, both of whom were deeply shocked by her revelations, soon provided the answer. On Tuesday the 17th of February the girls had had spent the first class of the morning arranging displays of their work in the schoolrooms. They had then taken part in a final rehearsal of the dance display, something which had required them to express the spirit of flowers, fans and ribbons. After luncheon the visitors had arrived and the girls had conducted them about the school. A light tea had been served in the music and art room and the dance display had been performed to universal acclaim. Sometime between the evening of Monday the 16th and nine o'clock on Wednesday the 18th, for part of which time the school had been entertaining visitors, someone had spent no more than a minute dropping the pamphlets into the girls' desks. Since there had been some displays of embroidery in the classroom, anyone found in there could easily have accounted for their presence.

Frances could do no more than ask all the members of staff to try and recall as much as they could about the time in question and make a list of the visitors they had seen and to whom they had spoken. She returned home in a mood of despondency to find that two new letters had arrived.

One was a note from Chas and Barstie advising her that the suitor whose intentions they had investigated was an earnest individual who made a habit of paying violent court to pretty young women with whom he had persuaded himself he was in love, only to take to his heels when the wedding day arrived. He was, however, the heir to a fortune, and if the anxious mother could only prevent his escape, they thought he might make a fair prospect.

The second letter was more controversial.

Dear Miss Doughty

Forgive me for thus writing to you. I most earnestly entreat that you do everything in your power to prevent a terrible crime. The wedding of Mr Roderick Matthews to the Duchess of Kenworth must not take place. Mr Matthews, who masquerades as a widower and single man, has a wife living, but is ashamed of his humble connection and does not make it known.

The wedding took place on 6th October 1874 at the church of St Mary's Havenhill, near Mr Matthews' country estate. The bride was his ward, Caroline Clare, and the witnesses were a housemaid, Mary Ann Dunn, and Mr Matthews' farm manager, Joshua Jenkins. Mrs Matthews was an unhappy lady and soon left her husband and now resides abroad.

I am,

Very respectfully

A friend of the family

Chapter Thirteen

Frances stared at the letter for a while, then examined the envelope but it was quite plain, with no stamp, no post office cancellation and no clue as to the sender. There was not even an address, just her own name. She consulted Mrs Embleton, who was able to advise her only that it had been brought to the door by a messenger boy.

Frances wondered why the writer had sought her out, as it would have been the easiest thing to obtain a certificate of the marriage and send it to the proper authorities. It was possible, however, that the writer was unfamiliar, as she herself had been not so long ago, with the method of obtaining a certificate. She was obliged to wonder if there was any possible connection between this letter and events at the school. Matthews took little interest in the affairs of the school, never went there and used it only as a convenient and respectable place for the education of his daughters and wards, so any wrongdoing of his could not, she thought, affect the school in any way. The principal result, if the letter was accurate and the contents became known, would be the collapse of the planned marriage, the loss to both Matthews and his friend Paskall of the funds that depended upon it, and quite possibly also the end of Paskall's parliamentary ambitions. It was a development Frances could not afford to ignore.

She could go to Somerset House on Monday and order the certificate, but realised that since she knew the exact date and location of the wedding, a quicker way to resolve the matter was to go to Havenhill church and ask to see the registers. She examined her timetable of trains from Paddington and found that there was a train to Havenhill the next morning, a journey of only thirty minutes, which would enable her to attend the Sunday service.

Sarah was anxious to accompany her, but as the new apprentice detective was making good progress in her own enquiries, Frances reassured her that she would be perfectly safe going to visit a church alone, and as the journey was not a long one, promised faithfully to be home by tea time at the latest. The only other thing she needed to do that day was write to her new client, the lady with the Hyde Park romance, to arrange a meeting, warning her to make no changes to her circumstances until the investigation was complete. She was sure that a 'Friend to Women' would approve of her caution. If, reflected Frances, she turned out to be not so much a detective as a preventer of bad marriages that would be a highly commendable thing.

Havenhill had once been a small farming village, little more than a row of cottages on either side of a cart track, with narrower paths carving their way up across the fields. The steam-belching monsters of the Great Western Railway had raced uncaringly past the modest hamlet, since the transport amenities of horse and cart and the Grand Union Canal had been more than adequate for its requirements. In the last thirty years, however, the transformation of Bayswater from a quiet semi-rural backwater to the thriving western outpost of fashionable London had created an urgent demand for fresh produce in abundance. The result had been a rapidly spreading patchwork of market gardens streaked with rows of hothouses, and elegant country homes with their own kitchen gardens, where a tradesman might retire when his week's work was done and imagine himself a gentleman. Trains began to call at Havenhill, and a station was newly minted, smiling with tubs of spring flowers, like colourful corsages on the gown of a debutante.

The main street of spruce little homes would, thought Frances, be quite a bustling place during the week, and there were recently constructed lanes leading from it with newer cottages, so the village was growing outwards from the high road, like the roots of a tree.

At the centre of the village was a public house, the Havenhill Arms, with a sign depicting a cornucopia of fruit and flowers, and a small church with a square tower, a pretty arched gate and well-kept graveyard. The sign named the incumbent as the Reverend Charles Farrelly, and the paint was sufficiently weathered that Frances felt hopeful that this was the same man who had officiated at the wedding in 1874.

The Reverend Farrelly was a bespectacled man of about forty who looked out from the pulpit upon his congregation with the benevolent expression of a fond father. The people, she judged, were all folk from the village and estate, since there was a sociable ease about them that came of long acquaintance, family ties, and shared toil. There was no hint, as she had often detected in Bayswater, of attendance merely from a sense of duty, of obligation not to church and community but to outward show. The congregation came willingly, almost eagerly. The sermon was on the subject of the weather, the variability of nature, the gladness that came with the lifting of the cold hand of winter, and the promise of spring, that brought hope to all their hearts. There were hymns sung lustily, and a final closing address, then everyone rose and strolled out into the cool, cloudy lane, where a pale sun was making a loyal effort to add to the warmth of the Reverend's sentiments.

Frances stayed by the door as he spoke to members of the congregation, and it was clear that he knew them all well, as he asked after their health and that of relatives unable to be present. As soon as he was free Frances approached.

'Good-day, and welcome to Havenhill,' he said. 'You must be new to the village.'

'I am Miss Frances Doughty, and a visitor only,' said Frances, 'but I would like to say that I find your church most delightful, and your sermon very uplifting after the recent chills.'

'I hope we may see you again,' he said, obviously curious as to the reason for her visit.

'I would like to consult the marriage register for October 1874,' said Frances, 'would you be so kind as to allow me to look at it?'

'Oh, please come in, I have all the registers to hand.' He led the way back into the church, where a side door admitted them to an office the size of a linen cupboard with a small desk, a chair, and shelves of books and papers.

'Were you officiating here at that time?' asked Frances, hopefully.

'Yes, I have been here since 1871,' said Farrelly, peering at the leather spines of the registers and lifting one off the shelf. He placed it on the desk.

'Then I am sure you will remember the wedding in question,' said Frances, opening the book. She turned the pages, trying to look as if it was the simplest enquiry in the world, yet could not help but feel a strange little thrill of excitement as she anticipated the discovery that was to come. She found the page, as Reverend Farrelly stood by quietly on hand to assist her if required, but when her eyes scanned down the paper, she found a clearly written entry for October 1st and then no more until a week later. She took the letter from her pocket and studied it in case she had made a mistake, but the writing was very clear and said 6th October 1874.

'Is there some difficulty?' asked the Reverend.

'I have the date written here, but there was no marriage then,' said Frances. 'Of course the writer may be in error.' She looked further on in the month and then earlier, but without result. 'That is very curious.'

'Sometimes people recall the day and month but are mistaken as to the year,' said Farrelly. 'I keep an index of names that may help you. Who were the celebrants?' He lifted another volume from the shelf.

'The groom was Mr Roderick Matthews,' said Frances.

Farrelly had opened the book but in his astonishment allowed it to fall shut again. 'Mr Matthews of Havenhill House?' he exclaimed. 'There must be some mistake. Mr Matthews has not been married here. Mr Matthews is a widower. He was married in London I believe, some years before he lived here, and his wife, who was afflicted with consumption, died in Italy. But you are right in one thing. Had he been married *here* I would certainly have remembered it.'

'Do you know the date of his wife's death?' asked Frances.

'It was in 1873. There is a plaque to her memory in the church.'

Frances re-read the letter. 'In your index, is there a marriage of a person with the surname Clare?'

He examined the book and shook his head. 'No. But the Clares are connections of Mr Matthews' late wife. There was a ward who he placed at school in London, and later he brought her here to look after the house following Mrs Matthews' death. But the country life did not suit her.'

'When did she leave?' asked Frances.

'Oh, I doubt that I could recall the date. She came here after Mr Matthews returned from Italy, which was at the start of 1874 I believe.

'Was she living here in October 1874?'

'Possibly, yes. In fact, yes, I am sure of it. She was here when Mr Frederick – that is Mr Matthews' eldest son – came of age, and we had a very pretty little celebration for him. I recall it well because his birthday is at Christmas. He was quite a favourite of Miss Clare's, and I did wonder if they might make a match, but he went to look after some family business in Florence soon afterwards. I think it was not long after that that Miss Clare went away.'

'This letter says that she lives abroad,' said Frances. 'Perhaps she is in Florence, too.'

'May I see it?' asked Farrelly. Frances handed over the paper and he studied it carefully, then shook his head. 'I do not recognise the hand,' he said, 'but the contents are clearly false and may, I fear, be inspired by malice. Someone wishes to prevent Mr Matthews from marrying the Duchess of Kenworth, and has made up this story to place doubt in her mind. They have quite probably written to her, too.'

'What of Mary Ann Dunn and Joshua Jenkins, the supposed witnesses?'

'Mary Ann Dunn was then maidservant at the house, and she lives there still, as housekeeper. Joshua Jenkins managed the estate, but he died – hmm, let me see . . . ' Farrelly found a burials book. 'Yes, Jenkins was buried here on the 9th of October 1874, and I always make a point of recording the date of death as well as burial. He died on the 6th of October.'

'So according to the letter he witnessed the wedding on the day that he died,' said Frances. 'Was his death unexpected?'

'Oh no, far from it. Jenkins – and I recall this very well – fell down in a fit some two weeks before his death, and had to be carried to his bed, from which he never stirred. The man was unable to walk or speak, let alone come to church and witness a wedding. I was sent for early on the morning of his death. Mrs Dunn used to call in on him several times a day, and that morning she found that he had taken a turn for the worse during the night and was quite clearly dying. I sat with him, but he passed away peacefully very soon afterwards. I think the person who wrote to you knew enough of the locality to give the man's name, but was ignorant of his condition, and has now been caught out in a lie.'

'I expect that anyone living in Havenhill at the time would have known he was unwell,' said Frances.

'Indeed, I said prayers for his recovery two Sundays in succession.'

'So, we are agreed that no such wedding took place and the letter is false and designed to injure Mr Matthews,' said Frances.

'It is a very serious matter,' said Farrelly. 'You should show this letter to Mr Matthews, who may decide to consult a solicitor. But why was it sent to *you*?'

'I am a private detective,' said Frances, who was still finding the words unfamiliar and like something more out of a novel than reality. 'I have been undertaking some work for some friends of Mr Matthews.'

'I see,' said Farrelly, 'well that is quite extraordinary!' He pondered the matter for a moment, then said, 'I will ask my wife if she knows of any person who bears ill-will against Mr Matthews, although I think it most unlikely.' He put away the books and they returned to the church, where a lady was refreshing an arrangement of flowers. On the way he pointed out the plaque in memory of Agnes Matthews, deceased in Florence Italy, on 10th August 1873, much missed by her sons, Frederick, William, Edwin and Horace, her daughters Selina, Lydia, Dorothea and Amelia and wards Wilhelmina Dancroft and Caroline Clare.

'My dear,' said Farrelly to the lady who turned around with a smile, 'allow me to introduce you to Miss Frances Doughty, who has an interesting mystery to discuss.'

'Delighted to make your acquaintance,' said Mrs Farrelly. She was a small round lady, with a plump, almost circular face, framed by crisp brown curls like the crimped pastry edging around a pie. 'I am all attention. We are very quiet here, not that I am averse to that, but a mystery sounds very engaging. How may I help you?'

Frances showed her the letter and explained the possibility that an enemy of Mr Matthews wished to prevent the planned marriage, and Mrs Farrelly listened with wrapt attention and gave it considerable thought. 'Well,' she said at last, 'that is an interesting conundrum, to be sure. While I think about it, Miss Doughty, you would be very welcome to walk with me to the vicarage. I must hurry back to make sure that my dear little dog Benjie doesn't get hungry. He can get quite cross if I neglect him!'

The Reverend Farrelly smiled indulgently as if to say that the likelihood of his wife neglecting their pet was somewhat remote.

Frances would have liked to go up to Havenhill House and ask Mrs Dunn about the fact that she was named as a witness to a wedding that had never taken place, but there was just a possibility that the writer of the letter had been partially correct, and a wedding had occurred elsewhere. If Matthews was concealing the connection then the servant he had entrusted to keep his secret would simply maintain her silence. Frances decided that her best course of action if she wished to pursue the matter was to go to Somerset House and look at the registers.

The vicarage was a pleasant cottage close by the church, its garden showing abundant evidence of loving attention having been lavished upon it. Mrs Farrelly looked about her with pleasure and glowed at Frances' compliments, gently touching the faces of the flowers as if greeting a cluster of children come to welcome her.

They were met at the door by a small but determined dog, who had obviously spent his moments of captivity attempting to paw a ribbon from his long-haired coat, and who leaped up at his mistress with enthusiasm, barking loudly. 'That's my darling boy!' said Mrs Farrelly. 'Isn't he quite the best dog in the world?'

Frances, who lacked acquaintanceship with dogs and found it hard to warm to them, thought it polite to agree that Benjie was both handsome and intelligent. Despite this accolade, Benjie did not approve of the stranger in the house and turned to Frances, quivering like an angry mop, setting his little feet firmly on the ground, arching his back and setting up a sharp insistent rhythmic yap, almost as if someone was at his back working him with a pump.

'Oh don't worry about that, once he is used to you, you will be friends in no time!' smiled Mrs Farrelly. 'Now then, I will see that Susan brings us some refreshments. Our dinner will be at three and we would be very pleased if you could join us.'

'That is very kind,' said Frances, 'but I have promised to return home by this afternoon.'

Susan, who was a plain young woman of about thirty, brought tea, bread and butter, a pot of jam, and a little dish of scraps. Benjie sat at Mrs Farrelly's side, confident that he would be included in the arrangements, and was soon allowed to jump up onto her lap.

'Oh he is such a naughty boy, but he knows I can't deny him,' exclaimed the lady, feeding him titbits of ham. Frances glanced about her at the portraits on display, photographs of a very much younger Reverend and Mrs Farrelly at their wedding, and posed groups of venerable persons, probably relatives. There were no pictures of children.

'I cannot imagine,' said the Reverend Farrelly, who had been very thoughtful, 'anyone who might wish to cause any harm to Mr Matthews. He is not perhaps here as often as he might be, as I believe he prefers the town to the country, but his managers have always looked after his affairs here very diligently and with great fairness. I am wondering if the writer of the letter is some lady who is in love with him and wishes she might marry him herself and hopes to deter a rival.'

'Do you know the name of any such lady?' asked Frances, but having made the suggestion he was unable to justify it with any useful detail.

'Daisy Trent,' said Mrs Farrelly suddenly.

'Daisy Trent?' echoed her husband. 'But she never set her cap at him, and indeed how could she, the daughter of a black-smith?'

'No, that was not what I meant, my dear, only that she was the only person ever to say a word against him, and that was because her mind was in a very unhappy state, poor thing.'

'Tell me more,' said Frances.

'Oh it was quite some years ago,' said Mrs Farrelly, 'before they went out to Italy for Mrs Matthews' health. There had been some thieves on the estate, not from round here, but the next village, East Hill so it was thought, boys or young men, stealing and causing damage. It was all very upsetting. So Joshua Jenkins sent one of his men, Daniel Souter – a good, reliable sort of person – to frighten them off with a shotgun.' She shook her head. 'It was a very bad business. They must have crept up on him, and he was killed.'

'The details were very unpleasant,' said Reverend Farrelly. There were a few moments of silence while husband and wife looked sorrowful, and Frances awaited the unpleasant details in vain.

'I could of course read about the incident in the newspapers, but it would save me considerable time if you could enlighten me with some more information,' said Frances at last. 'I promise I will not faint.'

They looked at each other, and Mrs Farrelly rose to see about more tea with Benjie scampering after her. 'It was thought there were at least three of them if not more,' said Reverend Farrelly. 'One of them came up behind poor Daniel and shot him – a handgun of some kind, it was never found. The inquest said that the shot did not kill him, indeed had that been his only injury then he might well have recovered. But as he lay on the ground he was shot again with his own gun, and after that – it seems that there was further violence done to the body. Sad to say the culprits were never discovered.'

'And Daisy Trent?'

'She was sweet on Daniel and it was thought they might be wed. She was angry with Joshua for sending Daniel out alone, and also with Mr Matthews as she said it was for him to see that his men came to no harm. Of course neither of them could have known that the gang carried arms. We did what we could for her of course. If you are interested I might have some cuttings from the newspapers at the time. I know I do tend to keep material about local matters.'

'That would be very helpful, thank you.'

Mrs Farrelly returned bringing a freshly charged teapot to the table and a plate of fruit buns, and her husband disappeared to his study. 'Poor Daisy,' said Mrs Farrelly, 'I heard her say that she hoped Joshua and Mr Matthews would never be happy after all the misery they had caused her.'

'I would like to speak to her,' said Frances.

'Oh, she went away about five years ago. She said there was too much here to remind her of Daniel.'

'I hope she found happiness again, wherever she might be,' said Reverend Farrelly, returning with a small bundle of papers, 'and peace in her heart that she might forgive.'

'Does she still have family here?' asked Frances.

'No, her father passed away and her mother remarried and moved to another village,' said Mrs Farrelly, holding a bun so Benjie could gnaw at it. 'I could try and find out where she went if you like.'

'That would be very kind of you,' said Frances and wrote out her address on a slip of paper.

Reverend Farrelly had brought the parish journals for the period in question, which recorded how prayers had been offered for the soul of Daniel Souter and Daisy's recovery to health. Folded into the journals were cuttings taken from the Middlesex county newspapers. The facts of the murder were as Frances had been told, and she learned that after Daniel had been shot the body had been beaten with the butt of his own gun, an act of quite savage and unnecessary violence. One of the newspapers had a sketch map of the area and Frances studied this with interest and copied it down into her notebook. It was Daisy herself who discovered the body, which was found in a small copse about two hundred yards from Havenhill House. Later that night she had been seen wandering in the village in a state of distraction, weeping and hammering on the doors of the houses as she went. Her mother had been fetched, as the girl had been so hysterical it was impossible to discover what the matter was by questioning her, and it was assumed at first that she had been assaulted, as there was blood on her clothing. She had been able only to point in the direction from which she had come, and some men had been sent to search. The map showed a footpath leading like a narrow thread across the fields from the copse to the village and another breaking off to East Hill, the place from which it was suspected the thieves had come and to where they had fled. The only other thing on the map was a line of small buildings near the manor house and Frances was told that only two had been occupied, one by Daniel and one by Joshua Jenkins, the others being stables and storage barns. Daisy, said Mrs Farrelly, had been placed in the care of her mother and had been too ill to attend the inquest.

There seemed to be nothing more to learn, so Frances finished her tea and rose to take her leave. 'Oh let me come some of the way with you!' said Mrs Farrelly. 'It's time for Benjie's walk, and he does so enjoy his walks!'

Frances and Mrs Farrelly set out for the railway station, with Benjie, so far from enjoying healthful exercise, being carried by his owner, who explained that this would ensure he did not get dirty. 'He is so naughty sometimes, aren't you my darling?' she said, nuzzling her face into the dog's hairy coat. 'He will try to get into rabbit holes and ditches and then he is all over mud and I have to bathe him.'

Frances said she imagined that must be a difficult task and Mrs Farrelly was kind enough to regale her with all the details of Benjie's daily toilet. 'Charles had to expressly ask Mr Matthews to place a fence around the foundations of his new buildings as Benjie *would* try to play there and he was so dirty and smelly I thought he would never be clean. You can see it there,' she added, pointing to a pathway that climbed uphill between some fields. 'That is the way to Mr Matthews' manor house, although it is really no more than a large cottage but very well-appointed and comfortable.'

Frances saw part way along the path a sizeable rectangular area with boards around it. 'What is being built?' she asked.

'Oh at the moment nothing at all,' said Mrs Farrelly. 'The intention was to build a fine row of model cottages for the men who tend the hothouses, and we all thought it would make a handsome and sanitary addition to the village, but no work has been done on it for some weeks. I have heard,' she added, 'that it was an arrangement between Mr Matthews and Mr Paskall, whereby Mr Matthews provided the land and Mr Paskall the cottages, and there were men hard at work, even in the cold weather, digging the foundations, but then quite suddenly they stopped. It is rumoured that Mr Paskall lost a great deal of money with that terrible business of the Bayswater Bank, and there is no more money to be had to finish what has been started. Oh Benjie!' she suddenly exclaimed, as the dog began to squirm in her arms with fierce determination, and before she could secure him he leapt down to the ground and ran up the pathway as fast as his little legs could take him.

Mrs Farrelly held onto her bonnet and ran after him, calling out 'Benjie! Benjie! Oh you *bad* child!' and Frances decided to follow.

The path was crushed gravel well stirred with dried mud, and rutted with cart tracks so as to be very hard to traverse without accident. There were sturdy and ancient hedgerows on either side, protecting fields tilled into ridges, the nature of the crop being as yet a mystery. Frances quickly caught up with Mrs Farrelly and helped her along as she stumbled over the treacherous ground. Benjie had got as far as the wooden fencing and was trying to jump up, barking loudly, but it was far too high, so he began to scrabble in the dirt at the base of the fence. Mrs Farrelly finally reached him, panting hard, and had just bent to scoop him up when a section of wood that must have split in the recent cold weather came away and left just enough space for Benjie to slip through.

'Oh no! What can I do?' wailed Mrs Farrelly. 'Benjie! Come here!'

Frances peered over the fence, which was very roughly and unevenly constructed from wooden boards of different sizes.

The ground within had been laid out and well dug with the foundations of four cottages, and some of the walling was already in place. Benjie was nowhere to be seen, but from one of the ditches came the sound of excited barking, and sprays of dry earth showed where he was digging furiously. 'There must be a gate so we can enter,' said Frances, and she walked around the fence until she found one with rope hinges on one side and secured with a padlock and chain on the other. Mrs Farrelly, who was very much shorter in stature than she, was unable to see over the fence and stood by, helplessly wringing her hands. 'I am sure he will come out again when he is hungry,' said Frances, deciding not to add that she did not think they would have long to wait. 'Perhaps if you could bring one of his favourite titbits he might be tempted out.'

Benjie was growling now and Frances could see his tail waving like a pennant caught in a gale as he backed out of the ditch with something clamped between his jaws.

'What is he doing? Can you see?' asked Mrs Farrelly. 'Is he hurt?'

'No, he seems to have found something – a glove I *think*,' said Frances, unsure because if the object, which was undoubtedly glove-shaped, really was a glove he was having unusual difficulty with it. It was a few moments before Frances realised two things – the object in Benjie's jaws was a glove, and the reason he was obliged to tug on it so hard was that there was something to which it was attached, a bundle of clothes that someone had flung into the ditch, or even an old scarecrow.

Whether or not it was recent events that had led her imagination into unexpected areas she did not know, but she was suddenly struck with an unpleasant thought, and knew that at the very least she had to satisfy herself that she was mistaken. Briefly, she considered fetching some men from the village to help, but then she decided that if she thought herself capable of exercising the vote she was certainly capable of scrambling over a fence.

'What are you doing, Miss Doughty?' exclaimed Mrs Farrelly as Frances moved a lump of abandoned building stone to give herself a step up. It was a lot heavier than she had anticipated but having started she was not about to admit defeat and managed with some effort to drag rather than carry it near to the fence. 'I'm going to fetch Benjie,' she declared, and started to haul herself over the top of the fence, which was not, she discovered, as robust as it looked. The boards sagged alarmingly, and creaked as if they were about to snap and impale her on splinters. Mrs Farrelly watched her with alarm.

'Oh, Miss Doughty, do you think that is really advisable? I think we may need a man to assist us. Perhaps I should fetch my husband!'

The Reverend Farrelly, while undoubtedly a man, was, Frances had observed, shorter and stouter than she and twice her age, but she declined to mention this. One advantage he did have was the wearing of trousers and she thought, as she struggled to manoeuvre her heavy skirts over the fence, that the sooner a more rational mode of clothing for women became acceptable the better. There was a brief moment of difficulty as her skirt caught on a protruding fence post and Mrs Farrelly hurried up and released it, then Frances swung her long legs to the ground.

Benjie had temporarily stopped pulling at the glove and was standing barking at it. Frances took the opportunity to pick him up, surprised to feel how tiny his body was under the matted and muddy hair. She carried him to Mrs Farrelly, who received him with sighs of gratitude, then returned to what had captured his attention.

The neglected foundations had been considerably damaged by the bad weather of the last two months. Heavy rains, snow, and frost had caused the earth to collapse in places, and most of the trenches were filled with a heavy mud, much dried and caked about the edges, but treacherously soft in the middle. The object that Benjie's sensitive nose had detected would have lain underneath the top layer, and he had succeeded only in dragging out what Frances was now sure was a gentleman's leather glove, albeit thickly slimed with mud. As she approached, a stench of decay reached her nostrils and she was obliged to place a handkerchief over her nose, the scent of laundry soap affording some relief. Even under the thick dark crust there was no doubt that the glove contained something solid, and she thought she could make out the cuffs of a shirtsleeve and coat, and the flesh of what could have been an arm, very much discoloured. Frances had seen death before and was not afraid, but had never encountered it like this.

'Mrs Farrelly,' called Frances. There was no reply and she returned to the fence and peered over it to see that lady absorbed in cooing over Benjie, who was quivering with indignation at being thwarted of his prize. 'If you would be so kind as to assist me, I think we need to send for a constable.'

As Frances struggled back over the fence, she realised that she was now very unlikely to be home by tea-time.

CHAPTER FOURTEEN

It was late when Frances stepped wearily from the train at Paddington. Sarah, alerted by telegram, was waiting, her face a portrait of concern, which changed almost as if by magic into relief when she saw at last that Frances was safe. 'I've got a cab waiting,' she said, 'and I've made cocoa with brandy.' Frances could only nod gratefully.

Earlier that day, Mrs Farrelly had taken Frances to see Constable Clayborn, finding him at ease in his High Street cottage, enjoying a peaceful Sunday afternoon. To do him credit, he at once recognised the seriousness of what the ladies had to say, and transformed himself into a man on duty in an instant. He was too respectful, especially of the Reverend's wife, to suggest that the report of finding a body in Mr Matthews' ditch might be due more to over-excited female imagination than any palpable truth, although Frances felt certain from his expression that the thought was in his mind. He accompanied them to the spot, climbed the fence with some agility and, after peering into the muddy trench, agreed with a startled expression that he too could see the remains of a deceased gentleman, and departed immediately for the nearest police station, which was two miles away at Hillingdon.

There was nothing else to be done immediately, so Frances and Mrs Farrelly returned to the vicarage, where Mrs Farrelly handed Benjie to Susan to see to his bath and took it upon herself to ensure that the large battalion of men, who she had no doubt would soon be descending on Havenhill, would not want for tea.

Reverend Farrelly was astonished at his wife's news and both were in agreement that whoever the unknown person was, he could not have been an inhabitant of the village as no one was unaccounted for.

'A visitor, then,' said Frances. 'And we may be able to estimate when he arrived. I doubt very much that he would have lain there unnoticed while the foundations were being dug. So whatever it was that happened took place after the digging stopped. Do you recall the date when the men last worked there?'

'They stopped a day or two after the bank crashed,' said Mrs Farrelly emerging from her larder, where she been searching for cake, and bringing out her largest teapot. 'I remember that very well because it was the talk of the village.'

'And when was the fence built?'

'Not long afterwards,' said Reverend Farrelly. 'The weather was very cold and misty all through January, and then came the heavy frosts and snow, and I was worried, because I could see that anyone who walked up to the house from the station, especially if they were a stranger to the area, might easily stray off the path and fall into the diggings and break a leg. So I wrote to Mr Matthews to ask if a fence could be put round, and that was done. It was completed very promptly, within a day or two of my letter. In fact, I may have made a special mention of it in my sermon, thanking Mr Matthews for his kindness. I will consult my book.' He went to his study and returned after a few minutes. 'Yes, I have it,' he said. 'I spoke of it on the 1st of February, the work having been carried out the day before. It was the Monday before that, which would have been the 26th January, when we saw that the men had not returned to work.'

So, thought Frances, the area had therefore been unattended but open from Sunday the 25th of January to Friday the 30th, Had someone fallen into the trench and been stunned and unable to cry out, and then frozen to death, the body would have been quickly obscured by frost and snow. Mr Matthews' men could have put the boards in place without realising that anything was amiss. It was possible, of course, for someone to have brought the body there afterwards if he had the key to the padlock, or if more than one man was present, to lift it over the fence, but from what Frances had seen the remains were stuck deep in mud and had been there for some weeks.

'Since it must have been a visitor, he would most likely have come here by train,' said Frances. 'The line terminates at

Paddington in the east, so he might have come from London or any station in between, or if from the west —,' she tried to recall the route.

'Could be as near as Slough or as far as Bristol,' said Mrs Farrelly, proudly. 'Or down the little branch line from Uxbridge. It's Mr Brunel's railway and he meant it to be a good one.'

It was nearly dinnertime when the police cart from Hillingdon clattered up the main street bringing an inspector, Constable Clayborn and a doctor. Frances knew that the police would want to speak to her about the discovery, but despite Reverend Farrelly's considerate suggestion that it might be better for her to wait at the vicarage, she was determined not to sit meekly indoors and miss all the activity. She wanted to see the police at work, and was out of the door and hurrying up the street before he could offer any argument, with Mrs Farrelly impulsively rushing after her.

The arrival of the cart had already caused some stir, and the Sunday afternoon strollers had veered in its direction, followed it down the street, and become a crowd, speculating all the while on what had brought its occupants to the village. 'What's the matter, Clayborn?' asked someone of the grave-faced constable and was told gruffly that he would 'know soon enough'. Surrounded by excited chatter, the cart turned off the High Street and proceeded up the track to the foundations, where Clayborn alighted and, standing with folded arms and a stern look, became a one-man barrier, making it quite plain that the crowds were to go no further. Everyone gathered as near as they were permitted and gazed in fascination at the unfolding events.

There was no niceness about preserving Mr Matthews' fence, part of which was torn down to give access to the site, the doctor being far too stout to permit him to climb over it. He squatted beside the trench with much grunting, and after a while, arose with an effort and pronounced the remains to be human, adult and male, but beyond that he was unable to say without closer examination. A portion of the fence was employed as a kind of pallet, on which the mud-encrusted corpse was laid, and two of Mr Matthews' men volunteered to carry it down the track, where it was deposited in a stable attached to the Havenhill Arms, the villagers, all dressed in their gay Sunday best, forming a cortege like mourners at an unconventional funeral.

The medical man, who was called Naresby, briefly questioned both Frances and Mrs Farrelly about how they had discovered the remains, but seemed less impressed with the merits of Benjie's detective instincts and fine nose than the dog's owner.

'What will happen now?' asked Frances.

'I have notified the coroner and Mr Matthews has been sent for by telegram, since the body was found on his land and he may know the identity of the deceased. In the meantime, anyone who wishes to view the remains and suggest who it might be is free to do so. The body will remain where it is, and I will engage an assistant and make a full examination on Monday afternoon. Under the circumstances I don't expect the inquest to open until Tuesday. Please leave your name and address with the police, who will let you know when and where to attend.'

There were many late dinners in Havenhill that Sunday. The police remained on hand to supervise the queue of people waiting to see the body. Both Mrs Farrelly and her husband felt obliged to look, and Frances, too. Someone had brought dried flowers to strew around the stable to hide the worst of the smell, and some villagers fetched lavender bags and bunches of herbs to carry. One lady, green-faced but determined, held an open jar of cloves under her nose, and Mrs Farrelly refreshed herself with a smelling bottle. The body, still on its pallet, was laid out on the straw. The face had been washed, but it was very swollen and dark, the features distorted by decay and could not have looked as it had in life. Frances braced herself for the sight, but it resembled a broken thing more than it did a man, and she felt more sorrow than revulsion. The clothing was undoubtedly male, but she thought that the coat was of an unusual cut. There was a subtle difference about the shape of the collar that made it unfamiliar to her. It was not the kind of coat gentlemen were wearing in Bayswater and she wondered if it was a country fashion.

Frances and the Farrellys returned to the vicarage where, they had been told, the inspector would shortly visit them, and an overcooked dinner was served, for which no one had much appetite. Inspector Eaves was polite, intelligent and gentlemanly, quite a contrast, Frances thought, to Inspector Sharrock, but then she supposed that Hillingdon was not quite as active in the sphere of crime as Paddington, and he had fewer matters of importance pressing upon him. Informing the Farrellys that the body had not yet been identified and was, almost certainly, that of an outsider, he consumed prodigious amounts of tea and several fruit buns, promised Frances to send a telegram notifying Sarah of her late return, made a fuss over Benjie and then departed. The Farrellys promised Frances to write with any news and walked her to the station for the evening train to Paddington.

On their way home, Sarah recounted to Frances the details of her very successful day's detective work, although she was almost as outraged by the state of the fashionable lady's kitchen floor as she was by the unexplained absence of her silver. Sarah had identified the transgressor, who was not the suspected serv-ant but a member of the lady's family. Under the circumstances she had chosen not to denounce the thief, but had instead laid a trap, which would be sprung the following morning and offer undeniable proof.

The following morning Frances received a letter from Miss Gilbert assuring her that she quite understood Frances' hasty departure, which she was sure was on a mission of very great importance. She had made enquiries about the Soho Printworks in Dean Street but had not discovered anyone who could supply any information. She added that she would be greatly honoured if Frances and Sarah could accompany her to a meeting at Westbourne Hall at 7 p.m. on Tuesday. There was to be a platform discussion about the forthcoming election at which the Conservative candidates were to appear. It was her intention to distribute leaflets in the hall, and question the candidates about their position on female suffrage, asking whether, if elected, they would vote for it in parliament. Frances, hoping that she might discover something to further her enquiries, replied saying that she would attend.

At nine o'clock that morning she again appeared at the boardroom of the Infirmary in Mount Street, where the inquest on Matilda Springett was due to reconvene. The board-room was not large, with seating for about twenty, which would normally have been more than adequate for an enquiry into the death of a maidservant whose body had been pulled from the Serpentine, but that morning was an exception and the room was becoming more crowded by the minute. Inspector Sharrock was already there when Frances arrived, as were two constables and a medical man.

As Frances took her seat, Mr Fiske arrived, no doubt having been deputed by the school governors, if not his wife. He was followed by Mr Rawsthorne and his clerk, a young individual, thin as a stick, with hair like rusty bed springs and ink-stained teeth. Mrs Springett, Jem and Davey made their own little group of black-clad desolation, accompanied by a man and a woman who were probably Davey's relatives, as they were busy comforting him. Their solicitor, Mr Marsden, Rawsthorne's bit-terest rival in Bayswater, surveyed the scene with unconcealed ill-humour at having got the meaner bargain. Mrs Venn, who might have been expected in the circumstances to approach the Springetts and utter some words of condolence, was sit-ting alone with her dignity and refusing to cast her eye in their direction. Frances doubted very much that the headmistress's bruised feelings would ever permit her to admit just how much money the Springetts had obtained from her over the years for support of the Professor's supposed child.

The *Chronicle* had sent Mr Gillan, who was already scribbling busily in his notebook, his expression softening from boredom to pleasure as what must have initially promised to be a dull assignment was transforming before his eyes into a matter of more than ordinary interest. The arrival of Frances placed the crown on his anticipation and he rose quickly to his feet and greeted her. 'I look forward, Miss Doughty, to an interview as soon as the proceedings have closed,' he said, noting where she was sitting so as to be sure she would not escape without supplying him with material for another sensational feature.

'Good morning, Miss Doughty,' said a familiar voice, and she saw Theodore Paskall taking a seat beside her. 'Bad business this; father has sent me to keep an eye on things.'

The coroner for Westminster, Mr St Clare Bedford, called the meeting to order. At the last meeting, he said, the deceased had been formally identified as Matilda Springett aged twenty-four, maidservant at the Bayswater Academy for the Education of Young Ladies. He asked the first witness to appear, a constable who had been patrolling in Hyde Park on the evening Matilda had last been seen.

The constable stated that as the night was cool, there had not been a great many people in the park, but he had seen a young woman who might have been the deceased walking alone in the direction of the bridge shortly after eight o'clock. He had also observed several respectably dressed men who all appeared to be walking briskly as if crossing the park, a tall woman strolling down the carriage drive going out of the park, and a couple standing at the western end of the bridge not far from the Magazine, 'spooning'. His route had then taken him away from the bridge area and he did not return to it for another hour, at which time he saw a man he thought might be a footpad and escorted him from the park.

On the Saturday another constable had spied something lodged underneath the arch of the bridge and alerted a boatman. They had rowed out and recovered the body, which was quite cold. He had taken it to the Receiving House, where it had been examined by Dr Blackett. No attempt had been made to revive the young woman, who was quite clearly dead.

Dr Blackett said that he had been called from his home in Park Lane to examine the body and had later performed a post-mortem examination. At this, Mrs Springett wailed and was soothed by her son. The coroner asked if the lady might like to retire from the room, but Jem frowned and shook his head. 'If you don't mind, Sir, this is Matilda's mother and she has more right than anyone to be here,' he said.

The coroner indicated that Blackett should continue. The doctor, carefully avoiding gazing at the family group, went on. 'My preliminary examination suggested that the deceased had been dead for at least a day if not more. She was a healthy and well-nourished female. Although she was found in water she did not die from drowning. There was no water in the lungs, which were in a collapsed state, and the heart was healthy. There was considerable bruising of the tissues of the neck, the marks suggesting that she had been seized about the throat. On dissecting the external integuments of the neck I found a quantity of extravasated blood under the skin, and three of the cartilaginous rings of the windpipe were flattened. I am as certain as it is possible to be that she was already dead when placed in the water. The cause of death was asphyxia as a result of manual strangulation. From the marks on the throat, which show the impression of thumbs at the front and fingers to the side, it is clear that she was strangled by a single assailant, who stood facing her. Apart from the marks of the attack she was quite uninjured, and her clothing was not disarranged.'

'Are you saying that there was no sign of any struggle?' asked the coroner.

'That is correct. I believe she would have been unconscious within moments.'

'Was the strength required for the attack beyond that of a female?'

'It would not be impossible for a strong female, especially as the victim was a small person, but in my experience strangling with the hands almost always indicates a male attacker.'

Mrs Venn was called and stated that she had last seen Matilda at about eight o'clock on the Thursday evening. She was not aware that the maid had left the school premises until she was discovered to be missing the following morning.

Inspector Sharrock gave evidence next. He confirmed, pausing frequently to wheeze in an alarming fashion, that the police did not have any information to suggest who might have been in Matilda's company on the evening of her death.

The coroner summed up, pointing out that the evidence showed beyond any doubt that the injuries could not have been self-inflicted, and that some other person had been present to put the body in the water. The jury had no difficulty in returning the verdict that Matilda had died from manual strangulation, and that it was a case of murder, by a person or persons unknown.

Once the proceedings were closed Frances approached Sharrock. 'Inspector,' she said, 'I strongly advise you to go home and rest.'

'I've got six babbies at home,' he growled. 'I get more rest at the station with the villains of Paddington!' He stamped away, coughing loudly.

Frances looked around to see Mr Gillan by her side, note-book and pencil at the ready. 'Good morning Miss Doughty, and what, may I ask, brings you here?'

'I was acquainted with the deceased,' said Frances. 'I have been engaged as a teacher at the school.'

'For appearances only, surely?' he said with a knowing smile.

'For a salary,' Frances replied.

'Ah, but I hear whispers that more is involved. It seems that you are setting yourself up as a veritable Dupin and the Paddington police may soon be out of business altogether!'

'I hope you will not publish that,' said Frances, sternly.

He affected a sad expression. 'My editor is a hard man and he will have his hundreds of words and column inches, no matter what. And if I cannot find a story to engage his interest then I am expected to conjure one up from nothing at all. It is very trying.'

'I believe,' said Frances, 'that the composition of material for the newspapers is very taxing upon the imagination.'

'Which is precisely why I prefer facts,' said Gillan. 'Have you any for me? This may surprise you, Miss Doughty, but I do have principles, and I can be as discreet as the next man when it is called for. I am not in the business of libel, neither do I wish to cause pain. I only wish to inform.'

Theodore Paskall appeared at her shoulder. 'I hope this fellow is not annoying you, Miss Doughty?' he asked anxiously. 'Did you know he is from the *Chronicle*?'

Frances smiled. 'Mr Gillan and I are already acquainted,' she said.

'Then you will know to take good care of what you say to him,' said Theodore. 'And Mr Gillan will take care what he writes or Mr Rawsthorne will know of it.' He gave a curt nod and walked away.

Frances knew that Gillan would write his piece for the newspaper whether she spoke to him or not, and considered whether it would be to her advantage to maintain a friendly dialogue. Information could, after all, pass in more directions than one.

'I imagine,' she said, 'that you are on good terms with the Paddington police.'

'I have many good friends in the police force,' said Gillan. 'They are a worthy body of men. It is a matter of great regret to me that it is expressly forbidden for police officers to give information to the press, even though sometimes it is in the public interest to do so.'

Frances felt sure that a small libation would quell any difficulty on that point. 'But you may not know anyone in the Hillingdon police,' she went on. 'I assume, therefore, that you have not been informed that yesterday morning I was visiting friends in Havenhill and chanced to discover the body of a man. It appears he may have stumbled into foundations being dug on Mr Matthews' property and expired.'

Gillan was clearly astounded. 'My word, you are a calm young lady,' he exclaimed. 'Does nothing discompose you?'

'Only lies, Mr Gillan. Let us find a suitable place to talk and I will tell you all my story. But for my part I shall ask you to tell me the things that you know which other people keep from me. Are we agreed?'

He gave a smile of great satisfaction. 'We are indeed!'

It was a short stroll to Hyde Park, where at its eastern tip, large crowds had assembled to hear the political speakers, making so much noise that scarcely a word of what was being said could be heard. There were banners in profusion snapping in the wind, and eddies of leaflets whirling up into the air. They stood on the bridge gazing into the Serpentine, and Mr Gillan rested his notebook on the parapet and wrote his looping notation as Frances gave him the full story of her adventures on the Sunday.

'I suppose,' he said, 'you are disinclined to tell me the real reason you were visiting Havenhill?'

'It would be unwise of you to speculate,' said Frances.

'The gossip in these parts is that the girls at Mrs Venn's school were given literature of a scandalous nature to read and that your true position there is not that of teacher but detective. Since Mr Matthews is a governor of the school, it seems reasonable to me to assume that your visit was in connection with that enquiry.'

'I advise you to tread carefully,' said Frances. 'You know better than I the consequences of slander and libel. I have given you enough, and wish to have your assurance that you will wait until I think it safe to say more.'

'Very well,' Gillan said grudgingly.

'And now I hope you will keep your part of our bargain. I would be interested to know what actions the police have been taking concerning the death of Miss Springett. Although it has only just been declared to be murder, I know that they have believed that to be the case from the start.'

'They have, and many persons have been interviewed, but no suspect has emerged. I too have been making my enquiries. I even interviewed Mr Paskall under the guise of writing about his candidacy, and I found him to be very exercised about the business. He believed the girl to have been a courier employed by his political enemies who has been silenced because she knew too much about their plots. I pointed out that if he believed that the girl was working against him, that would make *him* an excellent suspect, and he became very unhappy and threatened to have me arrested if I wrote it down. But of course everyone knows the Paskalls are almost chained to their desks at present, and most unlikely to have spare moments for murdering housemaids even if they were inclined to.'

'I only wish,' said Frances, 'that I had the freedom to ask people any question I liked, irrespective of their rank in society or whether they considered it polite. Since we can assume that Matilda was killed during the evening of the 4th of March, or possibly the morning afterwards, what I would dearly like to do is ask everyone who might have known her where they were at that time.'

'And then you will have your murderer,' said Gillan. 'And I will have another chapter of your story, only to be found in the *Chronicle*. I'll see what I can do.'

CHAPTER FIFTEEN

Sarah had completed her business that morning and returned home with a strong sense of justice done. The thief had been unequivocally revealed as the fashionable lady's cherished only son, who had pawned the family silver to pay his gambling debts, thus showing that he had a greater sense of responsibility to his bookmaker than his mother. Frances wondered if the client, who was currently too distressed to discuss remuneration, was entirely satisfied with the outcome. Any problem that could be solved by the dismissal of a servant was by definition a trivial one, but one which took the heart out of her own family was a hurt from which she might never recover. Frances decided to wait awhile before she sent a gentle reminder about payment. Before attending the inquest she had sent a note to Mr Matthews' townhouse asking for an interview, and on her return from seeing Mr Gillan received a reply that he was from home that morning but would be available to speak to her at two o'clock. In the meantime, Sarah was eager for further employment, and so Frances decided to send her to Somerset House to look at the marriage registers. It was something she had felt daunted by the first time she had gone there, as she had had no advisor to explain where she should go and what she must do, so she made sure to instruct Sarah carefully.

There was just time to meet the lady with the Hyde Park romance, who was an unprepossessing spinster of fifty-five with attractive investments. Her devoted swain had told her only that he worked in the City and boasted considerable expertise in finance. Frances discovered when the next tender assignation was to take place, warned the client not to part with a farthing, and sent a note to Tom asking if he could track the ardent gentlemen back to his lair.

After a luncheon of bread and cheese, Frances hurried to Roderick Matthews' townhouse on Gloucester Terrace and was shown into the study, where she was unsurprised to discover its occupier striding up and down, with a glass of brandy in his hand and very much out of humour.

'I have just had to go down to Havenhill this morning,' said Matthews irritably, 'where I was obliged to look at a most disgusting object and I suppose I have you to thank for that, you and that unpleasant little dog.' He swallowed the rest of the brandy at a gulp and put the glass down. The thought of offering any refreshment to his visitor did not occur to him any more than he might have offered it to his parlourmaid.

Frances had not warmed to Benjie but was far from terming him 'unpleasant', neither did she feel personally responsible for the body in the trench. She could see, however, that Matthews, a man who felt that stirring himself to make an effort was a task best delegated to others, might have been annoyed.

'Did you recognise the man?' she asked.

'No,' he replied brusquely, 'and nor does anyone else.'

'He must have come there after the workmen had stopped digging but before the fence was built,' said Frances. 'That was in the latter part of January. Were you at Havenhill during that time?'

Mathews flung himself into a chair and fidgeted. 'What is all this about?' he said. 'What has all this to do with you? Or me for that matter! Why do I have policemen tramping all over my land, not to mention an artist from the *Illustrated Police News*. He wanted to go into the stables and make a sketch of the body! The impudence!'

'I know that I am supposed only to be investigating the incident with the pamphlets —,' said Frances.

'Yes, how is *that* progressing?' he said, insolently.

Frances maintained a patient demeanour. 'I have some clues, which I cannot reveal at present,' she said, 'but the issue of the pamphlets may be more complex than at first thought and I have to take into consideration anything unusual connected with the school, its pupils, its staff and its governors. Miss Springett's death, for example. I attended the inquest this morning, where it was declared to be a case of murder.'

'Oh, Paskall won't be happy about that!' exclaimed Matthews, with a derisive snort.

'And it is possible that the man found dead on your land was in some way involved with the subject of my enquiries. *Were* you there in January? I understand that the last day on which digging was carried out was Saturday the 24th.'

'That sounds about right.' He pulled his cigar holder from his pocket, contemplated it and pushed it back in again. 'I went down there with Paskall on the Monday after, and we had a look at how much had been done and discussed whether or not we should stop or go on. We decided to stop until we knew more about how the work was to be paid for. The weather was against us in any case.'

'What was the weather like that day?'

'Abominably cold, even colder than London. Frost almost as thick as snow, ground solid as a rock.'

'Do you think, if the body had been there then, you would have seen it?'

'Yes, I'm sure of it. Paskall had a better look than I did, and he saw nothing.' Frances had a mental picture of Bartholomew Paskall tramping about the site while Matthews hovered impatiently nearby, muffled up warmly and taking sips of brandy from a flask.

'And after that visit, did you go straight back to London?'

'No, Paskall did as he had people to do business with. I stayed at the house that night. There were some estate matters to attend to.'

'And you had no visitors?'

'No, nor was I expecting any. Had I been, I would have sent a man with the dog cart to fetch them from the station.'

'When did you return to town?'

'Early the next morning. My manager drove me down to the station. It was still dark, and if there had been a body there then it would have been impossible to see it.'

'And then, I understand, not long afterwards, Reverend Farrelly sent you a letter asking for a fence to be put up so no one could stumble into the open trenches.'

'Yes, and I gave instructions for it to be done. But what I do not understand, Miss Doughty, is why you were in Havenhill interviewing the Farrellys. Perhaps you could enlighten me?'

Frances prepared herself to introduce a difficult subject. 'I think we are all agreed that the person who deposited the pamphlets may have done so with the intention of causing some harm to the school. But that may be only one avenue through which this individual will exert his or her malice. It may also be directed at those closely connected with the school. I received a letter recently which alleged that you are a married man, and therefore not free to marry the Duchess of Kenworth.'

'What?' he exclaimed, suddenly tense and upright in the chair, small spots of red anger appearing on his cheeks. 'That is an outrageous libel! Supposing that person had also written in such terms to Margaret!'

'Have they done so?' asked Frances, coolly.

'She has said nothing of it to me,' he said, 'but she is a highly prudent lady and might have reserved her comments until she had made her own enquiries.' He favoured Frances with a dark stare. 'I hope you have not spoken to her?'

'No. I have taken the view that if the matter is a libel I should not spread it. But I did go to Havenhill and examined the marriage registers and was able to satisfy myself that the allegation is false.' Frances in fact was not yet satisfied, and would not be until she received Sarah's report, but did not feel it wise to expose all her thoughts or methods to Matthews or anyone else. Nevertheless, she could see from his reaction that while he was understandably angry about the accusation he was not threatened by it. He clearly did not fear the discovery of any obstacle to the forthcoming wedding.

'Do you know of anyone who might have a motive to stop the wedding, or delay it, or indeed to harm your interests in any way?'

Matthews slumped back in the chair pensively. 'Margaret has had other admirers, of course, although she entertained no man's addresses but mine. She is an excellent woman in every respect and highly esteemed. There have been many who hoped to deserve her, and they must envy me my good fortune. But this foolish libel makes no sense, since it can be disproven by the easiest of methods, as you have found. May I see this letter?'

Frances handed it to him and he read it without a change of expression. 'Were you at Havenhill at that time?' she asked.

'The date of the supposed wedding is the day of Joshua Jenkins' death. I understand that for two weeks prior to that he was too ill to stir from his bed.'

'Yes, I recall that was the case, and I was there then.' He handed back the letter. 'The hand is not familiar to me.'

'And your ward, Miss Clare – she was living there at the time?'

'She was.'

'She must therefore have known of Jenkins' illness?'

'Indeed. I recall she used to carry him hot soup.'

'Where does she reside now? The letter claims that she is abroad, and Mrs Venn has confirmed this. If this libel is spread further then it may be necessary to interview her, and of course she may be able to suggest the identity of the person who wrote the letter.'

He gave a scornful grunt. 'I really have no knowledge of where she is. She left my house and told no one of where she was going. I did my best for her but was poorly repaid for my generosity.'

'How did this come about?' asked Frances.

He looked ill at ease and Frances suspected he would have liked a cigar or another brandy or even both. 'Miss Clare, as you probably know, is a relative of my late wife, and I promised that I would care for her and also for her cousin, Miss Danforth. Miss Clare has no fortune – her mother made a most inadvisable marriage and was living in very reduced circumstances after her husband died in debt – but Miss Danforth will one day come into a very handsome legacy. Miss Clare, I am sorry to say, was envious of her cousin, and unhappy with her position in life. I had promised her mother that she would receive a good education and hoped she might become a governess but that, it seemed, was not to her liking. I thought then that she might stay here as housekeeper and assist with the care and education of my youngest, Horace, but that too she declined to do. No, she had set her sights on a loftier prospect; she wished to marry my eldest son, Freddie. They had always been on affectionate terms, much as brother and sister, and I confess I had not realised where her ambitions lay. For his part, Freddie, who is a gentle and affectionate boy, loved her as a brother might, but had no wish for any closer alliance. Freddie became enamoured of Italy when we were there in '73, and as soon as he came of age he departed for Florence and now has a flourishing business there. I anticipate that in time he will advise me that he has courted and won a Florentine lady of good family with wealthy connections.

Miss Clare left Havenhill not long after Freddie's departure without so much as a letter or a word. I feared at first that she had pursued him to Florence, but that, he assures me, is not the case. She was eighteen at the time, and I still therefore had a guardian's duty of care. I wrote to her mother to discover her whereabouts but my letter was returned, stating that the occupant had gone away.'

'Where did her mother live?'

'It was a most insalubrious lodging house in Dalston. I sent a servant there to make enquiries and while Mrs Clare had lived there for a time, she had departed leaving no address to which letters could be sent.'

'Is there any other family?'

'None for whom I have an address.' He shrugged. 'I did what I could, but Miss Clare is now of full age and her own mistress. I therefore take no further interest in her.'

'What about Daisy Trent?' asked Frances.

He stared at her in astonishment then gave a rueful smile. 'You know of all my family ghosts,' he said. 'I suppose Mrs Farrelly has told you about that. I feel guilty of course, young Souter was a good employee, but neither Jenkins nor I had any idea of the danger we sent him to. But Daisy Trent felt that she needed to hold someone to account, and since the criminals were never found it was Jenkins and myself who were blamed.'

'Might she have sent this letter to revenge herself?'

'Assuming a mind unhinged with grief, perhaps. But that was many years ago and I cannot say where she is to be found now.'

The door opened and Selina and Lydia entered. The transformation in her languid host took Frances by surprise. She could see that he was lazy, selfish and irritated about anything that disturbed the smooth running of his life, but the arrival of his daughters at once moved him to action. He rose from his chair and became at once concerned and attentive. For all his faults, he appeared to be a dutiful and affectionate father.

'I had heard that you were here, Miss Doughty,' said Selina, as her father took her hand and drew her to a chair. 'I was hoping you could tell us what transpired this morning.'

'Selina, my dear, are you sure this is quite appropriate?' asked Matthews. 'There are some things you really ought not to ask about.'

'It is the most ridiculous fancy I ever heard!' said Lydia. 'I have done my best to dissuade her, Papa, but she will not listen. Miss Doughty may think that it is prudent for a female to go to such places, but I cannot agree. There may be things said, expressions used that it would be quite wrong for any respectable person, whether man or woman, to hear.'

'You forget,' said Selina gently, 'I have visited the school many times and take a great interest in it. I am anxious to know what became of the poor girl.'

'She must have been quite stupid to go walking there at night, alone!' said Lydia. 'She was not, I think, a decent person. We encountered her out walking the other day and she was very rude about Horace. I refuse to think of her any more!'

The servant entered at that moment with a note. 'Message from Mr Paskall, Sir,' she said, handing it to Matthews.

'Oh, what is it *now*!' he said testily, tearing it open.

'Is there to be an answer, Sir, the boy is waiting,' asked the maid.

'I suppose so,' said Matthews, looking about for a pen and ink. 'I for one will be very happy when this election is done with.'

'Come,' said Selina to Frances. 'Let us leave my father to his work. We will be more comfortable in the parlour and I will have some tea brought.'

Lydia twitched her nose and gave a sniff of disapproval, but went with her sister, as if appointed to be her personal attendant.

'I always felt,' said Selina, when they were cosily settled, 'that Matilda had some sorrow in her life. You can always tell, even with a servant.'

'She did have sorrows,' agreed Frances, 'but they were long past, and I understand that she was anticipating wedded happiness. Her sweetheart is a very good sort of person. Her only concern was saving enough money to give him a good start in a carpentry business. Had you noticed anything unusual in Matilda's behaviour on your recent visits?'

'Yes, the last time I was there I saw that something was troubling her. She had been doing her best to conceal it but a woman always knows, don't you think? When I heard of the terrible thing she had done, I wished I had said something to Mrs Venn, who might have prevented it. I assume that my fears have been found to be correct?'

'I do not wish to say anything that might distress you,' said Frances, awkwardly.

'We cannot avoid sadness and loss,' said Selina. 'Men seek to protect us, but we can be stronger than they. Please tell me.'

'It appears,' said Frances carefully, 'that Matilda did not make away with herself.'

'She was probably intoxicated with who knows what nasty compound,' said Lydia.

'As to that I really couldn't say,' said Frances.

Selina seemed relieved. 'Oh it is such a terrible thing to contemplate another's agony of mind. Thank you, Miss Doughty. You have comforted me. It was an accident, then, and the girl not suffering at all.'

'I believe she did not suffer,' said Frances. 'But it was not an accident. It appears that another person was involved.'

Selina's creamy pale visage seemed to bleach white. Lydia took the teacup from her sister's trembling fingers. 'And now, Miss Doughty, we will wish you good day,' she said.

Frances made a wise retreat.

Sarah returned from Somerset House with the news that the registers contained no marriages of a Roderick Matthews from 1873 onwards, and while several ladies named Caroline Clare had married since that date, none had done so in 1874, or in any location in the vicinity of Havenhill. The information in the letter was undoubtedly false.

CHAPTER SIXTEEN

The inquest on the stranger found in the ditch opened at the Havenhill Arms on Tuesday morning. Frances had only once and quite against her will entered a public house, the Redan on Westbourne Grove – an incident which still made her blush with embarrassment, and she recalled with some distaste its clamour and alcohol-fumed atmosphere, not to mention the unpleasant headache that had followed. The inside of the Havenhill Arms was, by contrast, like a welcoming inn out of a child's story book, a place in miniature, with ancient polished wood, brass lamps, low beams suitable only for the easy passage of small folk, and quiet nooks for contemplation. She half expected to see a copper-skinned gnome with a pointed hat smoking a clay pipe in one corner.

Frances and the other witnesses climbed a small winding wooden stair whose treads had been made for finer feet than hers, and reached an upper room where a table had been placed ready for the coroner and rough wooden chairs were assembled in rows. As Frances went to take her place she found that the floor sloped alarmingly on sagging beams, and creaked at points of dangerous weakness, something the villagers regarded with unconcern.

She was first to be called to give evidence and made sure to state only that she had come to Havenhill on a private matter, and had discovered the body because she had been recovering Benjie. Mrs Farrelly told the same tale.

The Havenhill stationmaster was a jovial fellow with rosy cheeks, but was slow to answer questions, and his replies were curiously vague and unhelpful. He could not recall the arrival of any strangers, or the timetable, or how many tickets he had taken, or, it seemed, a great deal of the month of January. There were some hard looks from the coroner and the other witnesses.

The next to be called was the landlord of the Havenhill Arms, stout and hearty and a fine advertisement for his own ale, who said that on a cold, dull day towards the end of January a stranger, aged he thought about thirty, with a foreign-sounding accent and carrying a small leather gentleman's handbag, had asked him the way to Havenhill House. He directed the gentleman towards the path and told him to take care as the weather was very misty. He had viewed the body found in the ditch, and while he could say nothing as to the features, he believed the suit looked very like the one worn by the visitor and also thought he recognised the bag found with the remains.

Mr Matthews, looking awkward and uncomfortable in the cramped interior of the little room, told the court that although the body had been found on his land the man was a stranger to him. At the period in question he had been in his house on one night only, that of January 26th, but there had been no visitors, and neither had any been expected.

Mary Ann Dunn, the housekeeper, was a mannish looking woman of about forty with a hard but handsome face, black brows and a figure that looked as if it was encased in steel. She confirmed that no stranger had visited the house on any day in either January or February.

The next witness was Dr Naresby, whose bulk was such that he had to be pushed up the stairs by the substantially lighter coroner's officer, at no small risk to both of them being the subject of the next proceedings. The doctor's preliminary examination of the remains had suggested that the cause of death was a fractured skull, which could well have been the result of the man's stumbling into a trench and hitting his head on the stone foundations. There were no other injuries on the body. A full and detailed report would be available in due course.

The evidence of Inspector Eaves was of most interest since he had made a thorough examination of the man's clothing and effects. Those garments which bore a manufacturer's label had been made in the United States of America. The leather bag had also been made there. It contained a clean collar, a change of linen and the usual gentleman's requisites. There was a pocketwatch of inexpensive make, which did not bear a jeweller's mark, and a leather pocketbook containing both American and English money, and some receipts from a shop in New York. A letter and a railway ticket and what looked like some business cards were found in the pocket of the coat, but these had been so soaked with water and mud that any writing or printing on them was no longer legible. It was impossible therefore to say who the man was. The inspector said that he would be circulating a description in the hope that someone would recognise him, but the police were working on the theory that the visitor was an American, and quite possibly recently arrived. He might have left a trunk either at a railway station or hotel, but without a name it would take some time to trace.

The coroner adjourned the inquest to the following Monday, expressing his confident belief that by then the identity of the dead man would have been discovered.

Frances spent her train journey to Paddington considering the evidence and what it must mean. The unfortunate man had clearly never been to Havenhill House before, since he had been obliged to ask the way, but there was no doubt that this was his intended destination. It had been assumed by the court and indeed everyone else, that the stranger had gone to Havenhill to see Matthews, but that was not necessarily the case. Had he wanted to see Matthews he would surely have called at the Bayswater townhouse, since Matthews was hardly ever out of town, and any enquiries the stranger had made would have suggested that he should try there first. During the critical period Matthews had only been at Havenhill for one night, and that visit had been arranged for business reasons brought about by the bank crash, something that could not have been anticipated. It was therefore far more probable that the visitor had called to see Mary Ann Dunn or one of the farm servants who lived on the estate.

And yet, Frances reflected, the visitor was carrying business cards. What was he – a seedsman – a dealer in horticultural equipment, or something in the world of finance, property or insurance? If that had been the case, then it was more likely that it was Matthews he wanted to see. Supposing, she thought, the American had called at the townhouse first while Matthews was away and then been redirected to Havenhill?

She decided to call at the townhouse on her way home. The housemaid recognised her at once, and said, 'Oh, I am very sorry but Master is not in.'

'As it so happens,' said Frances, 'it is you I wish to see.' She was in the hallway before the maid could recover from her surprise. 'I was hoping that you might be able to remember a visitor – it would have been towards the end of January, while your Master was away. He was well-dressed and probably called here on a business matter. He was carrying a gentleman's handbag, and he was from America.'

'Oh,' said the maid with some surprise, 'well, Master has a great many visitors but I can't say I can remember anyone of that description.'

Frances was disappointed, but there was nothing more to be said, and she went home. It was time to put all her paperwork in order. The only item of furniture she had brought from her old home was her father's writing desk, and she set about polishing the dark wood and shining the little handles on the drawers, brushing every speck of dust from inside and lining it with clean paper. It was while she did this that she noticed that one of the small drawers seemed shallower than the others. It took some prising with a letter opener, but she was able to remove a false base and there discovered a thin packet of letters. She carried them to the table, separated them carefully and opened them out. There were four, all in the same hand, and were addressed from her mother to her father. Three were little more than notes, dated prior to her parents' marriage, in which the future Mrs Doughty thanked her betrothed for gifts. The fourth was undated.

Dear William,
I know that I am entirely to blame, and that your actions were correct, my fate well deserved. I accept that in future we must be as strangers to one another. I have only one last

entreaty. May I – before our fates are severed forever – see my beloved children one more time? Perhaps Mr Manley might make the arrangements? I promise faithfully that V will not be there.

Respectfully

Rosetta

Frances read the letter several times. It had been only weeks since she had learned that her mother had not, as she had always been told, died sixteen years ago, but had instead deserted her husband and two children for another man. Frances had been both sad and angry, full of self-pity for the selfish cruelty with which she and her brother had been abandoned. Her mother might well still be alive, and one part of her had wanted to find her, while another had been afraid of what she might discover. It was a path she had hesitated to take. Now it seemed that there was more to the story than her uncle Cornelius, her mother's brother, had admitted. Perhaps even he did not know all the truth. What actions had her father taken? What was her mother's fate? Who was Mr Manley? Who was 'V'? She felt sure that the meeting for which her mother had begged had not taken place, or her brother, who had been five years older than she, would have recalled it. Several times she started to write to her uncle, but the right words eluded her. She was suffused with the knowledge that she had, after all, been loved.

While she considered what to do next, Frances carefully folded the letters and put them away, then she sorted all her materials neatly and assigned them their proper places. She had just completed this task when Tom arrived to report on his findings regarding the two part-time husbands, and Frances thought it best to write to the two mauve-clad wives and arrange a meeting where they might compare notes. It would be a painful interview, and would require the services of a medical attendant, a solicitor and, in all probability, a policeman.

That evening Frances and Sarah arrived in the Grove in good time to attend the meeting at Westbourne Hall, but found the supporters of women's suffrage standing outside in the street in some dismay, having been denied entry. Miss Gilbert and Miss

John were there, as she might have expected, as was Jonathan Quayle, and a smartly dressed lady of mature years who he introduced as Flora's mother, Mrs Gribling.

There were also a large number of men waiting outside, many of whom, judging by their clothing, represented local trades and it appeared that they too had hoped to attend the meeting and been disappointed. They had formed themselves into groups which new arrivals were swelling in size by the minute, making loud indignant complaints to each other and anyone else who would listen.

'Oh, Miss Doughty, here is a to-do,' said Miss Gilbert. 'Would you believe that entry is by ticket only, and that tickets are only to be had by Conservatives? This is most shameful, as it means the candidates are not to be challenged in any way, but will simply have their own kind about them, and what good is that, and of course it disqualifies ladies entirely.'

There was a sudden rush as Frances heard a familiar voice and saw Tom with bundles of tickets in his hands, offering them for sale. He was no longer in the shop uniform but in a suit of clothes he had been bought by Chas and Barstie some weeks ago when running messages for them. His hair, which would not lie flat without an application of anything less than the greasiest ointment, had been cut short and stuck up all over his head in glistening spikes.

'Tom, where did you get those tickets to sell?' asked Frances, when he had disposed of his stock.

He stuffed coins in his pocket and winked. 'Private business,' he said, 'all straight, mind, nothing funny. Wish I'd 'ad more, now, could've sold a 'undred, there's that much of a pother.'

It soon turned out, however, that the mere purchase of a ticket was insufficient to ensure entry, and disappointed and increasingly frustrated Liberals crowded about the double doors, forming a solid mass of bodies and arguing that they had a right to be let in, which two stalwart doorkeepers were firmly resisting. Eventually, to howls of execration and language wholly inappropriate to be used in a public street, the doors were swung shut on the crowds and firmly locked. Miss Gilbert sighed. 'Oh dear, I had really hoped to ask the candidates to make their position known on the suffrage question. But all is not lost; I have some leaflets here which I will give them as they leave.'

The mass of men outside had not, however, given up hope of attending the meeting and kept up their loud and angry demands, while those at the forefront started pounding on the doors, which were not of the stoutest build, having been constructed to match the architecture and not to resist a siege.

'Do you really intend to remain here?' asked Frances above the escalating din. 'It seems to me that there might be a dangerous disturbance.'

'Ladies,' said Jonathan Quayle, his eyes bright with anxiety, 'please, I beg of you, let me conduct you to a place of safety! If I might assist you to a cab, it would be for the best.' Miss Gilbert, however, a bundle of leaflets in her hands, looked anything but concerned at the prospect of some excitement.

Miss John gave a smile. 'Oh,' she said softly, 'there is nothing to be gained without some risk of danger.'

'Marianne is right, as ever,' said Miss Gilbert firmly. 'I will not stir until I have done what I came here to do.'

The frustration and anger of the crowd was rapidly boiling into rage, a position from which retreat was no longer possible. The men had given up hammering on the doors with their fists and were now attempting to enter by the expedient of charging them down with weight of numbers, loud cheers and exhortations accompanying their efforts. 'Let me at least place you under my protection!' urged Quayle above the pandemonium. As he spoke there was the sound of splintering wood and shattering glass and the doors burst inwards, the hapless doorkeepers were swept aside, and the mob charged into the hall with roars of victory.

'Well,' said Miss Gilbert, appreciatively, 'it seems that we may enter after all.'

Before anyone could say another word, she hurried in on the heels of the mob, followed closely by Miss John and Mrs Gribling. Quayle waved his arms in despair and ran after them. Frances held back for a moment then, emboldened by example, joined the crowds, with Sarah at her side.

The meeting, thought Frances, if its object was the dissemination of information, was unlikely to be a success since the hall was too crowded and noisy for any voices to be heard. She wondered if election meetings were always conducted in this way. Every seat was occupied and there were more patrons standing at the back, their numbers increasing with the sudden violent incoming crush of Liberal supporters. Frances' height enabled her to see the platform, on which there were a number of men seated behind tables, amongst whom were Bartholomew Paskall and Mr Matthews. A man she did not recognise was on his feet attempting to make a speech. Someone in the body of the hall was calling out for the intruders to be ejected, but the doorkeepers were in no position to do so as they were lying dazedly on the floor with bloodied noses, and even when they managed to stagger to their feet a hostile crowd made it impossible for them to move. Mr Paskall rose up and, judging by his arms, which were moving in a jerky semaphore, seemed to be appealing for calm, but to no effect. Miss Gilbert, realising that there was no chance that her prepared questions might be heard, was taking the opportunity to throw leaflets into the air, scattering them like seeds in the wind, in the hope that they might alight on a fertile mind and take root, while Miss John, whose normally timid expression had achieved a quite alarmingly determined aspect, was preparing to defend herself with a bodkin. At the front of the hall, a man jumped from his chair, climbed onto the platform and started to speak, but the crowd roared for him to leave and as he did so, someone picked up a table and flung it at his retreating figure. There was a loud and unified shout of disapproval and the next moment the crowd surged into motion. Chairs and tables, both whole and in pieces, were flying through the air and there were outbreaks of arguing and pushing and fisticuffs all over the hall, with not a Queensberry Rule in sight. The candidates and their friends, led by Bartholomew Paskall, ran from the platform and made for a side exit, and those members of the crowd not engaged in their own private confrontations, pushed forward and tried to go after them. Frances, cushioned from much of the shock by Sarah's large form at her side, felt a firm hand on her arm. 'Time to go,' said Sarah, in the sort of voice that had once made a bookish young girl clear her dinner plate, and Frances at once complied. They squeezed through the surging crush of humanity, heading back towards the Grove, Sarah swatting aside over-excited Liberal voters with the back of her hand. On the way they encountered Jonathan Quayle, helpless in a pack of bodies and gasping for air. Sarah extricated him but he was too weak to stand so she draped his limp form over her shoulder and marched grimly on.

At last the little party reached the street, where they saw Mr Paskall, his fellow candidate and their supporters hurrying away as fast as they could go, desperately trying to attract a cab, while a mob of Liberals ran after them hooting in derision.

They moved away from the broken doors to allow the crowds to emerge and Sarah sat Quayle on the pavement, propping him against the wall where he drooped like a wilting flower.

'Oh dear, we must take him home at once!' exclaimed Mrs Gribling, mopping the poet's brow with a handkerchief.

'I'll fetch a cab,' said Tom, appearing from nowhere.

'But are there any to be had?' asked Mrs Gribling anxiously.

'Sixpence says there are,' said Tom with a wink.

The sixpence was provided and he hurried away, returning a minute later with an empty cab.

Mrs Gribling was putting the handkerchief into her pocket when Frances realised that she had seen something like it before. Even in the gentle glow of the street lamps she recognised the pattern – the little scallops of blue and white that Mlle Girard had assured her was of her grandmother's invention. How had Mrs Gribling obtained it? Was it the same one that Mlle Girard had been making or another?

Frances could think of nothing to do except snatch at the item and when Mrs Gribling turned to stare at her in astonishment, said, 'Oh, I am so sorry, I thought it was about to fall to the ground.' She handed it back, but had seen enough to satisfy herself it was indeed the same design. 'How delightful,' she said, 'where did you obtain it?' Frances knew that she sounded like a thoughtless girl, concerning herself with a trifle in the midst of more serious matters. It was a part she had played before, and would no doubt play again.

'I really cannot remember,' said Mrs Gribling impatiently and she took the handkerchief back a little too quickly for politeness. Quayle, who had partially recovered, was being helped into a cab and Mrs Gribling followed him. As they drove away Frances found Tom.

'Another sixpence for you if you follow the cab,' she said. 'I need to know where the lady lives and anything else you can learn about her.'

He nodded and scampered away. It was late that night when he returned to report that Mrs Gribling lived in Fulham, not far from her daughter, and was the widow of a coffee-house proprietor who had once owned a flourishing business in Soho.

Frances determined to consult Mrs Venn's directory as soon as possible, but also looked in her father's old volume, and thus learned a valuable lesson; that new was not always best for her purposes. Ten years ago there had been a business called Gribling's Coffee House in Dean Street, just three doors from the Soho Printworks.

CHAPTER SEVENTEEN

The next morning Frances returned to the school, where she at once sought out Mlle Girard. The teacher of French was poring over some translations and shaking her head with little sighs of regret. She at once greeted Frances, who suspected that few visitors who distracted her from this unrewarding task would have been unwelcome. 'I would very much like to see the handkerchief you were working on the other day,' said Frances.

'Ah, the one you admired so much,' said Mlle Girard with a smile. 'It is not yet complete I am afraid.' She took it out of her work-box and Frances could see that while a great deal of progress had been made, it was unfinished.

'I saw a lady only yesterday with one very like it – in fact, identical, but I had imagined that this was the only one,' she said.

'There was another,' said Mlle Girard. 'I made it for the Christmas bazaar, and it was sold to a lady there.'

'How interesting,' said Frances. 'The lady I met yesterday was a Mrs Gribling. What is her connection with the school?'

'I do not know,' said Mlle Girard, 'but Mrs Venn will tell you. She knew the lady and greeted her by name, not, I think, Gribling, but I do not recall what it was.'

Frances went to see the headmistress at once. Mrs Venn, who was preparing some papers for a history lesson, seemed to have aged since they had first met. Her face was worn, like old wood that had lost its varnish, and it was an effort for her to maintain her dignity and composure. Frances wondered if she had even eaten breakfast, something Sarah always insisted she do, and took the liberty of sending for tea and buttered toast.

'Mrs Venn, I believe I may have made some progress towards solving the mystery,' said Frances, when they were settled more comfortably. 'What can you tell me about Mrs Gribling?'

'Why, I do not know anyone of that name,' said Mrs Venn.

'But I am given to understand by Mlle Girard that this lady attended the Christmas bazaar where she purchased a handkerchief and that you greeted her and addressed her by name.'

'How extraordinary,' said Mrs Venn. 'Of course there were many ladies there, aunts or parents of former pupils to whom I spoke, but none are called Mrs Gribling.' She thought for a moment. 'I do remember the table where Mlle Girard and Mrs Sandcourt were selling fine lace and needlework, and I stopped to admire it. Oh yes, I do recall now, and it was quite a surprise. I encountered Mrs Clare, Caroline's mother, and spoke to her, and she did purchase a handkerchief, but I hardly recognised her at first, and she seemed quite taken aback that I knew her at all.'

'Had she changed so much?' asked Frances.

'The Clares had been living in very humble conditions, and were dependant on Mr Matthews' kind charity. Mrs Clare, on the one occasion I had previously met her, was not fashionably dressed and neither was her hair quite so beautifully arranged, or so – dark. But I have a good memory for features and after a moment I realised that it was she. Of course I was careful to make no allusion to her altered circumstances. She did advise me, however, that she had married again, to a person with a business in Soho, but had since been widowed.' She sipped her tea. 'I remember now – Soho – that was the location of the printer.' Sudden comprehension made her almost drop the cup. 'Was it Mrs Clare who was responsible for the pamphlets?'

'I am not sure,' said Frances cautiously. She looked again at the photograph on the wall, the one of the governors presenting the key of the school to Professor and Mrs Venn. When she had first seen it the faces of the girls standing on the steps had seemed identical, unrecognisable, but that was only because she had not then met some of them. She studied the picture again, counting eleven girls, and was able to distinguish the promise of pale beauty that was Selina's face, the sharp nose and cheekbones of Lydia and one other, the sweet calm features of Flora Quayle. 'This must be Caroline Clare,' she said, and Mrs Venn agreed.

'Was Mrs Gribling, that is, the former Mrs Clare, at the dance display?' asked Frances, 'because that is when I think the pamphlets were left here.'

'No, I have not seen her since the bazaar. She has not been here since, I am quite sure of that.'

Frances, feeling that she was drawing closer to the answer, took a cab to Fulham and called again at Flora and Jonathan Quayle's home. She knew she went to fetch away the truth but did not know what it was she might be bringing with her. There was a very great risk that she carried unhappiness and discord. The truth, as she was well aware, was not always a source of contentment. It would be best to speak to Flora alone.

She knocked at the door, and a moment later saw a curtain creep carefully aside and a face glowing like an opal within, then, after a pause, the door opened. 'Miss Doughty,' said Flora timidly, 'I had not expected you. But you are very welcome, please do come in.'

Frances entered and Flora conducted her to the parlour, where she busied herself with the kettle.

'Mrs Quayle,' began Frances.

'Yes?'

'You may know that I have been teaching at the Bayswater Academy, where you were once a pupil.'

Flora stopped what she was doing and her shoulders stiffened, but she did not turn to face Frances and remained silent.

'In Mrs Venn's study there is a photograph of the governors handing over the key to the premises, and you are there. I am told you were once called Caroline Clare. Is that correct?'

Flora looked around, and she was clearly afraid. 'I had forgotten about the picture,' she said. 'I suppose I cannot deny what you say. Yes, I was once Caroline Flora Clare.' Her mouth trembled. 'Have you told anyone else of this?'

'No. I assume you would prefer it if I did not?'

'I must *beg* you not to!' she said earnestly.

'Very well, I will respect your wishes, but in return you must answer my questions. Do you agree?'

She nodded.

Frances took out her notebook. 'First of all I would like to know when you were married.'

Flora began darting about with teacups and saucers and plates and spoons. 'Oh, my dearest Jonathan and I were united less than a year ago,' she said lightly.

Frances, concerned that she could not see Flora's expression, said, 'Please, do not trouble yourself about refreshments; I would like just to sit with you at the table and talk.'

Flora put the cups down with a nervous clatter, and came to sit down, biting her lips, the knuckles of one hand grinding into the palm of the other.

'You have not previously been married?' asked Frances.

'I have been married only once,' Flora said.

Frances unfolded the letter and placed it on the table in front of her. 'Do you know of this letter? Is it in your handwriting?'

Flora glanced at it briefly and looked away. 'That is not my writing,' she whispered.

'Aren't you curious to see what it says?' asked Frances. 'Or do you already know? Perhaps it is your husband's writing – or your mother's – it would not be hard to make a comparison.'

'No, please!' begged Flora. 'Please say nothing to Jonathan!'

'If there is something amiss which concerns Mr Quayle, then that is for you to tell him,' said Frances. 'Now, perhaps you would like to talk to me about what is in the letter.' She held up the paper so that Flora could read it, but the girl stared down at the tabletop.

'Who wrote it?' Frances demanded.

'It is my mother's hand,' said Flora quietly, 'but written at my behest.'

'And can you tell me why it was written, for the contents cannot be true.'

'But it *is* true,' Flora insisted, looking up, emotion colouring her pale cheeks. 'Roderick Matthews is my husband.'

'Mr Matthews denies the connection,' said Frances, 'and there is no proof that it ever occurred. There is no marriage certificate at Somerset House, and no record in the register of St Mary's Havenhill. I have spoken to Reverend Farrelly and he is adamant that he did not conduct the service, and Joshua

Jenkins could not have been a witness on 6th October because he was dead.'

Flora gave a little gasping intake of breath. 'It happened!' she cried. 'You must believe me! Roderick and I were married as the letter describes. Of *course* he will deny it, and Mary Ann will say whatever he directs her to say. He would not want the Duchess of Kenworth to know that he is another's lawful husband or that he abused his responsibilities as my guardian. When I wanted my freedom my mother went to Somerset House to get the certificate and found none, so I had to remain content in my present circumstances, but when I heard of the proposed wedding I knew I had to say something, even at the risk to myself.'

'I don't understand,' said Frances. 'What risk is this? What are you afraid of?'

It was a few moments before Flora could whisper 'My husband.'

'Do you mean Mr Quayle?' said Frances.

'No!' exclaimed Flora. 'Jonathan is the best creature in the world and I love him dearly. He is kindness itself. But – and it pains me to admit it – he is not my husband as the law understands it, although he is the husband of my heart and mind. The law has bound me to a monster, a wicked monster – not a man – and I am afraid, Miss Doughty – afraid for my life!'

Frances began to seriously wonder about the sanity of the young woman before her. 'Perhaps,' she said soothingly, 'you could tell me from the beginning how this wedding in Havenhill came about.'

Flora nodded and her agitation subsided a little. 'I first came to Havenhill soon after Roderick returned from Italy,' she said. 'I was eighteen then, and had just left school. He told me I was to be his housekeeper, but in reality,' she blushed, 'he attempted to make me his mistress.'

'Attempted,' said Frances, leaving the question unasked.

'Naturally I refused him,' said Flora quickly, 'and he did not try to force me. But then he asked me to be his wife. I have no fortune, Miss Doughty, and – so I thought at the time – no prospect of marriage. He said that he would secure a fortune for me in his will and also – and please believe me this was what decided me – he promised to ensure that my mother was never free from want. His only condition was that as I was not of full age, and he was my guardian, the wedding must be kept a close secret from all except those immediately involved, and even those few would be trusted persons who would be sworn to secrecy. I did not love him but, to my eternal regret, I consented.' She heaved a sigh. 'It did not occur to me that he would carry out his purpose so soon. Barely a week later, I was awoken very early one morning by Mary Ann Dunn, the maid.'

'The morning of the 6th of October?' asked Frances.

'Yes. I cannot say what time it was, only that it was dark. She said that I was to be married to her master at once and helped me to dress. It felt so very strange, as if I was still asleep and dreaming. We walked down to Havenhill, with a lamp to light us. There was no sound anywhere. It was dark in the church, but Roderick was there and Joshua and the clergyman. And so we were married.'

'But Joshua Jenkins was a sick man,' said Frances, 'he could not stir from his bed. Reverend Farrelly was called to him that same morning and sat with him until he died. There is no mistake; he recorded the date in the register.'

'Joshua Jenkins was there,' Flora insisted. 'I can only say what I saw.'

'You knew that he was a dying man?'

'I knew that he was very ill. When I saw him sitting in a pew, wrapped in a great cloak against the chill, I assumed that he had rallied. And of course he was a person in whom Roderick placed a very great trust. It seemed quite natural that he would be there.'

'Did you sign the register?' asked Frances.

'I – I'm not sure. There was a paper, and I signed it, but it was too dark to see what it was.'

'And the witnesses signed too?'

'I don't know. I couldn't see.'

'But there is no record of the marriage,' said Frances. 'I have seen the register for myself. How do you explain that?'

Flora shook her head. 'I can only imagine that Roderick used his influence to ensure that it went unrecorded.'

'Are you suggesting,' said Frances, with considerable astonishment, 'that Mr Matthews either induced or even bribed Reverend Farrelly to conduct a secret wedding in the middle of the night, not to enter the event in the parish records, and then to see that no certificate was ever registered with Somerset House? I am not sure but that may be a criminal offence.'

'I think,' said Flora uncertainly, 'that the clergyman was not Reverend Farrelly. Sometimes, in my dreams, it comes back to me, and then I see his face clearly, but when I awake it is gone again. I can only say that I have never seen him before or since.'

Even Frances' firmest stare was insufficient to move the girl from her unlikely tale. 'And then, some three months later, you ran away,' she said. 'Can you give a reason?'

Flora paused. 'I am not sure if it would be of any advantage to speak to you further. I can tell by your manner that you think I imagined the wedding.'

'I am sorry if I have given that impression,' said Frances. 'Do not let it deter you from finishing what you have to say.'

Reluctantly, Flora went on. 'A few days after my marriage we attended Joshua Jenkins' funeral at St Mary's. In the congregation there was a young woman hardly more than my age who caused a great disturbance. She kept calling out that it was a good thing that he had gone. It was very shocking, of course, and many people tried to comfort her and tell her to hush, but all she could do was laugh and then she turned to Roderick and pointed her finger and said that he would be next. I asked Roderick what it all meant and he told me that the woman was drunk or mad or both. Some friends of hers took her outside, but later as we came out, I saw her running about the graveyard laughing and then she went to the grave and threw stones into it. I asked someone who the young woman was and found that her name was Daisy Trent. The next day I sought her out and spoke with her. She lived in a room in the blacksmith's cottage that had once been her father's. She was much calmer then and told me a terrible thing. She said that Joshua Jenkins and Roderick had killed her sweetheart, Daniel Souter.'

'She said that they had actually killed him?' asked Frances, incredulously.

'Yes.'

'I have read the account of the inquest,' said Frances, 'and I have spoken to Reverend and Mrs Farrelly, and it was well known at the time that Daniel Souter was killed by a gang of men from East Hill who had been roaming the area thieving and causing damage. Joshua Jenkins had sent Daniel to find the thieves and frighten them away, but had not realised that they were armed. Daisy found her sweetheart's body and it sent her out of her wits. I know that she blamed Joshua Jenkins and Mr Matthews for Daniel's death, but it was not because she thought they had actually done the deed themselves but because they had put him in danger.'

'That isn't true,' said Flora firmly.

'But what makes you so certain? Did Daisy say that she had actually witnessed Daniel's murder?'

'No. The only witnesses were the murderers themselves.' Flora's face drew into something approaching a scowl. 'I can see that you don't believe me. Just as no one has ever believed Daisy.'

'If there is a single shred of evidence, one thing that would stand in a court of law, I would like to know it,' said Frances.

She waited, but Flora was silent.

'You were not living at Havenhill when Daniel Souter was killed?'

'No, I was at school, and living in Bayswater.'

'And it was after you spoke to Daisy that you ran away?'

'Yes, of course – as soon as I could! Can you imagine my feelings? I was terribly afraid. A man like that! But I had no money and I dared not place a burden on my mother. Then, not long afterwards, Freddie turned twenty-one and came into some money of his own. I told him I was very unhappy, but of course I could not tell him the reason, and he gave me enough to be able to leave. He was a good friend to me, and I do miss him.'

'Was Freddie at Havenhill at the time of Daniel Souter's death?'

'I believe so.'

'I expect you will tell me that Freddie is also under the control of his father and will say whatever he is directed to.'

'No. Freddie dislikes his father. He went abroad as soon as he was able.'

'Florence, I am told.'

'Yes.'

'Has he ever spoken of what happened on the night of Daniel's death?'

She shook her head.

Frances pondered the puzzle. If one discounted anything Mary Ann Dunn might have to say, as she would undoubtedly support her master, it left two conflicting accounts both of the murder of Daniel Souter and the supposed wedding. If Flora was telling the truth about the wedding, then there had been a conspiracy in which several people, including a clergyman, had been involved. The other and rather more likely explanation was that the marriage had never taken place and that Flora was lying or insane or had dreamed the entire thing. As for Daisy Trent, it seemed very probable to Frances that the unhappy girl, distracted by grief, had not given the most coherent expression to her feelings and that Flora had made some unwarranted assumptions.

'There is one other thing I need to speak to you about,' said Frances. 'The pamphlet, "Why Marry?"'

Flora said nothing.

'It was obvious when I read it that it was written by someone who knew the school well, and was there in some capacity, either teacher or pupil, during the lifetime of Professor Venn. Someone with the ability to compose such a document. Someone who had good reason to want to warn young girls against a hasty marriage. It was printed by a business in the same street as the coffee shop owned by your mother's second husband. I do not think that is a coincidence. I believe that you are the author and Mrs Gribling the lady who arranged for the printing. Am I correct?'

Flora appeared to be considering the option of a flat denial.

'For the avoidance of doubt, I could, of course, ask the printer to visit Mrs Gribling and identify her,' said Frances.

A moment or two passed and Flora capitulated. 'There is no crime in it,' she said. 'No one should marry unless for love. It was my duty to tell the girls that.'

'Did you pay Matilda to place the pamphlets in the desks?'

'Pay Matilda?' repeated Flora, mystified. 'I don't understand.'

'But it was she who put the pamphlets in the girls' desks?'

Flora hesitated. 'I don't know,' she said at last.

Frances did not press the point, since she believed that Mrs Gribling might be better able to supply the answer. 'Did you or your mother, or anyone you know, ever meet with Matilda or send her messages?'

Flora shook her head.

'You should know that Mrs Venn is very upset about your accusations against her late husband. Did you observe his indiscretions yourself? Did you ever go into his study?'

'No, but there were those who did.'

Frances gave a despairing sigh. 'Mrs Quayle, you must not write such accusations and then distribute them based on another person's unsupported word. The only defence against a charge of libel is that what you have said is true. From what you have told me you have no proof at all. Even though Professor Venn is dead and therefore beyond any considerations of that kind, the school has been defamed, and if Mrs Venn wished to, she could institute proceedings against you. I assume,' she continued, 'you refuse to name the actual accuser.'

'I do,' said Flora.

'I must tell you that the appearance of the pamphlets has caused the gravest anxiety to the school governors, the teaching staff, the pupils and the parents,' said Frances severely. 'I understand that you felt the need to utter a warning, but now that you have done so, I wish you to assure me that this incident will not be repeated. If you can tell me that, then I will go to the governors and inform them that the matter has been resolved and I promise that I will not disclose your name.'

There was a spark in the girl's eyes, a flash of defiance, a hint of fire, and though in that context it was not welcome, it warmed Frances to think that perhaps Flora would not always think of herself as a victim, that she might one day, even within her happy association with Jonathan Quayle, be a woman who could also belong to herself.

'And supposing I did the same thing again?' asked Flora. 'What would you do? Would you hand me over to a murderer? Or tell my dearest Jonathan about my past?'

Frances realised that she had no authority with which to ensure compliance with her request, and no weapon other than one which she was not prepared to use. 'It is not for me to tell Mr Quayle your secrets,' she said, 'neither do I wish to place you in more fear than you are already. I can only entreat you to desist from any further contact with the school, its staff and its pupils. And perhaps I may also offer my help. If in the future you should feel impelled to impart another message, write to me first, and we will talk about it, and work together and devise a better means of achieving your object. There. Do I have your promise now?'

Reluctantly, Flora nodded.

CHAPTER EIGHTEEN

rances was beginning to feel that she was swimming in very deep waters. She had accepted a commission to investigate an incident which was not even a crime, and before she knew it had found herself looking at two murders, a suspicious death, blackmail and an allegation of planned bigamy that could threaten a politician's career. Tempting as it was to try and uncover the truth, some of this, and quite probably most of it, was not her concern at all. While Matilda's death might well be connected with the pamphlets, Frances anticipated that despite Mr Paskall's hysterical fears, the inquest on the man in the ditch would find him to be the victim of an accident. She had no obligation and no explicit reason to investigate the circumstances of Daniel Souter's unsolved murder, but felt that if she could cast some light on that event, it might ease Flora's mind, which was at best distracted, and at worst suggestive that close confinement might be her best position. It was Flora's hatred and fear of Roderick Matthews that had prompted the composition of the pamphlets and until those feelings could be resolved, Frances did not feel sanguine that some further incident might not take place.

Frances made a careful list of all those persons to whom she had not yet spoken who might know something of the events on the night of Daniel Souter's death. She had no doubts that Mary Ann Dunn would support anything her employer might say on the matter, Joshua was dead and Daisy Trent vanished. The only other possible witness was Matthews' eldest son Freddie, who lived in Florence. The English community in Florence was, Frances believed, a close-knit society in which all the members might well know one another, and there was one person of her acquaintance who had lived there for most of his life.

Cedric Garton was an anomalous man of whom it could be said that he was unlikely ever to marry. Frances had first met him in January when he had come from Italy to represent the interests of his family following his brother's tragic death. They had first become acquainted under circumstances which Frances now blushed to recall, since she had accosted him impersonating a newspaper man while dressed in one of her late brother's suits, and calling herself Frank Williamson, a circumstance Cedric frequently reminded her of with mischievous relish.

The legal difficulties that had ensued following Frances' enquiries had necessitated his indefinite stay in Bayswater. He had taken rooms not far from Frances in Westbourne Park Road, where he lived a bachelor existence with his manservant, Joseph. Frances knew that his unusual tastes might render him loathsome in some circles, yet she also found him witty, charming and very much cleverer than he pretended to be.

Frances sent Sarah with a note asking if she might call, and settled down to work on her business accounts. Compared with the ledgers she had once kept of the chemist's shop this was simplicity itself. Soon she had all the books neat, precise and up to date and felt very happy. Perhaps, she thought, as her fingers brushed the drawer where her mothers' letters were kept, there were some things better left alone.

Sarah returned with a message saying that Mr Garton was engaged with an appointment of very great importance, which would afford him far less pleasure than Frances' company, which he looked forward to with keen anticipation the following morning at eleven.

At nine o'clock on Thursday morning, Frances was at the school to take an arithmetic class. The work was not, when one compared it with the long hours serving in a shop or indeed trying to solve a murder, arduous and in the case of the cleverer pupils, quite satisfying. After the recent revelation of their organised mendacity the girls were subdued and obedient, although the chief culprit, Sophia Fiske, showed no signs of remorse.

That morning Frances had received a letter from her uncle Cornelius approving her choice of profession and deploring the dreadful and thankfully false rumours he had heard that she had become a private detective. He invited her to dine with him at her earliest convenience. Frances felt sure that this was a ruse to question her but could hardly take offence, as she knew he was concerned for her welfare. She replied, accepting the invitation. Would it, she asked herself, be such a very bad thing if she abandoned her strange endeavours? She knew that she was supposed only to be teaching in a temporary capacity but Mrs Venn had been so kind as to intimate that she had great promise in that profession. No one had as yet been engaged to replace the teacher who had found that she preferred the married state to respectable work. It seemed quite possible that Mrs Venn might offer her a permanent engagement, and if she did, thought Frances, she might give the matter some very serious consideration.

Frances had never visited a single gentleman in his apartments, but found that it was very little different from visiting a lady, except that Cedric was kinder and more welcoming than many ladies she knew. The rooms were furnished in impeccable taste, and since Cedric was exceptionally well travelled – indeed he often cited travelling as his only profession – there were many souvenirs of Italy, France, Germany, Greece and other countries.

Cedric ordered Joseph to bring tea and thin-cut sandwiches for their refreshment. The manservant, who had never quite forgiven Frances for intruding herself into the home of his previous employer under the pretence of delivering a cake, treated her with cool dignity, although the effect was, to her mind, slightly diminished by the fact that he was wearing rouge.

'Your manservant does not approve of me,' said Frances.

'He disapproves of everyone,' Cedric assured her.

'Except you, of course,' said Frances.

'Oh, most especially me. But he has a delightful sister who often calls and she *adores* me. I think she would like to be introduced to your associate Mr Williamson. They would make a fascinating couple.'

'*That* gentleman is unlikely to be seen again in these parts,' said Frances.

'Such a pity. If you think he might ever reappear do let me know and I will offer him some friendly advice on the correct cut of a suit.'

The refreshments arrived, giving sufficient pause for Frances to enquire about Freddie Matthews.

Cedric carefully smoothed his silky blond hair and brushed a minute speck of dust from his sleeve before sipping tea from an elegant china cup. 'Oh yes, I remember the family very well, and Freddie was a very particular friend of mine, a sweet boy and a great admirer of classical art, especially all things Greek. The parents took him travelling to broaden his education.' He smiled fondly at the memory. 'I think they succeeded.'

'Did you see much of Mr Roderick Matthews and his wife?' Frances helped herself to a sandwich made from hothouse cucumbers, which was quite a treat.

'I saw little of Mr Matthews and cared to see even less. Freddie detested him. His father was constantly trying to make him into a market gardener – imagine!' Cedric inspected his fingernails closely, as if the mere suggestion had contaminated them with soil.

'I am told that Mrs Matthews was an invalid, and died there?'

Cedric nodded. 'Yes, she was very ill, consumption I believe. The family did not entertain visitors in the villa for that reason, apart from doctors, who seemed to be there almost every day. I saw her on a number of occasions when Freddie invited me there – well, smuggled me in, if you must know – for a secret *tête a tête*. A pale little woman, very thin and frail, forever lying on a chaise longue in the shade of the verandah. Her condition was such that a permanent daily nurse was required, to be followed soon after by an undertaker.'

'Did Freddie ever mention a cousin of his called Caroline Clare?'

'Oh dear, you are forever taxing a fellow's memory,' sighed Cedric, 'I shall have to employ a private secretary to write down my every conversation. That would make very amusing reading and I could publish it afterwards for selected friends in a brown paper wrapper.'

'And what would it say on the subject of Caroline Clare?' persisted Frances.

Cedric bit into a sandwich and chewed thoughtfully. 'As I recall, when Freddie was first in Italy he was not well acquainted with her. I think he mentioned that his father had two wards whom he was educating in Bayswater. About a year after the family returned to England Freddie came back to live in Florence, where he established a business as a dealer in fine art and became quite the thing in society. He has *very* engaging manners. I did learn one morsel of scandal from a gentleman who knew the family, and of course I *had* to find out the whole thing from Freddie, but he was not very inclined to speak of it, and once I persuaded him I could tell why, as it turned out to be very sordid. A servant was killed on their estate by some brutes, and a mad woman who lived in the village told stories that so frightened one of the wards, who was, I think, the Miss Clare you mention – a charming girl but highly strung and very imaginative – that she ran away in a great bother and was never seen again.'

Frances had been intending to ask Cedric for Freddie's address so she might write to him, but now saw that this might not be required.

'I assume you saw nothing of the other members of the family?'

'Nothing at all. There were two younger boys away being educated somewhere fashionable and expensive, and, no doubt very depraved, and a sister at school in Bayswater. Freddie said she was a sharp-tongued little witch, born to make some unhappy man even unhappier. And there was another sister with a face to enthrall a thousand noblemen, who was away being finished somewhere like a gown. I heard a rumour that she had married a *Viscomte* who fell down a mountain and was dashed to pieces. No doubt his bliss was unendurable.'

'And of course,' said Frances, 'the child that was born at that time.'

He mused on this. 'I did hear a child cry once, but I do not know whose it was. Freddie said he thought a relative of the maid had brought it in to be admired.'

'No, I meant the youngest Matthews child. He has a son called Horace who was born in Italy.'

Cedric shook his head. 'I never saw any such child, nor was one mentioned. And Mrs Matthews was most assuredly not about to become a mother.'

'How very strange,' said Frances. 'There is a child living with the family, a boy called Horace who Matthews has said is his youngest.'

'I would not be surprised if he was the father,' said Cedric, 'but his wife could not have been the mother. A servant perhaps, or a mistress.' He leaned forward as if about to impart a very great secret. 'I believe it has been known.'

There were, thought Frances, a thousand reasons for people to conceal truths or tell lies, and she wondered if the mystery about Horace's birth had any significance. She recalled Lydia stating that Matilda had once said something rude about the boy. Could that be of importance? Perhaps she might try and see him for herself. 'Do you recall the name of the maidservant in Italy?' she asked.

'Really, what would you think of me if I did? She was elderly, Italian and female, and that is all I can say, although now I think of it, she did have a very unattractive moustache.'

'Do you still correspond with Freddie Matthews?'

'I do.'

'Has he ever mentioned his father marrying for a second time?'

'No, only his pursuit of the Duchess, which everyone knew about although no one ever thought she would have him. But the lady is fifty and I understand that that may do strange things.'

Frances, not yet twenty, wondered if her life could be any stranger than it already was.

That afternoon she met briefly with Mr Gillan, who called upon her and professed to admire the new apartments, although she always felt there was something calculating in the way he looked at everything, as if he had his own motives which were nothing at all to do with the empty words of polite conversation.

He had the advantage in his profession, thought Frances, not only of being a man but more impertinent than she, and of having the power of the press behind him, not to mention his friends in the Paddington police, whom, of course, he was careful never to mention, so he had been successful as far as was possible in discovering where persons of interest were on the night of Matilda's murder.

Roderick Matthews had been at his club in the presence of about twenty witnesses. Mr Fiske, together with several of the most respectable gentleman in Bayswater, had been interviewing Mr Miggs as a candidate for his lodge, the Literati, while Paskall and son were working late at the office. Of the teachers Mrs Venn, Miss Baverstock and Miss Bell had been meeting over a light supper to discuss school matters. Both Mlle Girard and Mr Copley were at home in their respective apartments and neither had company. Selina Sandcourt had been visiting her sister, but was unable to say where her husband was that evening. Mr Sandcourt had claimed that he was out of the house on a business matter and declined to say more. Mr Gillan said he suspected that he had been visiting a mistress who was a married woman. He did not say if he had specific reasons for this suspicion or whether it was what he always expected a married man to be doing when away from home without a witness.

Jem Springett had been having a glass of beer with some friends, and had been joined by Davey later that evening, while Mrs Springett was at home and noticed nothing unusual about either of the young men on their return. To this list of possible suspects Frances could have added Mrs Gribling, and Flora and Jonathan Quayle, but could not advise Gillan of this.

That evening Sarah confessed to Frances, with some embarrassment, that ever since Constable Brown had shown them his late father's collection of the *Illustrated Police News* she had become a regular and devoted reader, exchanging copies with friends. 'It's the pictures, you see,' she admitted, proffering the most recent issue, 'and I think you ought to see this.'

Frances had no objections to this sensational but informative reading matter, but was alarmed to find that the main item on the front page was entitled 'The Sagacious Dog and the Lady Detective – Horrible Discovery!' The artist had executed three pictures, which took up the entire width of the page.

The first showed Benjie discovering the body while two startled ladies peered over the fence. One portrait was a good likeness of Mrs Farrelly, presumably sketched from life, the other, for which the artist only had a verbal description, was thankfully sufficiently unlike Frances to allay any fears she might have had of being recognised in the street. The caption was 'A Clever Dog Finds the Body'. There was nothing too remarkable about this, but another picture showed Frances clambering over the fence with more display of ankle and petticoat than she would have thought appropriate. The caption was 'The Lady Detective Investigates'. A third picture showed two men carrying the body on its makeshift pallet, under the direction of the police, captioned 'The Body of a Stranger'. There was a cameo insert of Benjie looking almost humanly intelligent, and another of the face of the body, which Frances thought to be in poor taste, although she appreciated that its object was not so much to shock the public as to assist in identifying the deceased. Not, she thought, that anyone would recognise the swollen features.

The following morning brought a fresh bundle of letters. Many of the writers were intimate friends of the lady who had been so recently disappointed in her thieving son, but who had found herself impressed not only by Sarah's discretion and rapid solution to the difficulty, but by the scrubbed spotlessness of her floors. The apprentice detective's services had accordingly been highly recommended to the ladies of the carriage class and Frances realised that she would have to revise her thoughts about what might be an appropriate fee.

One note, however, was from the Matthews' housemaid.

Dear Miss Doughty

After your call here on Tuesday asking after an American business gentlemen I remembered something that might be of interest. A few weeks ago, there was a visitor asking for Master but he was an Englishman, although he did have a slight accent and I knew he was not from London. He said he was Master's brother-in-law and wanted to see him on urgent family business. I said that Master had been called away unexpectedly to Havenhill and I could not say when he would return. The gentleman seemed very upset. He gave me his card and I said I would put it on Master's desk so he would see it on his return, and the gentlemen said he would come again. As far as I know he did not come back. When Master returned the next day I told him about the gentleman and showed him the card.

I spoke to the other servants in case any of them remembered the American gentleman you were asking for, and Mary, the parlourmaid, told me that she thought that the gentleman who said he was Master's brother-in-law was from America. After he had called she was taking out the waste paper and saw his card in the basket in Master's study, and it had an address in America. Unfortunately she can't remember anything more about it.

Respectfully yours

Jane Parkinson

Frances was not sure what to make of this. Was the visitor at the townhouse the same man who had died at Havenhill or another man entirely? Was the London visitor really a brother-in-law or could he have been lying to get an entry into Mr Matthews' home? The man who had visited Havenhill had been young – the landlord of the Havenhill Arms had estimated about thirty. Frances examined her notebook, in which she had recorded the details on the plaque in Havenhill church. Mrs Agnes Matthews, had she lived, would have been forty-eight. It was not impossible that the visitor could be her brother, but unlikely. He might also be a brother-in-law if he was married to a sister of Matthews, but she was not even sure if Matthews had a sister, and if he did, she too might well be considerably older than the caller. If the caller's story was a lie, she thought, then it was a very ill-judged one, which explained why the card had been disposed of.

She decided that the best way of finding out more was an interview with Mr Matthews and sent him a note, receiving a reply to say that he could afford her ten minutes of his time at four o'clock.

She found him in his study, with more paperwork about him than he obviously felt comfortable with.

'I wished to ask you,' she began, getting straight to the point, 'whether you think the incident at Havenhill has anything to do with the business at the school?'

'What a peculiar notion,' he said. 'It had not occurred to me as it seems very unlikely.'

'I understand,' Frances went on, 'that shortly before the man at Havenhill met his death there was a caller here, who stated that he was your brother-in-law.'

Matthews bridled. 'Have you been questioning my servants?' he demanded.

Frances, finding herself in dubious territory, nevertheless decided to brazen out the situation. 'I did, because I am a detective and that is what detectives do,' she said. 'I can assure you that they were very discreet.'

'And what drew you to this mode of employment?' Matthews asked rudely.

Frances felt that this question did not require an answer. '*Do* you have a brother-in-law?' she asked.

'None living, which is why I knew the man was a fraud. Agnes, my late wife, had two brothers, both older than herself, and both are long deceased.'

'You do not have a married sister?'

'I have two sisters, both spinsters and I wish they *would* marry,' he said testily.

'Who do you think the caller was?' asked Frances.

He shrugged. 'A salesman looking for business. They call all the time. I never see them. The maid was quite right to send him on his way.'

'Did he leave a card?' asked Frances, who was not about to disclose that his parlourmaid examined the contents of his waste paper basket.

'He did, but I threw it away. There was scarcely any reason to keep it.'

'Did you look at it – do you have any recollection of the name printed on it? Or the man's profession, or his address?'

'No – it was such an obvious ploy that I didn't trouble myself.'

'And yet it is very possible that this is the same man who died at Havenhill. In which case his business was so pressing that instead of waiting for you to return to London he pursued you there.'

'I cannot explain it, except to suggest that he may have been driven to desperation by some business reversal.' He took out a pocket watch. 'I believe that is all. And now I have other matters to attend to, my forthcoming wedding. Do not trouble yourself about purchasing a new bonnet, you are not invited.'

CHAPTER NINETEEN

On the following day Frances called upon Mr Fiske to report her progress. She was unsure of what to say since she had effectively solved the mystery she had been engaged to undertake but not to her own satisfaction. She had found a copy of the pamphlet, and discovered the culprit, and could reassure the governors that the incident was not an attack on the school, but she was unwilling to show them the pamphlet or divulge the reason for its composition, and was quite unable to guarantee that a similar event would not occur in the future.

Mr Fiske was in a state of very great distraction. He hesitated for a time about seeing Frances at all, even though they had an appointment, but eventually he consented.

'It is really too bad, too bad!' he exclaimed. 'Tell me, Miss Doughty, have you had any communication with Mr Miggs? You recall that he is the young man who has been about to publish a book by Mrs Venn.'

'As a matter of fact he did write to me,' said Frances. 'It was a most unusual request. He sent me a review of a book of poetry that he had published, not a very complimentary one I must admit, and wanted me to discover the identity of the writer, who has adopted the name *Aquila*.'

'Did you tell him?' demanded Fiske with an alarm that almost approached severity.

'No, I declined the commission,' said Frances. 'I have not read the poems in question but I take the view that an opinion is merely that, an opinion.'

Fiske sank into a chair. He was perspiring and drew a hand-kerchief from his pocket and passed it across his brow. 'I wish I knew how he discovered it,' he said. 'It is no secret now, he has made enquiries and found that *Aquila* is myself, in fact very often *Aquila* is my dear wife, who does not mince words when she dislikes something. I have spoken to Edith and she assures me that had she been entirely honest about the volume her words would have been even more distressing to the author than they were. Of course, she has my entire support. But the result is that Mr Miggs is very unhappy – no, not unhappy, I would say enraged would be a better description. You might almost imagine that *he* is the author.'

'I expect he is,' said Frances. 'They do have the same initials.'

Fiske paused and stared at her, then he clasped a hand to his head and groaned.

'Surely this is not as bad as you suppose,' said Frances. 'I assume that Mrs Venn's book will have to find another publisher, but with the lady's reputation there should be no difficulty about that. I can also reassure you that Mr Miggs has no grounds for a case of libel, if that is what you fear.'

'Oh, it is far worse than that!' said Fiske. 'Miggs demanded that I print an apology for the review and indeed substitute another one that pleases him, but that I told him I can never do. And now he has taken his revenge. Of course he had heard the rumours about the pamphlets and until now he has been pleased to dismiss them, as I personally assured him that the matter was a trivial thing blown up by foolish gossips and rivals envious of the school's success, but now all that has changed. Following our disagreement, Mr Miggs has started listening to and believing the rumours. He is an ambitious young man and so he wishes it to be known to everyone that he is the very model of moral rectitude, which of course he may well be, and he has printed a pamphlet of his own, saying that he has severed his business connection with the school because of the scandal. He is sending this terrible paper to everyone he knows and is even taking it to election meetings, where there are hundreds of people. I have seen one, and shown it to Mr Rawsthorne, but he tells me that Miggs has been very careful to stop short of actual libel and there is nothing we can do. I am besieged with parents demanding to know the truth, and the worst of it is that we have no copy of the pamphlet to reassure them.'

'But supposing you did find one and it was not reassuring?' asked Frances.

He sighed. 'I really do not know what to do!'

'What is Mrs Fiske's opinion on the matter?' asked Frances.

'She has suggested that a quiet meeting between the parties with solicitors present might result in some amicable arrangement.'

'That sounds very sensible,' said Frances.

'And if all else fails, a public meeting.'

'At which you may ask Mr Miggs to read some of his poetry and let the public judge for themselves,' said Frances.

'Do you know, I never thought of that,' said Fiske, his brow clearing. 'It is quite dreadful, you know, all affectation and no substance.' He shook his head. 'But there – we must turn to the reason for your visit. Have you discovered who placed the pamphlets in the school and why?'

'You will appreciate that this is a very delicate matter,' said Frances. 'I have made considerable progress but I cannot tell you all that I have found without causing unnecessary pain and embarrassment to others.'

'I understand, of course, but we do need reassurances.'

'Those I can freely give,' said Frances. 'The incident was not and was never intended to be an attack on the school. It was simply the work of a misguided individual, to whom I have spoken, and I am doing everything I can to ensure that it will not happen again.'

'I see,' he said. 'A misguided person – but what of that poor girl – the maidservant?'

'I have discovered no evidence that her death was associated in any way with the school.'

'Well of course, we would not expect you to try and find her murderer; that is a question for the police.' He nodded. 'I will speak to the other governors. We have a meeting first thing on Monday morning, and I think we can agree to settle your account and say that you have been successful in your endeavours. In the meantime,' he added mournfully, 'I shall have to see what I can do about Mr Miggs.'

As Frances left, she thought there was a matter of significance that she had missed, and it had been the mention of Mr Miggs' name that had brought it to mind. She puzzled over it all the way home, but without result.

On Frances' return she found Jonathan Quayle waiting for her. He looked tired and strained, and as he rose from the parlour chair she thought for a moment that he might fall. 'Flora has told me everything,' he whispered.

Frances sent Sarah out to fetch brandy. 'What can I do for you?' she asked.

It was a moment or two before he could say more. 'Oh, Miss Doughty, I do so hope you can help us! My poor, poor darling girl, what she must have been suffering all this time! When I first asked if she would consent to make me the happiest of men, she told me that she could not be my wife, because she had an aversion to the married state. Of course I respected her wishes and as it was plain that we were both entirely devoted to one another we determined on a course that I know many would disapprove of, but we could not bear to be apart. And all this time, my dearest love wanted to marry me, wanted it as much as I did, but was too afraid to tell me.'

Frances felt a great sense of relief. She had feared that Flora's revelation might alter Quayle's feelings, but it gave her great pleasure to see that he remained true. How many lawfully wed people might envy them now?

'I assume that what you both most desire is to be free to marry,' she said.

He was too moved to speak but nodded vigorously.

'And you are both convinced that the wedding at Havenhill took place as —,' she hesitated, 'Mrs Quayle has described?'

Although Flora was not Jonathan Quayle's wife in law, Frances reflected, the affection and constancy of the young couple merited her the respect of that status and name.

He applied a handkerchief to his eyes, unembarrassed by his display of emotion. 'Oh, yes, Flora is quite adamant on that. She could hardly be otherwise. Miss Doughty, I have heard so much of your prowess as a detective, indeed Miss Gilbert has hardly spoken of anything else since she met you. We have a little money and we would like to engage you to find the papers we need so we may be united under God's holy law. Flora has told me of Mr Matthews' great wickedness, and how he is even now seeking to ensnare a good and virtuous woman for the sake of her fortune.'

'When I first received Mrs Quayle's letter,' said Frances, 'I made some enquiries but so far I have not found any document which would prove that the marriage took place. But I will persevere. Can you tell me if, apart from those who were present, any other persons knew about the marriage at Havenhill?'

'Flora told Mrs Gribling, although since it was a matter of great secrecy she made her promise most faithfully not to tell anyone, and I believe she has kept that promise. And she also told her brother Harry, imposing a similar condition.'

'I will have to speak to them both,' said Frances.

Jonathan readily supplied Frances with Mrs Gibling's address. 'Harry is in America, where he has been these ten years,' he said. 'Flora was hoping he would visit and help resolve matters, and he did write to say he was coming but she has heard nothing from him for some weeks. He may have been detained by business.'

'Oh,' said Frances. She did not want to alarm anyone without good reason but was wondering if the man whose body had been found at Havenhill was Harry Clare.

Quayle soon departed, saying he did not like to leave Flora alone for long, and Frances tried to fit together what she knew. If the unfortunate man was Harry Clare he might well have sailed from New York, where, she recalled, the deceased stranger had made some purchases, but she did not know where he might have disembarked. Once on English soil it would surely have been natural to send a telegram to his family to advise them of his arrival, but this he had failed to do. Had he forgotten to do so or had there been some urgency about catching the train that had prevented him? Supposing he had then arrived in London, at which terminus she could only guess, she thought he would in all probability have deposited his travelling trunk at the left luggage office and gone to visit his family. This, too, he had not done. So far the failure to either telegraph or visit his family argued against the man being Harry Clare, but there remained the visit to the Matthews' townhouse claiming to be Matthews' brother-in-law, something only Harry Clare could have had reason to believe. On being told that Matthews was at Havenhill he had taken the next train there, and, if he was Harry Clare, his intention must have been to confront Matthews about his sister's marriage.

Frances wrote a note to Inspector Sharrock, informing him that she believed that the man found dead in Havenhill was called Harry Clare and that they might well find his trunk at a left luggage office.

Having determined to see little Horace for herself, and not feeling able to insist upon it, Frances devised a plan to do so by underhand means, which she would be able to carry out on the Sunday. The Matthews family lived in the parish of St James, and would, she surmised, worship at the church of St James the Less. As soon as the service at her own parish church of St Stephens was over, Frances hastened to where St James' lay, at the meeting of Gloucester Place and Grand Junction Road, just north of the gates to Hyde Park, and placed herself where she might see the family as if by chance, as they left the church. As groups of friends formed outside the church doors and sociable interaction took place, Frances saw Bartholomew Paskall having a long and animated conversation with Matthews, and it was plain that whatever information Matthews had imparted was causing Paskall considerable displeasure. Theodore approached them, but Paskall distractedly waved his son away, an action that occasioned him both surprise and annoyance. He didn't leave but turned aside and waited for his father. Eventually, however, Matthews went to speak to Mr Fiske, then Paskall and son conversed together, Theodore shaking his head in some dismay at whatever he was being told. The two then hurried away furtively. Frances felt certain that despite the fact that it was a day of worship they were headed towards the office.

The conversation between Matthews and Fiske was altogether lighter in content but while they paused, Selina, Lydia, Mr Sandcourt, the nursemaid and little Horace strolled amicably together in the direction of Hyde Park. Cautiously, Frances followed, but realised that to satisfy her curiosity she would have to engineer a chance meeting for a closer look.

Fortunately, the little group stopped near the Magazine while Mr Sandcourt engaged Horace with a flamboyant tale of soldiers and battles, which passed on to the child the quite inaccurate idea that most of the major conflicts in history and several others that had never happened, including an encounter with Napoleon himself, had occurred on that very spot.

'Good afternoon!' said Frances, approaching with what she hoped was a pleasant smile. 'The weather is very refreshing today!' She had never had the skill or the inclination for the small talk of polite society, and realised as soon as the words left her lips that this was, at best, a weak effort, since the weather was cold, dull and hazy, with a biting wind nipping cruelly at the spring flowers. There was a moment of silence during which Frances began to doubt that the little group would even acknowledge her presence, then Lydia and Selina, in deference to the requirements of the situation, turned to look at her and inclined their heads, while Mr Sandcourt beamed broadly and raised his hat. 'Well if it isn't Miss Doughty!' he exclaimed.

Lydia twitched her mouth and wrinkled her sharp nose. 'Oh, and I suppose it is *you* we must thank for sending that nasty policeman to our house. He actually dared to come to the front door! The impudence! And he did nothing but sneeze all the time – it was positively unsanitary!'

'Well that is very interesting,' said Frances innocently. 'I wonder what he could have wanted?'

Lydia snorted. 'Only to ask about a very distant cousin who none of us has seen in ten years and who we don't care two-pence about in any case. It seems that he has been found dead in a ditch but *you* should know all about that. I have been told the story is in all the penny papers.'

'Mr Harry Clare,' said Frances. 'Are the police sure it is him?'

'It's a bad business, but yes,' said Sandcourt. 'Matthews told me all about it.' He sighed and shook his head. 'Promising young fellow with a nice line in neckties and cravats, so I understand.'

'Really, that police person spoke to my father as if he were some sort of *criminal*,' said Lydia. 'I am pleased to say that Papa is going to make a complaint to someone *very* senior.' She gave a satisfied smirk.

'It seems,' said Selina softly, 'that the police called upon my father because a letter was found in Mr Clare's luggage, in which his mother asked him to pay a visit when he came to London.'

'To borrow money, I expect,' said Lydia, derisively. 'The Clares have done nothing but live off my father's charity, and have ill repaid his generosity.'

'You were at school with his sister Caroline, I believe,' said Frances.

Selina frowned, a brief dimpling of her milky skin. 'We have not seen her for some years.'

'You were not close friends at school?'

'The Clares were to be tolerated, not made friends of,' said Lydia contemptuously. 'We had no time for them. They had no fortune and were jealous of those who do. Such gratitude! I pitied poor Wilhelmina – she is our Danforth cousin – Miss Clare made a great pretence of doting on her, said she loved her dearer than a sister, made her into a plaything, a puppet, the poor child would do anything she wanted. It was disgraceful!'

'So, tell me, Miss Doughty,' interrupted Sandcourt, 'have you found out who wrote those pamphlets and put them in the school?'

'I believe I am making some progress,' said Frances, who was not prepared to reveal anything of moment to someone who not only had not employed her, but did not have an alibi for the night of Matilda's death, 'but the matter is far from resolved, and I fear it may never be.' She glanced at the child, who had been standing silent and motionless beside his sister. There could be no doubt that the boy was Roderick Matthews' son. Tall for his age, and with the dark eyes and hair of his father, the child had a solemn very serious look, as if he was watching the world very carefully and recording everything he saw with the intention of producing a treatise just as soon as he could afford to buy enough ink. He did not, thought Frances, see the world with any great optimism, the lugubrious mouth seemed incapable of smiling. He was clutching a small wooden boat but did not seem to care much for it. She wondered who the mother could be. There was something about the child's features which was familiar, something she had seen very recently in another face, but she could not recall where or whose.

Later that day Frances dined with her uncle Cornelius and regaled him with an account of her new career as a teacher. Alarmingly, she felt not one quiver of guilt at the slight deception. She was unable to resist broaching the subject of her mother's letter, but Cornelius, who assured her that he had never seen it, or even known that it existed, was able to enlighten her upon only one of her many questions. Mr Manley had, until his death in 1864, been her father's solicitor, Mr Rawsthorne then being only a junior partner, albeit one with expectations since he was affianced to Manley's eldest daughter, whom he later married. Cornelius did, however, have in his library a Westminster directory even older than her father's dating from 1862, and said that Frances could have it as a gift.

On her return home she examined the directory and made a list of every name which began with the letter V. It did not include the Venns who, she had been informed, hailed from Oxfordshire and had first arrived in Bayswater in 1867. No insight followed and she put the list in the drawer with the letters. As it closed she felt that she was finally shutting away her past, a past that she was perhaps never intended to understand.

CHAPTER TWENTY

On the Monday morning Frances again took the train to Havenhill to attend the resumed inquest on the man found in the ditch, and was surprised to see Theodore Paskall on the platform at Paddington station boarding the same train.

'Surely you are not going to Havenhill, Mr Paskall,' she said after they had exchanged greetings and settled themselves in a carriage.

'I am my father's messenger boy,' he said ruefully, 'and until I encountered you, Miss Doughty, I was thinking how much rather I would be at my desk renting properties and arranging insurances, but now I have such good company on my journey,' he smiled, 'I feel I may have a pleasant morning after all.' Frances took his comment as a polite gallantry.

'I presume you will be inspecting the foundations of your father's cottages?' she enquired.

'That, and attending the inquest on the poor man found there.'

'I understand that the police now believe him to be Harry Clare, a relative of Mr Matthews' late wife,' said Frances. 'Did you know him?'

'No, I am not acquainted with that family,' said Theodore, 'and Matthews is not convinced that the man is Clare at all. My father, I am afraid, has got a strange fancy in his head that some enemy of his has conjured up a body from somewhere and put it in the foundations of his cottages to cast a slur on him, and has ordered me to come and watch the proceedings.' He gave a troubled shake of the head. 'The election has been a great strain on him, that and the fact that in these difficult times we need to attend to business almost night and day, and I for one will be very pleased when he is safely in parliament, as he is bound to be soon.'

The train gave a great hiss and began to pull out of the station.

'But he cannot be in both places at once?' said Frances.

'Most assuredly not, but he has given me to understand that when he is a member he will devote all his time to politics and thereafter Paskall & Son will be mine to manage,' he added more cheerfully. Though he had his father's hawk-like features Frances thought that his sunnier disposition made the narrow face and prominent nose almost handsome. 'I have worked for my father since I was sixteen, starting with the humblest of tasks and working my way up until I am very nearly a full partner, and though I am just twenty-four now, I know the business very well and have my own customers and can run things very nicely.'

'And perhaps one day you might follow your father into parliament?' asked Frances.

'Oh that will be many years from now,' he laughed. 'For today I am content merely to have plenty of work to keep me busy, and good prospects.'

They whiled away the half hour journey with more similarly engaging conversation, Paskall saying that his father was the hardest working man he had ever known, and Matthews the most idle, except for his undoubted devotion to his family. Frances said that she believed a wedding to be in the wind for Miss Lydia and he replied that he knew nothing about it, but hoped for the sake of the groom that he was a deaf gentleman. As the train pulled into Havenhill, Frances thought that if Theodore could advertise himself as he advertised properties he could have written, 'Pleasing aspect, well situated, suit single lady'.

As they descended from the train Frances saw that a number of somberly clad passengers had also come expressly for the inquest. They did not include Matthews, and Frances assumed that one of the gentlemen present was his solicitor. Mrs Gribling, heavily veiled and clutching a small wreath was leaning on the arm of a lady of her own years – a neighbourly friend Frances guessed – and was walking with slow, almost tottering steps towards the church. Frances went to offer her condolences.

'He's buried there,' whispered Mrs Gribling, gesturing towards the church, 'and me not here to see it done, never knowing . . .' She stumbled unsteadily onwards, her companion patting her arm.

'Is it certain it is he?' asked Frances.

'Oh yes,' she sighed, 'they showed me his watch. I bought it for him before he went away. A simple thing but all I could afford. He said he would keep it always, and he did.'

Frances let the grieving woman go on to the church for her own private moment by the grave. Theodore stood by respectfully. 'I take it that is the mother of the poor fellow?'

'Yes,' said Frances. 'Even though I too have suffered terrible losses, I cannot imagine what she can be feeling at this moment.'

There was a little while before the inquest was due to begin and so Frances and Theodore walked up the rutted path to the building work, with its broken fences and weather-scarred trenches. He inspected the scene gloomily, while Frances told him how she had come to find the body.

'Father will be very displeased,' he said. 'All that expense and nothing to show for it. He told me that he was all for abandoning the work last January. He'd have taken a spade and filled it in himself if necessary, but Matthews wouldn't hear of it, and now it seems that father was right after all.'

Frances thought it best not to allude to the expected arrival of new capital once Matthews had secured the Duchess's fortune. 'Is there nothing to be done?' she asked.

'In a few months, if matters improve, we may begin again,' he said, 'but for now I will take steps to ensure that no one else comes to grief here.'

He offered his arm and they walked back to the Havenhill Arms, where Frances was glad of his assistance in negotiating the narrow winding stair and lurching floorboards. The inquest began with Mrs Gribling stating with tearful certainty that the watch found on the dead man was the same one she had given to her son when he left for America. The men of the jury glanced at each other and nodded and it was clear that the court would formally identify the body as that of Harry Clare.

When Dr Naresby, mopping his face from the effort of climbing the stairs, rose to be questioned, the coroner leaned towards Mrs Gribling and suggested that as there was medical evidence to be heard she might prefer to retire, but she shook her head and stayed where she was. A glass of water was provided.

Dr Naresby said that he and his assistant had completed the post-mortem examination of the body and found a single wound above the right ear consistent with either a blow or a fall on some hard surface. On removal of the outer tissues of the head he discerned a clear comminuted fracture of the skull. The bones had been depressed inwards and there was considerable effusion of blood. Apart from this injury the deceased had been in perfect health at the time of his death. He had no hesitation in attributing the cause of death to the injury.

'I think we are agreed on that point,' said the coroner, 'but the remaining question is whether the injury was accidental or the result of some criminal act.'

'I have,' said Dr Naresby, 'seen many injuries caused by a variety of implements and have observed that each implement, be it a hammer or a spade or an iron bar, will leave a very characteristic mark. That was not so in this case, where the wound was very irregular. I came to the conclusion that the object that caused the injury was a stone. Had the deceased been struck by a stone and then thrown into the ditch I would have expected to find the stone nearby as people almost never carry away such items with them, but I found none. I therefore concluded that the object that had caused the injury was the stone of the partly constructed foundations, which no individual could have wielded. Of course the passage of time and the muddy conditions meant that any traces of blood have been washed away, all the same, it is my opinion that death was due to an accidental fall when the deceased, no doubt confused by the misty conditions, stumbled into the trench and struck his head.'

'Was death immediate or would he have been able to call out for assistance?' asked the coroner.

'I believe that initially he would have been stunned by the injury. He might have regained consciousness but by then he would have been confused and might not have been able to cry out.'

'So the actual cause of death might have been exposure?'

'I believe the primary cause of death to be hemorrhage and injury to the brain. The freezing temperatures would have hastened matters.'

The jurors conferred, the court very quiet apart from the sound of Mrs Gribling's sobs.

Frances looked around at the others present and saw that Mary Ann Dunn was silent and rigid, yet her eyes slowly turned to look at the distraught mother and just for a moment the hard exterior softened and a look of compassion passed across her face.

As expected, the jury found that the deceased, Harry Clare, aged twenty nine of New York City, had died from a fracture of the skull and injury to the brain caused by an accidental fall. They deplored the fact that the open trenches had not been fenced off earlier, and the coroner, who, unlike many of the residents of Havenhill, had no reason to be in awe of the land-owner, concurred, and made some very pointed comments. Frances, with her new commission from Jonathan Quayle, determined to question Mary Ann Dunn and, as the hearing ended, hurried over and introduced herself.

Mrs Dunn, who was not discomfited by the approach, asked Frances to take a turn with her about the churchyard. 'I had expected you sooner,' she said. 'Master said that you would want to speak to me, although I am sure I don't know how I can help you. I know nothing at all about the poor young gentleman.'

'He has never been to the house?'

'Not to my knowledge, and I have been here twelve years. And we had no visitors at all in January apart from the usual tradesfolk, all of whom I know very well.'

Frances heaved a great sigh and touched a handkerchief to her eyes. 'His poor mother!' she said. 'What she must be suffering!' In truth the masquerade required very little in histrionic ability, since Frances had only to think of her own family, those she had lost and those she had never known, to produce a genuine tear or two.

Mary Ann nodded and there was an answering moisture in her eye. 'We have all had sorrows,' she said, 'some worse than others. My sister's boy was just twenty two when he was killed, and that was seven years ago, but the pain is as bad now as the day it happened.'

'Do you mean Daniel Souter?' Frances enquired.

'Oh, so you've been told about it. A fine, handsome, honest, hardworking boy, and no one called to pay the price, and my poor sister dead of grief within the year. I tell you, Miss Doughty, if ever they found out those who did it and gave them the sentence they deserved, I'd stand on the scaffold and pull the lever myself!'

There was a sudden flare in her dark eyes and Frances was left in no doubt that she meant what she said. 'I believe he was going to be married to Daisy Trent,' she said.

'Yes, and the lass almost lost her wits for a time.'

'Almost?' queried Frances. 'For a time? Do you mean she is well again?' Flora's description of Daisy's behaviour had led Frances to think it very possible that the girl had been confined to an asylum, possibly permanently, but if she was recovered and could be found, then she and Flora might meet, and then the misunderstanding would be dispelled.

'Oh she had wits enough when I last saw her, although the burden on her heart will never be gone.'

'Do you know where she is now? I should like to call on her.'

Mary Ann shook her head. 'No, she went away, and never said where.'

'Surely her mother knows where she is?'

'I expect she does, but no one here knows where her mother went.'

Frances tried her best to conceal her disappointment. She felt sure, however, that Mary Ann, a loyal housekeeper, would always be concerned about the interests of her master. A good, useful and discreet servant was an asset who could prove her worth in a quiet way every day of her life, and expect a comfortable pension when she was too old to work.

'Daisy said some hard words about your master after Daniel's death,' said Frances.

'As I said, she had lost her wits. We all knew it was her sorrow speaking.'

'But people still remember what she said. There are even some who believe that Daisy was telling the truth, and that your master *was* to blame for Daniel Souter's death. I am sure that now some time has passed and Daisy is well again, she would welcome the chance to admit that she was mistaken. No one would blame her for what she said in her grief and they would applaud her honesty. Mr Matthews, I am sure, would be very much relieved if that were to happen.'

'That may be,' the housekeeper admitted.

'If you were ever to learn where Daisy Trent is living, would you write to me and let me know? I could arrange for her to meet your master's accusers and tell them that they are in error.' Frances wrote her address on a page of her notebook and handed the paper to Mary Ann, who nodded thoughtfully and put it in her pocket. 'But I think you know what it is I have come to talk to you about,' she went on.

'A letter, I was told,' said Mary Ann, contemptuously, 'with some foolish lies in it, by someone who dared not sign their name.'

'The letter said that your master was married to Caroline Clare at St Mary's on the 6th of October 1874 and that you were there as a witness,' said Frances.

Mary Ann folded her arms and looked immovable. 'As I said, lies plain and simple.'

'It claimed that Joshua Jenkins was also a witness, but of course, that cannot be right as that was the day of his death.'

The housekeeper gave a satisfied smile. 'Then that just goes to prove it.'

'And Reverend Farrelly says he knows nothing about it.'

'Of course not, because he wasn't there,' said Mary Ann firmly.

There was a moment of deadly silence, then Mary Ann coloured deeply and said, 'What I meant to say was, he couldn't have been there because it didn't happen!'

Frances, the consequences of what she had just heard flooding her mind, stared keenly at the woman before her. 'Mrs Dunn, in all our interview you have been very precise. I think that precision has not deserted you.'

'I don't know what you mean!' said Mary Ann defiantly, but there was a break in her voice, a note of panic. 'If that is all, I will take my leave!' She turned and almost ran away, heading towards the little lychgate but Frances pursued her with some determination, her long legs striding across the grassy mounds of the burial ground, gathering her skirts to leap over a row of little stones that sprouted from the earth like ancient teeth, and finally overtaking and facing the housekeeper at the gate, blocking her way.

'How dare you! Stand aside and let me go!' gasped Mary Ann. 'I will call for assistance!'

Assistance, Frances knew, was not far away, so she spoke quickly. 'Listen to me first. I think that the wedding *did* take place. I think that you were there and that somehow you fooled Miss Clare into believing that Joshua Jenkins was there as well. Reverend Farrelly is innocent in this matter, indeed I never suspected him to be guilty, so some other clergyman must have conducted the ceremony. All I now require is the name of the man. Give me that and I will stand aside.'

Mary Ann recovered her breath and, with that, her composure. 'It never happened, and you can't prove that it did,' she said.

'I can't prove it now,' said Frances, 'but one day, I promise you, I will. Very well, if you will say nothing today, I will return home, but when you feel ready to tell me the truth, please do so.'

'I have nothing more to say to you,' said Mary Ann obstinately, 'not today or at any time!'

'Nevertheless,' said Frances, 'you have my address.' She stood aside, and the housekeeper hurried away.

Frances made the journey home alone. If Flora's account was true, she thought, then Matthews, after failing to make the girl his mistress, had arranged a secret marriage in order to possess her. No reputable clergyman would have agreed to take part in such an underhand proceeding, and Frances wondered if there was such a person as a disreputable clergyman. She rather feared there might be – one addicted to drink perhaps, or with debts to pay. Even if she was able to find this man, and she had to admit that without Mary Ann's unwilling testimony she could not imagine how she might do so, he would hardly confess to what he had done. Supposing, however, he was not even a genuine clergyman, but had been defrocked for whatever sin might result in that unsavoury situation. If that was the case, then the marriage was not lawful and Flora would be free to

marry Jonathan Quayle. The more Frances thought about it the
more she believed that this was the answer. If Matthews had
indeed contracted a lawful marriage with Flora, would he have
dared to court the Duchess? The perils of discovery were far
too great. The mere fact that not one scrap of paper existed to
say that the wedding had ever taken place led Frances to conclude that it had been a sham.

That afternoon Frances was due to teach a chemistry class at
two o'clock, and with no time even to return home or refresh
herself with a biscuit, presented herself at the school at a quarter
to the hour. To her surprise, however, there was no answer to
the bell. She waited for a while and tried again, but the house
was silent. Mystified, she went to see Mr Fiske, but the maid
said that he was unwell and could not be disturbed. 'In that case,
I wish to see Mrs Fiske,' said Frances.

'Mistress is not at home to visitors,' said the maid, as if chant-
ing a nursery rhyme.

'Then I will wait inside until she is,' said Frances.

'Mistress says she can't see anyone at present, but if you were
to send a note —,'

'Rose,' said a quiet voice from the hallway, 'you may conduct
Miss Doughty into the parlour.'

'Yes Ma'am,' said Rose without turning a hair, and stood
aside to let Frances in. 'This way, if you please.'

Frances and Mrs Fiske made themselves comfortable and tea
was sent for. Mrs Fiske looked weary and troubled.

'I have come from the school,' said Frances. 'I was due to
teach a class but it is all closed up.'

'And may well remain so,' said Mrs Fiske. 'There has been a
disaster of the greatest magnitude.'

'I hope no one is injured?' Frances asked anxiously.

'No, it is nothing of that nature.'

'Where are the pupils and the teaching staff? Have they all
gone away?'

'I have sent Charlotte and Sophia to stay with my sister. The
Younge girls, who have no female relative, have gone to a board-
ing school in Kent. The others I believe are with their families.
Those of the staff who reside on the premises remain there, but

as you have discovered, they are not answering the door to visitors. I don't know where Mlle Girard is and I don't particularly care. Mr Copley the art teacher is in the custody of the police. He has been charged with murdering the maidservant.'

Frances gaped in astonishment. 'I have spoken to him on only two occasions and I cannot say that I held him in any esteem, but I cannot imagine that he is a murderer.'

'I assume,' said Mrs Fiske dryly, 'that your experience of murderers, while greater than mine, is necessarily limited.'

'That is true,' said Frances. 'I have known murderers, and somehow they seemed outwardly to be little different from anyone else. But what evidence do the police have against Mr Copley?'

'I am afraid it all stems from the activities of the pretentious Mr Miggs,' said Mrs Fiske. 'He came here the other day in a great state saying that I had insulted Mr Mellifloe's mother. I pointed out that I had said nothing to the detriment of that lady, but he replied that he did not appreciate the tone of my comments, and I ought not to have mentioned her at all. I was blunt with him and said that Mr Mellifloe had brought odium upon himself by having the effrontery to publish under the guise of poetry lines utterly devoid of merit, and then expect the public to part with money for them. As to Mr Mellifloe's mother, if he did not want her mentioned then he ought not to have dragged her into the matter himself.'

'All of this is very true,' said Frances, 'but I expect it did not please him to hear it.'

'Not at all. He then revealed that he had made enquiries amongst all the printers of his acquaintance to try and discover a copy of the pamphlet, and he had found one that he was sure was the one distributed at the school. He read some passages to me and I could not deny that they sounded very like what Sophia had been saying. The allusion to Miss Baverstock was unmistakable. He then revealed that under normal circumstances he would not choose to make the contents public, however the pamphlet referred to an evil man in the school, one addicted to nameless vices. He felt it his duty to inform the police, if only for the protection of the girls.'

'But —,' began Frances and stopped before she revealed more than she ought. 'But the only man associated with the school is Mr Copley and surely he is not addicted to vice?'

'Oh, but he is,' said Mrs Fiske severely. 'Mr Copley is addicted to seeing the female form in a state of nature. Some call it Art, and I understand that there are many paintings of that sort in the Royal Academy, which is a place where those who wish to indulge themselves may do so without fear of arrest. The police, however, have found pictures in his portfolio purporting to be —,' she paused, 'purporting *only*, you understand, to be of the pupils of the school. It is surmised that he exercises his talents in drawing the forms of dishonest females, and then for his own amusement appends to these filthy things the faces of innocent young girls drawn from memory.'

The tea arrived and fortunately it was accompanied by thin slices of sponge cake. Mrs Fiske ate nothing, but Frances was hard pressed not to devour the entire contents of the plate, which would have been very impolite.

'That was a most shocking discovery,' she said, 'and I can understand your distress, but what has it to do with Matilda's death?'

'There was, amongst his other imaginative work, a drawing of the maidservant. Her mother has confirmed that there are certain features which convince her that it was drawn from life. It is suspected that the girl was paid to pose for him. However, the police also believe that being a prying young person, she may have seen the other drawings when visiting Mr Copley at his lodgings, and demanded money in return for not reporting what she saw.'

'Thus giving him a motive to murder her,' said Frances.

'He admits drawing her, indeed he can scarcely deny it, but he denies murder.'

'One hardly knows what to believe of a person like that,' said Frances.

'Precisely,' said Mrs Fiske.

'Poor Mrs Venn!' said Frances, thinking of all the people who had by now seen the dreadful pamphlet and what would ensue when it was realised who the man referred to really was.

'She employed the man, and as a result her judgement is now seriously in question,' said Mrs Fiske. 'I doubt very much that she will be retained.' She put her cup down. 'I must not forget – my husband asked me to pass on an envelope to you. I believe it is your account.' She rose and took the item from a side table and handed it to Frances.

'I hope Mr Fiske is not too unwell,' said Frances.

'A headache only – he does not deal well with upheaval, and I regret to say that there is more to come. Mr Younge has just returned from Malaya, where I understand he is something in rubber, and he has engaged the services of a solicitor. It appears that there will be a public enquiry. They have lost no time and an announcement will be in tomorrow's newspapers. It should take place very soon.'

'Before the election?' asked Frances.

'Sooner than that – before Easter,' said Mrs Fiske. 'Thursday, if they can secure a suitable room. And the formal nomination of candidates takes place on the following Tuesday. I wonder what romance of the imagination Mr Paskall will make of *that*.'

Frances decided that she would call upon Mrs Venn as soon as that lady felt able to receive visitors. Once home, she relayed all the events of the day to Sarah, who soon saw that Frances had barely eaten and plied her with more cheese and pork pie and cake than she could comfortably manage. Sarah's detective duties had continued to meet with success, and Frances anticipated that her apprentice might, in time, become so well known for her work amongst the servant class that it would be necessary only for her to enter the door of any establishment to procure the abject terror of the culprit, who would instantly confess.

Frances opened Mr Fiske's envelope, the contents of which were very satisfactory, but represented, she knew, a dismissal from the case. The payments she had received for her other work had also been more than handsome, and she found herself obliged to visit the bank, although not before she had given Sarah a bonus, which was received with considerable astonishment. Perhaps, thought Frances, one day they would be sufficiently settled that they might think of investing funds to ensure their comfort in old age. But even the most prudent of plans could all come to nothing, as she knew from her father's example, and to which she now had to add that of Mrs Venn.

She wrote a letter to that lady, expressing her sincere condolences and the hope that in due course she would be permitted to call upon her, not in any professional capacity but as a friend.

Tom called to advise Frances that the lady he had been following had kept an appointment with her Hyde Park swain but the tender moment had been interrupted by his arrest on several charges of fraud at the behest of a whole posse of disappointed females. The client, being the only one of the gentleman's victims to retain possession of her investments, was naturally grateful, if still suffering from the effects of lost love, and was entirely under the impression that the drama she had just seen enacted had been brought about by Frances' almost miraculous prowess as a detective.

Frances had not planned to go and see Flora until she had something more tangible to report than her own suspicions, but in the dying light of the evening she took up the pamphlet again, as there was an expression she had heard recently that was an echo of something in its pages, and she wanted to be sure that it was no more than coincidence. There was an awkwardness of phrasing at its centre as if there was something the writer wanted to say that she could not place comfortably, but it sat there, standing out as if it had been underlined, and was, perhaps, the most important part of the document. Frances saw now that Flora had not been entirely honest with her, and that the pamphlet had not after all been prompted by a desire to warn all girls against the dangers of marriage without love. She determined to go and see her immediately after breakfast the next morning.

Frances had sent a note to the Quayles to announce that she would be calling, although she knew that Flora would be at home as she almost always was. To her surprise, the knock at the door of the little Fulham home was answered by Jonathan, and he was utterly distraught. 'Oh, Miss Doughty, come in, it is the most terrible thing in the world, my darling has been cruelly attacked – someone has tried to kill her!'

Frances, knowing that poets were often by their nature inclined to embellish the truth, was suitably sympathetic but kept her doubts about the seriousness of the situation to herself. She was conducted to the bedroom where Mrs Gribling sat by the bed holding her daughter's hand. Flora lay white and still, her head bound about by bandages, her secrets inaccessible and possibly even lost forever.

CHAPTER TWENTY-ONE

'She is sleeping now,' said Mrs Gribling softly, 'the doctor says that it is best for her. We hope she may heal.' Jonathan hovered in the doorway with a look of anguish, torn between the desire to be at Flora's side and fear of disturbing her rest. At last he came in and sat by the bed, staring intently at the face of the unconscious woman.

'What happened to her?' whispered Frances.

Mrs Gribling rose and drew Frances from the room. 'We think that she may have surprised a thief in the house. A neighbour who was passing heard my poor girl screaming and knocked at the door. That may have saved her life, as it seems the thief heard the knocking and ran away. When the neighbour went to the back of the house she found the door open. That must have been how the thief got out because Flora would never have left it like that. Flora was lying on the parlour floor – she had been struck on the head with a poker. It seems that she had the presence of mind to pick up a cushion and tried to shield herself with it, and that may have saved her from the worst. There are bruises on her head and arms, but no broken bones. She is very fortunate to be alive.'

'Has she been able to describe what occurred?'

Mrs Gribling shook her head. 'She has spoken, but can recall nothing, not only of the attack itself, but, strange as it may seem, for several hours beforehand. The doctor told me that that is sometimes the case with such injuries.'

'What was the time of the attack?' Frances asked.

'It was about two o'clock. She was quite alone. I was at home and Jonathan at his office.'

'Did the neighbours see any strangers in the area?'

'The police have asked everyone hereabouts and there were the usual delivery boys and men putting up election posters, but that was all.'

'Your daughter would not have admitted a stranger to the house,' said Frances. 'Was there any sign to show how the thief broke in?

'There were no locks or windows broken,' said Mrs Gribling. 'I can't account for it.'

'Was anything stolen?'

'Not as far as I know. The police asked Jonathan to look around the house but nothing had been either taken or disturbed. There is little enough here to tempt a thief.'

'Then perhaps he was not a thief,' said Frances. 'Your daughter has secrets and there are those who would prefer her not to tell them. I will be open with you, Mrs Gribling, please be open with me. Mrs Quayle has told me of the clandestine wedding in 1874 and has confessed all to Mr Quayle, who stands by her. I am a private detective and he has engaged me to discover the truth so that they will be free to marry.'

'Oh I do so pray that it will happen!' said Mrs Gribling with a great gush of relief. 'My poor girl has been living in fear. But who would know where to find her? Who would know that Flora Quayle is really Caroline Matthews?'

Frances thought about this. 'Apart from ourselves, only those persons present at the wedding knew of it.'

'Mr Matthews may have engaged spies to find her out,' said Mrs Gribling. 'What with his betrothal to the Duchess, he is the one most afraid of what she has to tell.'

'Perhaps someone came here appearing to be bringing a packet in the post, and then forced his way into the house,' Frances suggested, 'but surely then she would have cried out sooner.'

'Even my poor dear Harry did not know Flora's address as she had not long been living with Mr Quayle,' said Mrs Gribling. 'He used to send his letters to my house.' Tears trickled down her face at the thought of her son and she made no attempt to dry them. 'He called on me last January – I have found that out, now. I had told my servant to admit no one from Mr Matthews. It seems that when I was away from the house Harry called and asked to see Mrs Matthews – meaning Flora. As soon as the girl heard the name she became alarmed and declared that there was no one called Matthews at that address and shut the door on him.'

'I wondered at the fact that you were not expecting him,' said Frances. 'You did not receive a telegram announcing his arrival?'

Mrs Gribling shook her head. 'I questioned my maid to see if there was anything at all that he had said at the door, and she thought that there was some mention of a telegram, and an apology, but she could not recall exactly what was said.'

Mrs Gribling peered into the bedroom again, where Flora looked peaceful, her devoted lover by her side.

'It was you who arranged for the printing of the pamphlet "Why Marry?", was it not?' said Frances. 'The printer was near where you once lived. You were not afraid of being recognised there?'

'I sometimes visit the area to see a sister-in-law, and saw that the printers had a new manager, so I knew that I was safe as long as I gave a false name.'

'And you took them to the school?'

'No, I —,' she paused uncertainly. 'You will excuse me but although I do know who put them there, the recent scandal suggests to me that it would be unwise to reveal the truth. I have seen a publication by a Mr Miggs and I cannot say more.'

'Was it not Matilda you engaged to place the pamphlets in the girl's desks?'

'No, it was not. But I think that under the circumstances it would be as well to allow people to believe that.'

'Your daughter told me that she wrote the pamphlet to warn young girls against a loveless marriage,' said Frances, 'but I feel sure that it was more than that. The pamphlet mentioned the reader being dearer than a sister. That was her cousin Wilhelmina, wasn't it – I understand that they were very fond of each other. The pamphlet wasn't a general warning at all, it was a letter to Wilhelmina, in disguise.'

There was a long moment. 'Flora and Wilhelmina were very devoted,' said Mrs Gribling. 'People misunderstood it; they thought that Flora was only friends with Wilhelmina because of her expectations. She will come into a fortune of £40,000 when she is twenty-one or when she marries, whichever is the sooner. But Flora cares nothing for money and anyone who claims she is jealous of her cousin is probably jealous themselves and does not understand true affection. Wilhelmina is a very timid girl and will do as she is told. Flora feared that she might be hurried into a marriage for which she had no inclination so that her husband could acquire her fortune for his own purposes.'

'Was there any such marriage planned?'

'Flora thought so; indeed, she had been told that her poor cousin was due to be affianced to a man who cared nothing for her. It was out of the question for her to go and see Wilhelmina. She wanted to write to her with a warning but knew that any letters might be intercepted. Also, she did not wish to reveal that she was still in London. So she devised the idea of writing a pamphlet, something that would seem to be a general address to unmarried girls but which Wilhelmina would recognise as coming from her loving cousin.'

'As soon as Mrs Quayle is well enough, I would like to speak to her,' said Frances. 'When she first told me of the wedding in 1874 I confess I thought it might all have been a dream, but I am now convinced that it did occur.'

'Have you found the documents?' asked Mrs Gribling excitedly.

'No, and there may be none to find. It is my belief that the wedding may have been a sham. If I can find the man who conducted the ceremony then I might be able to prove it, and I am hoping that Mrs Quayle might recall something that would provide a clue.'

'Come tomorrow,' said Mrs Gribling. 'I am sure she will be a great deal better then.'

There was a sigh from the bedroom, and Frances saw that Flora had opened her eyes and was smiling up at Jonathan, who was caressing her hand. Mrs Gribling went to her daughter, and Frances quietly slipped away.

Frances next called at Paddington police station to find if Inspector Sharrock was willing to part with any information about Mr Copley. To her annoyance the desk sergeant greeted her with a snigger more appropriate to a schoolboy than a grown man in uniform. He waved her towards Sharrock's office with a smile that threatened at any moment to break out into a chortle.

'Your sergeant has been most impertinent!' said Frances, walking into the office before she could be announced.

Sharrock was at his desk with a pile of papers clutched in his hands, and his young constable was leaning over his shoulder staring at the contents, his eyes standing out of his head like marbles. Both men started in alarm when Frances entered the room and the papers were very quickly turned over on the desk and a ragged blotter moved on top. Sharrock indicated the door with a jab of his thumb and the constable hurried away.

'Evidence,' he said. 'And how may I help you today? We've got the murderer of Miss Springett so that's one up to us.'

'I can see your cold is improved,' said Frances, 'did you try the Friars Balsam?'

'No, I tried brandy.'

She looked at the papers on the desk. 'Are those Mr Copley's drawings?'

Sharrock placed his hands on the pile. 'And why would you want to know?'

'I want to know everything, Inspector.' She removed a large pair of mud-encrusted shoes from a chair, wiped the seat with a handkerchief and sat down. 'What evidence do you have against him?'

'Well he deserves to be locked up for his pictures alone. Disgusting.'

'Does he admit to murder?'

'Not yet, but a few days in the cells might lead him along the right path.'

'Was Matilda blackmailing him?'

He leaned back in his chair. 'Miss Doughty, you seem to think that it is a part of my job to answer your questions about private police matters. Well I have to inform you that it is not. What possible interest can you have? The murder is solved.'

Now that Frances came to think of it, she could have no possible interest. She had not been engaged to find Matilda's murderer, and had nothing other than a feeling that Copley was not guilty of *that* crime at least. Despicable as he was, he did not deserve to die for a crime he had not committed.

'Not sweet on him, are you?' insinuated the inspector.

'Of course not!' she said angrily. 'I just need to know, in connection with another matter, whether he ever gave Matilda money.'

Sharrock drummed his thick fingers on the desk. 'If I tell you, will you go away?'

'Yes.'

He puffed his cheeks out in exasperation. 'You'll finish my career one of these days,' he said. 'Well, according to the prisoner she asked him for £5 not to tell what he was up to, but he didn't give it to her. He says he was about to lock away his pictures in a secure place so as to be safe from blackmail, when she went missing.'

Frances wondered if Mrs Venn had told the Inspector about the £20 found in Matilda's slipper. There was now surely no reason to withhold the information apart from the difficulty that might ensue from the fact that she ought to have mentioned it before.

'There are places he could get that for each drawing, I have no doubt,' Sharrock went on. 'And by the way,' he grinned, 'you might not have been sweet on him, but he was certainly sweet on *you.*'

It was a moment or two before she realised the implication of his words, and Frances quickly took her leave, her cheeks burning red with embarrassment.

Next morning the London dailies advertised a public meeting which was to take place at the Great Western Hotel on Thursday at 6 p.m. to discuss the recent events at The Bayswater Academy. Admission was free of charge and all, including members of the press, were welcome. Frances determined to go, and, in view of the fact that the event might occasion some excitement, decided to take Sarah with her.

Frances returned to Fulham, and was delighted to see Flora out of bed and recuperating by the parlour fire with a cup of cocoa. So far from being in a state of nervous debility as might have been expected, Flora had a new light in her eyes, and a firmer set to her mouth. Both Jonathan and Mrs Gribling were, she knew, inclined to treat Flora as a fragile creature in need of their constant protection, but Frances could not help wondering if the girl was stronger than they realised.

'I recall so little of Monday,' said Flora regretfully, 'although the doctor tells me that it may come back in time. There was a man here from the newspapers yesterday and he was so insistent that I told him a made-up story to make him go away.' She gave a mischievous smile.

'Oh he will not mind if it is not the truth as long as the story amuses the public and sells more copies,' said Frances. 'I hope, however, that you will tell me all you know.'

'There is almost nothing,' said Flora. 'And what there is seems very confused. There are pictures that come into my head and pass across my eyes and keep changing almost like a magic lantern show, and what happened on Monday and the wedding have got mixed up together and sometimes I can't tell them apart. Perhaps as the days pass it will all be clearer.'

'The pamphlet, it was a letter to Wilhelmina,' said Frances. 'I know that now.'

'You are very clever,' said Flora.

'But there are a great many things still hidden from me and I know you have the answers. What was it that made you believe that Wilhelmina was about to be forced into a loveless marriage so that her husband could secure her fortune?'

'She will be eighteen soon, and was due to leave school in a month or two.'

'That is the prelude to an entry into society, and not necessarily a forced marriage.'

'There are men who look at her and do not see the young woman. They see only a bank on which they might draw. So many have lost their funds recently with the failure of the Bayswater Bank, and are seeking marriage as an answer.'

'You describe a general anxiety, which I can understand,' said Frances, 'but the action you took suggests to me that you knew of a planned wedding and felt you needed to act with urgency. Is that the case?'

Flora stirred her cocoa carefully, as if hoping that the pause could make Frances forget her question, but she looked up to see no change in her visitor's expression. 'Yes, it is,' she admitted.

'Do you know the name of the man in question?'

'No.'

'I am surprised that Mr Matthews did not claim her himself, but of course his ambitions were already set on the Duchess.'

'If it is fortune alone that concerns him, she better suits his purpose. The Duchess is fifty and there will be no future obligations as there would be if he married a much younger woman. I was such a child when I married him, and did not understand these things. I really believed that he loved me. Had there been issue of the union, I cannot say what he might have done.'

'Now, allow me to guess the answer you will give to my next question, and I hope I may be wrong,' said Frances. 'I must ask you for the name of the person who told you of the wedding that was being planned for Wilhelmina, and you will refuse to tell me.'

Flora smiled.

'Can you at least tell me who took the pamphlets to the school and put them in the desks?'

'I am not at liberty to say. Does it matter?'

'I can hardly know that until I have the answer,' said Frances with some frustration. 'One thing I have discovered, however, is that it appears Daisy Trent has recovered her wits. I do not know where she is, but I am hopeful that if I can find her she will clarify her account of Daniel Souter's death.'

'She was not mad, Miss Doughty. People thought her mad because she was distraught at the loss of the man she loved, and angry that those who murdered him walked free. If she had been calm and shed a quiet tear when her man was killed so brutally, *then* she should have been locked away as a dangerous lunatic. I spoke to her and though her manner was strange she was very clear in her mind about what had happened, but she was doomed not to be believed. Too many people in Havenhill rely on the market gardens for their livelihood, and would never speak out against Roderick for fear of losing their income and being thrown out of their cottages.'

'I know she accused Mr Matthews and Jenkins when you spoke to her, but that was more than a year after the murder – did she do so at the time?' asked Frances.

'Yes, she did, over and over again, but people said it was the grief speaking. Even Mary Ann, who is Daniel's aunt, is,

I believe, a little bit in love with Roderick, and would not hear a word against him.'

'But don't you think that what Daisy *really* meant was not that that they had actually committed the crime, but were responsible because they had sent him into danger.'

'That is the story that was told in the village. That is why Daisy was not believed. Everyone thought they knew what she had said, and when she did speak her manner was such that people found it easy to dismiss her as a mad woman. Even her own mother used to apologise for what she had said. I was the *only* person who sat with Daisy and talked to her, and when she saw that I believed her she was calmer and her mind was as clear as anyone's. But there was nothing I could do, so I ran away.'

Frances was impressed by the earnestness of Flora's address, but knew that allegations fell a long way short of proof. 'Do *you* know where Daisy Trent is now?' she asked.

'I am afraid not.'

'The difficulty is that it is so well known that she was distracted in the past, that even if she is well now, her words will not be seen as having any value.'

'So you are set against her, too?'

'I perceive that there are difficulties, but I will try not to be prejudiced if there is more you can tell me. Is there more?'

Flora set her cup aside and smoothed her dress. 'On the night of Daniel's death he and Daisy were due to meet and walk together, but Daniel was told by Joshua Jenkins to take his shotgun and go and look for the young men from East Hill who had been causing damage to the estate. He met up with Daisy as arranged but told her that their walk must necessarily be cut short as he had his duty to perform and did not want to put her in danger. She agreed and after a while they parted company, and he walked on. She was returning home down the footpath to the village. It was night, but there was a full moon. All was quiet but then she heard Daniel's voice. She could not tell what he was saying but it sounded as if he was challenging someone. Then there was a shot – but it wasn't Daniel's gun, it was something more like a pistol, and she thought she heard a cry. A few moments later there was another shot, and this sounded like a shotgun. She was terrified as you can imagine, but she hoped that all that had happened was that Daniel had seen the men and frightened them away. She walked back up the path hoping to see that he was safe, and waited for him at the door of his cottage. Then she saw two men emerge from the woods and walk towards her. They were Roderick Matthews and Joshua Jenkins. Roderick was holding a pistol and, as he drew closer, she saw the expression on his face and it frightened her.

He stopped, and Jenkins spoke to him. "Have courage, Sir," he said. "The —" he used a word which Daisy declined to repeat, "scoundrel" is perhaps the nearest, "the scoundrel is dead and he deserved what he got. And if the East Hill crew get the blame and hang for it, I won't lose any sleep!"

Daisy hid in the shadows and saw them go past. Joshua went back to his cottage and Roderick returned to the house. Daisy knew that something terrible had happened, something a man might hang for, and she was afraid that Daniel was involved, but it never occurred to her that someone might want to murder him. So she waited by the cottage, but all was silent. At last she decided to go and look for Daniel. She found his body amongst the trees.'

'How long did she wait after seeing the two men?' asked Frances.

'A few minutes only.'

'And she saw no one else?'

'No.'

'And heard only the two shots?'

'Yes.'

Frances took out her notebook and looked at the map she had sketched from the newspapers. 'I should have noticed this sooner,' she said. 'Why was it when Daisy found the body she did not run to the nearest house for help, which would have been Jenkins' cottage or the manor house, but instead went along the path to Havenhill, which was much further away?'

'People said she did it because she wanted to go to her mother,' said Flora. 'But of course she would hardly run for help to two murderers.'

'The pistol that Daisy saw Mr Matthews with – where did he obtain it? What did he do with it afterwards?'

'It may have been the ornamental one that usually hung in a glass case on the wall of his study. I suppose he put it back.'

'And his son Freddie – he saw nothing?'

'I told him what Daisy had seen, and I did feel that he knew something, but he would never speak of it. But he, too, left home as soon as he came into his money.'

Frances felt certain that any case against Matthews was lost almost before it was begun. Daisy, even if she could be found, would not be a believable witness, while the accused would be able to cite the activities of the East Hill gang in his defence. And there was another issue. A prosecution did not, she understood, have to prove motive but any defence would make the very sound point that there was none.

'What reason does Daisy give for Daniel's murder?' asked Frances. 'If he had been found stealing, for example, and I don't suggest that he had, the usual consequences would be dismissal. Why go to such lengths?'

'I don't know, and Daisy doesn't either. Perhaps Joshua had a reason.'

'No, if Joshua had some reason to murder Daniel he would have done it by himself. Mr Matthews is not a man who undertakes other people's tasks for them, in fact he hardy likes to undertake his own. If he did kill Daniel there is some reason why it gave him a very particular satisfaction.' She thought carefully. 'Who was living at the manor house at the time of the murder?' She consulted her notebook. 'It was on the 14th of March 1873. That cannot have been long before the family went to Italy.'

'No, they went later the same month. Only Roderick and Freddie were at Havenhill then, and Mary Ann, of course. Freddie was there because Roderick wanted to instruct him in the business, but he didn't take to it. Selina and Lydia and Wilhelmina were at school, as was I, and the younger boys and girls were at the townhouse. Mrs Matthews was at a resort on the South Coast for her health.'

'So the family went to Italy in March, where Horace was born and Mrs Matthews died there the following August.'

'Yes, that is correct.'

Frances recalled the wasted consumptive Cedric had seen in Florence and an unpleasant thought crossed her mind. It shocked her that she could have entertained such an idea and she wondered if she had over the last few weeks been so exposed to evil that the most depraved imaginings were now commonplace to her. There was, she felt sure, just one thing that could have stirred the normally indolent and apathetic Roderick Matthews to commit murder. 'When is Horace's birthday?'

'In the summer – July, I think – his mother died just weeks after he was born.'

'Did you or Mrs Sandcourt or the other children spend much time at the manor house?'

'Very rarely, why?'

Frances did her best to grapple with her horrid thoughts. 'Was there a harvest festival or something very like it in the village, which all the family attended in the October before they went to Italy?'

Flora, puzzled by the question, gave it some consideration. 'Yes, there was, I remember it now. There were church services and a great gathering, and a merry dance. Why do you ask?'

'Was Mrs Matthews there?'

'No, she was too weak to travel. She had been at the South Coast for some time.'

Flora seemed to find nothing strange about this and Frances realised that, as she had mentioned in the pamphlet, the school taught the girls everything they did not need to know and nothing that they did. She was thankful that her years of toil in the chemist shop had given her a more realistic understanding of the experience of women.

'You seem very troubled,' said Flora.

'I am sorry,' said Frances, 'I know I am tiring you with too many questions. And sometimes I find that the most tiring thing is the answers.' She rose to leave.

'But Miss Doughty, you haven't told me —,'

'And there are things that *you* have not told me,' said Frances, 'so I know that you will understand.'

❧

There was, thought Frances, as she made her way home, only one circumstance that explained both the abrupt removal of Selina abroad for several months and the impossible fiction that Horace was the son of Agnes Matthews. Horace was undoubtedly a Matthews, but not, as she had at first supposed, because Roderick was his father but because Selina, who had inherited her father's height and colouring, was his mother. In March 1873, sixteen-year-old Selina, knowing that she could not hide her shameful plight much longer, must have confessed all to her father, and named the author of her shame as Daniel Souter.

Matthews would not have countenanced for a moment the public exposure that would have resulted had the culprit been arrested and brought to trial, but neither could he have tolerated leaving the crime unpunished, and the criminal free to tell his secrets. Frances could picture the stricken and agitated father, a man unused to physical confrontation, holding the ornamental pistol in trembling hands, shooting Daniel Souter in the back, wounding but not killing him, and Jenkins coolly finishing the task.

Chapter Twenty-Two

Frances had by now become a regular reader of the *Illustrated Police News* and the town edition issued that Thursday did not disappoint her. Engraved across the front page in large letters were the words 'Disgraceful Scenes at Election Meeting in Bayswater', and there was a very detailed picture of the turmoil inside Westbourne Hall with broken furniture sailing through the air, and a surging mass of bodies. Much comic effect had been produced by featuring a stout lady brandishing a women's suffrage poster in one fist and giving a man a black eye with the other. Frances especially admired the excellent likenesses of Bartholomew Paskall and Mr Matthews, both looking very afraid and running down the street away from the angry mob. A small and less well executed picture at the bottom of the page was captioned 'Cowardly Attack in Fulham'. Flora, whose bosom as imagined by the artist was rather more prominent than it was in life, was shown cowering on the parlour floor, while a hideous scoundrel hovered over her wielding a cudgel. The accompanying article consisted of short paragraphs copied from the daily papers, saying simply that a woman had been found unconscious after surprising a burglar, and could recall nothing of the incident.

What edifying pictures might she anticipate in future editions, Frances wondered. Roderick Matthews ruminating on his sins in a police cell. Matthews in the dock of the Old Bailey. Matthews on the scaffold. Somehow she doubted it. It was not so much that she felt unable to find proof of his guilt, but that the proof itself might not exist. She consoled herself with the fact that if he was, as she suspected, guilty, he would eventually pay for his crimes, and in a more terrible place than Newgate Prison enduring ministrations far less humane than those of Mr Marwood.

Frances tried to imagine the terrible scene in which Selina had confessed her shame. A girl in such a situation would not, she thought, as a first instance ever consider going to her father, even if eventually driven by necessity to do so. A mother would have been the natural choice, but for Selina that was not possible, and she had no older sister. That led Frances to wonder if Selina had confessed to another person first, someone she might have regarded in a similar light as a mother, someone who might offer sympathy, advice and help. There was one obvious mother figure – Mrs Venn. And there was another person who might have known, not by being told, but who might have guessed because she was a mother herself and would have recognised the early signs – Matilda. Had Matilda been blackmailing Selina? The maidservant had not seen Selina since she had left the school, but Selina's new position as patroness and her visits to award prizes and sell lace at the bazaar had brought them back into contact. Was it Selina who had provided the £20 as the price for Matilda's silence? Whatever Selina's youthful failings, Frances did not see her as a murderess, especially as she was protecting an unborn child.

It was while she was engrossed in these less than wholesome thoughts that Cedric called for Frances quite unannounced and declared that he would like nothing better than to take a turn along Westbourne Grove, which he said was becoming the most fashionable promenade in London. The West End was too *passé*, too serious; only the Grove answered all the requirements of an elegant and adventurous man about town. Frances did not especially want to go on a frivolous tour of the shops, especially as there was nothing she wished to purchase, but allowed herself to be persuaded. For Frances to go out required only that she put on a coat and bonnet but Cedric needed several minutes in front of the mirror, surveying his form from every possible angle, whether it was convenient or not. Finally he pinched his cheeks and pronounced himself ready.

'You should go out in society more, my dear Frank,' said Cedric as they strolled arm-in-arm. 'We make a wonderful couple. You would sting with your intelligence and I would astonish with my golden hair. The world would be at our feet – or Bayswater at least, which is the only part of it that counts.'

'Oh I shall be going out this evening to the society event of the year,' said Frances teasingly. 'Everyone who is anyone will be there, I am told. You should come, it will be very shocking.'

'Shocking? How interesting! Will there be dancing girls – or better still, boys?'

'I expect fisticuffs at the very least.'

'Oh, so I expect you are taking your pugilistic lady friend. There are backroom mills where she could earn a good purse. But do tell me more.'

Frances explained about the public meeting at the Great Western Hotel, and Cedric admitted that it could supply a pleasing antidote to the boredom he often experienced when five minutes passed in which nothing sensational had occurred.

'It starts at six o'clock prompt,' said Frances.

'Perfect!' exclaimed Cedric. 'It will fill those disappointing hours between tea time and dinner.'

'But there is something you might do for me,' said Frances. 'Could you write to Freddie Matthews and ask if he would correspond with me? There are a number of questions I would like to ask him, albeit of a somewhat delicate nature.'

'I am afraid I cannot comply with your wish,' said Cedric solemnly.

'Oh!' said Frances, disappointed. 'Well, if that is the case . . .'

'You misunderstand. There is no point in my writing to Freddie as he is newly arrived in London on business, although I understand and indeed earnestly hope that pleasure is also to be involved. He is even now at a tailor's being measured for several suits at once in which I anticipate he will take the capital by storm. He is staying with me. Whatever indelicacies you wish to whisper in his ear you may do for yourself.'

Frances left Cedric in Whiteleys, agonising over the choice of a new cravat, and returned home to find that a messenger had brought a reply to the note she had sent Mrs Venn, from which she learned that the headmistress would be at home receiving visitors that morning. Frances went to the school with some trepidation, since the original purpose of the suggested visit had been to offer some friendly comfort and she now had quite another mission.

Mrs Venn was in her study and appeared, under the circumstances, to be remarkably calm. It was as if the explosion of rancor that had fallen upon her had, now that the event had actually happened, alleviated the stress of anticipation. She was at her desk with a heap of papers in front of her, including letters from Mr Rawsthorne, and insurance documents from Paskall & Son.

'So many things to take care of,' the lady said with a sigh, although Frances detected that Mrs Venn was happier for being busy, 'so much to do, but if I am to resign my post, as I fear will be necessary, then I wish to leave everything in the most perfect order for my successor. I trust and hope that it will be Miss Baverstock who is approved, but of course I can have no say in that.'

Frances hesitated, as there was some difficulty about the question she was about to ask. 'Mrs Venn, there is a matter of some delicacy I feel it necessary to discuss with you.'

The headmistress smiled. 'Oh, do not be reticent, Miss Doughty, it seems to me that in the past weeks we have talked almost exclusively about matters of that nature.'

'I fear that is true,' said Frances regretfully, 'and I do hope that a time may come when we may meet and talk of happier things. There is no easy method of introducing this subject, so I will be direct. I have a question for you about Mrs Sandcourt – or Selina Matthews as she was when a pupil here.'

There was no change in the headmistress's expression, as there might be no change on a man's face who was about to be shot, and was making a brave thing of it.

Emboldened, Frances pressed on. 'Did she, perhaps during the early part of 1873, shortly before the family departed for Italy, come to you for advice on a personal concern? The kind of advice that she would, under other circumstances, have sought from her mother? I must assure you,' added Frances, 'that I have no wish to make public anything you might say.'

Mrs Venn took a long time to form a reply. 'I cannot imagine what has prompted you to ask that question,' she said at last, 'but of course I believe you would never have broached such a subject unless you already knew or suspected what my answer would be.'

'Then I am correct,' said Frances. 'Can you tell me what your advice was?'

Mrs Venn gazed back at her in wonderment and more than a hint of admiration. 'You are the most extraordinary young woman,' she said. 'You seem to take in your stride things that another of your tender years might feel faint just to hear mentioned.'

'That may be true,' said Frances. 'I never had the guidance of a mother, only an aunt who saw me fed and clothed and little else. I had a brief schooling and thereafter educated myself. I never moved in society, to be told what to think, to make myself presentable. My thoughts, such as they are, are my own.'

'Your very presence in this room, your character and address and words challenge all that I have ever believed about the education of girls,' said Mrs Venn.

'But you educate them to be married,' said Frances, 'not to ask questions, which you then try to avoid answering.'

Mrs Venn gave a light laugh. 'That is true. Well, Miss Doughty, the answer is that my first action was to call Dr Montgomery, whom I knew to be discreet, as I thought it possible that the girl was mistaken. I had hoped he would reassure her and the matter would go no further. Unfortunately he only confirmed her fears. I advised her to go and see her father and tell him the truth. She was terrified, of course, so I agreed to go with her. His reaction I am sure you may imagine.'

'Did Mrs Sandcourt reveal the name of any individual?' asked Frances.

'Her father naturally demanded it, and she did mention a name, but I am quite unable to recall it after so long. It was not a name that was known to me.'

'Was this a person who lived at Havenhill?'

'I believe so. Mr Matthews, on first hearing the news, suggested that I had failed in my duty of care – indeed he threatened to have me removed from the school, but Mrs Sandcourt said that the school was not in any way to blame. She said something about a festivity at Havenhill which had been attended by the whole family. Mr Matthews' expression when he saw that the failure of care was his and not mine, was a picture I shall never forget.'

Frances nodded. 'Was Matilda at the school then?'

'Yes, I believe she had not long returned to her position after the birth of her daughter.'

'I assume that Mr Sandcourt knows nothing of these events.'

'In all probability. I think that such a man might be prepared to forgive a pretty young wife, but I doubt that she would wish to test that assumption. He is, however, a man of the world. I do recall hearing a rumour that Mrs Sandcourt had been briefly married while in Italy, no doubt a fiction to persuade Mr Sandcourt that his bride was a widow and not a spinster.'

'Have you ever seen the boy – he is called Horace.'

'No, I have not. It would hardly be appropriate for Mrs Sandcourt to bring him here.'

'I saw him when I chanced to meet the family out walking in Hyde Park,' said Frances.

'Chanced,' said Mrs Venn, nodding. 'Do you rely on chance a great deal?'

'It has its uses,' Frances admitted. 'I think the boy will be a credit to the family. He is a true Matthews, tall and dark-haired and with a very intelligent, thoughtful look about him. He will be a great man of business some day, or a politician or a scholar.'

It was as those words left her lips that Frances realised in a great explosion of thought what she had failed to observe earlier. Her gaze moved to the pictures displayed on the wall of the study and she was both shocked and disgusted when she saw that she was right, and knew what it meant.

'Miss Doughty?' asked the headmistress anxiously.

Frances, almost numb with dismay, rose to her feet. 'I – have just recalled something I had forgotten and must take my leave of you. Forgive me for this sudden departure.'

'Not at all.' Mrs Venn rose and proffered her hand. 'When this is all settled I will write and let you know where I am living and we will take tea.'

'Oh, I hope we might!' said Frances.

She hurried away, this time her steps taking her in the direction of the Matthews' townhouse.

The maid was astonished to see her standing on the doorstep in a state of some emotion. 'Master is out,' she said.

'It is not him I wish to see, but Miss Lydia,' said Frances. 'Is she at home?'

She could hear in the distance the sound of a very fine piano being played very badly. 'Miss Lydia is taking a music lesson,' said the maid, unnecessarily. A reedy voice began to commit a crime of violence on a sentimental song.

'You will not, I think, mind my interrupting,' said Frances, walking in and heading down the hallway.

'Oh but —,' exclaimed the maid, scurrying after her.

It was not difficult to locate the source of the noise and Frances threw open a door, behind which she found a beautifully appointed drawing room. Lydia sat at the piano and beside her a lady teacher, with a fixed expression of great patience not unmingled with pain.

'What is this?' exclaimed Lydia, turning to view the intruder. 'How dare you force your way in here!'

'I need to speak to you,' said Frances. 'Privately.'

'This is outrageous! I will inform my father!'

'Oh, I think he will know about this without your assistance very soon,' said Frances.

The music teacher rose. 'I will return tomorrow,' she said, nervously.

'But my lesson!' protested Lydia.

'The world of music can wait a little longer,' said Frances as the teacher, with a look of fright, hurried away.

Lydia almost jumped to her feet. 'I will call a footman and have you escorted from the house,' she said, flushing with the expectation of excitement.

'Oh, but aren't you even a little bit curious about what I might have to say?'

Lydia hesitated and her mouth twitched. 'Really, Miss Doughty, do you take me for a common gossip?'

'As a matter of fact,' said Frances, sitting down, 'I do.'

Lydia gasped. She had been reaching for a bell-pull but withdrew her hand and sat down again. 'Very well, say your piece and begone, but you will not hear the last of this!'

'When we last spoke you mentioned a meeting with Matilda Springett. You said that she had made some impertinent comments about Horace.'

'And what of it?'

'You did not say what those comments were.'

Lydia snorted. 'They were scarcely important, and indeed hardly comprehensible. It was a stupid incident and I did not note it.'

'I think you did and I will not leave until you tell me,' said Frances.

'It meant nothing!' insisted Lydia. 'Selina said that the girl was quite addled in the head and she had to humour her or she might have had a brainstorm.'

'Then it must have been memorable,' said Frances.

'Oh very well,' said Lydia reluctantly. 'I recall that she praised Horace, saying he had a very intelligent look, or some such words. Then she said that his mother must be very proud of him – which only shows the girl's ignorance as the boy has no mother – but I saw no point in correcting her.'

'But Mrs Sandcourt spoke to her?'

'The girl said some nonsense about how there were twenty good reasons to be proud of him and she thought there would be more in future. Selina said she thought there might be fifty, and the girl said *she* thought more nearly a hundred. It was like some stupid parlour game.'

Or, thought Frances, the negotiation of blackmail. 'And was that all?'

'I believe so.'

'And the words that Matilda used – that the boy had an intelligent look – were those her actual words?'

Lydia grimaced at having to soil her lips with a common expression, an action that neither enhanced not detracted from her natural beauty. 'I think she said he looked like a proper little Professor.'

Later that afternoon Frances was preparing to go to the meeting at the Great Western Hotel when Jonathon Quayle arrived in a very distressed state.

'Oh Miss Doughty – is Flora with you?'

'No, I have not seen her since my visit yesterday. Is she not at home?'

'Oh dear, oh dear!' he exclaimed, 'I don't know what to do! She seemed so very much better this morning – quite her old self – indeed more than her old self if you see what I mean, but then she read the newspapers and became very excited and rushed out and we have not seen her since. I thought she might have come to see you.'

'I am afraid not. But does she know of the meeting at Paddington?'

'Of course, but she would scarcely have gone there, it is hardly the kind of event she would choose to attend. She is such a timid soul.'

'There will be a great many people there, most of them connected in some way with her old school,' Frances observed. 'Perhaps if you were to go you might find someone who knows where she is. I am taking a cab – you may come with me.'

'I will do that,' he said, 'but if I learn nothing I will alert the police.'

They were about to depart when a letter arrived postmarked Hillingdon, and Frances opened it. It was from Mary Ann Dunn and she read it eagerly. 'Wonderful!' she exclaimed. She thrust the paper and some coins into Sarah's hands. 'Sarah, I want you to hire a cab and go to the address in this letter. You must fetch Daisy Trent – admit of no denial – and take her *at once* to the meeting at the Great Western Hotel.'

CHAPTER TWENTY-THREE

As the cab rattled its way towards Praed Street Jonathan Quayle, almost hysterical with anxiety, enumerated all the places he had been to in search of Flora. 'I tried all the neighbours first, but none of them had seen her, and Mrs Gribling's house, and then I wondered if she had gone to Miss Gilbert and Miss John and so I went there, but they were out and the maid on a half day holiday. And then I thought, of course I am being very foolish, it was something in the *newspaper* that alarmed her, although whether that would have sent her *to* a place or *from* a place, I really didn't know.' He pulled a crumpled copy of the *Illustrated Police News* from his pocket and stared helplessly at the front page. 'I looked at all the pictures and I didn't know what to think, so I tried as many things as I could − I went to Westbourne Hall, but that was boarded up, and the school but they were closed. Mr Paskall's office, only he was out of course, but the young gentleman was very sympathetic and said if anyone of Flora's description came there he would alert Mrs Gribling at once. And then of course I thought she might have come to you.'

'Did she seem afraid when she ran out?'

'No,' he said, with a puzzled look, 'and that is the strangest thing. For the first time since I have known her she didn't look afraid. She seemed − I suppose I would say that she seemed determined.'

Frances considered the possibilities. 'Did the suffrage society hold a meeting today?' she asked.

'I am not sure.'

'Does Mrs Quayle receive literature from the society?'

He nodded emphatically. 'Yes, she does, very often, and reads it with great attention.'

'Then,' said Frances, 'if there is a meeting today she would have known about it and might have gone to the place where it was being held. And Miss Gilbert and Miss John would be there and not at home.'

'Oh – I didn't think of that!' he said, brightening. 'Yes, of course, you may be right.'

'Do you know where they hold their meetings?'

'There are many halls in Bayswater which they might have used, depending on the numbers expected.'

'If she is with those ladies she will be quite safe,' Frances reassured him.

He mopped his brow with a handkerchief. 'I did learn one thing before Flora ran away. She said she wanted to confess everything to me, so that we might have no secrets. It seems that she is the author of the pamphlet you came asking about. I was very surprised as she has never done anything like this before, and she told me all about how she came to write it. And of course it is those very pamphlets which have caused all the excitement at the school.'

'Did she tell you who took them to the school?'

'Yes, it appears that it was Mrs Sandcourt.'

'Mrs Sandcourt?' said Frances, with very great surprise.

'Flora told me that they had been corresponding using Mrs Gribling's address, although she was careful to maintain the impression that she was living abroad. It was Flora and Mrs Sandcourt, who thought of the plan to write the pamphlets. Mrs Gribling had them printed and then delivered them to Mrs Sandcourt who took them to the school.'

'However did the correspondence commence?' asked Frances. 'And why? I don't believe they were very great friends at school.'

'Mrs Sandcourt chanced to meet Mrs Gribling at the Christmas bazaar and asked if she could write to Flora. Flora said she hoped that because Mrs Sandcourt was so often there as a patron she could give her news of her cousin Wilhelmina, who is still there.'

Frances recalled that at the bazaar Mrs Venn had approached Mrs Gribling under her previous name of Clare. Selina must have overheard this and taken the opportunity to make her acquaintance. But why, she wondered, had Selina wanted to start a correspondence with Flora? Was she trying on her father's behalf to trace the elusive Caroline Clare? Had she known of the secret wedding? And while Frances knew why Flora would want to distribute the pamphlets she could not understand why Selina, as a patroness of the school, would connive at any action that might bring the establishment into disrepute.

As they reached the hotel it appeared that the prospect of the meeting had excited all the citizens of Bayswater – either that or they had sensed that some free entertainment might be on offer – and the street was almost choked with carriages and cabs, while omnibuses were being brought to a halt and men on laden dreys with goods to deliver were rapidly losing patience with the crowds and each other. Anyone who had an opinion on anything had decided that this was a good place to be. There were groups of Liberals and Conservatives getting up little meetings, and the temperance society was trying to persuade passers-by to sign the pledge. A small party of anti-vivisectionists were carrying placards and shouting out their appeals, and one had a large board with a chalked message urging people of the good sense of vegetarianism. A lady was scurrying about pushing pamphlets into people's hands, denouncing the dangerous practice of vaccination, while a lone man paraded grimly up and down with a placard complaining about Mr Whiteley's new building in Queen's Road, which was obscuring its neighbour's light.

Frances and Quayle left the cab and somehow inserted themselves into the throng, looking about for Flora, but it was hard to discern anyone in the great crush of people.

Vendors were everywhere, with newspapers, pamphlets, matches, flowers, buns, pies, and fruit. As the crowd grew so it attracted still more people, who swarmed like flies around a nutritious piece of meat; singers, jugglers, beggars, people with some novelty to display. They appeared to come out of nowhere but most probably spent a great deal of their day lurking around Paddington station, and they had all suddenly seen the excitement and descended on the one spot. Tom was there, his buttons so shiny they almost glittered, offering to carry messages and parcels, and Frances also spotted Chas and Barstie, who appeared to be doing nothing at all other than watch the scene with enormous satisfaction. She greeted them and they doffed their hats with great gallantry.

'Are you overseeing Mr Paskall's interests?' asked Frances.

'His and others,' admitted Chas.

A cab drew up at speed and Theodore, looking very anxious and so engrossed in his own concerns that he noticed no one else, jumped out and hurried into the hotel.

'Now that is curious,' said Barstie. 'Son not minding the shop for his father. I wonder what he's about?'

'Running from the amorous designs of Lydia Matthews, perhaps,' said Frances. 'If the fathers hope to make a match there, I think they will be disappointed.'

'Oh I found out that that was never a match,' said Barstie. 'Something else was in the wind, but I never heard what.'

A person in motley danced by to the tune of a tin whistle. 'Well,' said Frances, 'it is quite a carnival. It lacks only a brass band.'

The words were no sooner spoken when she heard the rhythmic thudding of a drum, coming from the direction of Craven Road. There were three firm beats, a pause, then three more, followed by a regular continuous pounding which, judging by its increasing volume, was drawing closer. As she looked about for the approaching musicians, there began a sound that Frances had never heard before, like a hundred insects all loudly buzzing in tune, to be joined almost immediately by the voices of women raised in song. Marching towards her down the middle of the street were the ladies of the Bayswater Women's Suffrage Society, arrayed in their purple sashes. Some were singing a rousing melody called 'Women of England Unite!' – some, with puffed cheeks and red faces, were blowing heartily on instruments like flattened metal pipes. Miss John had outdone herself with a new banner, a pure white silken flutter almost the width of the street, with the name of the society stitched in glowing scarlet and she and Miss John supported it on either side with tall poles, so it paraded almost ten feet above the ground. Leading the company, her bandaged head held high, was the proud and valiant figure of Flora Quayle, beating a drum.

'Oh – my – good – Lord!' exclaimed that lady's adoring husband. 'My darling girl! Oh, she is a miracle!'

Carriages continued to arrive, and Frances saw in quick succession Cedric handing down an auburn-haired youth, a sunburnt gentleman she guessed was Mr Younge, then Mr Miggs, swollen with his own importance, brandishing his silver case which clicked and snapped as he distributed his little white cards to anyone who would take one. It was as she watched him that the unresolved thought that had been sitting at the back of Frances' mind came up polished and complete, and she determined that as soon as the meeting was over she would write to Inspector Eaves of the Hillingdon police.

Miggs was soon flanked by his supporters; Mr Younge, Reverend Day – the chaplain of St Stephens Church – Dr Collin a respected Bayswater physician, and Inspector Sharrock. Frances suspected that Sharrock was there as much to see that order was kept and the law observed as any great liking for Mr Miggs. Mr Rawsthorne arrived with his clerk, and since he greeted everyone with great friendliness it was not immediately apparent for which side he was acting. Four of Sharrock's largest constables strode up, and he quickly gave them their orders before they went inside.

The great phalanx of women halted outside the hotel, the buzzing instruments – which Quayle said were an American novelty called a kazoo – continuing to accompany the song, the drum beat thumping away while the banner danced on its poles. The end of the song was met by wild cheers and a scattering of leaflets.

Quayle rushed up to Flora. 'Oh my darling, I have been so afraid for you!' he exclaimed.

Flora looked him in the eye. 'I shall never be afraid again,' she declared.

He touched her hand appealingly. 'And will you come home, now, my dear?'

'When the meeting is over we will march home together,' she said.

Quayle, who would have denied her nothing she asked at that moment, nodded and kissed her flushed cheeks. Frances felt sure that he would remain outside with her.

She turned to see if Chas and Barstie were about to join the crowds who had started flowing into the hotel for the meeting, but found that they had both vanished. She looked about her and saw something – a shadow at the corner of the street – a stain of dark grease by the wall, the flash of a knife and the hint of a broken-toothed grin. It was the Filleter. In the next moment, he was gone.

Frances hurried indoors, where anxious commissionaires were directing everyone through a handsome high ceilinged foyer past large rooms from which the scent of tea and coffee wafted tantalizingly, and the murmur of polite conversation muffled by pastries and self-satisfaction told of another life that might be lived. They were shown to a room with seating for about a hundred persons, which soon became uncomfortably packed. At one end was a row of three tables. Miggs and his supporters sat on one side of the room and Mrs Venn and the three governors on the other. Between them was Mr Flood, an auctioneer by trade, whose extensive experience on the Paddington vestry – a group of gentlemen whose discussions often led to some conflict and comments of a personal nature – it was hoped would enable him to keep the meeting civil. Nevertheless, Sharrock was taking no chances and had stationed his constables about the perimeter of the room.

With the chattering assembly in their places, some seated and some being obliged to stand at the back, Mr Flood gave a firm and authoritative tap of his gavel and called the meeting to order. There was an obedient hush and he proceeded to intro-duce those on either side of him. 'I also see in front of me many ladies who have been pupils at the school, and are now pleased to be its patrons, as well as parents of past and present pupils, and the current teaching staff.'

'Not *all* of the teaching staff,' said Miggs pointedly, and a titter went around the room.

'Everyone who wishes to make a statement will have ample opportunity to do so,' said Mr Flood. 'I would like to begin by calling upon Mr Miggs to say a few words about the reasons for his dissatisfaction with the arrangements at the Bayswater Academy.'

Mr Miggs rose and surveyed his audience with an unat-tractive smile and Frances thought for an unpleasant moment that he might begin by reciting a poem, but, fortunately for the assembled company, he did not. 'My friends,' he said, 'I have brought you all together to address a matter of very grave concern. It will not have escaped your notice that there have been rumours afoot lately that reading matter of an unsuitable nature has been distributed to the innocent young girls of Mrs Venn's academy. Many of us who know and respect the lady will have dismissed the charge as the fiction of a jealous rival. Some will have satisfied themselves that the report was in error, or that the material, if it existed at all, was not as dangerous as supposed. I have to inform you that I, through my own efforts, have succeeded where all others have failed and obtained a copy of this item of literature, and today I can advise you that it is very much worse than even I had feared.'

There was the sound of a number of gasping intakes of breath. 'But I do not ask you to accept my unsupported word.' He took a copy of the pamphlet from his pocket and placed it on the table before him. A few heads on the front row craned forward to try and read the words. 'I hope you will be able to make your own judgement. I propose to read it aloud.'

Mr Flood cleared his throat and tapped his gavel again as the audience muttered excitedly. 'While I cannot prevent Mr Miggs from reading the item, I would like to remind him that Inspector Sharrock will be exercising his judgement as to the legality of the proceeding. I also suggest that any ladies present, if they do not wish to be offended, should now take the opportunity to retire.'

There was a brief pause during which the ladies had to decide whether they were motivated more by the need to demonstrate their moral superiority or by curiosity. It was a difficult choice, and apart from one or two venerable matrons regaled in fur and Parisian hats, who rose from their chairs and made a great show of leaving the room with self-conscious dignity, curiosity won.

'Very well,' said Miggs, 'I will proceed.'

Frances saw Mrs Venn grow pale. Her hands were resting on the table in front of her and one was very tightly gripping the other. Frances thought that this ordeal was too much for any individual to bear, and decided that before anything was said, she must appeal to the meeting and ask if at the very least the pamphlet could be studied in private.

'The title of the pamphlet —,' began Miggs as Frances was preparing to rise to her feet and make her plea, but both were interrupted by the loud boom of a drum from inside the hall. While every eye had been turned towards Miggs two more people had entered the room; Jonathan Quayle, who was now carrying the drum, and Flora, who was holding the two poles of the Suffrage Society's banner, one in either hand. Such was the length of the strip of silk that it might have trailed on the floor behind her so she had wound it about her slim waist, and held the two poles so that the white fabric with its red embroidery rose from her high on either side. Her long golden hair was streaming loose and the bandage was a halo around her head. She looked like an angel with bloodstained wings.

As Jonathan stayed at the back of the room, Flora, marching to the beat of the drum, advanced down the aisle between the rows of seats to the front, and so startling was her appearance that the occupants of the room, mesmerized by the apparition, said and did nothing until she paused in front of Mr Flood. The drumbeat stopped.

Sharrock rose from his seat, his eyes upon his constables, ready to instruct them if required.

Matthews gazed on Flora with some discomfort, and then he leaned to one side and had a whispered word with Flood, who nodded. Beside him, Paskall, paralyzed with horror, stared at the angelic figure as if she was a demon conjured up from the depths on purpose to torment him.

'Young lady,' said Mr Flood kindly, 'I am afraid you may not be in the best place to make your exhibition. Might I ask you to withdraw?'

'No,' said Flora, 'because I have something to say, and I *will* be heard!'

Flood glanced at Sharrock and shook his head. 'I really think, Inspector —'

'This can have nothing to do with our business here,' said Miggs. 'I suggest she be removed and her family advised to look after her better.'

It was the moment in which the game could be lost or won. As Sharrock made to signal his constables, Frances stood up. 'Allow me to ask that this lady be permitted to speak. Inspector – you know I would not lightly make such a request.'

'Let her speak!' came a voice from the back of the hall, which sounded like Cedric's.

'Yes, let the lady speak!' came another voice and then another, and eventually by popular demand, Flora faced the crowd. Sharrock shrugged and sat down. Matthews was staring at the floor, his expression dark as a thundercloud, while Paskall squirmed in his seat and looked as if he was about to run away.

'This man,' said Flora, pointing a wing at Matthews, 'was once my guardian. I was entrusted to his care by a cousin, and he repaid that honourable duty by making an assault on my virtue!'

There were little cries of horror from the crowded room. 'The woman is obviously mad,' growled Matthews.

'But *were* you her guardian?' asked Flood and Matthews grudgingly gave a sharp nod. Flood motioned Flora to continue.

'When I resisted him, he offered me marriage,' said Flora, 'and as I was young and ignorant, I accepted. A wedding took place, one which I believed at the time to be lawful, but I have since found that it was a sham, devised only that he might achieve his reprehensible purpose, and that the clergyman was no clergyman at all, but a friend of his who connived at the foul plot.'

'You can't prove that,' said Matthews. 'Really, how long must I tolerate this attack on my character?'

Theodore, who had been lurking at the back of the room, hurried forward and addressed Mr Flood. 'I beg of you, stop this charade at once! Can you not see that this unfortunate young woman has suffered a violent injury to her head? If she was to be examined by a physician it would be apparent that her memory is disarranged, and nothing she says is to be trusted. Dr Collin, please could you see that this unhappy female is removed to some secure place where she can be cared for. It would be the kindest thing.'

'I am not so sure,' said Dr Collin, drily, 'that your father does not also require some attention.'

Bartholomew Paskall was cowering in his seat, his whole body shaking in fright. 'That is the man!' cried Flora. 'The false clergyman. I did not know who he was until today, when I saw his portrait in the newspaper, and now I see him again in the flesh, I know him without any doubt.'

The room erupted with exclamations and Flood hammered with his gavel. At last the tumult subsided.

'Mr Paskall?' said Flood, but the aspiring Member of Parliament, looking as though he was about to suffer a fit, was unable to speak. 'Young lady,' said the chairman, 'do you have any proof of these allegations?'

'Of course she doesn't,' said Theodore. 'Would you believe her unsupported word against that of my father? A poor lunatic who has had her brains stirred with a poker and no more memory of what happened to her than a new-born baby?'

Flora gazed at him calmly. 'Oh, but my memory is clear again. I remember everything. I remember when you came to my door last Monday and I admitted you because your face looked familiar to me. I thought at first that you were the man who had performed the marriage and you would be able to answer all my questions, but then I saw that you were too young. And that was when you struck me down.'

In the middle of a fresh tumult, Jonathan Quayle threw his drum aside, bunched his fists, and ran up to confront Theodore, but two burly policemen seized the anguished husband before another crime could be committed, and Frances got to Theodore first. He was backing away from the struggle, sweating with agitation and there was a dangerous light in his eyes. Theodore, thought Frances, who would do anything to protect his father, who had been alerted to Flora's disappearance by Jonathan Quayle's frantic searches and who had abandoned his work to hurry to the meeting and prevent just such a scene as this.

'Perhaps you would like to explain how you know that Mrs Quayle was struck with a poker?' she asked.

'Whatever do you mean?' demanded Theodore. 'Everyone knows it. It was in the newspapers.' There was another outburst of discussion in the hall, and Frances took the folded copy of the *Illustrated Police News* from Jonathan Quayle's pocket and handed it to Mr Flood.

'No one knew it except the police and the family and the man who attacked her,' said Frances. 'You wanted to silence her, didn't you, so she would not reveal your father's crime.'

'It wasn't a crime!' squeaked Paskall. 'It was a joke, that was all, a masquerade. We had many a jape when we were schoolboys together. I thought he would tell her afterwards and then do the honest thing, but . . .'

'You fool!' bellowed Matthews.

'I suggest,' said Inspector Sharrock, holding up his hands for quiet, 'that this is a discussion best continued at the station.' He signaled two more constables to apprehend Theodore. 'Best to come quietly, Sir,' he advised.

Theodore stared about him and as the ponderous officers of the law advanced towards him, he made a run for the door. The men holding Quayle dropped the poet and charged after him, but he was slender and fleet of foot, dodging around chairs, and pushing startled people aside, until suddenly he tripped and fell headlong, his legs tangled in Cedric's best silver-topped walking cane. He was at once seized and hauled to his feet.

'Bring him here,' said Sharrock, and Theodore was dragged forward. 'Now young lady, are you prepared to swear that this was the man who attacked you?'

'I am,' said Flora.

'Well,' said Sharrock, 'I am very glad that I thought to bring four constables. I think we can safely say that the meeting is over.'

'But what about —,' demanded Miggs, waving the pamphlet.

'Oh we can leave that particular piece of nastiness for another day.' Sharrock dispatched one of his men to hire a four-wheeler. 'I just hope Paddington has enough upper-crust cells. Mr Matthews, Mr Paskall senior, you'll both have to come with me as well.'

'I really can't see why a harmless peccadillo is treated with such seriousness,' Matthews protested.

'Harmless, Mr Matthews?' growled Sharrock fiercely. 'The young lady doesn't seem to think so. And no father of daughters would either.'

'I have more to say,' said Flora, but there was such a buzz around the room that she could hardly be heard, and all eyes were on the three prisoners being removed. Frances ran forward, snatched the gavel from an astonished Mr Flood, and banged it until everyone was silent.

'This man is worse than you can imagine,' said Flora, pointing at Matthews again. 'I fled from his house in terror because I found that he was a murderer.'

Matthews rolled his eyes. 'Idle gossip of foolish country folk and the ravings of an imbecile,' he announced. A constable had his elbow but he was able to stab an angry finger at Flora. 'Another word and you will be sued for slander. '

'There is a witness,' said Frances.

He turned to her, 'Oh, *really*? Well I don't see one!'

'Daisy Trent.'

He laughed contemptuously. 'That is your witness? She is *insane*!'

'She is here,' said a voice from the back of the hall.

Everyone turned to look. Sarah had just arrived, and beside her stood a young woman clad in the sombre habit of a nun. 'I was once Daisy Trent,' she said, 'and betrothed to a good man whom this man murdered. I am now Sister Evangeline of the Church of St Augustine, Kilburn.' She walked forward and placed one hand on Flora's. 'My poor dear friend,' she said. 'I know that you have suffered, but with justice comes an end to suffering. I have told my story many times, and never been believed.' She turned to Sharrock. 'Inspector, if I was to tell you all I know, would you listen to me?'

'I wouldn't miss it for the *world*!' said Sharrock. He looked at Frances. 'This is your doing, isn't it? I can tell. Other stations get nice simple crimes, I get bamboozlement and you!' He started to sneeze. 'I think I need another cab!'

The prisoners were led away, although in Theodore's case he was half dragged. As he passed by Selina Sandcourt his eyes turned to her, and Frances saw that the young woman was staring at him in a very direct manner, with a look that seemed to be either asking or demanding. She placed a finger to her lips and the other hand lay in a graceful gesture, her fingertips resting on her abdomen. He nodded and was taken away.

Frances did not know if anyone else saw that rapid exchange, but it told her more than she could absorb for the moment. Theodore and Selina – not merely known to each other but so close that they could speak without words.

As the crowds filed out, already honing their gossip, and reporters hastened back to their offices with the news, Frances could only stand by and watch as Mrs Venn was comforted by Miss Baverstock and Mrs Fiske. The headmistress had been spared the humiliation of having the pamphlet read out in public, but with the arrest of two of the school governors the Academy's days were at an end. Poor Mrs Venn, thought Frances, had only wanted to be useful to society, both protecting and educating girls, and now she would never again be entrusted to do either, or see her labours bear fruit under another's care.

Freddie Matthews was looking dejected as Cedric introduced him to Frances. 'I know that father will be getting what he deserves,' he said, 'and it's time he did. I am only relieved that it did not come about through my actions.'

'May I ask you something?' said Frances. 'Did Mrs Sandcourt ever tell you her secret? I am speaking of Horace.'

'I don't know how you could have found that out,' said Freddie, astonished.

'Oh Miss Doughty is the *nonpareil* of finding things out,' said Cedric. 'Beware or she will tell you things about yourself that even *you* did not suspect!'

Freddie blinked at Frances in some alarm. 'Well, yes, she did tell me.'

'And did she mention the name Daniel Souter?'

He nodded. 'But I was not sure at first if I could believe her.'

'Oh? Why not?'

He hesitated. 'It was at the harvest festival the year before. There was a dance and people of all classes of society were free to attend. I saw Selina . . . she – flirted with Daniel. She knew, even so young, that her beauty gave her power to attract or torment men. But Daniel rejected her, he said he was affianced to another and would be true to his love. Later she told father that he was the cause of her misfortune, and I suppose it must be so, for I can't imagine who else it might have been.' He sighed.

'Selina hides her nature behind an enchanting face, but when her beauty fades she will be doomed. Lydia is the lesser witch, but she makes no secret of it.'

'What happened on the night of Daniel Souter's death?' asked Frances. 'You were at Havenhill, were you not?'

He was reluctant to say more, but Cedric patted his shoulder and nodded encouragement.

'Yes,' said Freddie at last. 'Father had the strange idea of turning me into a farmer, so I was there looking after things as best I could. Then he arrived from town and I could see at once that there was something terribly wrong. I thought that mother had taken a turn for the worse, and he told me he would be taking her to Italy for her health very soon. I thought about that and decided later that night to speak to him and ask if I might go to Italy, too, but when I came downstairs I saw him in the hallway speaking with Joshua Jenkins, and he was holding the little pistol he keeps as an ornament. They went out together and I waited for him, but when he returned he looked so upset I decided to go to bed and speak to him in the morning. The next day the police came and asked us questions and father told them he had never left the house that night. I decided not to ask him about it, and I don't think he even knew I had seen him. I thought perhaps there had been an accident with the gun and it was that he was hiding and not murder. I didn't know otherwise until Selina told me her story. Father actually told her – he admitted it, and he was proud of it – that he had dealt with Daniel. But how could I go to the police and say what I had seen? I would have had to tell them about Selina and I couldn't do that.'

'It will come out, now,' said Frances, 'and you *must* go to the police.'

'Must I?' pleaded Freddie.

'You must,' said Frances. 'Daisy has told her story but it may not be enough.'

He shook his head. 'I can't,' he said. 'Father only did what had to be done. The fellow had to be punished.'

'Daniel Souter was innocent of any wrong,' said Frances. 'He was true to his love and your sister lied. Another man was the father of her child.'

Freddie groaned with despair. It was some minutes before he was able to speak, but finally he promised Frances that he would tell the police what he knew.

'Well I will get this unhappy young fellow home and apply whatever restoratives come to hand,' said Cedric. 'And I must say, Miss Doughty, you *do* put on a good show!'

There was only one person Frances now needed to speak to and that was Mrs Gribling, who was almost too busy embracing her daughter to be questioned, but Frances extracted what she had suspected to be the case, that after attending the inquest on Harry, Mrs Gribling had first called upon Flora to report on what had occurred before going to her own home.

At last the crowds were gone, and Sarah came to tell Frances that a cab was waiting for them.

Frances accompanied her outside. 'Was it very hard to persuade Daisy to come?' she asked.

'I thought I'd have to bring her in a sack,' said Sarah.

Over a late supper and a small glass of sherry Frances quietly pondered on all that she had learned, and at last committed her thoughts to paper. In time, she knew Inspector Sharrock would send for her and she would be ready for him.

CHAPTER TWENTY-FOUR

On the morning after the meeting a placard was placed outside the Bayswater Academy for the Education of Young Ladies informing the public that the school had been permanently closed and any enquiries should be addressed to Mr Rawsthorne, solicitor.

Rumours were rife around Bayswater as to the fate of the teaching staff. Mrs Venn, when representatives of the newspapers went to interview her, was nowhere to be found and it was believed she had gone to live in the country. Miss Baverstock had withdrawn into quiet retirement with an elderly sister in Norwich. Miss Bell had gone to live with a cousin, and, so it was said, was hoping to find a deserving husband as soon as possible. Mlle Girard had departed for Switzerland, where she planned to open her own school. The murder charge against Mr Copley had been withdrawn, and since he had not published his offensive drawings he did not appear to have committed any criminal offence and was, with some reluctance, released. His entire stock of art was to be destroyed, although there were whispers that items had exchanged hands in some circles for astonishing prices. He was rumoured to be about to leave the country and make his home in those districts of Paris, where it was thought his talents would be better appreciated.

The Conservative office was busy arranging for the printing of new posters and leaflets announcing that Mr Paskall was no longer to be a candidate in the General Election and that another man of unimpeachable respectability would be selected immediately. Rumblings of discontent in the neighbourhood were suggesting to interested parties that any undecided voters had, as a result of the Conservative candidate's downfall, established a new allegiance for the Liberals.

As Frances had anticipated, on the day following the meeting in the Great Western Hotel, a young constable called upon her asking if she might accompany him to Paddington Green station, where Inspector Sharrock wished to speak to her.

'I think my cold has come back,' said Inspector Sharrock hoarsely as she entered his office. Frances had prepared for this eventuality and handed him a box of lozenges. He had gulped down two of them before she could mention that he was supposed to keep them in his mouth.

In deference to her, he had had a chair emptied of debris and it had been buffed like an old shoe. She sat down while he pushed papers around his desk and stared at her disapprovingly.

'Now it has come to my attention that despite all my warnings you have been poking your nose into places you ought not,' he said, 'and I have asked you to come here so that I can make it very clear that you must stop before anything unfortunate should happen. There is work that is proper for females, and you seem to be making it your business to avoid it.'

'I *was* considering taking a post at the Academy,' Frances admitted. 'The instruction of girls is a very respectable occupation, but I am not sure that any school would accept a reference from Mrs Venn.'

Sharrock tapped his foot irritably. 'I suppose now you're going to try and make out that you're cleverer than the police, and tell me everything that's happened and why,' he grumbled.

'But that is not woman's work,' said Frances. 'Really, I wouldn't dream of it.'

'Not that I don't know all about it already, of course,' he assured her.

'I am sure you do.'

He fidgeted with a pencil. 'Well, there may be things that ladies talk about between themselves that I might not have heard, and if there were, it would be your duty to tell me.'

Frances smiled and took out her notebook.

✳

'So you're saying,' said Sharrock, some time later, 'that Mrs Sandcourt is the mother and not the sister of the youngest Matthews lad?'

'Yes,' said Frances. 'There was an unfortunate liaison with Professor Venn. She chose, however, to blame a servant, Daniel Souter, not because of any loyalty to Mrs Venn but because the young man had resisted her blandishments for love of his sweetheart, Daisy. That was her revenge for being spurned.'

'A cruel revenge,' said Sharrock.

'I do not think she anticipated how far her father would go to exact his retribution. The maidservant Matilda was a mother herself by then, and recognised the signs, but soon afterwards the Matthews family went to Italy, and Matilda did not encounter Mrs Sandcourt again until she reappeared as a respectable married woman and patroness of the school. I think that Matilda demanded and got £20 as the price of her silence. Mrs Sandcourt of course cared nothing about the school, but she knew that her patronage would be endorsed by her husband and it gave her some freedom to meet with Theodore Paskall, who was her real interest. Mrs Sandcourt, being married to a much older man, no doubt looked forward to a time when she would be a very wealthy widow and then she may have hoped to marry young Mr Paskall. But I do not believe he cared for her quite as much as she cared for him. I think if you ask Mr Matthews and Mr Paskall you will find that they had thought to unite Mr Theodore to Wilhelmina Danforth to secure her fortune, which will be hers, and therefore her husband's as soon as she marries. It would also appear, from Mrs Sandcourt's great anxiety to prevent the match, that he had no great objections to this. Wilhelmina for her part would do as she was told. Only one person might have been able to sway her and that was her cousin Caroline Clare, but she had disappeared.'

'And she, you said, is Mrs Quayle?'

'Yes. Matthews engineered a sham wedding, with Mr Paskall playing the part of clergyman. Mary Ann Dunn, out of loyalty to her master, was a witness and kept the secret. Joshua Jenkins was at the point of death and I think they dressed him and carried him to the church. It was dark enough that Mrs Quayle could not see his true condition. He died only hours later. When she discovered what part her supposed husband played in the death of Daniel Souter, she ran away as soon as she was able.'

Sharrock examined some notes. 'Young Freddie Matthews has just told us that he saw his father go out with a pistol that night. He claims that until now he believed his father not to be guilty of any crime. He is lying about that of course, but I can't prove it.' He rubbed his eyes and glanced at his desk drawer, where France suspected was a flask of some medicinal beverage. 'And you say it was Mrs Quayle who wrote the pamphlets that were put in the school?'

'She was concerned that Wilhelmina, who was of marriageable age, and due to leave school, might be forced into an unwanted match for her fortune, so she asked her mother, Mrs Gribling, to go to the school bazaar to see if she could find out if her cousin was well and happy. Unexpectedly Mrs Gribling was recognised by Mrs Venn, who addressed her as Mrs Clare, not knowing that she had remarried. Mrs Sandcourt was nearby and overheard the conversation. She later spoke to Mrs Gribling and established a correspondence between herself and Mrs Quayle. She offered to pass on news about Wilhelmina, which of course was very much what Mrs Quayle wanted. It was Mrs Sandcourt who, hoping to prevent Theodore Paskall's wedding, told Mrs Quayle about the plans to marry off Wilhelmina to a fortune-hunter and asked Mrs Quayle to use her influence to prevent it.'

Sharrock scratched his head. 'And what was the maidservant's part in all this?'

'The pamphlets? Oh, none at all. But Matilda happened to meet Mrs Sandcourt and her sister Lydia and Horace while they were out walking and saw at once what she may already have suspected, that the boy was the son of Professor Venn. To anyone who knew Professor Venn or had seen his portrait the resemblance was very striking. She suggested that Mrs Sandcourt might like to pay her more – she was hoping for a £100.'

'Now you're not going to tell me that Mrs Sandcourt strangled the maid?' said Sharrock dubiously.

'No, but I think she sent her a letter making an appointment to meet her in secret.'

'Only someone else kept that appointment?'

'Yes.'

Sharrock nodded thoughtfully and looked at his notes. 'There was only one person who had no witness to his movements that night, and who had a reason to protect Mrs Sandcourt's reputation, and that was her husband,' he said. 'I had better pay him a visit.'

Frances fingered a paper in her pocket, a recent message from Tom, which she was not about to show Sharrock. 'Mr Sandcourt has interests which take him from home and which he does not divulge to his wife,' she said. 'No, I think the person Matilda met in Hyde Park was Theodore Paskall. I know that father and son often worked late in the office together and I am sure they would have stood alibi for each other if necessary. And I think that Matilda may have recognised him. Whoever killed her was someone she knew, someone she allowed to approach close to her, even when she was alone and in the dark.'

There was a pause while Sharrock suffered a coughing fit and he opened the box of lozenges again.

'Try letting the lozenge dissolve in your mouth,' urged Frances. 'It will do more good.'

He grimaced. 'That can't be right. They taste like coal tar soap.'

'If you are in the habit of eating coal tar soap then I suggest you desist,' said Frances.

He put a lozenge in his mouth with obvious distaste. 'But when had young Paskall and the maid ever met? He had nothing to do with the school.'

'Young Mr Paskall once described himself as his father's messenger boy – he had worked for him since he was sixteen and learned the business from the humblest duties upwards. The Paskalls do insurance business with the school. I think he first met Matilda when he came to the door with messages from his father. He might even have been the father of her child, although until she saw him again and realised that he was a man with some prospects in Bayswater it suited Matilda to blame that on Professor Venn and use Mrs Venn's guilt to extract money from her. I think that when Matilda recognised Mr Paskall junior, she demanded money from him too. The last thing he wanted was a scandal when his father was due to enter parliament, and he knew that Matilda was the kind of blackmailer who would be a leech upon him forever. He decided to kill her. I doubt that he would ever admit it, but you might be able to persuade Mrs Sandcourt to tell the whole story if you can promise that she will not be prosecuted. Somehow, I don't think she will be too squeamish about sacrificing him. She may not have known that he would stoop to murder – she was certainly very shocked when she learned that Matilda had been killed.'

Sharrock nodded. 'But what about the attack on Mrs Quayle – she's been hiding away for years – why try to kill her now?'

'When the body in the ditch was identified as Harry Clare, and the police came to interview Matthews, he told Paskall about what had happened – in fact I may have witnessed that conversation outside the church on the day after your visit. Mr Paskall would have panicked in case the story of his fakery was exposed, after all, neither of them had realised until then that Harry Clare even knew about the sham wedding, and neither knew if he had told anyone else about it. Paskall probably confessed what he had done to his son, who saw the chances of his father getting into parliament vanish. And of course he very much wanted that for his father, as he would then have the sole charge of the business. With that and marriage to an heiress he would have been very well placed. He didn't want to wait for Mr Sandcourt to die.'

'Young Paskall might have murdered Sandcourt,' observed Sharrock. 'Then there would have been a fine uproar!'

'As you say, the death of a wealthy man always comes under very great scrutiny,' said Frances. 'No, Mr Paskall junior was content to marry Wilhelmina. But Mrs Quayle had to be dealt with. He attended the inquest on Harry Clare, hoping she would be there. She was not, but he followed her mother, who called in on her daughter before she went home. That was how he found out where she lived. He took his chance and fortunately he did not succeed.'

'And did Matthews murder Mr Clare? Might as well hang him for one as the other if you can prove it.'

'I think,' said Frances, 'that Harry Clare did come to the manor house, and that he died there, and his body was put in the ditch. But it is quite possible that his death may have been an accident, perhaps the result of a struggle and a fall. I don't think Matthews is a man who engages in violent combat. Even his shooting of Daniel Souter was not fatal and he was very shaken by it. When he found that Clare was dead, Matthews concealed the body with the help of Mary Ann Dunn.'

'Hmmph!' said Sharrock. 'She has a lot to answer for but no court would convict her – she can always claim she was working under her master's direction.'

'It may have been the other way about,' said Frances. 'It was very striking that although nothing appeared to have been stolen from the body, such as the money or the watch, something that would have at once told the police that there had been some foul play, all the items on his person that showed he came from America such as his banknotes and invoices, were in his pocketbook and so were protected from the wet, while all the things that might have helped identify him such as his rail ticket and business cards, were loose in his pocket and soaked beyond recognition. That suggests to me that the items were deliberately arranged in that way. The loose items might even have been wetted before they were put in his pockets. The watch was not a distinctive one and quite unmarked. Neither Matthews nor Mary Ann realised its significance. There was one thing that did occur to me, however. I have observed that gentlemen who carry business cards about their person do not keep them loose in their pockets where they might become damaged. They have a little case. Maybe they even have the case engraved. But no such case was found on Harry Clare.'

Sharrock made some notes, then he threw his pencil down on the desk and sat back. 'I wonder,' he said.

'Ask and I may be able to enlighten you,' said Frances with a smile.

'Well what I am wondering is this – did Mrs Venn ever suspect that her husband was – er –more friendly than he should have been with one of the schoolgirls? I mean, a maidservant is one thing but the daughter of a gentleman is quite another, so I am told.'

'I have never asked her that,' said Frances. 'She did consider him a possible danger, which was why she had him removed to a sanatorium.'

'Where, after a few weeks, he demanded to be allowed to return to the school,' said Sharrock.

'Oh? I wasn't aware of that.'

'Yes, well you don't know everything, do you? I have recently spoken to a nurse who had charge of Professor Venn during his stay. He was doing very well, I understand, until he died suddenly. Dr Montgomery certified death as due to a sudden paralysis of the heart, but the nurse was not so sure.'

'You know, of course, the reason he was there,' said Frances.

'Oh yes, morphine addict. And on a small dose while in the sanatorium. Not enough to kill him. And I don't think he died from disease of the heart.'

'Then what do you believe the cause of death to be?'

'That is what I am intending to ask Mrs Venn,' said Sharrock. 'She walked into the station this morning and confessed to murdering him.'

Frances was permitted to speak to Mrs Venn, who maintained a perfect dignity even in her cell, sitting with a ramrod straightness that Miss Baverstock would have admired, a Bible open upon her lap.

'Did I surprise you?' she asked. 'Only you seem to have devised the truth of everything else and I had hoped that I might have been able to keep just one secret.'

'I was quite astounded,' said Frances. 'I never suspected you for a moment.'

Mrs Venn almost laughed.

'I think,' Frances said, 'that any jury will feel sympathetic towards you, and a judge also. What I mean is —'

'You mean,' said Mrs Venn calmly, 'that you do not think I will hang. I have spoken to Mr Rawsthorne and he is also of that opinion. There will be a great many years in prison, which I am told will be very harsh to begin with, but in time I hope

I may be allowed to assist with the education of the women there to better fit them for their release. I may, after all, do a great deal of good.' There was nothing, she assured Frances, that she required, neither was there any service that could be performed for her. All her affairs were in order and Matilda's £20, which she was unwilling to touch as the proceeds of blackmail, had been donated to a charity for the education of the poor. When Frances left, Mrs Venn was more content than she had ever known her.

Frances later learned that Mary Ann Dunn, when questioned by the police, had nothing to say about Daniel Souter's death, since she had, with her master's permission, been absent from the house that night tending to a sick relative in Uxbridge. Matthews had later told her that he had not left the manor house and she had seen no reason not to believe him.

On being apprised of further information, Mary Ann Dunn had asked for and been granted private interviews with both Daisy Trent and Freddie Matthews, after which she had wept a great deal. She had then made a lengthy statement to the police in which she revealed the full story of the sham wedding which had occurred as Frances had speculated, with the barely conscious Joshua Jenkins being carried to the church and propped up in a pew with cushions, and Bartholomew Paskall costumed as a clergyman. She also told of how Harry Clare had come to the manor house at the end of January demanding that Matthews give his sister freedom from the marriage. The two men had argued, but, said Mary Ann, there had been no struggle. With her own eyes she had seen Harry Clare walking away, saying that he was going to London to consult a solicitor. Roderick Matthews, she said, had seized a marble statuette and struck his visitor on the head, killing him instantly, and had then terrified her into helping him put the body where it would be assumed that death was due to a fall, arranging the contents of the pockets so the remains would not be identified, and thereafter maintaining her silence.

Matthews, on being confronted with this statement, protested that he knew nothing of Harry Clare's death and that the young man had never been to the manor house. Mary Ann, however, was able to give the police Clare's business card case, which was engraved with his name. 'Master told me to throw it away,' she said, 'but that poor young man – I couldn't help thinking – he was somebody's son. So I kept it by me, because I thought that one day his family would want to know who he was and what happened to him.' Faced with this new evidence, Matthews was obliged to admit that he had lied, and that Harry Clare had indeed arrived at the manor house and confronted him, but he now claimed that the death was an accident, resulting from a fall after a struggle in which Clare had been the aggressor, and that Mary Ann Dunn had witnessed it and could confirm that he was blameless. Mary Ann, with an implacable gleam in her eye, maintained her original story.

As a warm spring finally blossomed into life, Frances was delighted to attend a wedding, where Jonathan Quayle and Caroline Flora Clare became husband and wife, and the happy bride confessed to her with some blushes that the lawful union had not taken place a moment too soon.

A few weeks later Frances entertained a venerable old gentleman to tea.

He regarded her sorrowfully, but she thought his eyes were very kind. 'I must entreat you to abandon this life, which is neither proper nor wholesome for a female,' he said. 'You live upon the very brink of an even graver sin.'

'I have neither beauty nor fortune and so I must make my own way in the world,' said Frances. 'And I am strong. I have looked evil in the face and it has not conquered me.'

'Pardon an old man who thinks only of your welfare. I hope you pray every day for the guidance of God.'

'I do,' said Frances.

'Then you may yet be saved from the abyss.' He paused. 'I profess myself astonished at the courage and insight you have shown in exposing the outrageous activities of Mr Paskall and his friends. I am quite confident that the Liberal victory in Marylebone owes something to your actions.'

'Or perhaps even the result of the election?' suggested Frances, not a little teasingly, since the Liberals had thoroughly trounced the Conservatives and would surely have done so without her assistance.

He smiled. 'I would not go so far as that.'

'Tell me,' said Frances, 'Would it be such a very bad thing if women were permitted to vote?'

'Oh, depend upon it, my dear,' he assured her, 'it would.'

'One thing I do urge you to consider,' said Frances, boldly. 'I am aware that if I were to marry, then any fortune in my possession, which I have earned by my own hard work and saved through frugal living, would at once become the property of my husband, who might choose to spend it on drunkenness or gambling or a mistress. Then if he died I would be left in far worse straits than I am now. I cannot think that is right.'

Her visitor nodded, gravely. 'I expect that similar representations will be made to me, and I promise to consider them.' He rose to go, and after a moment's thought, said, 'It may be that in the future, matters of importance may arise which by their nature are best suited to a woman's delicacy of touch. If they do, I will call upon you again, and until then, you may find that a small monthly honorarium will help to preserve the respectability of your endeavours.'

'I am very grateful,' said Frances.

They shook hands solemnly.

'Good afternoon Miss Doughty,' said the venerable old gentleman. 'My visit to you has brought me greater pleasure than you can possibly imagine.'

She smiled. 'Good afternoon, Mr Gladstone.'

❧ END ❧

AUTHOR'S NOTE

The Bayswater Academy for the Education of Young Ladies and Doughtys' chemist shop are fictional, but all street names and public buildings in London named in the book are or were real places.

In 1880, entrepreneur William Whiteley owned a row of ten shops on Westbourne Grove and was busy converting eight houses on Queen's Road (nowadays called the Queensway) into warehouses and shops.

Salem Gardens used to run east-west from Salem Road, which was a cul-de-sac in 1880. It was demolished in the 1890s.

Hyde Park is little different today from its appearance in the 1880s. The Serpentine is part of the improvements begun by Queen Caroline in 1730. The tradition of Speakers' Corner dates from 1872. The Receiving House of the Royal Humane Society (RHS) was built in 1835 to receive the bodies of people who had been pulled from the Serpentine, and was manned by volunteer medical staff. One of the examining doctors was Dr Blackett. It was demolished in 1954. The RHS also had its own boathouse for rescuing bathers in difficulties. The bodies of the drowned were taken to the mortuary at Mount Street and the inquests held in the Board Room there before the coroner, Mr St Clare Bedford.

Westbourne Hall was built in 1861 and was used for musical entertainment and plays as well as public meetings. The hall could hold 1,000 people. Today, the ornate frontage remains at number 26 Westbourne Grove. The riotous election meeting at Westbourne Hall on the 16th of March 1880 is described in the *Bayswater Chronicle* of 20th March 1880.

The villages of Havenhill and East Hill are fictional, although Havenhill would be on the route of the Great Western Railway, not far from West Drayton.

The 1880 General Election

In 1880, parliaments lasted a maximum of seven years and the previous General Election had taken place in 1874. The Prime Minister was Lord Beaconsfield (Benjamin Disraeli), although by the start of 1880 prospective candidates for the next election had been selected; it was generally believed that the election would take place in the autumn. When the parliamentary session opened on the 5th of February, there was no hint of the Prime Minister's intentions and the dissolution of parliament announced on the 8th of March took everyone by surprise, and telegraph offices were swamped. Bayswater was part of the constituency of Marylebone which put forward four candidates, two Liberal and two Conservative, for two seats. Recent Conservative by-election successes may have led to overconfidence on the part of the government. At the election the Liberals swept to victory and seventy-year-old Mr Gladstone accepted the office of Prime Minister. Daniel Grant, a former director of Grant & Co., a Farringdon printing firm, was elected Liberal MP for Marylebone.

The Women's Suffrage movement of the 1880s

The National Society for Women's Suffrage was formed in 1867.

While the Bayswater Women's Suffrage Society is an invention of the author, there were similar societies in the 1880s, which were holding well-attended public meetings and petitioning parliament to grant votes to women.

Mr Jacob Bright MP (1821–1899), Mrs Fawcett (1847–1929) the former Millicent Garrett and sister of Elizabeth Garret Anderson MD, (1836–1917) were all supporters of women's suffrage.

Isabella Skinner Clarke (later Keer) (1842–1926) was the first woman to become a full member of the Pharmaceutical Society.

In 1882, a new Married Women's Property Act finally permitted women to retain ownership of their property after they were married.

Reverend Benjamin Day (1850–1936) was a Paddington curate who looked after the parish of St Stephen's.

Mr James Flood (1828–1886) was the chairman of the Paddington Vestry (a precursor of the Paddington Borough Council).

The Community Sisters of the Church is an order of Anglican nuns which, in 1880, was associated with the church of St Augustine, Kilburn.